THE MALLEE

NOTHING IS EVER AS IT SEEMS

RICHARD EVANS

852
PRESS

852
PRESS

First published in 2022 by 852 Press,
an imprint of Corven Pty. Limited
Suite 12, 12 Eshelby Drive, Airlie Beach, Queensland Australia
www.852Press.com.au

10 9 8 7 6 5 4 3 2 1

 A catalogue record for this book is available from the National Library of Australia

National Library of Australia Cataloguing-in-Publication entry:

Author: Evans, Richard
Title: The Mallee / by Richard Evans
ISBN: 9780645554403 (Trade paperback)
ISBN: 9780645554410 (ebook)
Australian fiction.
Cover Design: 852 Press

Richard Evans' first book, Deceit, is a five-star thriller that brings the Australian political process to life. – *GOODREADS*

As well as being a ripping good yarn, Evans charts the course for establishing a homeland state for Australia's First Nations. Compulsive reading with action, drama and a seriously provocative political challenge. – *L. E, MELBOURNE*

Wow! Richard Evans has given us his best book yet with The Kill Bill. From the moment I picked this book up, I was hooked. I didn't want to put it down to go to work, — *BJ'S BOOK BLOG*

I absolutely loved it, couldn't put it down. I would love to see your book become a movie. – *IAN S., MELBOURNE*

Rich in ideas and provokes much thought about our parliamentary process, abuses of power, corruption, and the need, at times, for ordinary people to step up and take a stand in the name of honour and professional integrity. – *NADINE D., EDITOR*

Woohoo. Could not put down your book, *Deceit*, what a ripper. Kept me up late, then started again at breakfast, in time to read to the end. Better than any whodunit. What a delight to read such a great Australian book at last. – *JUDY C, QUEENSLAND*

A great read, fast paced and page turning. I found it difficult to put it down. What a great book! Well written with all political content relevant, it kept me reading till the very end. – *GOODREADS*

Just finished reading *Deceit* and it was gripping; I could not put it down. It was brilliant. I just loved the book and can't wait to read *Duplicity*.' – *FORMER CLERK OF VICTORIAN LEGISLATIVE COUNCIL*

Evans' writing is slick, tight, and unobtrusive. The dialogue is a joy to read. The characters are solid and believable. One of the best books I've read in a while, and a solid five stars from me. – *GOODREADS*

ALSO BY RICHARD EVANS

Democracy Trilogy

Deceit

Duplicity

Doomed

Referendum Series

Forgotten People

The Kill Bill

Stand Alone Books

Out of my Hands

Non-Fiction

The Australian Franchising Handbook

For Deborah

Ideas and your wisdom are always welcome.
I reckon this protagonist meets your expectation.

A MESSAGE FROM RICHARD

Motor neurone disease (MND) affects the nerves called motor neurones in the brain and spinal cord. These nerves tell muscles what to do. MND is an insidious disease and there is no cure. It afflicts many and does not show any preference as to who it chooses.

My cousin Lyne lost her much loved husband Robert Howell to the disease without warning and too swift. There are many other families affected by MND and most victims of this disease are way too young.

A group of loyal friends have worked for over ten years raising more than a million dollars for research into MND as a dedication to their dear friend Michael Rodger, another taken too early. This is a tremendous effort and legacy.

I want to recognise Louise Mogg, Stephen Giles, Georgia Rodger, Alannah Giles, Georgie Ross and Russell Higgins for their efforts every year.

What the MND cause needs is money for research to determine what causes the condition and whether there is a cure. Many provide funds and we all hope there is an outcome shortly, as we have the best medical scientists working on this disease. But they need money to continue their work.

In 2022, I donated two characters from The Mallee to the MND Charity Ball and Auction. I continue to support the cause as best I can. I would welcome others in the community to see the value in donating what they can to the cause of seeking a cure.

If we do it together, we may find a cure.

Tim and Jess Brown, and Jon and Charlotte Poore purchased the characters. Thank you for your support of the MND cause.

The Major Players

THE DOWERIN FAMILY

Rose	Member for Mallee
Peter	Criminal Investigator
Primrose	On the spectrum
Bobby	Real Estate sales

THE PERSIAN WATER COMPANY

Darius Hassidim	Director - Chair
Hosmand Shofet	Director - Legal
Taimar Saraf	Director - Finance
Maisil Ghassab	Director - Security

GOVERNMENT:

Timothy Brown	Prime Minister
Jock Garnsworthy	Deputy Prime Minister and Country Party Leader
Clare Spencer	Water Minister
Charlotte Poore	Rose Dowerin's Chief of Staff

OTHERS

Simon Dobbs	Criminal investigator
Phillip Jackson	Victorian Premier
James Lever	Farmer and candidate
Jack Fingleton	Cattleman and candidate
Wendy Hammer	Doctor - medical examiner
Denis Sadler	Radio Commentator

CHAPTER

1

Mallee locals say you get used to it. The heat never seems to bother them. Not like the tourists coming for the sun during a winter desert holiday and regretting it because of the temperature. The film of sweat smearing skin every day and most nights doesn't bother the locals.

Red dust cakes most things in the mallee and whenever a flywire door slams, a cloud of fine dust puffs out. There's never a complaint, just a howl to not slam the door. Whipped up dust from random gusts of parching breeze can turn a squint into a grimace. Town dogs pant in the shade of scarce trees and there never seems to be a cat around, only the snarling ferals out bush.

Locals plonk on heads ridiculous, soft-brimmed hats with weird shaped high crowns full of dust and damp salty stains. Young'uns roll the brim, but most know the value of its shade. Long sleeves, red stained moleskins and dusty boots are standard issue to shield the sun. Town folk shake heads, wondering why cherry pink tourists visit such a desolate place short of water. Locals prefer their holidays in rain country.

No, it ain't the heat in the mallee; it's the flies that kill enthusiasm.

Pesky meandering blights fossicking the smorgasbord of faces searching out saliva and mucus and crawling into eyes. Locals use a steady wave to move them on. They are found everywhere and often wallowing in feeding frenzies on the fresh meat of the rotting carcasses as the drought takes a firmer grip on the mallee, strangling the life from stock.

Locals can withstand the wind, the dust, and the heat, but it's the flies drawing the most verbal abuse. 'Fuck off' the common refrain as they try to escape the discomfort. To dent the inevitable invasion, houses and businesses fortify openings with flywire. Strips of gooey plastic flypaper dangle from ceilings and door frames with a massive swarm trapped in its sticky gunk. Some locals use the aroma of basil and lavender to rid the filth, others soak rooms with insecticides in a never-ending battle to be rid of the bastards.

Without flooding rains, the mallee desert becomes what it has always been, a worthless dust bowl. Its vast reddish ochre beset with shifting dunes blown in from central Australia offering little mineral content. Crop yields rely on superphosphate to eek out a living for aspirational grain growers. Farmers still hang onto the future as if it will shine a light of prosperity, but the mallee will never be their pot of gold, unless conditions and the economy change.

Diverting water from the mighty Murray River transformed nearby land into an irrigated oasis. Investment in crops like grapes, fruit and olives transformed the region with more resolute farmers running cattle and sheep. Many farmers further out from the river consider it a waste of time and money but never say it out loud. They would have gone years ago if they had the money.

Locals get used to the heat and learn to live with the flies in the mallee.

Bobby Dowerin recognised the days of a desert farming bonanza were long gone. No water meant no profit for thirsty farmers. He identified financial opportunity trading in real estate, taking advantage of rural despondency. Not just broad acre grain farms and hobby farms closer to town, but also the grand residential properties along the river. He travelled the region using his used car sales charm, convincing locals to surrender and leave the district, often selling to city dwellers seeking escape from the burdens of a big city. His family didn't know everyone, but everyone knew them. He traded on that legacy to create the gravitas to close deals.

Not everyone enjoys the stillness of isolation, so bigger, broad acre farms with little water were harder to move. The sting of dust was problematic for likely buyers, so he preferred selling property in the urban areas. Especially around Mildura, the large regional city on the Murray where dust doesn't worry traders.

Bobby cherished the handsome commissions from selling property to the local Iranian community, a mixture of immigrants and refugees settling in the region over three decades. Using government subsidises, the community toiled long hours to set up various commercial operations amassing ever increasing wealth. Community leaders recently directed him to buy unproductive acreages an hour from Mildura. He didn't know why they wanted the land and didn't care. Perhaps they knew something about the desert he didn't know. Or maybe they were crazy. He didn't care. He only did it for the money.

Money was always his escape. As a teenager, Bobby dreamt of getting out. He believed the prospect of working in the family business a backward step and didn't wish to be lumbered into a government job like his older copper brother. *Could there be anything worse than dealing with crime and justice?* Money remained his ambition. He would consider any opportunity to get his hands on it. He needed it. His gambling debts demanded it.

Bobby travelled to Merrinee to talk to a farmer who left a message to come discuss the sale of his broad acre farm. When he arrived at the homestead, the manager told him the boss was holidaying in the rain and wouldn't be back for days. The manager left speechless by Bobby's tactless suggestion the property was being considered for sale.

Rather than waste the day, he motored over to Ned's Corner to check whether contractors erected directional signs for his listed properties on the Sturt Highway. When he hit the first pothole on the dusty track, he questioned the effectiveness of council rates. *Did they not spend any money on roadworks on secondary roads? He would raise it with his mother.* He questioned his driving choices when he smashed too hard into a second deep hole, sending a warning light into a blinking sequence. He stopped in the centre of what they could describe as a goat's track.

The hissing up front bothered him when he dropped from the cabin. It looked like steam, or worse, smoke gushing from the front. He hesitated because it would be pointless to investigate. A hissing engine meant nothing to him. Bobby guessed it might be best if he lifts the metal thing to give the motor air. When he popped it, he tried to lift the heavy hood. It didn't register with him there could be another catch. He tugged the hood enough times before realising he needed a secondary release. As he finally raised it, a white cloud dispersed. He examined the engine, wondering what to do. He shrugged and stepped back.

The cabin had little to offer. The AC was not working, so he dragged open the back hatch, perching on the carpeted tailgate out of the sun. Flies were onto him, caking his shirt. They crowded his open vehicle, hunting for anything. He checked his phone again for reception, dropping it back in his pocket.

The constant buzz and flutter of flies drove him nuts as he waved and threatened them. Each time he slapped his thigh, he wiped out a cluster. Frustrated, he stepped away from his Jeep, thinking the bastards would stay, and most did. A second wave descended, providing little relief from his flaying arms.

He searched out across the sparse dusty acres. He squinted to the horizon, searching for any sign of movement. The shimmering fluid layers of air broke up the perspective, providing little confidence he would see anything. It would be a long trek back to Merrinee, so he'd wait until the day lost its sting.

As he strolled around the car, a distant glint of reflected sun caught his eye. He waved away flies and shaded his hand across his brow, trying to distinguish any hope of movement. Shimmering air distorted his view, but he imagined he could hear something. What he could see was dark and very thin, but a distant noise sounded like a motor. A cloud of dust and a vague shape created a recognisable silhouette. What was once black was now white and what he thought was a truck now a four-wheel drive coming at speed. He smiled, relieved, looking forward to quenching his dry mouth. He blew a cluster of flies away, waving a hand high.

The white Toyota slid to an inevitable stop, kicking up stones with the trailing dust cloud rolling forward, swirling about, forcing him to shy-away, cupping his mouth and nose. When the cloud passed, he moved to the passenger side. The window lowered for him.

'What a surprise to see you here,' Bobby said, when he recognised the driver. 'You're the last person I expected to see out here.'

The driver didn't respond, flipping away a towel from the seat, lifting the polished wooden stock of a shotgun.

'Wait! No!'

Bobby didn't have time to move before his face and much of his head disappeared, throwing him backwards, crumpling him off the track. The flies wasted little time coming for him.

CHAPTER
2

The relentless buzz broke the silence of the isolation. A blue tarpaulin over the corpse didn't stop them. Peter Dowerin leaned on the rear of his vehicle, waiting for uniformed colleagues to finish assembling a crime scene tent. He gazed out to the horizon, hoping the heat would ease soon. The Jeep belonged to his real estate brother, that's for sure. He wanted the victim under the plastic not to be Bobby.

He didn't need another one.

A panicked call came three hours earlier from a passing labourer. He didn't notice the body until he stepped from his van and heard the frenzied buzz. A little unnerved, he scampered from the area, calling the police when phone reception improved on the bitumen. Police dispatched two uniformed coppers to the scene and informed Mildura's CIB Detective Inspector Dowerin. It shattered him to recognise his brother's Jeep, expecting the worst. Now he waited, worried about what to tell his mother.

'How long will you be?'

A senior constable was tying off a stabilization line to the free-standing tent. 'Almost finished. Just need to get the fly screen over it.'

'Try not to get any spray over the body.'

'We've done it before, Pete. It'll be okay.'

Dowerin nodded, dismissing the conversation with a hand gesture, now more interested in a cloud of dust advancing along the track from the bitumen.

The small SUV drifted to a halt, kicking up a rolling cloud of dirt and grit, forcing him to squint and wave the dust away. He watched as the driver went to the rear of her vehicle, dragging out what looked like a toolbox, which she fastened to a fat-tyre trolley like the ones seen in warehouses. She grabbed a broad-brimmed hat from the rear seat, playing with its headband before trudging towards him, hauling her load.

Dowerin grinned, almost chuckling as he took a lengthy gaze at his visitor dressed in an oversized denim blouse with a leather belt, inadequate strappy shoes and a hat with netting covering her face and shoulders.

'Don't like flies?'

'You could say that. Where's the body?'

'Who are you?'

'The pathologist. I drew the short straw.'

'Where are you from?' Dowerin said, scratching his cheek.

'Mildura hospital. Who are you?'

'Pete Dowerin, CIB.' He smirked a hello. 'Where's Gordo?'

'On vacation in Melbourne or Sydney, who knows?' she sighed. 'Anywhere has got to be better than here.'

'Not a fan?'

'I'm in this god-forsaken place on locum relief.'

'Why?'

'Yeah, excellent question,' she replied. 'Fucked if I know.'

'Nice,' Dowerin snorted, peering at his boots. He squinted back and grinned. 'Did you really draw the short straw?'

'Look, I'm not here for the chat. Can we get this done?'

Dowerin cocked a thumb over his shoulder towards the tent. 'They're getting rid of the flies, won't be long.'

'How are they managing that? They're not contaminating the scene, are they?'

'They know what they're doing. Done it before. Couldn't be any worse than the dust storm you created.' Dowerin fisted his hip. 'What's your name?'

She pointed to the badge. 'Hammer, Doctor Hammer.'

Dowerin pulled a face and nodded. 'That figures.'

The senior constable ducked out from the tent. 'It's okay now, Pete.'

The tension broken, Dowerin turned and wandered off toward the tent waving off flies, leaving the doctor with her load. 'How's the flies?' he asked.

'Got most of them, but the body remains alive with wildlife.'

'She'll presumably take her own shots, but we should do ours as well. Can I leave that to one of you?'

'No worries.' The constable nodded and left the tent for a camera as the doctor came struggling in, hauling her trolley through the grass and sand.

'Thanks for your help?' she said, straightening and peering down at the sheet.

'No problems, Doc. Do you need me to get rid of the tarp?' Dowerin said.

'If you wouldn't mind,' she frowned, pinching her nose. 'It may help with my examination.' Dowerin clutched a corner, flipping it up and off, floating it to a heap to the side of the tent.

'Christ!' she said.

Dowerin didn't answer. He gazed fixated on the body.

The doctor unbuckled her large plastic trunk, yanking open the lid. She plucked out a small, sealed bag, ripping it open, putting on a surgical mask. She tugged two blue latex gloves from a cardboard box, stretching them on as she squatted. She then assembled several instruments and specimen slides and bags, ready for her examination.

The constable crouched, taking photographs. The doctor prompting him to take various perspectives and her preference for certain angles. She stooped over the body, examining the wound, paying particular attention to the insect activity.

'I would suggest the time of death at mid-morning, around eleven. I will be more precise once I have him back at the morgue.'

'Any idea of weapon?' the senior constable said, taking notes.

'I'm not prepared to say just yet but given the shape of the wound and embedded powder, I suspect a close-range shotgun.' The doctor bagged samples as she spoke. 'Get shots from in here, thanks constable.'

She pointed to the neck. The photographer bent in close, clicking several images, fiddling with the lens.

She bagged and tied off one hand and began doing the same with the other when she stopped. 'This is interesting.' The others glanced at her, then at what she examined. 'He's missing the pinkie on his left hand. Someone hacked it off.'

Dowerin turned and bolted from the tent, stumbling over the excessive fly screen. The doctor watched him go, then smirked. 'The big guy doesn't care for the hard stuff?'

'I wouldn't say that,' the senior constable said.

The doctor chuffed a laugh. 'Oh yeah? Why so quiet?'

The senior didn't respond until the doctor straightened and tossed him a *so what* expression.

'That's his brother.'

CHAPTER

3

EIGHT MONTHS EARLIER

The million-bushel silos storing the annual crop on the highway out-of-town offer Wycheproof a monument to the local economy. Wyche is a town folks speed through on the way to Mildura. No one really wants to live on the Calder Highway three hours northwest of Melbourne. Six hundred resolute people do to supply the local farming district. The Royal Mail is the only entertainment if you're old enough to be served a beer. Otherwise, brushing away flies fills the day.

Curious tourists stop for a delightful choice of pastries at the bakery, before checking out Wyche's famous mountain, the smallest recorded in the world. It's a pimple forty-three metres above the surrounding dry plains. Such a pointless thing to do.

Behind Wycheproof's hospital, Henderson Soils and Transport base its operations. Opened with one truck fifty years ago, now a grandson struggles to make a go of it. Tony Henderson took over from his father a few years back when they had six trucks. Using competitive pricing, he accumulated clients, and the company now runs ten trucks hauling anything local farmers need. The idea of spending his entire life in Wyche doesn't excite him. He preferred his girls to live in rain country, so worked hard building his business to fund their relocation.

An overlarge black SUV entered the extended lot, parking by vehicles near a workshop close to the front gate. Darius Hassidim and Maisil Ghassab kept the engine idling, enjoying the light flow of air-conditioning as they waited for someone to attend. It didn't take long for Henderson to appear in greasy blue overalls, squinting against the sun, a blackened hand shading his eyes as he walked towards the unfamiliar darkened window vehicle. When he almost reached it, Darius buzzed the window.

'Tony.'

'Mr Hassidim,' Henderson replied, holding a hand against his heart.

'Can we talk?'

'Sure, what do you want?'

'I want a quiet place to have a chat with you.'

'About what?'

'Oh, I don't know.' Darius played with him. 'Maybe business. How is business?'

Henderson checked around and wiped his hands against his overalls.

'Good. Getting better, I s'pose.'

'This is what I want to talk about, so where shall we go?'

'There's a work shed over by the soil's storage.' Henderson pointed across the hood of the SUV. 'Follow me.'

Ghassab reversed, then trailed behind, the throaty exhaust purring a deep resonance.

When Henderson unchained the rattling door, a cloud of heat enveloped them. Darius took a swig from his plastic water bottle, following Henderson. A wooden work bench across the opposite wall had various tools strewn over it. Henderson eyed the hammer. He turned, leaning against the bench facing his visitors, sweat forming on his brow. The grimy concrete floor adding to the grubby feel of the shed's remoteness.

'Nice,' said Darius, taking another swig. 'A little warm for me, but we won't be long. Please take a seat.' He pointed to a couple of folded chairs leaning against a wall.

Ghassab handed one to Henderson, as Darius pulled a white handkerchief from his pocket, wiping the other before sitting in front of him, their knees almost touching. Ghassab, dressed in a black suit and t-shirt, stood by the door, hands in pockets.

'Now, Tony, tell me.' Darius shoved the handkerchief back and took another swig. 'What have you been doing?'

'What do you mean?' Henderson asked, peeking back towards Ghassab.

'Let's see, what do I mean?' In a blink, Darius slapped Henderson on the ear. 'I suppose I mean; you were not listening when we explained our commercial arrangements.'

'What do you mean?' Henderson cringed, raising his arm. His ear buzzing and burning. 'I pay you each month,' he said, hoping to reassure Hassidim.

'Yes, that's true, and we are grateful for your donation, aren't we, Maisil?'

Ghassab grunted. Henderson stifled a scoff.

'But this donation is not the reason we are here.'

'What do you want?' Henderson said, still wary of a sudden lunge. 'Twenty percent not enough for you?'

'Twenty is the agreed amount. We never break our agreements,' Darius answered, leaning forward, resting his forearms on his tailored trousers. 'Can you say the same, Tony?'

'How do you mean?' Henderson said, scratching his cheek with his knuckles. He checked over his shoulder again, shifting back in his chair as Hassidim leaned into his personal space.

'We explained the rules.' Darius engaged Henderson's eyes. 'We think you have broken the rules.'

'No, I haven't.'

Darius jerked straighter. 'No? Are you sure?'

'You can check my books if you want.'

'It's not the books I'm worried about.' Darius leaned back. 'It's truth I trust most in business.' He paused for a moment. 'I'm afraid you have been untruthful.'

'What do you mean?' Henderson cleared his throat. 'I tell you the truth.'

Darius gazed at Henderson, searching his eyes. His own black eyes gave nothing away. As he stared, his face tightened, and said, almost whispering. 'I loathe when my business partners lie to me, Tony. All I want you to do is tell me the truth.'

Henderson shook his head. 'I don't know what the hell you are talking about.' He glanced back at Ghassab. 'Do you know?'

Darius snapped his fingers in front of Henderson's face to bring his attention back. 'I know you have been unfaithful to us, Tony.'

'What? No, I haven't. What are you saying?'

'You have been undercutting prices to *my* clients. Why are you stealing *my* clients?'

'Who? What are you talking about?'

'I'm talking about you quoting ludicrous prices to my freight company's clients. I have retained my clients for many years. I have a relationship with my clients, Tony. My family enjoys many benefits from my clients.'

'But you still get your cut,' Henderson said.

'This is not the point.' Darius continued staring as Henderson averted his eyes. 'You have stolen *my* clients, and I want them back.'

'It's a free market,' Henderson said, raising his eyes.

'Free market?' Darius nodded, dropping his head. Then smiled before standing in a rush, scooping away his chair. 'Maisil, please give Tony a free market lesson.'

Crouching like a fighter, Ghassab moved to Henderson. From high above his head, he drove a fist like a pile-driver into Henderson's face. Then hooked the other flush on Henderson's jaw, flaying him backwards. Ghassab grabbed him by the lapel of his overalls, straightening, then lifting him back into the chair. He then smashed his right fist into Henderson's nose, blood now flowing across his mouth and cheek.

'End of the first lesson, Maisil.'

Henderson rocked back and forward, swallowing blood, smearing his mouth with a sleeve.

Darius resumed his chair, patting Henderson on the knee.

'In the mallee, my companies run transport. My clients are my clients, and they are not to be touched by my competitors, especially those we allow to operate, like you, Tony. Do you understand?'

Henderson lifted his head, only one eye open, his sight blurred.

'Do you understand?' Darius repeated.

Henderson nodded, careful not to move and fall from the chair.

'This is good; you pass lesson one. Lesson two.' Darius stepped away again, allowing Ghassab to resume. This time knocking Henderson to the dusty concrete with the first punch, then flogging him with kicks to the chest, back, and head. He finished by stomping on Henderson's head scuffing it with the heel of his boot.

Darius leaned over him. 'Tony, I don't mind you getting new clients. I will help you if I can, but I insist they must not be in the mallee... do you understand?'

Henderson tried to respond but couldn't.

'Sorry, I can't hear you.'

He heaved in a chest full of air, then blew out, struggling to make a groan sound like yes.

'You now pass lesson two in the school of the free market.'

Henderson tensed for another kicking. He felt his left arm dragged from under him and raised. Darius squatted with one hand resting on Henderson's chest.

'You have passed our lessons. Now for graduation. I take the first knuckle after a misunderstanding. I take the second knuckle after a mistake. I take the third knuckle just before termination. As this is your first mistake, I never want to hear from you again, Tony. Is that clear?'

Henderson could feel Ghassab holding his hand tight. He didn't see him tugging small bolt cutters from his back pocket, springing them open. He didn't feel them position over then gripping the first knuckle on his little finger.

'So ends our free-market lessons and your graduation, Tony. Congratulations.'

Ghassab snapped closed the bolt cutters with a flick, and the tip of Henderson's finger dropped to the floor.

He screamed, more in panic than pain.

Ghassab tugged a gauze cloth from his pocket, wrapping the stump. He then dragged Henderson to his feet, assisting him to the door. Darius rushed through before them, getting to the SUV and opening the hatch. Ghassab was not far behind, pushing Henderson into the vehicle. The men hopped into the vehicle and were off, kicking up dust and stones.

They skidded as they fought for traction when they hit the bitumen. They navigated various turns before rushing into the forecourt of the hospital, stopping outside the emergency. Ghassab went to the back of the SUV, assisting Henderson from the vehicle, and guiding him to the entrance. They were gone before Henderson, clutching his left hand, reached the reception desk seeking medical help.

'Well, that was easy.'

Ghassab grinned. 'I'm sure he'll do the right thing from now on.'

'I like Tony. He's a good egg.'

CHAPTER
4

As the sun disappeared on the horizon, the SUV entered Tyrrell Cooperative Station out near Sea Lake. The respected Jed Musgrove set high benchmarks for animal welfare, and his crop yields were consistent no matter the weather. He survived drought before and reckoned this current weather event compared little to the millennial drought.

Musgrove anticipated his visitors and stood atop the stone steps as he watched the two men tumble out of the SUV, stepping forward with hearty smiles and friendly handshakes. He invited them to sit and admire the sunset, calling through the flywire for cool drinks. The men settled into the plump, cushioned wicker furniture at the end of the wide wooden veranda. The housekeeper placing lemon and soda glasses with a paper napkin before them.

'What brings you out here, boys?'

'Water.' Darius grinned.

'I have plenty and don't need yours, so looks as if you wasted your time.' Musgrove glanced at him, and then Ghassab. 'Nothing here for you,' he said, flicking a fly from his face with a wave.

'You haven't listened to my latest offer,' Darius said.

'Your offer is twice what I'm paying.' Musgrove lifted his drink, wiped the bottom with a napkin and took a long slug, ice clinking against the glass.

'I suppose that's because you irrigate it from the lake, which is handy,' Darius said.

'Sea Lake Irrigation provides fresh water from their desalination plant. I have two bores. So, we are good.'

'This is very good for you, and I wish you no malice.' Darius waved away a fly. 'But let me ask you this: if SLI could not supply water, what would you do?'

Musgrove didn't answer. He gazed out into the setting sun, following the orange ball as it sank beyond the horizon.

'Truck it in from Horsham.' He paused a little longer and added, 'Or maybe Renmark.'

'Not Swan Hill?'

Musgrove glimpsed over to Darius, and then flicked a quick eye to Ghassab, watching for any sharp movements.

'You own the water at Swan Hill. You own it at Mildura. Maybe you own it along the Darling in New South Wales. It wouldn't surprise me if you own much of it in South Australia.'

Darius smiled. 'You're right.'

'You manipulate the market, and you charge way too much.'

'It's business.' Darius shrugged, watching the last of the sun. 'The market drives the price.'

'That's bullshit, Darius. You drive the price. You've been holding back water for years.'

'I trade water.'

'You've held back access since the drought started. Now you are charging top dollar.'

'I charge market rates.'

'You screw farmers, and I can tell you, you are not going to screw me.'

'Don't be like that, Jed.'

'I don't need you or your water.'

Darius paused for a moment, then stood, Ghassab following his lead. He held out his hand as Musgrove remained sitting.

'Jed, you will need us soon.' Darius dropped his hand, accepting the snub.

'Why do you say that?'

'We bought a parcel of shares in SLI just the other day and now we are the major shareholder.' Darius smiled, but his eyes didn't. 'I suspect you will ask us to meet your water needs in the future.'

'Listen here, Sheik. Whilst I have fresh water from other sources, I will never deal with you.' Musgrove stood, stretching to his full height. 'I would rather drink the sand than deal with you friggin' A-rab camel jockeys.'

Darius smiled, pausing for a moment. 'Let's all hope you won't need to do that.'

Darius and Ghassab bounced down the steps, hopping into their vehicle, wasting little time hitting the highway for the hour's drive back to Swan Hill.

As the sun cracked the eastern horizon, Musgrove already moved to assess his ewe flock if they were ready for rams so he could start lambing in December. He stopped at a gate near the windmill bore and water trough. As he walked up the rise, the dawn light revealed more of the landscape. He noticed a mob about the trough, and as he closed in, they didn't skittishly move away. As he got closer, he realised why.

Death is common on a farm, but death from a tainted water trough appeared too much for Musgrove, dropping to his knees, looking to the heavens, shouting to no one.

CHAPTER

5

Living near water is instinctive for many people, especially in Australia. Most folks live or build holiday homes on its long sandy coast. The wealthier your family, the closer you are to the water. In the desert, it's the same. When the irrigation channels in the mallee opened in the 1890s, the Dowerin family were early settlers. They invested in large tracts of rich pasture for crops and grazing close to the Murray.

Gregor Dowerin served on local council, becoming active in the federation debates. He argued colonies needed to forge one united nation, ending disputes over water and trade. When the new Commonwealth parliament proclaimed the seat of Wimmera, Gregor stood for election. The family representing it and the renamed electorate ever since; except for one three-year term after the Great War, when repatriated soldier settlers drifted into the mallee, wanting one of their own to represent them.

Gregor's grandson, Newton, decided it was far more economic to create a business in agriculture supply and service then be at the beck and call of the weather with its fickle ways. Their wealth increased, and they invested in freehold land on both sides of the Murray.

Junior Dowerin, Newton's son, sold all interests in the family's cattle holdings soon after entering parliament and developed a family estate on the river for his wife Rosemary. Following Junior's tragic accident, Rose subdivided the property, delivering equity for her children.

Peter escaped family obligations early by joining the police academy, but returned to head the local CIB ten years ago, building an impressive home next door. To the continuing exasperation of his mother, he never entertained plans to marry, resisting her demands for a brood of grandchildren.

His sister Primrose, diagnosed as being on the autism spectrum, relied on Rose's support so still lived at home. Peter often speculated about Primmy's diagnosis, sometimes pondering if it was all an act. *Does she have a medical condition? If she does, why is she so clever?*

Peter considered his younger brother a total flake for seldom accepting responsibility. Bobby was often seen across the river gambling or drinking with the shady characters amongst the Iranian community. The less Peter saw of him, the better, although uniformed colleagues informed him whenever his brother transgressed.

They came together for lunch most Sundays at Rose's grand house on the river to catch up and gossip. Rose enjoyed the robust weekly chitchat with her sons. It provided an ear to the hearsay of the town and nearby districts. These days she remained in Canberra on ministerial duties during the week but enjoyed being with her children, although detecting that it might be a chore for them. The responsibility for lunch rotated each week. Today Primrose enjoyed the honour. The usual high standard of her fare put the boys to shame.

'Today we have fish,' she declared as the family enjoyed pre-lunch beverages.

Bobby grinned. 'Local or from elsewhere?'

'It's barra,' Primrose responded.

'In the desert?' Bobby scoffed.

'From Queensland, silly.'

'How did you get it? We don't have it in town,' asked Peter.

'Something special for you, Peter,' Primrose giggled, shrugging. 'I know you like it.'

Peter grinned at his sister, shaking his head, surprised she remembered. He may have only ever suggested it once.

'Where did you get it?' Bobby insisted.

'I brought it up from Melbourne last night,' Rose responded, returning from the kitchen with a fresh bottle of chardonnay sunk deep in an ice bucket.

'On the plane?' Bobby winced.

'Yes, in a foam box with a little ice. I bought the barramundi, prawns, and a couple dozen Sydney rock oysters online and picked them up in Melbourne during transit.'

'Aren't we lucky? What's the occasion?' Peter asked.

'Well, two things. Primmy has been pushing me for some time to bring barramundi home, and second, I wanted my family's advice on my political career.'

'Should be a brief discussion.' Peter shrugged as he took a slug of beer. 'Give it up; they don't appreciate you.'

Rose scoffed. 'I can't do that, darling. Who would replace me?'

'It's a mistake to think you're irreplaceable,' Peter said.

Rose sighed. 'The family provides the federal member for Mallee. We have since federation.'

'Well, I'm not putting my hand up for it, and Bobby is too young.'

'Bobby's at the age when I first entered parliament.'

'What's wrong with me?' Bobby shook his head with a pained look of confusion.

'Nothing, pet, but politics is not for you,' Rose responded, dismissing him with a flick of her hand.

'Why not?' Bobby replied.

'Because you're an idiot,' said Peter, as he stood to fetch another beer.

Bobby frowned. 'Hey, ease up, I'm doing okay.'

Peter scoffed as he stepped into the kitchen.

Bobby glanced at his mother, who arched a brow. 'I am, Mum. I promise. Those days are long gone.'

'I hear you're often at the club in Redcliffs and sometimes you drive to Swan Hill.'

'I like the pokies, so what?' Bobby scratched his chin. 'No harm in that.'

'There is if you can't pay your bills and they show up here looking for money.'

'Or they come to me wanting to press charges,' Peter said, returning with a beer, shoved into a foam stubby holder.

'Who does?' Bobby protested. 'I don't owe money, and no one wants me in jail.'

Peter whistled through his teeth. 'No one needs you anywhere near them.'

'Peter don't talk about your brother like that,' Rose said.

'The Arabs do,' Bobby said.

His brother didn't respond, averting his gaze, taking another mouthful.

'What are they doing for you?' Rose queried.

'They're closing heaps of property deals with me,' Bobby said.

'Where?' Peter asked.

'Out at Ned's Corner.'

'Why out there?' Rose said, now more interested.

'They've got something planned.' Bobby smiled at his mother. 'Anyway, who cares so long as they pay me?'

Peter cast an eye over to Rose, who conceded his querying look with a slow nod.

'What about me?' Primrose joined the conversation after sitting for a while with no expression, as if not caring.

Bobby snapped a glance, raising his voice. 'What about you?'

'Why can't I go into the parliament like Mummy?'

'What?' Bobby scrunched his face, shrugging, frowning at the others, seeking an explanation. 'What's she talking about?'

'Darling, you can serve lunch now.' Rose smiled, nodding at Primrose.

'No!' she barked and slapped the table, causing the cutlery to jingle. 'I want an answer. Why can't I be a politician?'

Bobby scoffed. 'Because Primmy, you are far too smart to be one of those fools.'

Peter placed a comforting hand on her shoulder. 'I'm looking forward to the barra, sis. Do you need help?'

She wriggled away. 'I'm smarter than any of you.'

Rose leaned into her. 'It's a good idea darling; let's talk over lunch?'

A satisfied, toothy smile appeared. 'Then best I go serve.'

'Do you need a hand?' Peter asked again.

'No, lunch is special for you. I'll be right.' Primrose bounced off and busied herself in the kitchen.

Rose perused the others. 'She'll forget about it before we even eat,' she said.

'How is she?' Peter asked.

'She's fine.' Rose lifted a glass and took a refreshing sip of chardonnay. 'She enjoys travelling with me but gets exhausted. She appears to care for herself okay when I'm gone.'

No one spoke as Primrose served a platter overfilled with seafood, rushing back to the kitchen.

'She's becoming a pain in the arse, though,' Bobby declared.

Rose directed a stern squint at him, about to say something, but Peter beat her to it. 'She could be the worst person in town, and she would still smell like a rose compared to you.'

Primrose returned, placing clanking condiments on the table.

'Fair enough,' Bobby said, bowing his head, averting his brother's gaze.

CHAPTER

6

Over lunch, the family discussed water and Rose's challenges in Canberra. She mentioned gossip about the party leader retiring. Bobby suggested she toss her hat into the leadership ring. Peter, cautious about her future, suggested it would be a waste of time, given her colleagues didn't appreciate her. He reiterated it might be a good time to retire. Primrose remained quiet, offering nothing.

Three hours after lunch, Rose headed for a meeting arranged by the local farmers' cooperative at the council chambers. The meeting becoming rowdy when discussion turned to water rights. Speaker after speaker complained about drought and water. The president struggled to keep order during debate concerning the Persian Water Company. The company crippling irrigators by increasing prices six hundred percent.

Rose tried to explain the challenges the federal cabinet faced when deciding to release cash grants on top of current drought funding. This did not placate the audience. Farmers wanted water, not government handouts. They didn't enjoy or need platitudes from their federal member.

As it was nearing six o'clock, the president nodded towards a colleague sitting behind Rose at the front of the auditorium.

'Mr President, I would like to move a motion.'

'The Chair recognises James Lever.'

'Hear. Hear,' the audience chanted.

'I move that this meeting records its displeasure in the manner the government is managing the drought, and we express serious concern that our voice is not being heard by ministers.'

Rose decided she wouldn't oppose or speak against the motion, accepting she needed to receive a slap from the meeting. They weren't happy and wanted to blame someone.

'I also move this meeting expresses disappointment with the Persian Water Company and the manner it raises prices beyond the economic reach of the farming community reliant on water.'

'Hear. Hear,' a few chants came again from further back.

'Good on ya, Jimmy,' someone shouted.

'I further move this meeting direct the federal member for Mallee, Rose Dowerin, to negotiate a satisfactory outcome with said company to benefit the community.'

'Hear. Hear.' The chant now firmer and louder.

'I further move that if we cannot achieve an outcome, then this meeting request the state and federal governments to resolve access to water by revoking the trading licence of Persian Water allowing a government managed scheme to replace it.'

'Is there a seconder?' The president scanned the room. 'Thanks, Harry. Seconded by Harry Brownfield. All those in favour?'

Hands shot up throughout the audience.

'Against?' Not a hand to be seen.

'I declare the motion carried.'

The solid round of applause unsettled Rose. She remembered being told early in her career that once the farmers turned against you, then nothing would stop their anger. *They'll fight you in the ballot box, lassie, and you won't survive.*

She heard the rumours about her preselection but dismissed them. Just a few troublemakers, she thought, seeking to upset her. She now recognised the next election may not be as easy as she expected; perhaps she should take her son's advice and give it up or at least confront any threat head-on as she always did.

Rose spent an hour after the meeting chatting with those who wanted to talk. Supporters reassured her, but friends were now challenging her, asking her to do more. Distracted by the overt politics, she recognised a significant threat to her preselection now existed. If a quality candidate stood against her, someone like James Lever, then she might be in trouble.

When Rose arrived home, she found Primrose waiting up. A glass of chilled chardonnay handed over as she flopped onto the couch, kicking off her shoes. The small first-floor lounge of the homestead took advantage of the view, overlooking the Murray River, festooned with lights of moored houseboats.

'Did you get what you wanted?' Primrose joined her, holding a glass of ice and soda with a couple of squeezed lemon wedges tossed in.

'It wasn't a meeting like that, darling.' Rose forced a tired grin. 'Lunch was terrific today, thank you.'

'Why don't the boys like me?'

Rose continued her fixed smile, pausing for a moment. 'They love you, darling. It's just that they are very protective of you.'

'You've always told me I can be whatever I want.'

'Ah huh.' Rose took a sip, gazing out onto the river.

'You claim I have a gift.'

'That's right, you do.'

Primrose paused, peering at her mother, still fascinated by the lights on the river. 'But you didn't mean it, did you?'

Rose snapped a glance at her. 'What's that?'

Primrose shook her head. 'A man rang for earlier.'

'Who was it?'

'He left a number.'

'Did you take a note?'

'I don't need to.' Primrose fetched the wine, chilling in an ice bucket on the sideboard. 'You should know that, except you don't.'

'Don't be like that, darling. Mummy's had a hard day,' Rose sighed, smiling, as Primrose refilled her glass. 'Anyway, who was it?'

'A man from Tyrrells, he said.'

'Musgrove, was that it?'

'He didn't say. If he did, I would know.'

Rose dropped her hand to the floor, dragging up the oversized leather bag dumping it on her lap. She rummaged through, searching for her phone.

'What is the number, darling?'

'555 5319.'

Rose pressed in the numbers and waited for a connection.

Musgrove answered. 'Who's this?'

'Jed, it's Rosemary Dowerin. I'm returning your call.'

'Bit late.'

'Yeah, just got home. Been at a farmers' meeting.'

'They moved a motion against you.'

'Well, that is a little too literal,' she grinned. 'What they are after is more government action.'

'Not what I heard.'

Rose squeezed a thumbnail into her lower teeth. She mused if Lever worked the numbers.

'Anyway, that's not why I rang. One of my bores has been tainted.'

'Oh, no. How did that happen?'

'That towel head mate of yours paid me a visit, yestie. Reckons I should buy water off him.'

'Who's supposed to be my mate?'

'That wanker Hassidim and his goon.'

Rose shifted in her chair. 'I'm no mate of Darius Hassidim.'

'He's got you and Jackson wrapped around his little finger. You know it. I know it. Everyone in the mallee knows it, so stop bullshittin'.'

'I'm not, and I'm offended by your implication.'

'Be offended you as much as you like. Fact is, he donates heaps of dollars to your campaign. Once you take his money, you're only ever negotiating the price.'

'I don't do his bidding; I can assure you. Never have, never will. He doesn't give me money. Never has, never will.'

Musgrove didn't reply straight away. 'The moron tainted my bore. I'm sure of it.'

'That's a serious charge. Do you have proof?'

'Almost fifty head, with blood spewing from their guts.

'Tainted from what?'

'The local coppers sent a sample to the city for testing. I reckon the way they look from the muscle spasms, I'm guessing they dumped a load of strychnine into the trough.'

'And you think it was Hassidim?'

'No doubt in the world.'

'Why would he do that?'

'Sending me a message.'

'And what's that?'

'Water. He wants me to buy water from him.' Musgrove shouted, prompting Rose to hold the phone from her ear, switching it to speaker. 'He drove out here yesterday, threatening me. Buy water from him or there will be consequences, is what he said.'

'You want me to speak to him?'

'Nope. I can handle him and his camel jockey mates.'

'Then how can I help?'

'Stop him at the source.' Musgrove paused. Rose glanced at Primrose, who now listened. 'Cut off his authority and stop these threats of intimidation.'

'How do I do that?'

'Buy back the water rights and take control.'

'State government issue; they own the water rights.'

'So what? Take the rights off them.'

'Yeah, nah,' Rose said, tightening her lips. 'We need a change to the constitution to do that. You should talk to the premier.'

'He does nothing. Promises everything and delivers nothing.'

'He is the person you need to talk to,' Rose insisted.

'So, you'll do nothin'?'

'The constitution ties my hands, Jed.'

'Bloody typical. No wonder we want change.'

The phone went dead.

Rose glanced at Primrose, smiling. A scowl wrapped across Primmy's face. 'He's mean, Mummy.'

'Oh, he's okay. He's just annoyed about a few of his sheep dying, that's all.'

Her daughter came over to her, squeezing into the chair.

'Will everything be okay?'

'Yes, darling. Everything will be fine,' Rose said, wrapping her arms around her.

'Let me know if I can help, okay, Mummy? I'll do anything you want.'

Rose smiled, stroking her daughter's head.

'I love you, Mummy.'

CHAPTER

7

To have any chance of being re-elected, politicians need to be close to their community, especially in rural electorates like Mallee. Voters want a say on important issues, demanding their federal member be their loud voice in parliament and seldom hesitate to voice a view whenever they have the opportunity.

City electorates seldom see their federal member, and voters generally don't give a toss about politics. They reckon politicians are often playing fast and loose with the truth and only in it for themselves with their snouts in the money trough.

Rural folks are different and retain the habit of asking tough questions. Although, admiration is never high for politicians, no matter the electorate.

Ninety minutes on the road to an event to think about questions constituents could ask can push any fragile political character a little nutty. Rose Dowerin embraced it. Road time providing an opportunity for a podcast or maybe her favourite music. It was a break from the telephones and the occasional local constituent demanding she quieten a neighbour's dog.

This was her time.

Over the years, she tried to get ahead of the curve with her community by improving staff operations and support. She could now walk into a community meeting confident her briefing notes included likely questions with a list of constituents and party members expected to be at the event.

Today, the miles tripped past as she listened to her political thriller audio book, admiring the author's depiction of the quirky machinations of the Canberra political bubble. The vehicle almost drove itself as she listened. She cast the occasional eye over the farmland as she raced by, observing its dryness. As she neared her destination she speculated on the major political issues constituents could raise at the Mallee Machinery Day event.

Water remained the only issue.

Four hundred exhibitors would set up on leased property just south of Speed, a little town with a population of eighty. Over eight thousand visitors visit during the two-day event to evaluate equipment and seek technical advice. What commenced as a line-up of farm equipment with gnarled farmers clambering over gleaming machines progressed into a high-class event with produce, crafts and fashion pushing their way into exhibition space.

It offered a chance for Rose to talk to supporters, and during the years it rained, she would argue over immigration policy and high taxes. Now it was only ever about water. She seldom provided answers they wanted to hear, creating a political problem for her. Constituents didn't like their local member ignoring their concerns, and wanted her to adjust her attitude and become more vocal.

The federal government managed water rights as best it could. State governments control water: the federal government took all the political heat. *'Do something!'* was the ignorant cry from city talk-back hosts demanding Prime Minister Brown allocate money or legislate relief for the farmers and rural communities short of water.

'We send millions, if not billions, to Indonesia and other countries during emergencies like a tsunami, but we can't provide water to our farmers,' Denis Sadler, the high rating Sydney breakfast shock-jock, sneered into his microphone, setting off xenophobic rants from his city listeners. He would have farmers crying when they called to talk about their breeding stock and not being able to feed them.

'Prime Minister! What are you doing today that will help our farmers? It's a national disgrace.' He often declared.

So, when they scheduled the biggest agriculture event in the mallee, Rose understood it was in her best interests to always turn up and face her rowdy constituents, otherwise they pilloried her.

The heat smacked hard as she stepped from her government vehicle parked in the reserved VIP section. She wasn't expecting the sudden drain after the chill of her AC, causing her to be a touch unsteady on her feet. She leaned back into the cabin, snatching a bottle of water, and slugged it down before stretching for another from her small ice-chest out of the sun. She grabbed the leather bucket bag containing her political tools and plonked her broad-brimmed hat on her folded hair. The flies found another target as she stepped off, feeling a little better, but the heat remained oppressive.

Walking to the back of the vehicle, pleased she wore work boots, as the dirt gust up with each step, she opened the hatch, pulling out a horsehair fly whisk from a side pocket. It might appear pompous flicking the rattan stick about her shoulders, but at least the flies didn't bother her.

She took another slurp of water, dropping the bottle into her bag, then slinging the strap over her head, squinted against the sun, searching for a greeting party, surprised not to see one, plunging an ominous sense of dread into her chest. *Did they see her arrive? What plans have they for her?* Doubt squeezed her as she headed off, searching for the president of the Lions Club.

When she found the event manager's tent, the staff seemed pleased to see her, although expecting her later, lessening Rose's angst.

'Do you mind if we record your presentation?' a jolly lady asked.

'Record or film?'

'Um, record I think.' The lady seemed confused, flicking through sheets of paper.

Rose touched the woman's arm. 'Don't worry, it'll be fine.'

'Okay, that's great.' The lady smiled. 'And right on cue, your guide has arrived. This is Jeremy, and he will escort you around the exhibition.'

Rose turned to meet a strapping young man with thick auburn hair and a face full of freckles.

'Hi. Jeremy Cartwright, how are you?' He offered his hand.

'You belong to the Cartwright Station family?'

'Yep.'

'What brings you down here?'

'I'm doing ag-science at Longy.'

'Enjoying it?'

Cartwright shrugged. 'It's got its challenges.'

'Like what?'

'Oh well, too many international students, for starters.'

'You don't think we should send our farm education to the world?'

'It's not that.' Cartwright said, checking about to see if anyone was listening. 'They never come to class. I reckon someone who does want to learn could take that vacant chair. I mean, I have mates rejected who could do the work.'

'Longy needs the money.'

'Yeah, it probably does, but shouldn't the government be funding more agri places?'

Rose nodded. 'You on the electoral roll here or in the territory?'

'NT. Why?'

'Oh, I just wondered,' Rose said. 'If you don't mind, can we get the tour started?'

'Yes, ma'am.'

Rose learned long ago not to waste time talking policy with folks who weren't registered to vote in Mallee and followed the young man from the tent.

Ninety minutes later, weary from shaking hands, forcing a laugh, and smiling too much, Rose recovered off stage, scanning through papers, waiting for her call to address the meeting. Almost eight hundred farmers and agri-business people ventured into the tent keen to hear the federal member.

Organisers positioned more than a dozen hard working metal fans throughout the tent to generate air flow. Windows were wired tight and adventurous swarming flies were absent, to the relief of waving hands. Ice filled tubs of water bottles seemed to be everywhere.

When a Chamberlain John Deere agent wrapped up their presentation as part of a sponsorship deal, the Lions Club president came to the podium shuffling papers, searching for Rose's introduction. She insisted on one thing, an explicit statement: she was the federal member for Mallee, working hard for the community by securing funding grants.

When the hearty applause started, Rose stepped on stage, moving to the lectern without notes, knowing the message she needed to send. Before the applause dwindled off, she waved, lifted her hat, and smiled, facing the media cameras flickering to the side of the stage. Rose remained cynical enough to the adulation to understand she wasn't a celebrity, and a fickle electorate could turn against her at any time.

'Thank you for the kind words, Brian, and I want to acknowledge the work you and your club do organising such an outstanding event, which I note keeps growing year by year.'

'I also acknowledge the Traditional Owner peoples of this land; the Wotjobaluk, Jaadwa, Jadawadjali Wergaia and Jupagalk. I recognise the important and ongoing place all Wotjobaluk peoples hold in our community.' Rose didn't respond when she heard disapproving mutterings ripple through the crowd. 'I pay my respects to the Elders, both past and present, and commit to working together in the spirit of mutual understanding and respect for the benefit of the broader community and future generations.'

She paused, staring down any potential dissenters.

'It's not for me to talk about the long-term damage drought is causing and the impact on most communities in the mallee. We know, and many in the community accept that is the price we pay for making an agricultural living in the region. It's tough. My family knows it and we suffer just like everyone else.'

Rose didn't quite hear the interjection, so continued.

'Water is the golden staff of life for all of us, and without it, we have nothing. The drought is testing us, testing our resolve, and sometimes it has taken our hope for the future. Many of our community, especially cattle and sheep farmers, are reducing herds and flocks to cope with the financial pressure until it rains. They are shipping out breeders because of the cost of fodder and water. My worry is that if we lose our breeding stock, it will take years to build the herds and flocks back to a sustainable number.'

'This is the message I am delivering to the cabinet. We need water now, not in the future. We need action now, not in ten years and...'

'Let me stop you there, Rosie,' Jack Fingleton said as he stood in the middle of the audience. All eyes turned to him as a runner offered him a remote microphone. 'Thank you,' he said to the young lady. 'With respect to you Rosie, but what you just said is political clap-trap and frightens me a little.'

Rose had stopped speaking when she saw the cattle farmer stand and smiled at his comment. 'You're frightened, Jack? I find that hard to believe.'

'You are speaking in histrionics and again, there is no semblance of truth in what you are saying. It alarms me to think our federal member would say such rubbish.'

Rose stiffened. 'Are we not in a drought?' she said, her hands gesturing. 'Are our communities suffering because of it?'

'Of course, we are in drought. We are often in drought. This country has had droughts for centuries, but we have more than enough water to cope. We just don't have access to it. This is what alarms me about what you say. You must know the issues, or do we have a dud as our local member?'

Rose gnawed at the inside of her bottom lip, aware the media commenced recording the discussion. Fingleton watched, waiting for a response.

'The government does not control water allocations; this is a state government issue.'

'What a weak response from a respected community leader,' Fingleton said. 'Maybe you have been our federal member for too long.'

'Hear, hear,' several farmers repeated.

'Maybe you are tiring of being our voice and maybe we need a louder one that can get action on the water.' Fingleton commenced resuming his seat. 'Because Rosie, you are doin' nothin' for us.'

It did not surprise Rose when enthusiastic applause broke out in various sections of the gathering. She knew of the growing talk against her. 'What would you have me do? The leases are owned by Persian Water and operate under state water management regulations.'

'Change the law,' a voice demanded from down back.

'The law is the law. It is state law, and the feds have little control over the manner state laws are regulated, especially on water.'

'Rubbish.' A shout came from her left.

'Look...' she paused for a moment, dropping her head. 'The only way we could change the law is if the federal government gained control over water, and that means a referendum to change the constitution.' Rose scanned the meeting. 'And you know what happens in referendums, don't you?'

Fingleton jumped back to his feet, now without a microphone and raising his voice to be heard. 'At least try.'

'Your husband would have,' someone shouted.

Rose stared at the source of the voice but didn't recognise the person who yelled. 'This is not a gender issue, and shame on you for suggesting it.'

Several people dropped elbows to their knees, lowering heads and staring at their feet. They came to hear their federal member, and now the meeting whirled into a political scuffle.

'I'm but one voice in the cabinet. I cannot make the impossible possible,' Rose said.

'At least try,' Fingleton shouted again. 'Because if you don't, we will vote for someone who will.' Spontaneous applause erupted, much louder and more enthusiastic.

Rose perused the audience for a moment, then smirked, nodding.

'I have heard you and I promise you I will raise this issue at the next cabinet meeting on Monday in Canberra. I will provide a detailed response on my website.' Rose scanned the crowd, knowing it would be a waste of time to say anything further. 'Thanks for your time. Have a good day.'

The audience didn't clap as she left the stage. Many stood making their way from the tent. Others grouped for a chat. Rose just wanted to leave. As she reached the exit, Fingleton challenged her.

'You goin' straight back to Mildura?'

'I have farm visits to do on the way,' she lied.

'This water issue is hot in the community, Rosie, and you have to be seen to be doing something.'

'Why aren't you talking to the premier and threatening him, Jack?'

'We are. You just happen to be here today.'

'Advance notice would have been nice.'

'Yeah, maybe it would, but action might be better.'

'Are you leading the push to get rid of me?'

'No one wants you to go anywhere, but if you don't respond,' Fingleton paused, tightening his jaw, 'then we will find someone who will; trust me.'

'Trust you?' Rose scoffed as she turned away. 'I trust no one in politics, Jack, especially you.'

CHAPTER

8

The directors of the Persian Water Company often entertained, and tonight they intended to entertain the premier of Victoria, Phillip Jackson. They were his constituents and benefactors and whenever they beckoned, he would attend. When he could, he assisted them with various projects. In return, they remained generous to his election campaigns for Murray Plains.

The private dining suite in the executive wing had no window, dark in its colour palate, rich in texture. A long central hard wood dining table, big enough to entertain twenty, dominated the room. Lounges surrounding gas-fired replica wood fireplaces were set out at either end, adding grandeur. Art works adorned the wood panelling, highlighted by a recessed lighting system. Only the directors knew CCTV cameras in concealed positions recorded everything.

The jarrah table, often used for board meetings and presentations, was now set for five with Waterford crystal, Persian bone china and Christofle gold cutlery. The directors preferred formal dinners and Jackson always tossed a dinner suit into the car when he travelled to Swan Hill, just in case he received a call to join them across the river in New South Wales.

Well-dressed staff loitering about the downstairs foyer ushered the premier to a private elevator when he arrived. Jackson remained unsure if they were hospitality greeters or security. When he stepped from the elevator, a gloved attendant bowed, escorting him through a dimly lit corridor to the foyer of the dining room.

'Welcome, our friend.' Darius Hassidim stood stretching out his hand. The three others standing to welcome their guest. 'It is always nice to see you and I hope your room is satisfactory.' Darius moved closer for a hug.

'Chairman, it is always a pleasure to share a dinner with you and your directors.' Jackson shook each hand. 'The accommodation perfect, as always.'

'Come, please sit and let's relax before we have dinner. Would you care for a drink? Anything. What would you like?'

'A vodka martini, please,' Jackson replied, then turned to the attendant. 'A little dirty, please.'

'Of course, what an excellent choice. Please sit and let us talk about what you have been doing. How are the teachers treating you?'

Jackson sighed, then smiled as he flopped onto a leather couch. 'Ah, the teachers... they are fine. It's the fireys who are causing me pain. Their union boss is a bullying moron.'

'Anything we can do?' the muscled Maisil Ghassab asked, flicking lint from his knee.

'Noohohoho, Maisil, we will not get involved,' Darius laughed. 'The premier has it all under control, don't you, Phillip?'

'It's the usual pattern after any election.' Jackson nodded a thanks to the serving attendant. 'They follow each other. The coppers will be next, then the nurses. Here's cheers.'

Throughout dinner, the five men chatted about politics and the effects the drought affected the company. Then, as attentive, almost invisible staff cleared, the discussion came to the inescapable reason the premier attended the dinner. Darius winked across the table with a slight nod to the club's director of finance, sitting beside Jackson, encouraging him to begin.

'Mr Premier, as you know, I have the unenviable task of managing the finances of our organisation.'

Jackson tapped his mouth with his napkin, placing it on the table, turning so he could see Taimur Saraf. The bespectacled finance guru already needing a shave.

'Over the last thirty years, we have expanded our business interests to incorporate much of the economy of Swan Hill and Mildura,' Saraf said. 'We own the gaming clubs, the hotels and the liquor outlets.'

Jackson laughed and glanced across at Darius. 'Is that even legal?'

Darius tossed his head in a silent scoff, then nodded but said nothing.

'We have bloodstock holdings, and we own the regional transport fleet. We operate most of the pathology services outside of the government hospitals.' Saraf smiled as he paused. 'Although we have plans to expand further into the medical field, including another private hospital.'

'Impressive.'

'We own most things, Phillip,' Darius added. 'We even own the water, and because of the drought, it is becoming a major revenue stream. Excuse the pun. Continue, Taimur.' He nodded.

'We have significant holdings, as the chairman implies, but this does not transfer into a solid consolidated revenue base. Cash flow is a challenge, and our profits struggle.'

'The drought?' Jackson said.

'No, not at all.' Saraf rubbed his chin. 'Our expenses are high, affecting profit and cash flow because we provide significant funds to our community.'

'Very generous of you,' Jackson said, laying a finger across his lips to disguise his smirk. 'The tax benefits from those donations must be substantial.'

Hosmand Shofet, the legal director opposite, cleared his throat, leaning into the table. 'Our issue is beyond taxes. You must realise we pay our fair share.' He clasped his hands, rolling over the fingers as if to warm them. 'Mr Premier, our focus is on our community. We support their assimilation into the broader society, which generates a substantial cost to us.'

Jackson shook his head, frowned, pouting his lips. 'What type of expenses would you incur from services the government doesn't already provide?'

'You're kidding, right?' the big guy beside him asked.

'Maisil, be patient, my friend.' Darius cocked then waved his resting hand. 'Let Taimur explain.'

'The federal government-funded programs do not offer enough for resettlement. Local schools do not support religious studies, so we establish our own. Employment opportunities do not exist for settlers who don't speak English. We provide jobs. We also offer subsidised food and pharmaceuticals in Swan Hill and Mildura.'

'You do all that?' Jackson stared at Darius.

'Of course,' Darius said. 'We are not barbarians. We were the first to civilise, even before the Greeks.' He laughed. 'We are proud of our heritage, and we support our communities... our people.'

'We've taken Swan Hill's population to somewhere near fifteen thousand, and I estimate Mildura is sitting at around fifty thousand,' Shofet said.

'It's been a significant influence on the economy to have the Iranian community settle in the region,' Jackson said.

'We prefer to use the term Persians,' Ghassab grunted.

'Sorry.' Jackson fell back to the opposite arm of the chair.

'No matter, Mr Premier,' Shofet replied. 'The point we want to get to is this...' He paused, glancing at Darius, who nodded. 'We are seeking alternative channels of revenue and we have developed a plan to create employment, by increasing tourist visitations to the region, creating a new economic model for the mallee.'

Jackson didn't respond. His eyes darted about the directors. He could not fathom any ideas they could be talking about. 'You already explained you are into everything. What are you suggesting that might be different?'

Darius rested his head on his thumb, his forefinger scratching his cheek as he studied the premier. 'We have plans for a tourist precinct.'

Jackson didn't reply, doubting a few hotels would create a booming economy.

'We have identified land at Ned's Corner Station.'

'The nature reserve?'

'If scrublands are a nature reserve, then yes,' Shofet said.

'You want to buy the nature reserve?' Jackson said, shaking his head.

'We own most of the surrounding property, but we need the reserve,' Shofet replied.

Jackson tipped his head with a querying look back at Darius.

Darius continued, 'Our plan is to invest in the reserve. We will preserve the land and native animals. We shall fence it off, then rid it of the foxes and feral cats.'

'Gargantuan task,' Jackson said. 'Why?'

'We want to establish a tourist precinct at a bend in the river where some old homestead buildings are right now.'

'It's a flood plain.'

'Yes, we know; we own the water usage rights,' Darius responded.

'Why would you want to develop a nature reserve as a tourist precinct?' Jackson said, again shaking his head. 'Sounds crazy to me.'

'Our plan is to develop that bend in the river to include a marina with canals and other boating services. We will then create a more functioning nature reserve in the vast land we don't use. We also plan to develop other land we own nearby, which will service the tourist precinct.'

'I don't get it. Who would want to spend money to see a bearded dragon?'

'Phillip.' Darius breathed in, then smiled. 'Our plan is to generate four million visitors a year, but we anticipate that figure to increase to something like twenty million within ten years. We think the population servicing that standard of tourism to be around one hundred thousand.'

'You're kidding?' Jackson laughed out loud, looking at the ceiling. 'Must be some nature reserve.'

'It will be tourism, conventions, entertainment and...' Darius paused for a moment, 'gambling.'

Jackson's face dropped; he shifted in his seat and squeezed his napkin, avoiding looking across the table.

'We want to develop the Australian equivalent of Las Vegas, but without the criminals running it.' Darius smiled as he thumb-nailed his teeth.

No one spoke.

Jackson stared at the centre of the table.

'We want nothing from the government,' Darius added.

The premier smirked a little as he continued his stare. *He was here for a reason; he knew it was coming and was waiting for their call upon him.* He swallowed hard against his tightened throat, hoping they didn't detect it.

'Phillip, we want nothing from the government.' Darius said again, waiting for the premier to look at him. 'We just want to be treated fairly.'

'Is that something you can offer?' Shofet asked.

Jackson tightened his lips and nodded, suspecting there would be more to come.

'Relax, Premier.' Ghassab placed a reassuring hand on the premier's, who snatched it away. 'We are all friends here.'

'Who do you expect to work at the resort?' Jackson said, still not engaging with Darius.

Darius grinned. 'Well, not just a resort, more like a city. We plan an airport for freight and domestic travellers and expect international guests to fly direct from Asia.'

'Workers?'

'Given we already pay our community, we expect those who don't have work to be employed in the new city.'

'Living where?'

'On site for some, but mostly they will use more affordable living in Mildura. If we must build housing and community infrastructure on the land surrounding the reserve, then we will.'

'Services?' Jackson asked.

'All under our control. We will develop our own renewable energy plant and introduce the latest environmental technology for waste.'

'Medical?'

'We will supply it.'

'Law enforcement?'

'Unless the state wants to invest in these things, we will provide them.'

Jackson frowned, screwing his face. 'A private police force?'

'If we need to.' Darius leaned forward. 'Why all these questions? I expected you to be more supportive.'

'I need to know more detail.'

'And you will have it; presentation files that will answer all your questions are already in your room, but first let us have ghahve and dokha and relax. Maybe some arak... yes?' Darius opened his welcoming hands as coffee and small carafes of arak arrived. The staff placed individual wooden medwakh pipes with a silver tip and bowl before each of the diners.

The discussion mystified Jackson as he glanced at the directors. His leg bouncing as he tapped the table with a finger. He owed them, but this idea seemed more extensive than the information and support he had already provided. He massaged a thumb into a palm. Before entering parliament, he crossed the Persians a few times and knew all about their retribution.

As the staff left, Darius clapped.

The lights dimmed to spotlight the centre of the table. A hand drum beat from a darkened end of the room. Fingers flaying the skin captivating the men, now settling into sipping arak and smoking pipes, anticipating a performance.

Jackson shook his shoulders, enjoying the dokha. He glanced up; above him on the table stood a woman, matching the rhythmic beat, shuddering her hips. As she moved with the beat of the drum, her voluminous black hair whipped about.

The movements captivated Jackson as the dancer performed in front of him. Her chest covered with a sequined black top, heaving to the beat of the drum. Her arms waved to the rhythm, jewelled with armlets and bracelets forming alluring shapes above her head, then outstretching.

She stopped, and the beat paused. The drum then beat time, as she bounced her chest to the amusement of the others, encouraging her with grunts and claps. She flicked her body in time with the rhythmic, exotic beat. Her striking hair fell over her shoulders and down her back, beyond her hips. She held it back as she turned to face Darius, dropping to her knees, pulsating her hips. Then back on her feet, spinning with her grey chiffon skirt, offering an intoxicating waving movement. She stepped to the side, her hips regaining the beat of the drum, with her belly moving up and down in rhythm.

She peered at Darius, then turned to smile at the premier.

Her bejewelled hips still pounding a beat. Or was the drum leading her hips? The gawking men didn't care as they watched with broad smiles.

The drum changed beat again, and she bent over, her hair touching the table. Her hands snatched at the chiffon on her hips, pulling it to the side and spun as if with wings. Or did she spin a web? The drum stopped. She dropped her chiffon wings. It then beat gradually, building to a fast tempo. The dancer flicked her head, sending her hair into a rhythmic spin, faster and faster towards exhaustion. Then she stopped to return to the beat, her hips in a frenzy. The men's ears pulsating to the drum as they watched.

The beat stopped. She dropped to the table, flat back on her heels, her hair draping over Jackson's cup and glass. The directors clapped, and she opened her eyes, the blackness staring at the premier catching his gaze. She then stood, spun gracefully, smiled at the premier and tip-toed away.

The premier cast an eye over at Darius. 'She is good.'

'She is very good.' Darius nodded, arching a brow.

Jackson understood the gesture and smiled, then shook his head. 'Not tonight.'

'We hope you have enjoyed your evening, Premier,' Darius said, rising to his feet.

The other directors stood as one. Jackson did not move, confused by their sudden exit.

As they congregated by the door, leaving Jackson still seated, Darius said, 'Our presentation is in your room. We look forward to talking more about our strategy.' His tone changed and seemed menacing. 'We need your help, and we expect it. Mohammad will see you to your room.'

As they left, Ghassab turned and smiled back at the premier, lifting his hand to wave goodbye, but waggling his little finger instead.

Jackson watched them go, leaning on his fist, elbow on the table. He sighed, exhaling hard. He poured the last of his arak and slugged it down. As he moved to leave, the lights dimmed. Salome's seven veils music stopped him.

CHAPTER

9

Rose preferred to leave a wardrobe of parliamentary clothes in Canberra, enabling her to travel light, with an over-large leather briefcase on wheels her only responsibility. To connect with the Canberra flight from Melbourne, she needed to make the early six o'clock shuttle from Mildura. A tiring commute but much better than the gruelling nine-hour road trip.

When Rose arrived, her ministerial chief of staff, Charlotte Poore, waited with her daily schedule, a file of correspondence to be signed and information about a constituent requesting a chat already making five calls.

'Okay, who is it?' Rose said.

'Darius Hassidim.'

Rose's chest tightened, steadying herself on the side of her desk.

'Did he say what he wanted?'

'It was creepy, to be honest,' Charlotte chuckled. 'He whispered, and it was like I could feel his lips in my ear. Totally weird, and he just hasn't given up calling.'

'Okay, let's do him first.' Rose moved to her chair. 'Is the PM seeking meetings?'

'His office claims he is busy. Cabinet is scheduled after lunch. There are visiting dignitaries from the Pacific Forum, and apparently, he is meeting one leader late in the afternoon.'

'Where from?'

'Cook Islands, I think.'

'Do we need to do anything for them?' Rose winced.

'Only the formal dinner in the Great Hall.'

'Great, let's get Hassidim on the line. We had better have Roger join us.'

'Expecting trouble?'

'I may need a legal view.'

'I'll get it organised.' Charlotte stepped off to allow her boss to settle in.

Ten minutes later, Charlotte trailed Roger Newgreen into the office, settling with the minister at a meeting table by the window. She stabbed in numbers and it surprised Rose when Darius answered.

'Minister, good morning.'

'Huh? How did you know it was me?'

'I prefer not to be on speaker phone.'

'I prefer to be hands free.'

'Are you alone?'

Rose raised a finger to her lips. 'Yes, of course. How can I help?'

'Minister, I'm very concerned about many rumours I am hearing.'

'What are you hearing?' Rose shook her head and shrugged at the others.

'I am hearing there's a lot of unhappiness in your electorate, and this troubles me.'

'What have you heard?'

'Scandalous comments about water access and citizens blaming you.'

'There's been talk about your water prices; I can confirm that.'

'The economic market controls the price, does it not?' Darius said.

'Farmers reckon your price is too high.'

'They have options.'

'That means carting water, which is horrendously expensive.'

'Exactly.'

'But you control the transport companies.'

'A free market, is it not?'

Rose flicked her eyes across her staff. 'Some would suggest a monopoly.'

'I prefer to call it a diversification of business interests to protect my company from market fluctuations.'

'Your clients want me to raise the issue in the cabinet and I intend doing so.' Rose nodded towards her staff. They nodded with a *we'll work it out* shrug.

'I heard about the motion last week and even the trouble at the field days on the weekend,' Darius replied. Rose smiled at Charlotte, pinching and flicking her own ears. 'I do not want you to raise the issue if you wouldn't mind.'

Smiles disappeared with Newgreen leaning forward to scribble notes.

'You don't want me to speak about you manipulating water prices in the mallee?'

'It's a state government issue. Your government can do nothing. If you insist on raising water in the parliament, then I must advise you of the potential consequences. Hence my call.'

'I want water to be released at a price meeting the community's need for water.'

'You want?' Darius snapped, then paused. 'This is an interesting proposal.'

Rose gulped, then cleared her throat. 'I want my communities to have water that has travelled miles before you have gotten your greedy hands on it. I want what mother nature intended.'

'If this is what you want, what are you prepared to give?' Darius said in a hushed tone.

Rose said nothing, glancing at her staff. 'I tell you what I can assure you.'

'Assure me?' Darius scoffed a laugh. 'What is it you can assure me, Minister?'

Rose ignored Charlotte's placating hand gesture. She then leaned in and spoke slowly. 'I can reassure you that unless you offer more water at a reasonable price, I will do all I can to have your so-called water rights stripped from you.'

Darius whispered, 'Good luck.'

'If I don't get a conciliatory sign from you this week, then I will act.'

'I am disappointed with this aggressive tone, Rose.'

'You ain't seen nothing yet.'

Darius paused for a moment. 'Minister, it seems you wish to start a fight.'

'I will do whatever it takes to end your manipulation of water leases and profiteering from misery and hardship.'

Darius paused, then lowered his tone. 'Allow me to reassure you... if you move against me, I shall end your parliamentary career, just like your husband's.'

Rose glanced at the others, eyes wide and flicking about. The knot in her chest tightened. Her face went ashen as her jaw dropped.

'Goodbye, Minister.'

The staffers remained quiet as she panted through her nose.

'You okay, Rose?' Charlotte asked.

Rose glanced at her. 'Are you thinking what I'm thinking?'

'He just threatened your preselection?' Charlotte said.

'No,' Newgreen interrupted. 'I think the minister thinks the threat might be a little more... how shall I say, vigorous than that,' he said, finalising a note.

Rose leaned back and stretched, reaching her hands to the ceiling to rid herself of the energy she had internalised from the call. 'How safe do you think my numbers are?'

Charlotte cast an eye at Newgreen, who shrugged. 'The party will support you.'

Rose tossed her head back, looking at the ceiling, her hands linked behind her head. 'How sure are you, Roger?'

'As sure as I can be,' Newgreen said, twiddling his pen. 'None of the preselection delegates have changed since last time, so we should expect the same support.'

'No one was ever going to back the environmentalist, so the sample is a little jaundiced,' Rose said, straightening.

'Is it worth having a ring around to get a feel of how they are thinking?' Charlotte asked.

'You might be right.' Rose crossed her legs. 'Just be careful, though.

The pretence for any call should be something other than preselection. I don't want anyone getting nervous.'

Newgreen began packing. 'Who don't we want, standing against us?'

'They'll be serious if they use a party delegate,' Rose responded.

'Best we kill off any threat,' Charlotte added.

Rose scoffed a laugh. 'Just be careful what you promise them.'

'Noted, boss.' Newgreen withdrew, leaving Charlotte to discuss water policy and whether Rose should raise it at the cabinet meeting.

After the discussion, Charlotte paused by the door as she was leaving. 'What did Hassidim mean when he referenced your husband?'

Rose circled her desk, preparing to sign various correspondence. As she sat, she glanced at Charlotte, waiting by the door. 'I suppose he wanted to remind me folks die doing their job.'

'Your husband's death was an accident, wasn't it?'

Rose grimaced, clenching her teeth, glancing out the window. 'No conclusive answer, to be honest.'

'What did the police report?'

'Suicide is the formal response,' Rose said. 'They found him in the river after a two-day search.'

'Why would Hassidim suggest otherwise?'

Rose glanced at Charlotte. 'Look, we shouldn't read too much into what folks might say under stress.'

'Tea?'

'I should have these signed by the time you get back,' Rose said, patting the yellow file.

She watched Charlotte go, then stretched out of her chair, wandering over to her window, looking through the wooden slats out over the courtyard and into its greenery. She dragged the blinds up.

Peter provided cautionary tales to her about Hassidim. She knew him from the early years and heard the stories but had yet to see any evidence of the savage nature people alluded to. Rose wrapped her arms around herself, as if feeling the chill from outside. As she sat at her desk to warm up, she pondered the reality of the Hassidim threat.

CHAPTER
10

R ain showered the window as Rose watched from her desk. Her allocated office on the first floor of the ministerial wing allowed her to watch the cloudy mist of rain rolling in. A stark difference to her electorate in the mallee suffering from a dilapidating drought ruining not only landscape and livestock but lives.

The stark paradox of her life did not pass at such moments.

She could escape the desperation. Others she loved could not leave Mildura, and they hadn't experienced in years what she now watched. A touch of guilt rushed through as she examined droplets of water trickling down the glass, chilling her arms.

'Minister?' her chief of staff interrupted. 'Your meeting is in ten minutes; do you have questions?'

Rose ignored her for a moment and then turned into her desk. 'What is the gossip?'

'I've heard nothing, so don't expect any surprises.'

'Any movement on water?'

'The only thing I've heard is that the PM will table a new drought funding package, but I'm unsure what it is.'

'No papers?'

Charlotte laughed, then corrected herself. 'Sorry Minister, but no, we don't have a briefing paper.'

'Right then, what should I be looking out for?'

'We think something is happening in the leader's office, but we could not get any information, so expect an announcement.'

Rose fell back into her chair. 'How do you obtain this information?'

'Knowing who to talk to and at what time to do so.'

'It never ceases to amaze me how this place works.'

Charlotte remained standing, just nodding, lips withdrawn and eyes wide, promoting her boss to get moving.

Rose took the hint. 'I guess I should be going.' She bounced up, collected her cabinet briefing files, and left. 'Thanks, Charlie, I appreciate all you do.'

'Don't let Spencer get to you.'

Rose left the office, stomping down the internal wooden stairs. She dashed past the PM's media entrance and then into the cabinet room. The prime minister was yet to arrive and only half her colleagues were present, chatting or reading briefs. *Why were they still reading them?* Rose could never figure it out.

She ambled to the far end of the room and flopped into her normal chair before placing files on the long, oval-shaped cabinet table. The prime minister's leather chair was positioned on the opposite side, with his red leather compendium prepared for him.

On the button of one o'clock, Prime Minister Brown strode to his chair, checking papers before him, taking immediate command. No pleasantries, no attendance listing, just straight into the agenda.

'Item one, finance. Joe, your report, please.'

The treasurer explained the current state of the budget and outlined his proposed legislation. Several ministers asked questions. Why they still needed to ask confused Rose, as his replies were always the same: 'That answer is in your briefing notes'. The treasurer relished exposing colleagues.

Rose learned the cabinet political game early and kept her counsel, rarely asking a question during briefings from ministers. She saved her questions for important policy impacting her portfolio.

According to the agenda, five ministers were to provide a brief on the intended consequences of legislation they were proposing to table in the House of Representatives. The agenda then welcomed spending proposals from departments submitted by the relevant minister. It then listed political issues for discussion. Drought being the last agenda item.

'Before asking Bernie to brief everyone,' Brown said, leaning into the table, 'I want to announce the government will increase drought funding by a little over three hundred million dollars over a three-year period. We will focus on providing drought-stricken farmers with financial support to care for families. We will also provide an additional fifty million in mental health services. This is a significant issue not only for farming communities but also the towns of regions affected. The government will offer funds from the Drought Future Fund for the construction of dams and other irrigation infrastructure to aid in the sustainability of our agri-sector. I believe a solid funding program and will help farms in trouble.' Brown paused for questions, not expecting any.

Rose waited for colleagues to speak; none did. She tugged her seat to the table, leaning on her forearms, fiddling with her pen. She waited for an opportunity, seeking the prime minister's attention. He rarely cast an eye in her direction, so she cleared her throat and called for recognition to speak.

'Thank you, Prime Minister. I'm pleased to hear about these important initiatives, although no detail has been distributed.'

The prime minister sighed, dropped his pen, and leaned back in his chair. 'You will have papers after the announcement.'

'After is not before, so ministers and members who represent communities suffering from drought could make contributions. I note Canberra has rain today, which I suspect is inconvenient for many in this place, given the constant downpour. But these inconveniences are nothing compared to the zero rainfall in the mallee for the last three hundred and twenty days. Indeed, regions have gone without solid rainfall for much longer.'

The prime minister cast an eye at the treasurer, who shrugged. 'What's your point?'

'My point, Prime Minister, is this... your announcement of funding, whilst welcomed, doesn't go to the very heart of the problems out bush. The fact is, these are future funds. Not for today's needs, such as water.'

'Clare?' the prime minister called upon the water minister, interrupting a frowning Rose.

'Prime Minister, I hadn't finished.'

'Oh, I'm sorry. I thought you wanted an answer to the water question.'

'No, not at all,' Rose said. 'We have enough water in the mallee, but what we don't have is access.'

'How is this possible?' Clare Spencer said.

Rose smiled with a sigh. 'Well, I wouldn't expect a city member to know what was happening with water out bush.'

'I'm the water minister.'

The prime minister watched the discussion; he glanced across to the treasurer and winked.

'If that is the case,' Rose continued, 'you could explain why the cost of water access has escalated sixfold in the last six months, rising from around one fifty a mega-litre to an astonishing eight hundred and sixty dollars? It's outrageous, and we can't allow this to continue.'

Her statement surprised treasurer Joe Haslam, and he turned to Rose. 'Why is this happening?'

'Speculators, not landowners, have secured the leasing rights and they're manipulating the market to force irrigators and the farming community to pay a premium price.'

'How do they get the water rights?' asked Haslam

'It's a regulated open market and they buy low, then sell high. The joke is that these speculators don't even own land.'

'Legally?' The treasurer glanced towards Spencer.

Spencer shifted, then dragged her chair to the table. 'What Rose is saying is provocative. The system of water rights has been operating for decades, allowing farmers to manage water and carry over their allowances rather than sell or lease their allocation. The trouble comes from investors in Sydney or Melbourne trading water rights, driving up the price and denying access.'

'They aren't in Sydney or Melbourne,' Rose interrupted. 'They're based in Swan Hill.'

Spencer ignored the interjection. 'The drought spiked the price, but farmers still have access.'

'Only if they pay an extortionate fee,' Rose said too loudly.

Haslam turned to Spencer. 'Is that right?'

She glanced towards the prime minister, shifting in her chair. 'Yes.'

Rose continued. 'So, Prime Minister, the farmers are struggling with making payments for fodder, and this increased water fee is cutting into them. Your proposed funding announcement will not resolve the angst out bush. Many are walking away from farms because they can't survive. They need cash now to save stock. Their breeding stock is being slaughtered because they can't afford them. No seeding is being done because they can't afford it. We are in crisis, but all we hear is that you are paying for mental health aid.'

'Well, it's important,' Brown said, crossing his arms leaning back in his chair.

'They want fodder and water, not welfare,' Rose said.

'The states look after fodder, water and animal welfare,' Haslam said. 'We look after farmers.'

'The way things are going, we won't have any farmers left, at least not in the mallee.'

No one spoke. The silence of the room intimidating many around the table. Advisers ready to offer information sitting against walls scanned notes. Ministers avoided the discussion checking papers or looking at the prime minister.

'What do you think we should do, Rose?'

'I think you should shove a red-hot poker up the premier's arse.'

Smiles emerged; a few colleagues joked with their neighbour.

'We either send in the regulatory bodies to find out if there has been unconscionable conduct, or...'

'How many water companies are there?' Brown asked Spencer.

'Twenty.' She guessed wrong.

'There's five,' corrected Rose. 'We either regulate them out of existence or legislate the power from the states.'

'We should get onto it, Clare,' Brown said. Spencer took a note, nodding.

Rose hadn't finished. 'Prime Minister, this issue has the potential to kill the government.'

'It's only the mallee,' Haslam joked.

Rose took a deep breath. 'If you think it won't affect any of our marginal seats, then think again. What will folks like Denis Sadler do to the government once he sinks his claws into it?'

'Sadler has little interest in the bush,' Haslam said.

'He's not after ratings in the bush,' Rose said. 'He will be after you and will treat this fodder and water issue like a crisis.' She stopped for a moment, glancing around the table. 'I can just hear him now, complaining about the dollars we spend on overseas aid during tsunamis, and we can't even bother to treat our farmers with respect. I can just hear his talkback callers now.'

'Rose may have a point,' Brown said. 'We don't want this getting into mainstream media, so let's see what we can do with the water leasing rights.'

'Just buy the leases back and let's get water to the communities,' Rose said.

The treasurer nodded, then arched a brow towards Brown. 'We can look at it.'

'Okay, that's good,' the prime minister said, leaning forward. 'Let's move on. Bernie?'

Rose pushed her chair back from the table, bouncing the tips of her fingers on her upper lip as she leaned upon her elbow, paying little regard to the agriculture minister. She looked at Clare Spencer, her nemesis since they entered parliament together. Spencer served in the inner cabinet where the important decisions were made. Rose's ministerial career stalled as she floundered in the outer ministry.

Spencer remained the go-to politician to fill quotas. She lived on the north coast of New South Wales, parading her young family in every lifestyle magazine for the last ten years. She looked good in front of cameras; media often discussed her fashion choices. The only thing she didn't have going for her was policy gravitas, hardly ever across her department's brief. She didn't have to be as the prime minister favoured her.

The meeting continued for another hour. Rose penned a media release as she listened, more interested in the politics of her electorate than the Great Barrier Reef. The prime minister straightened to close the meeting when the deputy prime minister and leader of Rose's Country Party asked for a few moments.

'I suppose this is as good a time as any to announce that I will not be seeking re-election at the next election. I will step down from my role as leader soon after Christmas,' Jock Garnsworthy said, pausing for a moment. 'I shall leave it to my party to appoint a new leader and therefore deputy prime minister.'

Rose noticed Spencer bowing her head to hide from the nods and smiles sent to her from colleagues. She assumed the others weren't up to it and Spencer would get the job. One of the great paradoxes of politics: a regional and rural party appointing an urban politician as its leader. A woman elected because it was her turn, and nothing to do with merit.

Spencer cast an eye towards Rose and winked, releasing a sly smile as the prime minister thanked his deputy for his service, then closed the meeting with a flourish, departing the room with Spencer and Haslam struggling to keep up.

Rose stayed, thinking through the announcements. After years of low-ranking ministries, it seemed obvious her career had stalled. Perhaps she should be grateful for the regional development portfolio, but it didn't satisfy her long-time ambition. She wanted to be at the decision-making table. Much of the conspiratorial talk against her suggested she could go no further in the ministry, and they should make a change. The safer the seat, the more marginal the member, as the saying goes.

Rose felt very marginal at that moment.

CHAPTER
11

'The prime minister's office has been requesting you to go see him at once,' Charlotte Poore warned Rose as she walked in with a bundle of files.

'Immediately?'

'That's what they said.'

'Anything happen? What's happened to his diplomacy meeting?'

'They wouldn't say, suffice to say he wants you now.'

Rose never responded well to strong assertiveness, no matter who it was from, but realised when the prime minister called, perhaps she should be more welcoming. She finished signing the correspondence before heading off. She strolled past the Country Party leader's office to check if he will join the PM for the meeting. The news Garnsworthy would not be attending squeezed a knot through her chest.

She passed the principal private secretary's office. 'Hi Jon, do you know why the PM wants to see me?'

'No idea, Rosie.'

'I thought he was meeting the Cook Islanders?'

'He did have them scheduled but changed it thirty minutes ago.'

She knocked politely, then stepped through, gently closing the heavy door. The prime minister sat behind his desk talking to Clare Spencer.

'Ah, Rose. Come in, please sit down.' Brown gestured to a chair next to Spencer. 'Thanks for coming; you must have been busy.'

'How can I help?'

'Clare and I are considering a reshuffle.'

Rose glanced at her colleague, relaxing with an elbow resting on the back of her chair. 'A reshuffle?'

'Yes,' Brown grinned. 'I'm expecting Clare to be appointed leader of the Country Party. I thought it would be a good idea to take the opportunity for a reshuffle.'

Rose nodded. It seemed a reasonable suggestion. Spencer would likely stand for election unopposed. 'What did you have in mind?'

Brown still held his broad smile. 'I'm going to drop you from the ministry.'

'Say again?'

'We were just chatting, and it seems you are unlikely to be preselected. We reckon it might be an idea to move you on now rather than wait until your party dumps you.'

'What makes you say that?' Rose said, then cleared her throat.

'Information I have suggested you don't have the numbers to see off a challenge.'

Rose cast an eye at Spencer, who sat with a smirk, swinging a crossed leg.

'You told him this?'

'No, not at all. Tim asked me to join him, then we called your office.'

Rose turned to Brown. 'What have you heard, Prime Minister?'

Brown craned forward to look at scribbled notes. 'That you are not working on the issues. That you are lazy, which I can vouch for, given your performance in various portfolios.'

'Why haven't you sacked me then?' Rose said, tightening her lips.

'A gender thing.' Brown leaned back, rocking his chair. 'Now that Clare will be leader, I can bring in two girls. So, it's a positive.'

'I've done my job.'

'Not as well as you could have.' Brown picked his teeth with the nail of his thumb. 'Indeed, you say nothing in the cabinet, and reports from your department suggest you have a manner that does not create a positive work environment.'

'A manner?'

'Yes,' Spencer interrupted. 'You have a manner, and I don't like it.'

Rose nodded, tightly pressing her lips, trying hard not to respond. 'When?'

'When what?' Spencer asked, glancing towards the prime minister.

'In a couple of months.' Brown said. 'Once we have Clare settled in, so I'm thinking January, maybe.'

'This will kill any chance I had of winning preselection.'

Brown grinned, showing his teeth. 'Maybe. Maybe not.'

'Why are you doing this?'

Brown moved into his desk, ending the conversation. 'Rose, it's not personal. It's about business, and this decision is about what's good for my government. It has nothing to do with you personally.'

'I can keep my portfolio until January?'

'Yes, of course, but I would not be putting your hand up for too much travel. Work your electorate, I would suggest.'

Rose stood. 'Not the news I was expecting.'

'What were you expecting?'

'Oh, I don't know, maybe an announcement about water management, given the policy discussion we had in the cabinet.'

'Water management is a state issue. I said that in the meeting.'

'You know, I heard that exact same thing earlier today.'

'All done. When can I expect my money?'

'Prime Minister, thank you for your assistance.'

'When will I get my money?' Brown insisted.

'It is already in your Barbados account.'

'Nice doing business with you again, Darius.'

Rose didn't want to return to her office, so wandered off to Aussies Café at the other end of the parliament building's central core.

When she hit the timber floor, clomping past Members' Hall, she telephoned Charlotte, asking her to join her. She joined the queue for coffee, which weaved its way past newspapers and magazines, past the emergency food supplies and finally to the front counter. She ordered two lattes and waited. When she collected them, she walked out into the inside courtyard of tables and chairs.

Charlotte secured a table by the floor-to-ceiling wall of windows and waved as Rose searched about. She glided her way past the occupied tables and passed the coffee over. She needed a hit of caffeine, and as Charlotte drained a sleeve of sugar into her glass, Rose sipped a mouthful, washed it over her tongue and swallowed, then repeated the dose.

'That's much better,' she sighed.

Charlotte stirred her coffee, watching. 'What's wrong, boss? You appear frazzled.'

'Frazzled is not the word I would use, more like disappointed.' She sighed again as she checked about the crowded tables. 'I wonder why I keep doing this.'

'What's happened?'

'Reshuffle.' Rose took another sip of coffee.

Charlotte waited for more. It didn't come. 'And?'

'They are dumping me.'

'What? When?'

'When Jock retires.'

'Jock loves you.'

'Yeah, I know, but once he's gone, then Brown is going to... no wait, it's not Brown, it's Spencer who is knifing me.'

'Why?'

'Apparently not doing my job. Upsetting folks.' Rose crossed her arms and stretched out her feet, leaning back in the wooden chair. 'What did he say?' Rose dropped her head back for a moment. 'He said my manner upset people.'

'That's crazy.'

Rose stretched for her coffee and took another tongue-washing sip.

'That may be so, but he's effectively ended my career. There's no coming back.'

Charlotte said nothing for a while. 'What are you going to do?'

'Nothing much I can do. Once I leave the ministry, the local party folks will absolutely want to change the local member and my job is effectively over.'

'Mine too.'

'Yes, that's right,' Rose realised, a little embarrassed. 'Sorry, Charlie.'

'Don't worry about me. I'll get another ministerial position.'

Rose nodded. 'Of course, you will. Or maybe you could put your hand up and run for a seat. We need women like you in the parliament.'

Charlotte ignored the comment. 'You want to give up or fight?'

Rose sighed, glancing out the window at the rain. It had been a tough job since replacing her husband twenty-five years ago. 'Another battle.' She said, still gazing out the window. 'Do I have the energy?'

They sat quietly for a while. Charlotte gazing into her coffee, spooning froth from the side of the glass. 'Do you think the Arab had anything to do with it?'

Rose pondered the question.

'I mean, does it just sound like a coincidence that he threatens you this morning? Then a few hours after raising the issue in the cabinet, you lose your job,' Charlotte said.

'Yeah, nah. Not sure his influence would extend to the prime minister.'

'Why not? Money speaks all languages.'

Rose shook her head. 'Not likely. Nah. Couldn't happen.'

'It just sounds too convenient.'

'You've been reading Machiavelli again, haven't you?' Rose smiled.

'Everyone has a price, boss. You know that.'

'What's mine?'

'What would you do to get water?'

'Interesting.' Rose nodded. 'Maybe I would do anything if I knew it would make a difference.'

'Would you take money?'

'I suppose I already do when I accept campaign funds. But would I accept money from the Arabs?' Rose eyed her staffer. 'No, I wouldn't. I prefer to fight for what is right than get paid off.'

'What's right here?'

'With the PM do you mean, or the water?'

'Both.'

'I suppose I should fight and stop feeling sorry for myself,' Rose said, leaning forward.

'Then maybe we should tweak the water plan and go hard while you still have the opportunity.'

Rose drained her coffee. She then glanced up and smirked. 'Fancy another?'

'Battle or coffee?'

'Let's have a coffee first and then perhaps we can develop hostile battle plans.'

CHAPTER
12

No one expected Phillip Jackson's party to win the election two years ago, but it seems political miracles can happen. His party went to the election promising austerity with a policy focus away from Melbourne, in favour of developing regional cities. This simple plan caught the imagination of the voters in rural and regional seats, resulting in the party for the first time winning more seats than its coalition partner, resulting in him being appointed premier. The media called him the accidental premier.

Whenever Hassidim requested him to join them for an event, he did so, provided his diary was open. Today it was. He met the directors at Swan Hill airport for a flight to Mildura to attend a lunch with the local council. He walked across the tarmac apron waving to the men waiting by a Cessna decorated with the striking green, white and red colours of the Persian Water Company.

The luxurious nature of the cabin did not surprise Jackson; it had six plush leather seats with a bottle of water in the armrests. Taimur Saraf passed a little plate of Persian appetisers to him. A smiling Hosmand Shofet leaned forward. 'It should take us about an hour. We have a car waiting and Council will be ready for lunch.'

'The reason Council wants to meet with me is why?'

'We are meeting with them,' Darius Hassidim said, turning from watching the plane take off. 'I want them to learn of our plans for the tourist precinct and I would like you there to gauge reaction and add your government's point of view.'

'We don't have a point of view.'

Darius leaned out of his seat and patted the premier's arm. 'But you will.' He then smiled like a car salesman. 'This is a beautiful project and will offer jobs and growth for the region, which is what you want, isn't it?'

Jackson peered at the smiling Darius and flashed a benign smile, shoving a portion of soft cheese into his mouth, then gazed out his window to the dry land below.

The plane gave Mildura a wide berth, flying north across the river into New South Wales and then tacking in a direction that would take it over the nature reserve at Ned's Corner.

'We are there,' announced the pilot.

Jackson looked out at the desolate land; he wondered why anyone would be crazy enough to redevelop the area. 'Is that a flood plain?' The others looked down.

Shofet responded. 'The river is prone to flood in this region when water flowing downstream increases. Our plan is to build a channel for when we have over bank transfers.'

'You can see the natural flood flow, and the area we want to develop is safe from flooding,' Darius said.

'Where exactly?'

'See the point the bend in the river creates? Just near the junction of the other river.'

'The forested area?'

'Yes, that's it. The nature reserve encloses it. The government classifies the region as a high preservation zone. Although one wonders why,' Darius said.

'How much land do you need?'

'We will develop around twelve thousand hectares,' Darius added.

'The plan is to protect the rest,' Shofet said. 'We will develop any support sites needed for the precinct, such as industrial and residential estates, either across the river in New South Wales or outside the protected zone,' he continued. 'We are purchasing land for that use now.'

'Take it around again and much lower this time,' Darius told Saraf, sitting behind the pilot.

'Who lives on that property?' Jackson asked as they followed the river.

'The conservation park manager,' Shofet said.

'Indigenous?'

'No,' Darius said. 'We are planning to employ local aborigines either in the tourist precinct or as rangers within the conservation zone. We have spoken to local elders and expect they will agree to the project.'

'You seem to have everything covered.'

Shofet smiled. 'We wouldn't be doing this unless we set new standards in conservation, biodiversity and environmental protection.'

Jackson scoffed a cynical smile. 'But boys, you're planning Las Vegas.'

'A tourist precinct is all we have planned,' reassured Darius, as he peered out the window at the desolate landscape.

Jackson looked across at him. 'What do you want me to do?'

'Allow us to buy the land and then make sure the plans go through without too much aggravation.'

'What will be the cost to the government?'

'We are funding the entire development,' Shofet said. 'We will be happy to pay the relevant taxes once it's operational after a settling-in period.'

'How long do you expect the settling-in process to be?'

'Five years of full operation.'

'Tax free for five years?'

'That's our plan,' Darius said.

Jackson shook his head, tightening his lips. 'This sounds too good to be true.'

'To you maybe, but you are a politician,' Darius said, smiling. 'To us it is a hundred-year plan for the region and our people.'

'I don't like your chances of getting it through the bureaucracy and the inevitable protestors.'

'What protestors should we worry about?' Darius asked.

'The greenies, the anti-gambling lobby and maybe the churches,' Jackson said. 'Not to mention it will be a political hot potato.' He scratched his head. 'Permissions may never be given.'

'Never fear, Premier, we always get what we want... eventually,' Maisil Ghassab joined in the conversation.

'Hush now, Maisil,' said Darius. 'The premier knows we do everything by the book.'

Ghassab smiled, then gazed out his window. 'Yes, I believe he does.'

The plane banked again, heading for Mildura.

A bus-like black SUV with darkened windows met the plane as it taxied to a quiet section of the tarmac apron. Jackson stifled a laugh at the cliché when he saw it. They entered the vehicle through the side door and relaxed into the leather seats as the vehicle sped from the zone.

The premier wondered if the folks he could see walking the streets would care if their government leader was in town. It seemed so secretive; he questioned what his role might be. The plan seemed simple enough. He read their submission, and the flyover showed a nonproductive, desolate land, except to the plants and animals that called it home.

The vehicle drew up outside the Grand Hotel where a well-dressed aide opened the door. Another aide, also well-dressed in black, waited by the front entrance and led the group through to the famous Savino's restaurant in the cellars. Yet another well-dressed aide, female this time and wearing a hijab, led the group along a dark corridor with lit tables along one wall and memorabilia festooning the other. The group stepped out into a bigger, low ceiling, well-lit dining room with a table set for sixteen.

The long-retired founder, Savino de la Pieria, changed the food culture in the region, and they kept many of his recipes on the menu. The restaurant remained closed for the afternoon, booked for a private function.

The councillors stood as the group entered and made their way to greet them. They all deferred to Darius, before the premier, which

Jackson noted. Shofet asked them to sit; the premier sat with Darius at the head of the table. Restaurant staff fussed over guests serving wine and filling glasses of water. Once done, the chef stepped forward and announced his plans for lunch.

'It is the tradition of Savino that we only serve fresh produce every day. If we cannot get it fresh, then it will not appear on our tables. Poor ingredients will never make excellent recipes taste better and so we only use the best ingredients. We use the practice of cucina povera, which is a labour of love, to offer you freshness and full flavour. So welcome to our restaurant...' The chef paused, gazed at Darius. 'Or should I say, your host Darius Hassidim wishes you a plentiful and enjoyable lunch.'

The guests clapped as the chef withdrew.

'Gentlemen.' Darius glanced at the mayor, then nodded. 'And lady, of course. Welcome and thank you for coming. We are here to enjoy ourselves and I hope the food we have planned allows you to benefit from the many joys of the local produce. So, let us toast the occasion.' He raised his glass. 'And may we welcome the premier, who is here to listen and further understand the plans for a better future for the region of Mildura. Cheers.'

The councillors raised their glasses and responded.

Jackson considered it proper to say a few words. 'I am thrilled to see you all today. I am keen to get your feedback on the issues you consider important, and I want to make sure if any matters remain unresolved by the end of lunch, then we figure out how we can resolve them.'

The mayor looked at Darius, then smiled at the premier. 'The only issue we have in this region is water.'

Shofet sat straighter, leaning into the table. 'These are matters for the local independent state member for Mildura.' Ghassab tapped his right fist into his hand several times, which didn't go unnoticed by many at the table.

The mayor shrugged. 'Darius, we are grateful for the things your community brings to the region and indeed our city.' She glanced around the table. Her colleagues staring at clasped hands, avoiding eye contact. 'I know I speak for all of us when I say we need water, the irrigation farms need water, and the settlements further out-of-town need water.'

'Madam Mayor.' Shofet formalised his tone. 'These are issues we have raised with the chamber of commerce, the farmers' groups, the irrigators and we have even spoken to the country women's groups, and all are on the same page of understanding.'

'And what page is that?'

'There is plenty of water and they have access to it if they pay the going rate,' Shofet said. 'The market determines price, and high demand from the towns in South Australia and the cotton industry in New South Wales and Queensland has raised the price.'

The mayor glanced at Jackson. 'What are your views, Premier?'

'The government has agreements with the New South Wales and the South Australia governments to manage water. We cannot act unless legislation changes the current business terms and conditions, allowing a more regulated market.'

'So, nothing,' the mayor said.

Jackson glared at her, waiting for her to look away. She did not. He then glanced at Darius. 'Is the Council aware of your plans?'

'Some are.'

'Do you plan to brief them?'

'We shall eat first.' The staff began delivering the first of five courses.

Luncheon guests worked their way through the variety of pastas and meat dishes, the chitter-chat focusing on sporting feats of local teams, the new library funded by the Iranian community, and the development of a proposed retail precinct to the west of town. The food was taste-bud bursting; they caught one councillor licking his plate, sparking raucous laughter.

Coffees were delivered, and staff cleared the table. Darius called upon Taimar Saraf to address the meeting. Saraf moved to his leather case on a wooden sideboard, tugging from it a bundle of briefing papers. He handed one to each of the councillors. 'This presentation will not be too long, as I know you are all very busy. Let me point to our key objectives so we can have an in-principal discussion.'

Councillors leafed through the colourful pages. The mayor read the executive summary.

'In brief, we plan to develop a tourist precinct at Ned's Corner Station,' said Saraf. 'We estimate the development creating over one hundred thousand jobs for the region. Our modelling suggests we will have four million visitors yearly and this will rise to twenty million within ten, but more likely fifteen years. The plan is to enclose the entire reserve and raise the standard of tourism displays; we have engaged the local indigenous community to be active in designing the strategy. We expect significant benefit for the city and the regions with spin off tourism, especially on the river.'

The mayor interrupted. 'What are you planning to put out there in that godforsaken country?'

'A tourist precinct focused on the environment, and we expect significant visitations for conventions.'

'What's the attraction, a Disneyland type of thing?' a councillor asked.

Darius laughed and leaned forward. 'Disneyland for adults. We want to build a gaming and tourist precinct like Las Vegas, but much smaller. We think the city limits will be the size of Alice Springs.'

'How will they get there?' a confused councillor asked.

'In time, we will build an airport that will carry domestic and international flights.'

'Fuck off,' the mayor said, drumming her fingers on the folder. This prompted others to laugh, pleased someone expressed what they were thinking.

Shofet leaned forward on his elbows. 'Our plan is to put formal submissions to the Council within the month, and we expect your answer one way or the other within two months.'

'A little fast, isn't it?' The mayor sat back in her chair and sipped coffee. 'I mean, a major development like this would take years to get approvals.'

'We understand the usual process,' Darius smiled. 'But this project will be good for Mildura and the state, and especially good for the community.'

'I see the benefits, but I am a little soft on the idea,' responded the mayor. 'What say you, Premier?'

'I think the idea is out there.' Jackson smiled. 'I think it is attractive on many levels, but I also think it is problematic on many other levels.'

Darius frowned, squeezing his chin.

Jackson continued after a momentary pause and a deep breath. 'I believe it to be an interesting idea, but I'm sure all levels of government will need to work together to evaluate it. This first challenge is buying the land.' He arched a brow and stroked his chin.

'This attitude frustrates us,' Shofet responded, his tone sharp. 'We have a funded plan to provide growth and jobs, bringing prosperity to the region. Something I am sure all of you would agree and is a good thing. Do you not?'

No one dared speak.

Darius read the mood of the meeting and chose not to progress into a difficult discussion. He financially supported all of them, and now wasn't the time to ask for payback. 'This is the first step. Our next step is to submit documents to the council. We will have state government submissions ready at the same time.' He paused, then lowered his tone to a menacing register. 'Let me assure you all. We will do whatever we can to get the approvals for this project. I suspect you know what we can do.'

The silence hung like a shroud, sending a shiver along the spines of some.

CHAPTER
13

Shofet seemed anxious, fidgeting in the seat opposite Jackson as the plane headed to Swan Hill.

'What's up, Hosmand?' Darius asked. 'You seem keen to raise something.'

Shofet stopped fidgeting and stared at Jackson.

'What?' Jackson smiled, encouraging him to speak.

'Are we friends, Mr Premier?'

'Yes. What's wrong?'

'Do you like the idea of our tourist precinct?'

'I reckon it's problematic.'

'This is the word you said at lunch, is it not?' Darius asked. He tightened his lips, his face twitching as he glared at Jackson. 'Would you care to explain?'

Jackson stroked his upper lip his eyes flicking about the directors. As he did, Ghassab moved to the back of the plane.

'Well?' Darius said.

'I think it will be difficult to get the Trust to sell you the land. The government departments charged with approving the project will take their time. The environmentalists will ban it no matter what your assurances are. The churches will come down heavy on the gambling plan, and, just off the top of my head, I suspect the federal government will need to get involved.'

'So, you don't support it?' Darius asked.

Ghassab had not returned, tempting Jackson to check over his shoulder. The big guy made him nervous. 'I didn't say that.' Jackson stammered, giving away his anxiety.

'We want you to support it,' Shofet said.

'We want you to make sure it gets through the parliament without delay,' Darius said.

'My hands are tied,' Jackson said.

Darius smiled. 'Your hands are tied. That's funny.'

Jackson didn't understand the humour.

The gorilla stretched an arm, snatching Jackson's head into a head-lock. The premier struggled to breathe, feeling hard tendons pushing into his neck. Darius unclipped Jackson's seat belt with Shofet freeing it. Saraf squeezed through and clipped on handcuffs.

Darius moved to the rear of the plane and fiddled with the cargo door, undoing a few clips then rolling it open. The unpressurised cabin did not react to the sudden gust of wind whipping around them like skydivers. Ghassab released his grip, lifting a weakened Jackson to his feet, bashing his head into the plane's ceiling before pushing him backwards to the door.

Jackson panicked as he searched over his shoulder. 'What are you doing? Stop!'

Darius moved closer, shouting, 'Time for you to decide, Phillip. You either work with us or your life becomes problematic.'

Ghassab forced him to step further back until he felt his jacket flaying. 'No! Stop! This is crazy.'

'I tell you what is crazy, Premier,' Darius yelled. 'What is crazy is my community continuing to support you.'

'Stop! Darius, please.'

Ghassab braced himself against the hatch before letting go of Jackson, who began sinking backwards, surfing in the buffeting wind. As the premier lost his balance, Ghassab grabbed the handcuff links with one hand, placing a hand on the bulkhead above Jackson to steady himself against the tug of the breeze.

'Please stop this. No!' Jackson screamed like a child, eyes wide, searching for safety. 'Stop!'

'Will you work with us?' Darius shouted.

Jackson didn't respond, his shoe heels dangling from the edge of the plane, as he searched out into the country below. Ghassab gave him a jolt. 'All right. All right. I get your message.'

'It's not a message,' Darius shouted. 'It's a choice.'

'All right!' Jackson shrieked, his locked knees buckling under the strain.

'All right what?'

Ghassab smiled and released his arm a little more.

'I chose you.' Jackson screeched back into the cabin. 'I chose you. I chose you.'

Ghassab received a tap on his shoulder. He dragged Jackson back, then flopped him into his seat.

Jackson shook as he restored his breathing, the hatch now sealed. Saraf uncuffed him and the premier rubbed his wrists, already exposing enormous red welts. He rocked back and forward, then cupped his face, fearful of looking at the men. He ran fingers through his hair, combing it back to respectability. Shofet passed him a warm towel. The premier wiped his face, covering it for a moment or two with his head leaning back. The warmth helped. He cringed as Ghassab squeezed past.

Darius held a glass of wine before him with a broad smile. 'Let us toast our new arrangement.'

Jackson pursed his lips, nodded, and accepted the glass.

CHAPTER
14

'That's weird.' Rose replaced the telephone handset and leaned back as Charlotte Poore entered her office, an arm full of files.

'What is?'

'I just took a call from the mayor, and she appeared rather anxious about a meeting she just attended.'

'Mayor? Which mayor?'

'Mildura,' Rose sat forward, accepting the files. 'She just had lunch with councillors with a special guest sponsored by the Arabs.'

'Let me guess.' Charlotte took a chair to wait for the returned signed files. 'A sporting legend from long ago returning to his roots.'

Rose smirked. 'What? You think sports stars are the only special people to attend lunches?'

'It's in Mildura; the culture demands it.'

'What do you mean?' Rose said.

'They are so worried about water, the weather, the crops, the harvest and not having enough support or money. The only thing to get excited about is someone who escaped and made good; like a sports star.'

'I can see how you would say that, but I'm sorry you did.'

Charlotte smiled. 'Well, you get to know folks, and this culture drums through my mind when I think about the mallee.'

'You don't like Mildura?'

'I prefer Canberra,' Charlotte said. 'No flies in Canberra and plenty of rain.'

'Fair enough... where was I?'

'The mayor.'

Rose started signing files. 'The mayor had lunch with the premier.'

'You're kidding me.' Charlotte squinted an expression of distaste. 'We have been trying to get him to talk to irrigators for months.'

'The Arabs have him on a tight leash.'

'You can't say that,' Charlotte said.

'Well, they do.' Rose continued signing. 'It's common knowledge they fund his campaigns.'

'Why don't we get money from them?'

'I'm a woman, for one thing.' Rose peeked up at Charlotte. 'They're a tad misogynist in the way they do business. Plus, they don't like what I say about their water leases.'

'Is it true they use muscle to get what they want?'

'They have their good points,' Rose said. 'They brought wealth to the region, which benefits all of us.'

'I'm surprised they have so much influence.'

'You know them.' Rose signed her last file, stacking them and shoving them over to Charlotte. 'They own everything, and the Iranian community contributes to the communities of Mildura and Swan Hill. Without their economic influence, I'm not sure unemployment rates would be so low.'

'What did the mayor say?'

'Oh yes.' Rose leaned back. 'She said the Arabs presented a ridiculous idea to develop desolate land along the river as a tourist precinct and seek approval for it from the council within a couple of months.'

'Tourist precinct?'

'They want to build Mildura's equivalent to Vegas.'

'You're kidding me?'

'I kid you not.' Rose smiled at Charlotte's expression. 'According to their prospectus, they have done a heap of work with consultants, including engineers and urban infrastructure specialists.'

'Who's funding it?'

'They are,' Rose said. 'All of it.'

'So why was the premier there? I don't understand.'

'That's an excellent point,' Rose said, pointing a finger. 'I suspect something like this will need all levels of government involved. Given I'm the federal minister for regional development, I may have a say on its viability.'

Charlotte remained quiet for a moment, the files held against her chest, then said, 'Is this why you are being dropped from the ministry, do you reckon?'

Rose bounced her head around with a maybe expression. 'You think the Arabs have that influence in this place?'

'Perhaps.' Charlotte nodded. 'Maybe they worry you are the minister who will need to tick the development,' she said. 'Maybe they think you will use the approval to leverage water access.'

Rose turned to gaze out the window. 'Maybe.'

'Why do you think the premier was there?' Charlotte moved to the door.

'To add gravitas. No doubt he said all the right things. But...' Rose paused for a moment, gazing at her. 'It's a big but...'

Charlotte turned her back, checking over her shoulder. 'Are you saying my arse looks big?' she said with a grin.

Rose pointed a tapping finger. 'No, you jokester. If he's on the payroll, as I assume he could be, he will need to push it through state parliament. That will mean he will expose himself to criticism.'

'We have the strategy meeting in ten minutes,' Charlotte said. 'Why don't we put this on the agenda?'

'Good idea.' Rose picked up the telephone's handset, tapping a number. 'I'll just talk to Primmy and then join you.'

Rose swung toward the window and watched the trickling water.

'Hi Mummy, how are you?' Primrose sounded agitated. 'I've been watering the vegetables, and a man came past and told me to stop.'

'Who?'

'He said he was the water bailiff and gave me a card to give to you. He told me about the water restrictions, and I shouldn't be watering with town scheme water.'

'Did you keep watering?'

'I used tank water. Is that okay?'

'Yes, darling. That's okay.' Rose smiled, pausing for a moment. 'I've told you about the uncertainty of politics, haven't I?'

'Trust no one, you said. What's happened, Mummy?'

'The prime minister is going to reshuffle jobs and mummy could lose hers.'

'Why?'

'My leader is retiring, and the prime minister is switching jobs for everyone.'

'Jock's retiring?'

Rose raised an eyebrow; surprised she remembered his name. 'Yes.'

'Huh.' Primrose paused for a moment. 'Why are you being sacked?'

'Not sacked, retired.'

'Jock isn't doing it though, is he?'

'No, he's the leader.'

'Huh.' Primrose considered the issue. 'Mummy, if Jock is retiring, why don't you take his job?'

Rose pursed her lips. 'I don't have the support.'

'How come? Have you asked?'

'I don't want you worrying about politics, okay darling?'

'Okay, Mumsie.'

Rose thought about her daughter's throwaway line. *Did she have the numbers to have any chance of securing the leadership?* An interesting thought. She scribbled a note before strolling off to her meeting room.

After an hour of discussing ideas about how to save her preselection, Rose tired of the circular conversation. Politics is only ever about numbers, and Rose either had them or she didn't. No one suggested how she could secure the votes she needed. She stared at her staff and the whiteboard full of notes, her clenched fist resting under her chin.

'I had a mentor in school. She said that for me to do well in life, I had to think big.' She dropped her hand and flicked it across her staff. 'Are we thinking big?'

'You can't make it rain.' Roger Newgreen chuckled.

'Can I get them water?'

'Only if we break the commercial agreements.'

'And how can we do that?'

'We can't,' Newgreen said. 'They are state government regulated and they will not compromise their tax revenue.'

'I spoke to Jed Musgrove the other day.' Some of her staff didn't recognise the name. 'He suggested I am a liar in the employ of the Arabs. We talked about my hands being tied.'

'To what?' Newgreen asked.

'The constitution,' Rose said. 'He suggested if I didn't move to help, the party will sack me and as you say...' she pointed at Newgreen, 'the state government won't do anything.' She paused for a moment. 'What would happen if we amended the constitution to allow the federal government taking control of water management?' No one spoke as Rose waited. 'If the feds take control, we could legislate water rights and bust the entire market.'

Newgreen smiled. 'Giving drought-stricken towns and farms water.'

'Correct.'

'That would need a referendum, and there would be Buckley's chance of getting that through,' Charlotte said.

'Why?' Rose asked.

'History shows that unless the government leadership supports the question, then the Australian people won't vote yes.'

'What about the Country Party's leader driving the referendum?' Rose asked.

'It could make a difference,' Newgreen said. 'The PM would need to support his coalition partner.'

'Jock would never do it,' Charlotte said.

'He will not be leader soon,' Rose smiled. 'Think big, people.'

'Are you thinking what I think you're thinking?' Charlotte asked.

'And what am I thinking?'

'What a brilliant idea,' Newgreen said, seizing the idea. 'You become leader, promising a referendum to your colleagues to secure their vote. That kills any preselection issues in Mallee. You then get the referendum up in the cabinet because you are deputy prime minister and solve the water issues.'

'That sounds way too simple,' Charlotte said.

'Maybe, but why don't we think through what we might have to do?' Rose asked.

'You're brilliant, boss,' Newgreen said.

'Yes. Yes, I am.'

CHAPTER
15

Rose entered the cabinet room for the scheduled evening meeting of the Drought Emergency Committee, wondering if she should take her usual chair or sit where the prime minister normally does. The prime minister was not due to attend the informal meeting. Various ministers and influential backbench members whose electorates are in the grip of prolonged drought were attending. There was no red desk folder for the prime minister, so Rose sat in his chair.

Committee members filed in a few minutes before the allotted start time, and as the red second hand clicked over to nine o'clock, Clare Spencer, the water minister, entered the room, followed by three staff. Rose smirked at the sight of her entourage and figured Clare needed as much help as she could get.

Spencer swung around the table and stood at the prime minister's chair, waiting for Rose to vacate.

'Once I get a seat, we can start the meeting.'

Rose swung around and gazed at the impatient Spencer. She could either deny her the chair or comply. This wasn't a fight she wanted to have right now. She scooped up her folder and withdrew to an unoccupied seat further along the table.

Spencer flopped into the chair, pulling herself closer to the table. 'Now let us begin.' She smiled at colleagues opposite. 'Can we start by getting an update of fodder and water supplies? Can I also get an indication of the immediate need within each community?'

Each of the affected politicians reported to the meeting. Several public servants detailed funding proposals and allocation of benefits to farmers and communities suffering with significant revenue challenges.

Eventually, Spencer came to Rose.

'How is Mallee faring?'

'It's dry, it's hot, like it always is,' Rose responded. 'The growers aren't happy because yields will be down. Graziers aren't happy because fodder is scarce, forcing them to ship it in at increased freight costs. Herd numbers are down. Sheep farmers have reduced flocks, although the wool clip is expected to meet expectations. Irrigators complain about lack of access to water for fruit crops. The problem we have is water.'

'Don't we all,' a colleague said from the other end of the table.

'No, that's wrong,' Rose corrected herself, scanning around the table. Spencer stifled a yawn. 'Keeping you up, Clare?'

Spencer snatched in a breath. 'It's late. Do you have anything more?'

'Yes, I do.'

Spencer twirled her hand, encouraging Rose to hurry.

'You, see? This is the problem when we have a water minister who lives in a heavy rainfall area. We must hurry to discuss the water crisis we have in regional areas, otherwise it becomes a bedtime story.'

Spencer glared at Rose, gnawing her bottom lip. 'I was just encouraging you to get to your point.'

Rose smirked a slight smile no one could detect. 'We have plenty of water in the mallee. Water that can't be used flows past properties. We have transmission losses, which is code for too much water flowing down the Murray, breaking banks, and flooding at-risk forests.'

Spencer appeared puzzled by the comment. 'Why are forests at risk because of water?'

Rose sighed. 'Forests don't grow in wetlands, and we have over bank water flowing into forests when just downstream farmers are denied access.'

'How is this possible?'

Rose shook her head. 'You are aware of the current water management regime, are you not?'

'Of course,' Spencer snapped.

'Then you would be aware speculators have entered the market.'

'Water companies bid for licences,' Spencer responded. 'I don't think we should look upon them as speculators, do you?'

'These so-called water companies,' Rose air punctuated inverted commas, 'are driving up the price as they withhold flows. As I advised cabinet the other day, farmers were once paying one-fifty a mega-litre. They now pay around eight-sixty.'

'That's true, Minister,' confirmed a colleague.

Spencer glanced towards him and scribbled a note.

Rose continued. 'I have farmers who have had water costs increase by one hundred and fifty thousand dollars from last year.'

The minister peeked at her advisers, who jotted notes. Rose observed the by-play and shook her head. 'As I said, I raised this with the cabinet the other day if you recall. The PM directed you to do research. Have you done that?'

An adviser leaned over to the minister, passing her a note, which she subtly tried to read but failed as colleagues remained silent, waiting for a response. Spencer then read, 'The states manage water.'

'They have stuffed it,' Rose asserted, gaining the agreement from many nodding colleagues. 'We need to do it. We need to take control.'

'How do we do that?' Spencer asked.

'You ask them.'

Spencer scoffed.

'If they don't come to the table to improve the way they manage water, then we can do either of two things,' Rose said.

Spencer waited for Rose to elaborate, but she didn't. 'Okay, I'll bite,' Spencer sighed. 'What are they?'

Rose grinned. 'We either buy out the speculators and control the water, establishing a fair price.'

'Or?' Spencer sighed.

'Or we take full control via a change to the constitution.'

'A referendum?' a colleague asked.

'If required, yes,' Rose said.

'It'll never happen,' another colleague interjected.

'It would if the leadership group wanted it,' Rose said.

'The states will never agree,' Spencer said.

'It's the people who should decide,' Rose said. 'And I reckon we have a good enough democracy that will support the idea.'

'The prime minister would never agree,' Spencer said.

'Jock would,' Rose said.

'Yeah, but Jock won't be leader soon,' Spencer said. 'I'm not supportive of the idea.'

'Who nominated you leader?' Rose asked.

Silence.

Nothing moved except the second hand of the clock on the wall as it clicked a clear ten times before Spencer spoke. 'I'm not leader and the party room will decide who will be the next leader.'

Rose pushed harder. 'We are the Country Party. We are not the Regional Cities Party, and we should do all we can to get water to our communities.'

Spencer didn't respond, tapping the table with her fingers with a hand to her mouth. 'Okay, I hear you,' she said. 'Put a proposal to me within the week and I shall get it on the cabinet agenda.'

Rose nodded, and doodled on her pad, her head cupped in a hand, a concealed smirk hiding her strategy.

CHAPTER
16

'And the winner is...' The president of the Swan Hill Chamber of Commerce opened an envelope, extracting the name of the business of the year. He frowned as he read. 'Hafez Restaurant.'

The same ten tables of guests who cheered every announcement in the annual business awards clapped as Taimur Saraf, with an embarrassed wave, stepped to the stage to accept the Iranian community's sixth award.

'It has been a successful night.' Saraf smiled at the unsmiling tables of nominees. He paused and gazed at the trophy, then over to the guests, paying particular attention to the tables of officials of the Chamber and local councillors. 'It has been a long and hard road for us since we settled here over thirty years ago.'

The now seated president leaned over and whispered to his colleague, who chuckled and nodded.

'I must admit, though, there were early tensions, but I reckon what we achieved has been a benefit for all.' Saraf glanced over to Darius Hassidim, who nodded. 'My partners worked hard to establish ourselves in Swan Hill. When we achieved surplus funds, we invested back into the community. The medical centre we opened a month ago will provide a significant benefit to the city.'

The Iranian community tables clapped. Only a few on official tables did the same.

'Our plan is to bring even more services to Swan Hill and indeed Mildura. We intend public transport to increase. Our plan is for a twenty-first century library, and we are building a new public school. We are negotiating with the state government to move government departments to Swan Hill, and as part of that plan, we intend building office and retail space in town.'

The community tables applauded again.

'When I started this restaurant as a café ten years ago, my goal was to bring five-star chefs to the region and turn it into a Persian gastronomical palace. We wanted to offer affordable food. We remain grateful for the opportunity to work with the good citizens of Swan Hill to make that goal happen. As a way of celebrating this award, we will offer a free dinner service for the next week, so please come. But you had better book a table. Thank you.'

A photographer rushed to the stage as guests clapped. Saraf stood before the Chamber's banner and held the impressive trophy high.

Darius left his chair and wandered over to the president, offering his hand. The president responded but didn't bother to stand. 'A great evening, Mr President.'

'Congratulations, Darius. A clean sweep again this year.'

Darius smirked. 'The judges know a good business when they see one.'

'No doubt they do.'

Darius kept hold of his hand. 'Do you not think so?'

'In any business, money talks.'

'Ah, we now understand each other.'

'You do good work in the community, Darius, but do you have to be so ruthless?'

Darius shrugged and held up his hands. 'It's never personal; you know that.'

The president sat back and waved Darius away, the tip of his little finger missing.

Darius grinned as he left the table. He waved to several colleagues, who followed him through to the executive wing of the River Bend

Country Club. Not only the directors but community leaders followed to an isolated lounge, leaving families and staff to continue celebrating.

They had arranged the darkened room with comfortable leather chairs in a large circle. A wooden side table placed beside every chair, a dull lit gold lamp with a green shade on each, a chilled glass of water on a paper coaster waiting. When the men settled, an individual attendant asked each for their refreshment requirements; they set hookahs for those who asked.

'Gentlemen.' Darius called for attention. 'Thank you for coming this evening. We are here to discuss issues that may concern for you.'

The men were paying keen attention, some puffing ornate gold hoses, others sipping water or slurping coffee.

'We are pleased to advise we are in the initial stages of development approval for the tourist precinct. Early approvals are expected. Pressure may need to be placed on our politicians to get what we want. We are in direct contact with the premier and our discussion with the council is ongoing. Within the next two years, we expect construction to begin. indeed, we insist on it.'

Hosmand Shofet called an attendant, directing a briefing paper to be distributed. 'I'm passing out an overview of the plans and expected revenues within the first ten operating years.' He waited until the men had read the highlights. 'Our initial plan is for five casino and hotel complexes to be built. We will import labour and expertise from associate companies in Macau. We think this idea is better than relying on Australian labour.'

'Don't we own the unions?' someone asked.

'In theory, we do, but rates of pay are out of our hands,' Saraf said. 'Our preference is our own workforce from China. They are cheaper, quicker, and more reliable. We will seek formal federal government approval, which we have already received in principle.'

'Our plan is to always be modernising the new city, and we expect a total capital cost in the first ten years of fifteen billion,' Shofet said. 'We forecast our revenues to be around five hundred million per casino, around forty percent of our Sydney operation. We are then budgeting a net profit return of around twenty-five percent. This is a better return than any of our other investments, excluding narcotics.'

'The directors are doing what we can to secure approval,' Darius said. 'Questions?'

'Funding?' A question came from a cloud of smoke.

'We are receiving support from Macau, but our major banker is in Iran. The rate is very competitive and will not inhibit us,' Saraf said, as others nodded.

'Staff?'

'We want to use the community as much as possible, but if we have to bring in labour from Asia, then we will,' Shofet said.

'The Italians?'

'This is a good question,' Darius said. 'The locals are only interested in narcotics. The Americans have expressed an interest. Our offer to them is for our guaranteed access to celebrities in return for a small share.' He air-quoted with his fingers. 'It shouldn't be a problem.'

He glanced around at the silent group. 'Rest assured, we are moving forward rapidly, and we will make sure each of you will have a reasonable return. This is a legacy project for us.'

No-one spoke.

'Okay, the next item is water.'

Saraf began reading from notes. 'The current water leasing program is bringing in vital cash-flow revenue for the community, but we are seeing signs of infiltration into the market, especially down south.'

'Wassim, what is going on?' Darius asked into the smoky gloom.

'Khalif, the farmers are carting in water. Sorry...,' Iravani faltered, 'not just the farmers, but several villages. They have very little water.'

'Where is it coming from?' Maisil Ghassab queried, ready to take notes.

'Mostly from Gippsland, but also from Murray Bridge in South Australia.'

The group remained silent as Darius glanced towards Ghassab and then Shofet. 'That is our water, is it not?'

'Not once we send it downstream, Darius,' Shofet said.

'Are we not giving them enough reason to buy from us?' Darius glanced back at Iravani.

'Khalif, we do what we can, but they are complaining to the state government. They want Rose Dowerin to make an issue of it in Canberra.'

'Rose Dowerin,' Darius said. 'She will not be a problem after the next election,'

'There is talk of her being challenged,' a voice suggested.

'An independent member is no good for us. We need a government member,' Darius said. 'We need someone who can speak for us behind the closed doors of government.'

Shofet advised. 'We are trying to find a likely preselection candidate, so if you have ambitious folks who support the Country Party, then let us know.'

'I hear Jimmy Lever may put his hand up,' a voice said.

'Yeah, maybe, but he criticises us too much.' Darius frowned. 'In the meantime, give details of the transport companies carting water to Maisil.' He paused for a moment. 'Questions?'

'Khalif, there is increasing talk of a group of lads causing trouble in Mildura. It seems they are from our community. Do you have any instructions?'

Darius remained still for a moment. 'We are very lucky with what we have achieved over the years. Crime is down, meaning little interest from the cops. We have the Barbarian Brotherhood under control dealing our products across the state. We don't need kids threatening the community and our reputation.'

'Do you want me to go talk to them?' Ghassab asked.

'Not sure a heavy hand is what we need,' Shofet suggested.

Ghassab grunted. 'It has been in the past.'

'I agree,' a voice said. 'A good whipping will be good for them.'

Darius raised a hand to quieten the talk. 'They need something different these days.'

Iravani cleared his throat. 'Khalif, if I may; the winter crops are being harvested. Put them to work on our farms. Hard farm work will sort them out.'

Darius steepled his fingers, nodding for a few moments. 'Wassim has a good grasp on what is required,' he said. 'Let them work for a month and let us counsel them. If they do not understand their role, then we shall ship them to Hamadan, and they can examine their future for a year.'

The men nodded. Ghassab took a note. He would offer a valuable lesson with his whip when he delivered the boys.

Darius stood, ending the meeting. 'It is very important no one acts against our community,' he said. 'You all play a vital role; the successful management of your region helps us maintain our grip on power and influence. One crack and the entire community could fall. Do not allow this to happen in your region under your management.'

As they filed from the room, they took Darius' hand, bowed, placing his knuckles to their forehead.

'Khalif akbar.' each man said, before re-joining the celebrations in the ballroom.

CHAPTER

17

Darius' limousine entered his family compound, stopping at the iron gates to allow security to confirm passengers before being waved through once they recognised him. Within minutes, he dropped from the back seat and walked to the front door, which opened as he approached.

'Welcome home, Khalif. Your wife is in the study waiting for you.'

'Thank you.' Darius walked to the study, gently opening the door, wondering if his wife Razia might be resting. When he saw her against the fireplace, he said, 'You look lovely, my dear.'

She stared at him, thick lips pursed, waiting to say something. Dark eyes watched under an arched brow. A loose strand of hair from her tightly pulled bun followed her tightening jaw. She stood with a clenched fist on her hip.

'I can't tell if you are sad or mad.' Darius raised a modest chuckle. 'What's wrong, my love?'

'Nothing,' she said. 'The children have again expressed their displeasure at not seeing you.'

'Business gets in the way. I'm sorry, darling.'

'What's the point of having wealth if you cannot use it to spend time with the ones you love?'

'I've said before: business has its demands.'

'Yes, I'm sure it does, but so do we.' She turned away from him.

'What's happened?'

'Zana had an incident at school.'

'What type of incident?'

'They stopped him from hurting another boy.'

'Was he injured?'

'Zana?' She faced him. 'No, but the other boy was. It seems to be a regular occurrence.'

'What was he doing?'

'He was bullying a younger boy.' Razia glanced away. 'It's a game he plays so he can get what he wants.'

Darius walked to the window, then turned. 'What does he want?'

'Drugs.'

They considered each other. 'Do you want me to speak to him?' Darius asked.

'Let me think.' Razia put a finger to her lips. 'Do I want Zana's father to talk to him? What do you think?'

'When?'

'Now. He's waiting for you upstairs.' She crossed her arms, almost stamping a foot. 'I want him punished.'

'Of course. Let me take him out to the stables and horsewhip him,' Darius responded with a laugh.

'You idiot.' She sighed, shaking her head. 'You are too soft on them.'

'I will talk to him.'

'When?'

'Now?' Darius shrugged, raising his hands. 'You want me to talk to him now?'

'This is your fault.'

'How is this my fault?'

'You're never home, and you always give in to them.'

Darius conceded. 'Perhaps.'

'Not perhaps, Darius,' she continued as he glanced away. 'Everyone takes advantage of you all the time. You are too kind-hearted. Someone comes for your help; you give it to them, no questions asked. A servant drops something; you pick it up. It drives me crazy.'

'You are stressed way too much, my love.'

'Stuck in the middle of nowhere doesn't help.' She settled into her regular grievance list. 'We never travel as much as we used to. For instance, we have not been to Paris this year and only you have been to Tehran.' Razia moved to the leather lounge and flopped into it, billowing her frock.

Darius moved to the lounge and sat on the arm. 'I know it has been a lousy year for you and little to look forward to.' He smiled. 'But we are taking significant steps forward with our plans. Once it moves, the opportunities to enjoy more of the world will return.'

'Talk is cheap. We never seem to do much together. You always seem to work on sorting out one problem or another. You have no time for me.'

'I will make it up to you, darling,' Darius said. 'I'm travelling to Melbourne for meetings in a few days. Why don't you come? Do a little shopping. Maybe see a show.'

'Melbourne is not Paris.'

Darius shrugged and moved to the door. 'I'll make sure they inform you about my movements.' He stopped, turning to contemplate her. 'I would like to spend more time with you, my darling.'

'Make plans then.' She turned away.

Darius paused by the door, waiting for her to look at him. 'The sacrifices I make have always been for you.'

She didn't return his look. 'Yes, well, I've heard that before.'

'Shall I see you upstairs?'

'In a while.'

Darius left to deal with his son; to explain the importance of fairness and reinforce his usual message of gratitude and seeking forgiveness. Do as I say, not as I do, danced through his head, before knocking on Zana's door, not looking forward to what he was about to do.

CHAPTER
18

A houseboat chugged downriver as Rose watched. Children enjoying the sun on the top deck as parents worked in the cabin, mum preparing a snack and dad keeping a watchful eye on his bow. Just one of the many holiday boats using the river. All manner and standard of craft battled for river space: expensive cruisers, motorboats with skiers slaloming behind, and the chug-chug of a houseboat.

Rose perched herself at her favourite spot under a huge coolabah tree on an iron park bench overlooking the river, near the bridge. It offered an isolated place where she often came to think about things. She didn't do it very much these days. Experience and wisdom scaled back the worry wall of youth, and what might have seemed important once no longer demanded the stress.

She discovered this silent place when she first arrived in Mildura to pick fruit. The sun did no favours for her skin, but it was mighty preferable to the streets of suburban Melbourne. She thought of herself as a victim sick of abuse, realising there was little future in turning tricks as a sixteen-year-old. A regular celebrity client who enjoyed the company of young girls suggested she go fruit picking to earn big bucks because the streets were no good.

Hitchhiking outback could be dangerous, especially for a teenager, but she learnt how to manage men on the streets and watched for warning signs whenever someone stopped. When a truckie asked her name, she offered Rose. He liked it and so did she. It was her favourite flower, especially the yellow ones they wore each year during the Melbourne Cup festival. When she reached Mildura, she registered with a labour hire firm.

'Name?'

'Rose.'

'Rose what?'

The question stumped her. She needed a name for her application but couldn't think of one suitable until she saw a packet of cigarettes jutting from a handbag.

'Love? What's your surname?'

'Winfield. My name is Rose Winfield.'

'Age?'

'Twenty-two,' Rose lied.

The labour officer completed the application by filling out the back-packers' hostel as an address. She advised Rose to be out front at six the following morning. They would pay piece rate, with money settled at the end of each day. 'Make sure you bring this form and hand it to the coordinator tomorrow. If the farmer wants to keep you, they may offer you accommodation, which is a bunkhouse, no better than the hostel, but they feed you.'

'Thank you.'

When she finished with the labour hire firm, she wandered down by the river, finding the coolabah tree and the iron bench that would become her bed for the night.

It had been a unique journey for her since that first night.

She stayed the entire season, then found work on a sheep farm, helping the shearing team, cooking, and cleaning around the home-stead. She enjoyed the harsh nature of the work and didn't take crap from randy shearers. The older men shielded her, but she suspected they too would have a go if they had a belly full of beer. She never went to town, preferring the company of the flies.

One day, repairing a leak out by a bore, she picked up the sound of a horse. She straightened to see another girl she recognised riding up to water her horse. The animal gasping against the heat and effort when the girl halted. She stood in the stirrups, then sat high in the saddle, waiting for the horse to recover before leading it to the water. She inspected Rose as she squirmed in the saddle on the restless beast.

Rose stood with a hand shading her eyes, watching her.

'Are you going to the B and S Ball on Satdee?'

'No plans.' Rose glanced up at the girl.

'You wanna come with me?'

Rose eyed the rider before taking off her hat, dunking it, then dumping a load of water on her head, giving herself a soaking relief from the heat and dust before plonking it back. She walked over to the horse, gripping the halter, leading it to the trough, smacking its neck with affection. She gazed up at the girl sitting above her with a firm grip on the saddle horn as the horse gulped in water, the bit clanking with the effort.

'As a date, do you mean?'

The girl smiled. 'Nah, not yet. Just as friends.'

'Are we friends?'

'If we're not, we should be.'

'Sure. I'd love to go.'

'Can you pick me up on the way?'

Rose raised her eyebrows, then grimaced. 'Yeah, nah. I don't have a licence.'

'How old are you?'

'Old enough.'

'And ya don't have a licence?'

'Never needed one.'

The girl wheeled her horse and checked back over her shoulder as she walked off. 'I'll come get ya at sundown. Wear something pretty.'

'You too,' Rose smiled.

———

Saturday was the night that changed her life and steered her onto a different path; one that had its moments, but she soon learned life was much better without flies and dust.

She still had a tiny black number from her city life. As she looked at herself, she could not see any lines of underwear, nor would she. She waited on the step to her bunkhouse, scrunching and drying her hair in the last of the sun when the clapped-out Holden pulled up. The girl mouthed wow when she stared over. Rose didn't move and watched as the girl shook her head coming over.

'I was just thinking,' Rose said.

'What were you thinking, gorgeous?'

'I don't get into cars with strangers.' Rose smiled, waggling a knee. 'What's your name?'

'Roberta.' The girl straightened her sunglasses as she watched the knee and beyond, swiping away a fly. 'My friends call me Robbie.'

'I love your t-shirt,' Rose said with a grin. 'Are you a bachelor tonight?'

Robbie chuckled as she peeked down at her jeans and boots. 'I can see you won't be a spinster for long.'

'Well, Robbie, it's best we get going then.' She straightened on the steps, then sashayed down, passing close.

'You look great, by the way.'

Rose flicked her hair back and glanced over her shoulder. 'Do you reckon we'll get lucky tonight?'

'Maybe. With that cute arse of yours, I wouldn't be surprised.'

There were more bachelors than spinsters at the event. Set up in a paddock away from the large homestead, which Robbie explained the Dowerin family owned and organised the annual event for young folk. A steer revolved on a spit, attended by what seemed to be a professional cook. The well-stocked bar flowed, juicing up party goers. A band cranked and cowboys were getting off to the music.

Rose needed little encouragement to get on the wooden dance floor and was a willing partner for any cowboy who asked. She pointed out to Robbie that the best idea was to wear them out on the dance floor rather than chase grimy hands away later. Her enthusiasm encouraged the boring 'wallflowers' to get motivated and join the fun. The heat and rhythm of the beat increased the temperature as couples formed.

'I need water,' a sweating Rose panted.

'There's a bore yonder.' Robbie pointed to a windmill.

Rose lingered a kiss with her friend, then sauntered over, needing to cool down. She collapsed into the trough, feeling the water extract the heat from her. She turned over and lay back, almost floating, gazing up into the clear skies and studying the stars.

'You know that's a herd trough, don't you?' a voice from the dark offered.

Rose sat up and searched around but could see no-one.

'I wouldn't stay in there if I were you; not sure the scum would be good for your skin.' The voice said over by the squeaking windmill.

Rose stepped out of the trough gingerly, her dress clinging even tighter.

'You should have asked,' the voice said. 'I've installed an outside shower just to do what you have obviously done.'

Rose wrung her hair and flicked it back over her shoulder. 'And what is it I have obviously done?' she said to the shadowed figure.

'Washed away those grubby cowboys and their sweaty touch.'

Rose smiled. 'I don't mind a sweaty touch.'

'I bet you do. Which side of the saddle do you sit?'

Rose wondered about the question and thought about Robbie. 'I sit high on a comfortable saddle, near the horn, I suppose,' she said. 'But I may sit side saddle tonight.'

'That's a shame.'

'Who's asking?'

The man stepped out from the shadows. He wore moleskins and his shirt seemed well pressed. His boots clean, so not a cowboy. 'My name is Jeremy Dowerin. Must folks call me Junior.'

'Do you have sweaty hands, Junior?'

He laughed, causing Rose to laugh with him, a little embarrassed by her humour.

'Do you want to dance?' she asked.

'I don't dance, but I do like a wine. Would you like one?'

'Sure.'

'Follow me.'

Junior circled the dancing and the increasing mayhem, heading for the homestead. Rose trailed behind, searching for Robbie but unable to see her. As she reached the homestead, Junior had already entered the house. Rose hesitated. Before she could come up with an answer to what to do, he returned with a bottle and two crystal glasses, walking around the veranda away from the noise to a wicker lounge with plenty of soft cushions.

'Take a seat.'

Still damp, Rose flopped amongst the cushions, hoping to enjoy a touch of luxury. Junior stood above her, pouring a glass. He then stepped back to the other chair, pouring his glass as he went.

'Here's cheers,' he said, holding out his glass.

Rose leaned forward to clink the glass. 'Cheers.' She took a sip. 'Crumbs, that tastes fantastic.' She knew the taste of superb wine; a few clients showed her the difference.

'What's your name and where are you from?'

Rose didn't stay that night. She wanted to but was quick to recognise a long game opportunity. Think big, she was always told, and began scheming the start of a plan as she sipped her wine. She also felt a little obligated to Robbie and wanted to make sure they ended the night together.

Junior asked to see her again, and she agreed, but in a month. She knew men couldn't think straight when satisfying wanton needs. Rose understood she needed patience to get what she wanted. She knew the longer she avoided his sweaty hands, the better the success of her plan. Junior remained persistent, but respectful.

He thought her untouched as he asked around the region. No-one knew her. The only person she spent time with was Robbie, and Junior doubted they were anything other than close friends, just like his sister with her school mates.

When Newton Dowerin announced his retirement as the federal member for Mallee, everyone acknowledged Junior as the obvious replacement. His parliamentary career papers were well and truly stamped a long time ago.

'Rose?' Junior lounged on the same wicker chair on the evening they met almost two years earlier. 'A federal member of parliament needs to have a family. I need to bequeath Mallee to a son.'

'Why are you telling me this?'

Junior dropped from the chair to a knee, and as he did, extracted a red velvet box from his jacket.

'Will you do the honour of marrying me?'

The request astounded her; ten months earlier than planned.

The Dowerins married two months after announcing their engagement. It seemed a little rushed but became understandable to questioning conspirators when a bouncing bonnie boy arrived eight weeks early, seven months after the grand marriage with food provided by the newly settled migrants' catering firm.

Robbie left town soon after the wedding. No one heard from her again.

A toot from a passing craft moving upriver broke Rose's memories, and she glanced up, then around, to see if anyone was about. As usual, she could see no one, so checked her phone for the time and realised she needed to get moving.

'Mummy?'

Rose twitched on hearing the voice. She turned to the tree and saw her daughter kneeling behind the trunk, watching.

'How long have you been there?'

'I don't know, maybe twenty minutes. I was worried about you and thought you might be here.'

Rose smiled and waved Primrose to join her. She skipped down the slope, snuggling next to her mother.

'What's troubling you, Mummy?'

'Oh darling, I just have a few troubles at work.'

'Anything I can help you with?'

Rose put her arm around her daughter, who dropped her head to her shoulder. 'I am struggling to get the energy for another fight. I'm considering retiring, as I don't think I want to go through it again.'

Primrose lifted her head for a moment to ask, 'Who's giving you the trouble?'

'Everyone, it seems.'

'Why?'

'Well, that's an excellent question.' Rose tapped and stroked her daughter's head as she dropped it back on her shoulder. 'I have farmers wanting water and blaming me. Jimmy Lever is moving motions of no confidence against me and is likely to stand against me at preselection. The Arabs tell me not to get involved with water management. I have other party people wanting to take away my endorsement, and I have the prime minister telling me I can't be a minister anymore.'

Primrose thought about the list. 'So, five fights?'

Rose tossed her head back and gazed into the canopy of the tree. 'Yes, there are five battles, but only one war. They don't want me to be in parliament anymore.'

'But the Dowerin's are always in parliament.'

Rose breathed deep. 'Maybe it's time to give it up.'

'Who is telling you all this?'

'Oh, I don't know,' Rose sighed. 'It just seems the world is against me, and I need to move on. It's been a good life, but maybe I should just sell up and go live somewhere else.'

'But this is our home.'

Rose glanced down at her daughter, then cast an eye across the river as she brushed a persistent fly away. 'It has been kind to me and provided me with things I never expected.'

'Then why give it up?'

Rose paused for a moment, twirling a strand of her daughter's hair.

'I've done some mean things I'm not proud of in my life,' Rose said. 'I'm not sure I want to do it all again.'

'Politics is a dirty business, isn't it Mummy?'

'Yes, it is, darling.' Rose watched a small boat motor down river. 'Yes, it is.'

CHAPTER

19

A body splayed face down in a small irrigation channel beneath the shade of almond trees, heaving with a crop ready for the harvest. A forensic pathologist checked over the corpse as a uniformed police officer snapped photographs. Peter Dowerin crouched on his haunches watching, brushing away flies with a leafy stem snapped from a tree.

'Hey Gordo, when do you think you'll be done?'

The pathologist straightened and stretched his lower back, peering over at his friend. 'I need to bag him and get him back to the mortuary to confirm my initial analysis.'

'Which is?'

'Eggs, ants, and rigor suggest they knocked him within the last thirty-six hours. I'll know more when I do further tests.'

'Any idea how he died?'

'He has a massive contusion to the back of his head, which I presume fractured his skull.'

'Drowning a possibility?'

'Could be,' the pathologist said. 'No sign of a struggle so I suspect they knocked him before he hit the water.'

'So, an unexpected whack from behind and left for dead yesterday?'

'Sounds about right.'

The pathologist glanced over at the three police officers. 'Can we bag him, please?'

The officers rolled the man, lifting him then placing him on a black sheet with zipper sides.

'Let me have a look,' Peter said. He peered down at the man. 'Do any of you know him?'

Two officers shook their heads. The third said, 'I reckon he's a local farmer. I have seen him around town.'

'That's interesting,' Gordo said, as he bagged the hands which had been lying under the body.

'What do you see?' Peter asked.

'His little finger is missing.'

'Torn off?'

'Sheared off, by the manner of it.'

'An animal, like a cat, get to it, do you reckon?'

'Would not have thought so; it looks like a clean cut.'

Peter shook his head and frowned. 'Interesting. Ever seen anything like that before?'

'All the time,' Gordo chortled. 'Farmers lose fingers all the time. Or at least the tips of them. They get them caught in machinery all the time. The number of cases presenting at the hospital is almost endemic.'

'A machine ripped it off?'

'Nah, that's a snip.'

Peter allowed the officers to finish bagging the corpse and carry it to the pathologist's vehicle fifty metres away.

'What was this bloke doing out here in the middle of nowhere, getting his finger cut off and his head caved in?' asked Peter.

'You're the copper. That's for you to figure out.' Gordo laughed.

'Yeah, thanks, mate.' Peter placed an arm on his friend's shoulder as the pathologist removed his blue gloves. 'We need to know who he is first.'

CHAPTER
20

J ack Fingleton climbed out of his four-wheel drive, dressed in the formal garb of a wealthy cattleman: pristine white, high crown Akubra, blue shirt with thin green tie, brown herringbone jacket, moleskins with oversized leather belt, and buffed RM Williams boots. Rose Dowerin saw him and wandered over. He stepped across the gutter to shake her hand. 'Nice to see you, Rose. Are you coming to the meeting?'

Rose held his hand longer than he expected. 'Jack, nice to see you up this way.' Rose hadn't yet released her gaze. 'I am going to the meeting. I wouldn't miss it for the world, although it seems I may have missed my invitation. It's a long way for you to come. Why are you here?'

'The drought is killing us, and we need action. I'm here to put my view.'

'Government not doing enough for you?'

'Mental health funding is rubbish; we need water and fodder.'

'They're state government issues. The feds can only do so much.'

Fingleton thrust his hands into his pockets. 'Yeah, but you aren't doing much, are you?'

'I keep raising these matters in Canberra, you know that.'

'Talk is good, action is better.'

'And you have a better idea?'

'I reckon I do.'

'Which is what?'

Fingleton glanced to his boots, spreading his legs a little more. 'I reckon we should change our federal member.'

Rose knew Fingleton was itching to take her political scalp, and he lobbied to be the party's president in Mallee. 'And who do you think could do a better?'

The cattleman didn't respond; he checked down the street licking his bottom lip. 'I'm not saying there is a better person available. What I'm saying is we need different representation. If we can't get any improvement from you, then it's time we did something about it. It's not personal, you know that.'

Rose grinned; her eyes narrowing. 'Of course, Jack. Politics is never personal.' She paused for a moment. 'But I take any threat personally.' She turned and left him watching her go.

The club modernised its decor using the large profits from gaming machines. She heard the grinding of the machines and the pinging of false promise as she entered. She noticed most of the gaming staff seemed to be from the Middle East, and assumed the Iranians were involved.

Rose did a quick tour of the bars and dining rooms, shaking hands and smiling. Some thought her visit an intrusion; others complained. She received little praise these days.

The upstairs function room had a good crowd standing by the bar chatting and drinking before the scheduled commencement. Rose made her way to the front to speak to the chairman, who seemed embarrassed to see her. 'I thought you were in Canberra.'

'I thought the meeting important enough for me to attend, so I travelled home this afternoon.' Rose squeezed out a taut lip smile. 'I assume it's only a coincidence you called it when I would be in the parliament.'

He fumbled with papers. 'It's nice you made it. I should get it started.'

When the chairman opened the meeting, Rose checked over her shoulder, estimating the gathering to number around three hundred. She tugged a notepad from her bag, scratching notes to prepare a speech if they invited her to the lectern.

'Friends, before we continue, I reckon it right we recognise the work of James Lever,' the chairman began. 'James, as you know, was a passionate supporter of irrigators and celebrated as one of the most innovative citrus growers in the region. It is with great sadness I announce James' untimely death. They found him out at Landell farm earlier this week and it is now a police investigation.'

The room fell quiet, as if a shroud had descended. Rose didn't respond, but like everyone else, watching the chairman as he continued. 'With your permission, I would like to move that this meeting convey our deepest sympathies to his family and ask them to seek support if they need it over the next few months. All those in favour?'

'Aye.' A loud response came from the crowd.

'I thank the meeting.' The chairman shifted his notes. 'I would now like to invite Mr Jack Fingleton to the stage to make an address. For those who don't know Jack, he is a cattleman from down Stawell way. Please welcome Jack.'

'Ladies and gentlemen, we have before us a crisis.' Fingleton paused as the booming echo subsided. 'An emergency. A fight we must win.' Rose admired the strong beginning and rested her chin on one palm, the other supporting her elbow. 'The weather is not kind to us. It's stating the obvious that unless it rains over the summer, many of us will not survive beyond winter. I don't know what's causing it. It could be climate change as the scientists tell us or it could be mother nature having her say. I don't care. What I do care about is the way the federal government ignores us. They ignore our pleas and treat us as forgotten people.'

Rose smiled behind her palm, judging it as an election stump speech. No wonder they hadn't wanted her to attend.

'We have travelled to Canberra to discuss our needs, and we spoke to the water minister, but she has done nothing.'

This news surprised Rose, as it was the first time she heard of the meeting. She took a note to speak to Charlotte.

'We have met with the premier, but again we heard platitudes but got no action.' Someone interjected, but Rose didn't hear it. 'Let's face it, there's no drought in Gippsland, where there are more seats for the premier than the mallee, so no wonder he doesn't want to help us.'

Rose considered it an interesting point, but surmised she knew where Fingleton intended to go.

'I have read Hansard and watched the telly. I have listened to the radio, and I have scanned the local newspapers.' Fingleton paused. 'I'm not surprised with what I have seen or heard... or not heard.' He cast an eye down on Rose. 'I cannot see where our local federal member is standing up for us, nor have I read where she has ever spoken in the parliament on our behalf.'

Rose knew this to be true, but she had to preserve cabinet solidarity and could not speak on anything other than her portfolio in the parliament.

'The Member for Mallee talks about trains in Western Australia but is yet to talk about the water in the mallee. She talks about roads in Queensland but is yet to mention the drought.'

If only Rose could talk about the battles in the cabinet room. Even her own party members in the parliament did not know her position on the drought.

Fingleton waxed lyrical for another ten minutes, extolling the need for the local federal member to speak and represent the electorate's interests. 'We owe it to the communities and farmers who could not be here tonight to demand action. If the local member cannot, then let us elect one who can.'

The function room erupted with loud applause as Fingleton backed away from the lectern, waving with a huge cheesy smile. Already the politician.

Rose surged to her feet, calling for the attention of the chairman. 'Right of reply!'

The chairman appeared flummoxed; he gazed out into the crowd and then at his papers.

'Permission to speak,' Rose demanded. She then turned to the room and raised her voice. 'You want to hear from me? Then let me speak.'

There was a silence from the gathering until a female voice from down back shouted out permission for her to speak. The chairman then signalled Rose to step forward.

Rose gripped the side of the lectern and gazed out on the gathering. Most eyes were on her. She rubbed her thumbs along her forefingers, took a deep breath, filling her lungs through her nose, then smiled. 'Friends, thank you for having me here tonight. I appreciate the invitation to come from Canberra to speak.' She gazed out, smiling. 'I'm old enough to remember the last plague of locusts swarming from the north, eating everything in their path. They came after heavy rains, which broke the drought in New South Wales. There wasn't much feed for them north, so they came south and pillaged our crops. Throughout history, they have been a scourge and a sign of pestilence. They came so often that many fed off them as they were the only things left to eat. I'm not sure what they taste like, but I have seen them skewered and barbequed in markets in China. They tell me they are a delicacy.'

Rose chuffed a stifled laugh.

'The point I make is that they are pests who converge on the goodness of the land, leaving their mark.' Rose paused and gulped. 'Much like the Arabs who converged like locusts into our communities, taking our lives away. These pests own your transport, they own your retail, your health clinics, and they own most of the alcohol outlets, and maybe they own this and other gaming clubs. They have branched out into every aspect of our lives and now they own your water. They are the plague upon the mallee.'

Many in the meeting seemed astounded by her tone; nodding showed many agreed. 'You cannot say these things,' someone interjected. 'This is racist talk.'

'Why can't I speak the truth about these matters? What are we afraid of? Their bullying tactics to get their way? Their heavy handedness on those who resist? Tell me you have not felt the whip of punishment when you stand up to them. They are the modern pestilence of our community, and like locusts, they will destroy everything we have unless we respond.'

'This is crazy talk.'

'This is ridiculous.'

'What can we do?'

Rose scanned the interjectors. 'We can fight for our water.'

This prompted many in the audience to comment and chat with their neighbours.

'I'm not saying we get the shotguns out, but if we were in the wild west, then that is what the man with no name would have us do.'

'Ridiculous,' someone shouted.

'We need water and the Arabs have it, so why don't we go get it?' Rose said.

Jack Fingleton stood and in his booming voice said, 'Is this the best you have? To go to war with the Iranians. Is this all you offer?'

'I know how we can get the water back, but it needs all of you to fight.'

'How?' Fingleton shouted. 'How do you propose we get our water?'

'By referendum,' Rose said, then paused for a moment. 'We change the constitution to have the federal government take control of water management. We take control of the water leases, and we regulate the price.'

'Why can't we do that now?' someone queried from down front.

'Constitutionally, our hands are tied. The federal government has no authority over water. That means any water on land.'

Fingleton scratched his head. 'So, you are saying we can reduce the price if we get water regulated by the federal government?'

'That's exactly what I'm saying,' Rose said.

'Then why have you not said so in the past?'

'I have, but my colleagues ignored it.'

Fingleton saw his chance. 'You see...' He glanced around the room. 'Rosie says she provided the idea to the government, but they ignored her. This is why our voice is not heard in Canberra. It's not loud enough.'

Rose raised her voice to talk over him. 'I am but one voice. An army of voices is what I need to fight for this referendum. I need you. All of you need to speak up and demand a referendum.'

'How will our voice help?' a voice called from the side.

'I can tell you it won't hurt,' Rose responded. 'But here's the thing... there will be vehement opposition to it. The state government will reject the idea. Other farming regions will call us lunatics. And no doubt the Arabs will try to hurt us emotionally, mentally, and without question physically, to ensure they don't lose their rights. Believe me when I say this will be a fight to get the referendum legislated and an even bigger fight to get the yes vote.'

Rose paused for a moment, flicking her eyes around the room. 'Look, we cannot directly fight the Arabs. The only way we can disrupt their power is through legislation, and that means we need a referendum... so I ask you... are you with me?' Rose paused and stared out at the meeting, hoping for agreement. 'Will you stand with me and get our water back? Or will you do what Jack wants you to do and weaken your voice in the political race by changing jockey mid race?'

'It's not about you, Rosie,' Fingleton shouted from his seat.

'You're right, Jack.' Rose smiled and peered out, pointing and waving her arm. 'It's about all of you. I'm on the wall. Will you come and fight with me, or will you stay behind and do nothing?'

A farmer from down back stood and started slow handclapping. 'I'm with you, Dowerin.'

Another farmer nearby followed, then another, then another until everyone was on their feet clapping, except Jack Fingleton. He read the mood and gradually stood with a wry smile, clapping, but not as enthusiastically.

CHAPTER
21

'Listeners, you may recall me calling on the government to help our farmers during this devastating drought. You may also recall that they have been very silent and have done nothing. Oh, sure they have provided funding for mental health to help farmers who may struggle; but I can tell you, they are struggling because they have no water and fodder to feed herds and flocks,' said Denis Sadler, a fearless critic of government, and supporter of those in the bush struggling through unprecedented drought.

'You may recall me talking to the prime minister and almost begging for action. I recall I dropped to my knees here in the studio. You may also recall the arrogance of the water minister when she told me the current water shortage remained the responsibility of state governments. No, I said. I told her in no uncertain terms that the crisis we have right now is not the responsibility of the state governments, it is the responsibility of all Australians. We cannot continue to ignore the plight of farmers and the communities out bush that support them. We are in a crisis, and I want the government to act.'

Sadler had been pushing his plan on his syndicated breakfast show for weeks and was yet to get any traction with the government.

'There is no point in making money available to farmers when they have no income to pay it back and therefore do not qualify for loans that will buy them essential water. It's ridiculous. We offer interest-free loans to our students, and they pay them back when they have reached a certain amount of annual income. Why can't we do the same for the farmers? This is what I'm saying: there is no leadership in Canberra and whilst they sit on their hands and procrastinate never planning, our farmers do not have water and can't feed their livestock.'

Rose breathing deep, waiting on the telephone to speak with the Sydney-based Sadler. He normally spruiked a harrowing point of view, then cut to a minister, so she was ready to respond. Government media officers directed ministers to steer clear of him, as the well-researched commentator never held back criticism. He pilloried ministers for years who didn't take his advice. A prime minister once turned up late for an interview and he chastised her for twenty minutes. She never returned.

'Listeners, we are not in a climate crisis. Those arguments from the Greens are rubbish, but we are in a drought crisis. We must act now and make sure this will never happen again. I have with me the Regional Affairs Minister, Rosemary Dowerin. Minister, why is this happening to our farmers?'

'We have plenty of water, Denis.'

'Hang on, Minister.' Rose jumped up and began pacing as far as the taut telephone cable would allow. 'If you think we have enough water, then why are farmers screaming they don't have enough?'

'The state governments...'

Sadler groaned. 'Oh please, stop this rubbish.'

'If you would let me finish. There are two answers to your question. The first is immediate; that means now and the state governments can and should act.'

Sadler sighed. 'And the second?'

'The second answer means we can give greater relief to communities and farmers in the future.'

'What, ten or twenty years?'

'No Denis, ten or twenty months.'

'What? Are you a miracle worker, Minister? I see no evidence of your government having the nerve to act. It's only ever about money with you lot. People's lives are at stake here and the government is refusing to act.'

'As I was about to say, Denis,' Rose said still pacing, with Charlotte watching from a chair, 'the state governments control water management and they have sold off water rights to private speculators who retain water but withhold it to raise the price.'

'Listeners, what the minister is saying is correct. There are non-farming companies who control water rights and sell the leases to those wanting water, be it towns or farmers through New South Wales, Victoria, and South Australia.'

Rose continued. 'These water companies are not breaking the law, Denis. Nor are they acting against any regulations. We could argue, they are acting with no ethics by increasing prices during the current drought.'

'So why doesn't the government do anything?'

'We are.' Rose took a deep breath. 'We are ensuring water is being shipped to towns that need it and we are filling dams where livestock need water.'

'At what cost to the farmers?'

'This is being funded by the government,' Rose said. 'But it needs the state governments to do more with the water that is available and allow struggling communities to get access.'

'But Minister.' Sadler listening intently interrupted. He seemed exasperated. 'What will the government do to stop the speculators who are a scourge across the nation? It is not their water. It comes from the sky, but it seems once water hits land, it becomes a product that is manipulated to drive prices up for greedy businesspeople based nowhere near the drought-affected regions.'

'Denis, you are right.' Rose nodded her head and sat. 'The government can control water, and all it has to do is take the power for water regulation off the states.'

'Then why not do it? Why not do it today and release water?'

'It requires a referendum.'

'Are you saying the states have constitutional protection?'

'That's precisely what I am saying.' Rose chopped her hand. 'For the federal government to gain control of Australia's water, we need the majority of Australians to give us that right and change the constitution.'

'Have you put this idea to the prime minister?'

'I have discussed it with colleagues, but I have not put it to the cabinet.'

'Why not? It seems to make sense to me.'

'Australia is a federation, Denis.' Rose leaned back, more relaxed. 'As you know, we protect the rights of states as proposed by the founding fathers, and we want to preserve their sovereignty on matters over which they have control, such as water.'

'But if they don't act?'

'Then I reckon we should go to a referendum and have the people decide if they want the federal government to resolve these water leasing arrangements and never have this price controlled by speculators again.'

'This would be a perfectly valid question to ask the people of Australia.'

'Any support from you would be a good thing,' Rose said. 'I am sure your listeners worry, as I do, about the plight of the farmers and communities in the regions. My electorate, Mallee, has significant issues. We get a sprinkle of rain now and then, but it does not compare to the downpours the cities are getting. City folks just don't understand the urgency.'

'Well, I do, I can tell you,' Sadler said. 'I am pleased we have a government minister coming on air with ideas that can help our farmers.' He paused a moment, then added in a lower tone. 'They need it, I can tell you.'

'If it goes to a referendum, Denis, then it is your listeners who will change the water system that controls access for our farmers.'

'One last question before you go?'

Rose scrambled to her feet. 'Sure, Denis. Fire away.'

'Who is going to replace Jock Garnsworthy as the leader of the Country Party?'

Rose glanced at Charlotte. 'We have several quality candidates. I am sure we will work our way through those issues when the time comes to replace him.'

'Jock has been an outstanding leader for your party, but during this drought, he has gone missing, and we don't need another dud. I can tell you.'

'That's a little harsh, Denis, given Jock renegotiated to Australia's favour several trade treaties in the last two years.'

'Have you thought about standing?'

Rose paused for a moment. 'Not really.'

'That answer tells me you are considering it,' Sadler snapped. 'I will tell you this: if you are a candidate, you will have my support.'

'Thank you. Denis,' Rose said, beaming. 'I shall consider it.'

'Listeners, that was Rosemary Dowerin, the Regional Affairs Minister, and a worthy replacement for Jock Garnsworthy as leader of the Country Party. She is an honest politician, which is very rare these days. Time for the seven thirty news.'

Rose replaced the phone and stood with a broad smile as she looked at her staffer. 'Sadler said he will support my candidacy as leader.'

Charlotte smiled back.

The telephone rang before Rose had time to say or do anything else. She picked it up and listened, colour draining from her face as she rubbed her forehead with thumb and finger. 'Yes, prime minister, I'll be right there.'

'Anything wrong?' Charlotte asked.

Rose raised her eyebrows, widening her eyes and squirming her face. 'Yeah, he's not happy.'

'What are you going to do?'

'Well, I will not resign, I can tell you that.'

'Is this a fight you want?'

Rose grinned as she collected her leather folder. 'Bring it on, Charlie.' She nodded at her staffer as she strode from the room.

'Don't bother sitting; you won't be here long.' Brown sat with arms crossed, forearms resting on the desk. He had his jacket on, his face rigid with taut lips. 'I want your resignation on my desk by midday.' He stubbed a finger into the wood.

Rose could feel her knees weaken. Her eyes flicked about, eyelids blinking. She tried to speak but needed to clear her throat. 'Why would I do that?'

Brown sneered, his eyes narrowing. 'Let's start with breaching the ministerial code,' he snapped.

Rose nodded for a moment. 'How have I done that?'

'Announcing government initiatives that do not fall into your portfolio, thus breaching confidence and exposing the government to media scrutiny and ridicule.'

'The water delivery is already in the public. Spencer announced it last night.'

Brown's eyes darted about as he swallowed.

'Prime Minister, an announcement came from the minister last night around ten o'clock.'

'No, it wasn't. It is being announced this morning at ten o'clock.'

'Someone from the minister's office seems to have stuffed up. Or maybe it was the minister herself, given her track record.'

Brown picked up his phone and punched in a number. 'Jess, can you check the water minister's media and website to see if we have announced the government initiative regarding carting water?' He almost broke the handset as he thumped it back into the cradle. 'If you are wrong, then I will add wilful dishonesty to the list.'

Rose looked down on him, pursing her lips in a *wait and see* expression tinged with the slightest of smiles. She knew what the news was going to be. Roger Newgreen is a whiz kid when it came to digital hacking. The mistake had been sending out an embargoed media release last night instead of this morning.

Brown snatched at the phone when it rang and listened, then dropped it to the desk before putting easing it back in the cradle. 'It seems I am mistaken.'

'So, I don't need to place my resignation here,' Rose stepped forward and put her finger on the prime minister's desk, 'by midday?'

Brown fell back into his chair, gripping the arms taken aback by her assertive step forward. 'You may have been right about this, Rose, but that will not save you.'

'Tim, I know you,' Rose smiled.

Brown shook his head, squinting.

'I know men like you very well.' Rose leaned forward. 'They are full of bluster, and they bully the weak to get their way. You became prime minister because of threats and intimidation to your backbench. But I know you, and what may have passed between us in the past will not pass between us in the future.'

'What are you talking about, woman?'

'As your deputy prime minister, I will make sure you have a safe ride,' Rose said. 'But if you ever cross me again or demand anything from me, then it will be all over for you.'

Brown laughed out loud. 'Are you threatening me?'

Rose smiled, leaning even further forward. 'Yes.'

'You'll never be elected leader; Clare will.'

'There is much about Clare that is not public.' Rose straightened and moved away.

Brown dropped his smile.

'And you, for that matter.'

'You know nothing.'

'We shall see.' Rose left the office. 'See you in the chamber.'

CHAPTER
22

The Melbourne office of the premier moved from the old government building in Treasury Place to a more prestigious office in the towering state government building on Exhibition Street. The office commanded sweeping views of the eastern suburbs and Port Phillip Bay. Darius Hassidim soaked in the impressive view as he and his colleagues waited for an audience. He watched as a black and grey rain cloud swept the bay towards the eastern suburbs, then watching the scurrying city below still bathed in sunshine. 'Rain in the bay and none in the city, just like home,' he said to no-one.

A staff member clicked through a heavy security door and beckoned the four directors to follow her to an inner room. Unmistakable commanding views again, and the decor of the room suggesting taxpayers' money indulged the leader of the state. As they sat, the premier entered through a side door with an extended hand and a broad smile.

'Gentlemen, nice to see you.' He shook hands, asking if they would like a drink.

'Water is fine,' Darius said. 'We come to talk to you about our plans and wonder where we are at with our submission?'

'Well, good news about that.' Jackson smiled and leaned into the large, polished wood table. 'The department is completing a report, and it comes to cabinet in two weeks.'

'This is good news,' Hosmand Shofet smiled. 'What are the numbers in the cabinet?'

'Should be fine.' Jackson waved a hand.

A telephone shrilled, interrupting the conversation. Darius reached inside his jacket, holding up a hand. 'Timothy, nice of you to call.' He smiled at the premier. 'How can I help?'

'We have a problem with Dowerin.'

'What could be a problem with a woman of so little consequence?'

'She is fighting to stay in the cabinet.'

'How can she do that?' Darius frowned. 'You agreed to sack her.'

'This is the problem. I can only sack her if she is not in the leadership group, and she is making noises she will challenge to become leader.'

Darius said nothing and glanced over to his counsel, Shofet.

'The only way we can get rid of her is to take her out at preselection. Do you have a candidate?'

'I would have thought it was not up to me to organise such a coup,' Darius said, shaking his head. Jackson checked his watch. 'Look, Tim, I must go. Let me think about what we can do, and I'll get back to you. Did you get my gift?'

The prime minister paused. 'Yes, I did, thank you.'

'We have another for you when the submission for our new airport is before the minister.'

'We shall just have to wait and see,' Brown said.

'Always prepared to wait for your support, Timothy. You know that.'

'Let's talk soon.' Brown ended the call.

Darius slid his phone back. 'As you could tell, that was the prime minister.' He grinned at the premier. 'He is very concerned with the current member for Mallee.'

Jackson nodded. 'Everyone is concerned with the member for Mallee.'

'We are of the view that it's time for her to retire.' Darius glanced at his colleagues, who nodded. 'She has failed the local community during the drought and has criticised the water management scheme set up by your government. I am told she is about to be dumped from the federal cabinet.'

'She's lazy and takes too much for granted,' Jackson said.

'Exactly.' Darius flicked a pointed finger at the premier. 'We must challenge her preselection.'

'I agree.' Jackson nodded.

Darius smiled. 'This is why I like you, Phillip. We are always on the same wavelength.'

'It won't be easy to get rid of her,' Jackson said. 'She does her numbers well and the family name still carries weight.'

Darius didn't respond, dropping his head to rest on his hand. He gnawed his thumb nail. 'Would you consider standing against her?'

Jackson tossed his head back and laughed.

'You would be the ideal candidate to knock her off.' Darius observed Jackson's reaction. 'I can almost guarantee you the seat.'

'Look around.' Jackson waved a sweeping arm. 'Why would I want to go to Canberra?'

Darius dropped his head and scratched his cheek. 'How does deputy prime minister sound?'

Jackson dropped his sparkle, narrowing his eyes. 'I am not sure you can offer that job.'

'If I could?'

'Then I might think about it,' Jackson said. 'It would need me to be appointed once I entered the parliament.'

'I would ask you to consider your position.' Darius winked at Shofet. 'You get the tourist development plan through, and I shall make sure you are deputy prime minister.'

'You can do that?'

'This is easy,' Darius smiled. 'What is hard is having you get the planning approved.'

'I'll make sure it happens.' Jackson nodded and smirked. 'Are you prepared to negotiate if we get close?'

'Are you?' Maisil Ghassab asked, clenching a fist.

'Anything is possible. Let us take care of Madam Dowerin first,' Darius said.

'Guarantee me the leadership role and you will have your approval.'

'Ah, you see?' Darius stood, extending his hand. 'Everyone has their price.'

CHAPTER
23

W ater trickled down the side of the iced tea as Rose listened to her two elder children talking silly things, bantering about the fun they had when younger. She smiled at a comment and took a sip; the ice clinked against the glass and water dripped onto her blouse. She brushed it off, placing the drink on the table beside her then waving away a cluster of flies.

They were waiting for Bobby, again running late. The smell of lamb, rosemary, and garlic wafted from the open doors. Rose's chief of staff wanted a home cooked meal and offered to cook Sunday lunch for the family. It was hot but they could not resist the idea of a roast leg of lamb, so the family welcomed another to slave over an oven-baked meal in a hot kitchen.

Charlotte didn't mind. She liked Rose's kids, especially the boys.

Bobby's Jeep swung into the drive, sliding to a stop on the gravel. A metaphor for the way he lived his life, at speed and with little regard for others as they brushed away the dust clouding over them.

'Sorry I'm late. Just got a deal done in town.'

'Another city slicker seeking country living?' Peter said.

'As it happens, no.' Bobby took off his hat, banging it against his leg, sending up a brief puff of dust. 'Another Iranian family moving from Swan Hill. Better schools here, so they say.'

'They are everywhere,' Primrose said.

'They're a wonderful community,' Peter responded. 'They cause little trouble, few of them drink and they work to better the community.'

'Their community, you mean,' Primrose said.

'Maybe so, but their community is our community,' Peter said.

'Anyway, they have money, and plenty are prepared to pay top dollar for good properties,' Bobby said.

'We should have restrictions on them. They shouldn't be allowed to buy up the good ones.'

Peter raised his eyebrows. 'You can't say that Primmy.'

'Why not? It's a free country. I can say what I like.'

Bobby interjected. 'Anyway, I get a good commission, so another step towards Melbourne.'

'Why do you want to go to Melbourne?' Peter asked.

'Rain. Water. Cool air. Football. Do you want me to keep going?' Bobby flopped in a cushioned wicker lounge as Charlotte stepped from inside, announcing lunch being served. 'Right on time, as usual.' Bobby jumped up and tailed Charlotte into the house, poking her hip as he passed. 'Nice.' She looked over her shoulder and smiled.

The family sauntered in, getting comfortable to attack the feast, set with a white tablecloth and cloth napkins.

'You found the good stuff,' said Primrose, as she took her seat.

Charlotte smiled. 'I did.' She took a chair opposite her, next to Peter. 'I hope you enjoy it. The fan should keep us cool. I love a good roast. It's been a while.'

Bobby spooned several potatoes onto his plate. 'So, Mumsie, the word is that you are about to retire.'

'Mummy will not retire, will you, Mummy?' Primrose said.

'Charlotte and I have been plotting and planning various scenarios this week.' Rose peeked at her staffer and smiled. 'We remain unsure about the future and want to discuss it with you guys.' She glanced around them. 'Should I retire?'

'Yes,' Bobby said at once as he turned his attention to the carved lamb and gravy.

Peter asked, 'What does the party say?'

'There are loud voices against me. Fingleton, Toll, O'Brien, and Lever, but they don't have a quality candidate to nominate.'

'You mean James Lever?'

'Yeah, the loudmouth irrigator,' Primrose said. 'He moved a motion against Mummy, starting all of this trouble.' She scooped up peas from her plate with a spoon.

Peter took a mouthful of food. 'You know we found him out at Landells the other day. Indications are he was murdered.'

Rose laid her knife and fork on her plate. 'I am aware,' she said. 'Why would anyone do that?'

Bobby stopped chewing and glanced back and forward from his mother to his brother. 'Who owns his farm? Does anyone know?'

'You are kidding me?' Peter sighed.

'What? It's just a question.'

'Not the sort of question you ask in the same context as an announcement about a likely murder.'

'What's wrong? I just asked a question.'

Peter dropped his cutlery onto his plate, staring at his brother.

'Good riddance, I say,' Primrose declared.

Peter didn't respond.

Bobby waited for his brother to say something. 'How come you let that one pass?'

'She doesn't know better,' Peter said.

'I'm not stupid,' Primrose said, raising her voice.

'No one said you were, darling,' Rose said, patting her hand. 'Can I just ask you boys to settle down and let us finish this gorgeous lunch Charlotte has prepared?'

The brothers maintained their staring until Charlotte patted and rubbed Peter's thigh; he turned to her, embarrassed. 'Sorry, Charlie. Mum's right. This is beautiful.'

For the rest of the meal, the discussion ignored politics concentrating on the drought, the latest sporting results, and how long Charlotte would be in town. Once they finished a trifle dessert, they moved about the house cleaning up, with Rose and Peter shifting to the veranda for a wine.

'Any idea who did it?' Rose asked as they settled into the soft cushions.

'We are completing forensics and trying to get an idea why he was out there.'

'Was he in trouble?'

'Only with water leases; he's paying way too much.'

'Who would want to do him in?' Rose asked. 'Jimmy was harmless.'

'What was weird about the body was they took his finger.'

'His finger?'

'Yeah, they snapped his little finger off.' Peter said, shifting in his chair and crossing his legs.

'You're right, that is weird. Sounds like a mafia thing to do.' Rose laughed.

'You think the sopranos are in Mildura?' Peter said, chuckling.

'Who knows? They grow dope further north.'

'We've seen no evidence of them down here for years.'

'It's weird,' Rose said.

He peeked over at his mother. 'Yeah, it is.'

'Well, good luck with it. I'll check on his family this week.'

'Yeah, thanks.' Peter brushed a fly from his mouth. 'Are you thinking about retiring?'

'No, not at all,' Rose said. 'I'm being manipulated, and don't like it. Never have.'

'Why would you want to stay?'

Rose eyed her son, gnawing her bottom lip. 'I suppose duty. I have a duty to maintain the family name in the parliament and a duty to not let down your father's legacy.'

'You've done enough.'

Rose stood and stepped to the wooden sideboard where a bottle of chardonnay chilled in an ice bucket. She poured two glasses, handing one to her son.

'I never wanted to do this.' Rose slumped into her chair. 'I wasn't expecting to do this, but when your father died, your grandfather suggested, rather vigorously, if I recall, that it was my duty until one of you was ready.'

'We will never be ready.' Peter glanced over to Bobby, checking his phone, and Primrose, trying to snap with her hand the flies tracking above her.

'If I had known that years ago, I would have gone with my original plan.'

'What was that?'

'Sell up and move out of this desert country.'

'So, we let you down?'

'Not at all.' Rose took a sip of the chilled wine, brushing away a fly. 'I now realise I'm the last Dowerin, so I may as well make the most of it. Don't get me wrong; I'm ready to walk away, but those morons in the cabinet reckon I'm not up to it, so I reckon I might show them a thing or two and shove it up 'em.'

'Why?' Peter sipped his wine. 'I mean why bother?'

'I suppose it's how I feel about folks taking advantage. I won't put up with it. Never have.'

'But if you are ready to leave, then now could be the time.'

'It's not in my make-up to let folks take advantage,' Rose said. 'Those who do, regret it.'

Peter gazed at his mother, withdrawing his lips and nodding. He studied her stern expression. 'What are you going to do?'

'I'm going to run for the leadership and become deputy prime minister.' Rose gazed out towards the river. 'Nothing is going to stop me.' She drained her glass.

'Big ambitions,' Peter said.

Rose didn't respond for a moment as she stared towards the river. 'Someone once told me to always think big, so maybe it's time I did again.'

Primrose came to sit with her mother and brother. She turned to Rose with a querying look. 'When did you think big before?'

Rose glanced over at her daughter with what seemed to be a sad, tired expression. She pointed to her glass, and Peter brought the wine over, pouring a glass, topping up his own.

'Thanks, darling.' Rose sipped a little and settled back. 'I've always thought big ever since I can remember, always had big plans. Maybe I didn't think big when I started travelling to Canberra. Perhaps I thought I had made it.'

Bobby joined the conversation. 'If you were thinking big back then, why would you come to a dump like Mildura?'

'Bobby, you can't say that...' Primrose squealed. 'You're naughty.'

The others laughed.

'It's true. Why did you?' Bobby asked.

Rose dropped her head back and gazed at the twirling overhead fan. 'I was tired of Melbourne. I thought working up here could get me quick money to travel.'

'Why stay?'

'Your dad.'

'Were you thinking big when you met him?' Bobby laughed and winked.

'Not sure what I was thinking when I met him.' Rose took a sip of wine. 'We seemed to get along, so we married, and the rest is history.'

'You would have seen the dollars in the family and thought big, I reckon,' Bobby said.

'Ease up, Bobby,' Peter interjected. 'That's a tacky thing to say.'

'Why? I would have.'

Rose peeked at her youngest, perhaps recognising similarities. 'I played hard to get. I was working to save money.'

'He drowned; didn't he Mummy?' Primrose said. The boys shifted in their chairs at the comment.

'He went swimming when he shouldn't have,' Bobby said. 'Just remember that when you go to the river by yourself.'

'I can swim.'

'Dad could as well,' Peter said. 'That's what seemed so strange about him getting into trouble.'

'Your dad was a bit of a roustabout and took enormous risks,' Rose sighed. 'A little reckless, swimming early in the evening with plenty of river craft about.'

'Reckless.' Peter gazed out towards the river, brushing away a fly. 'Nice word.'

Charlotte stepped out onto the veranda, having cleaned the remnants of the meal, and cranking up the dishwasher. The others stopped their conversation. She helped herself to a glass of wine and sat next to Peter.

'So, tell me, Pete.' Charlotte lifted her knees onto the couch and leaned one arm on the cushion behind her, twirling her hair. 'What do you think about Rose standing as the leader of the party?'

Peter eyed her and smiled. 'Hey, thanks for lunch. It was great.'

'Brilliant, Charlie.' Bobby tossed her his salesman smile.

'And your mum running for the leadership?'

'Oh, she can do whatever she likes. She can look after herself,' Peter said.

Rose narrowed her gaze as she smiled at them.

'It's going to be a struggle,' Charlotte continued. 'We think we can kill off the party challengers if she wins the leadership.'

'Which comes first?' Primrose asked.

Charlotte turned to her. 'We are hoping we can have the leadership challenge before the preselection next year,' she said. 'But, if the party moves to have the preselection this year, then our plans may be in trouble.'

'Jimmy Lever said he would have been a candidate,' Rose said.

Bobby laughed. 'Well, that's convenient.'

'You could say that,' said Rose, glancing away.

Peter's interest sparked. 'He said that?'

'His wife told me he was making plans,' Rose said.

'Interesting,' Peter said.

Primrose peeked at her brother as she chewed a cushion, and then under a furrowed brow peered at her mother. Rose gave a slight nod and smirked.

'Hey, Mum? I was just thinking.' Bobby slipped his phone into his shirt pocket, grinning at his mother. 'You named Peter after Dad's younger brother and Primmy after you... who was I named after?'

Rose pushed her bottom lip out with her tongue as she paused for a moment, recalling her old friend. 'Robert was an early settler if I recall.'

'You don't know?'

'I recall your father suggested it.' Rose chuckled. 'Not happy with it?'

Bobby frowned. 'This is what I love about this family,' he said. No one responded. 'Hero here gets applause for fighting criminals. You get praise for being a pollie. I get nothing, even though I pull off a big deal today.'

'What about me?' Primrose complained.

'It's been the same since I was a kid. I never felt part of it.' Bobby stood, moving to the edge of the veranda. 'I don't know why I even bother.' He stepped off. 'See ya.'

'Don't be like that, son.' Rose watched him. 'Bobby, don't go.' He had already gone.

'He right to drive?' Peter asked.

'He had nothing to drink,' Charlotte said.

'Bobby doesn't like us, does he?' Primrose asked, prompting Peter and Rose to exchange a glance.

CHAPTER
24

'We have a problem.' Maisil Ghassab marched into Darius Hassidim's office, plonking himself opposite in a lounge chair opposite the expansive desk.

'Concerning?'

'The city council has asked for a planning and environmental impact report.'

Hosmand Shofet sitting in a hard chair at the desk said, 'Another?'

'They aren't using the one we registered,' Ghassab said.

'What are they doing?'

'They have a new planning officer. She asked to review the plans. She has the support from the greenies.'

Darius considered his colleague, stroking the tuft of hair under his bottom lip. He punched a button on the desk telephone. 'Could you join us, my friend?' A few moments later, Taimur Saraf came to the door. 'It seems we have a problem in Mildura.' Darius gestured for him to take a chair. 'Have the payments gone through to the mayor?'

'Yes, of course, a few weeks ago,' Saraf said. 'The mayor and the others have all received the agreed amount.'

'Maisil tells me they pushed it back to planning.'

'News to me; they were told to not hold up approval, and all agreed.'

'Then why?' Darius queried. 'This will delay the state government. They need the council's sign off.'

'It's the new girl,' Ghassab said. 'I can fix it.'

'Wait up,' Shofet interjected. 'We cannot be using a heavy hand on this, otherwise it will be all over.'

'It's not the planning officer we should talk to. It's the mayor,' Darius said. 'She must know we will come for her if they do not approve it.'

'No doubt she does,' Shofet said. 'She may just be covering her arse.'

'Fuck me!' Darius bounced out of his chair and walked to the window. 'Why are these women causing us so much trouble?'

'Who?' Saraf asked.

'The mayor, this planning officer and Dowerin.' Darius said, now leaning against the windowsill.

'Don't make Dowerin the issue,' Shofet counselled. 'We have set her up with her own problems. She has nothing to do with our plans.'

'She is causing us grief with the water.'

'What grief? The money is still flowing. Excuse the pun.' Saraf smiled.

Darius glanced towards Shofet, arching a brow. 'She might take that revenue stream from us.'

'Now you're doing it.' Shofet chuckled.

'Doing what?'

'Making puns.' Shofet said, smiling at Darius, who didn't respond. 'Revenue stream... water?' Still no response. 'Oh, forget it.'

Darius continued. 'She wants the feds to manage water.'

'She has little chance of succeeding,' Shofet said, now in focus.

'Brown mentioned she is proposing a referendum.' Darius frowned. 'If that gets up, then we may lose control of our water.'

'Relax, Darius. If we get our project up, we won't need water,' Saraf said.

Darius squinted at his colleague. 'There is no guarantee we get that approval.'

'Then let me fix it,' Ghassab said.

'We can't keep losing people,' Shofet sighed.

'We can if they are in our way.' Ghassab said, cracking a knuckle with his thumb.

'I'm told the government and the party want Dowerin gone,' Darius said.

'Hasn't she announced she is running for the leadership?' Saraf asked.

'We suspect that is her tactic to win preselection,' Shofet replied. 'She knows she is gone from the ministry, and if she loses preselection, she will be gone from the parliament. She thinks running for the leader will stop the move against her.'

'Stopping any contest at preselection?' Saraf asked.

'Exactly,' Darius said.

'On that basis there are two scenarios,' Shofet said. 'She loses preselection and is out of parliament, or she wins the leadership, guaranteeing preselection.'

'If she wins the leadership, she will push a referendum to have water regulation transferred to the federal government,' Darius added.

Saraf nodded. 'We need her to lose the preselection before the leadership ballot.'

'Exactly.' Darius slapped his hand.

'How likely is that?' Saraf asked.

'Brown is expecting the leadership ballot to be later this year,' Darius said. 'Jackson tells me the preselection contest will happen in the new year.'

'That's a problem,' Ghassab said.

The group remained silent for a moment. Darius pushed himself off the windowsill and returned to his desk. 'Who wants a sharbat?' he asked as he picked up the phone and fingered a number. Ghassab was the only one to shake his head no.

'If they schedule the preselection before the leadership ballot, will that help?' Ghassab asked.

Darius finished the order, then sat at his desk. 'It would terminate her career and she could not stand for the leadership.'

'We promised Jackson the leadership. Does he need to put his hand up for the preselection to knock her off?' Saraf asked.

'Hell no,' Darius answered. 'We kill her with a dud candidate, and then before the election we discover the dud in a scandal, and we swap in Jackson for election.'

'That doesn't give him the leadership because they will have already elected a new leader,' Ghassab said.

'That's likely to be Clare Spencer,' Darius said. 'We shall ask her to resign once Jackson is in the parliament.'

'How is that possible?' Shofet asked.

Darius held up his smart phone and flicked through to a file, pushing play. 'Remember when Taimur and I went to Canberra the other week?' He smiled as the file engaged.

'Thank you, Mr Hassidim, I appreciate your contribution to my campaign.'

'It is a gift, not a donation. We do not expect it to be used on your campaign. You can use it in any form you see fit.'

They could hear the rustling sound of items being removed.

'This is far too generous.'

'As I said, Minister. Use the fifty any way you want. We don't need a receipt or an acknowledgement.'

'Surely, I can help you with something?'

'Nothing at all, Clare. Just don't put it in the bank.'

'If you need help with your leases, then call me.'

'That day may never come, Minister, but if it ever does, then we expect you to do whatever you can to help deliver what we need.'

'I will be most willing to help.'

'As I say that day may never come.'

Darius swiped his phone, closing the file.

'I can guarantee Jackson will be the leader of the Country Party and deputy prime minister.' Darius smiled. 'If he gives us approval for our project first.'

Shofet and Ghassab chuckled. 'You are a worthy Khalif, aren't you?' Shofet said.

Darius grinned. 'It's never about the power. You know that my friends. We have done this together, and we have done well?'

Shofet smiled and looked over at Darius, nodding.

Darius perused his colleagues. 'We said we would do this thirty years ago. We had the plans, and we did what we said we would do. Tell us,

Taimur.' Darius nodded at the finance director. 'Tell us what we have done.'

'You already know.'

'Yes, but I like to hear it from you,' Darius said.

'We have capital assets of eight billion.'

They performed a whoop, and Saraf laughed.

'Cash sits around two-five million. We have shares or commission arrangements of around five hundred million and we have product passing through the warehouse with a street value of around fifteen million each month.'

'All from migrating here all those years ago.' Darius linked his fingers behind his head as he lay back in his chair. 'We left our desert and saw the potential in this godforsaken desert.' He smiled at his friends. 'We turned what Australians deemed miserable into a tremendous asset for our people. Now our community controls the economic strength of the region. And this is why we will have our Vegas.'

'It took time, but you said we could do it,' Shofet said, beaming.

Ghassab chuckled. 'We filled many holes in the desert.'

'Those problems we buried never saw what we saw.' Darius steepled his fingers in front of him. 'Now we are free to do whatever we want, and soon we shall have the deputy prime minister.'

'He learnt his lesson,' Ghassab said.

'When we have that position secured, and the precinct approved, we will expand further,' Darius continued.

'Let us take small steps, Darius,' Shofet said. 'As always, we must move stealthily and not upset the cart.'

'You still talk in horse-drawn carts, Hosmand.' Darius opened his hands. 'We can now buy the entire fleet.'

'Again, let us move with wisdom. We do not need to dig further holes.'

Ghassab grunted. 'The day we stop using our muscle and the manner we deliver messages is the day we start losing.'

Darius scoffed, pointing at Ghassab. 'I think he's right.'

An attendant walked in with the tray of drinks.

'We should go talk to the mayor and remind her of her duty,' Ghassab said.

'I think we should,' Shofet said. 'We don't need to touch the planning officer,' he continued. 'At least, not yet.'

Ghassab frowned. 'We can offer her a good reason to act to approve the plans.'

Darius hushed him with a gentle wave, took up the drink, and mouthed a generous slug. 'So good.'

CHAPTER
25

The black Land Rover thrashed along the gravel road towards the planned site of the tourist development. Most vehicles would take it easy, but it seemed Ghassab cared little about the vehicle hurrying to get to his destination. Relaxed in the front seat beside him sat Shofet. In the back seat, hanging on to whatever they could grasp, were the mayor and the town planner.

Shofet studied notes while Ghassab punished the tyres at a hundred kilometres an hour. The air-conditioning cranked to counter the baking heat and the wailing music of Iran set at a level to annoy the passengers.

'Can we slow a little?' the mayor asked.

Shofet glanced up and out the front of the vehicle. 'We're almost there.'

The mayor didn't respond and gazed out the tinted window and sighed. She had taken a call from Darius Hassidim, expressing his unease with the approval holdup, suggesting a site visit. What she thought would be a helicopter flyover turned into a forty-minute ride. She knew the likelihood of seeing anything of value shrunk with the flat landscape.

Ghassab braked, and the vehicle slithered to a stop. They sat for a moment, waiting for a cloud of dust to settle before jumping out and moving to the rear of the vehicle. Shofet opened the back hatch, taking out an umbrella, opening it up and passing it to the mayor. He did the same for the planning officer. He then passed each a bottle of water then pointing along the graded road.

'This is the proposed boundary of the planned city limits. The river is ten minutes that way. We'll see you there.'

'Hey, wait up, you expect us to walk it?' the mayor said.

'We want you to experience the land, so you understand the value of the development. Ten minutes, that's all.'

Shofet hopped into the vehicle and Ghassab took off at a pace that didn't worry the women, as it motored only twenty metres ahead. They trudged after it, pleased the men provided umbrellas. Although starting with confidence, their energy levels waned in the sapping heat. The planner finished her water, and the mayor stopped to recover her breath. The heat parched their mouths and hearts beat harder. Within ten minutes, the mayor was sitting under her umbrella and the planner had stepped off the road traipsing through the scrublands, a little disoriented having lost her umbrella now tumbling along the track.

The black vehicle returned after twelve minutes.

Shofet poured a bottle of water over the mayor and then let her guzzle a litre. Ghassab went off into the scrub, assisting the planner back to the car. She too gulped a litre of water. They assisted them back into the vehicle, chilled by the air-conditioning. Shofet positioned an iced damp cloth on their foreheads and offered a painkiller for the headaches he assumed they must have. Body temperatures eventually recovered, and Shofet turned in his seat to study the mayor.

'We brought you here today to reassure you of our intent to develop this rugged country into a tourist precinct.' Shofet flicked his gaze between them. 'As you can see, it is a wasteland. Good for nothing.' He encouraged them to drink. 'We want you to know that we have the money and the means to ensure this development project will be a success and meet all government requirements. Feel assured we will do whatever it takes to get approvals.'

The planner glanced away. A tear trickled across her cheek.

'I assume you know what to expect if we do not get them.' Shofet paused for a moment. 'I also assume you realise no one is immune.'

The mayor stretched and took the planner's hand, squeezing it.

'We expect to have approval for the project at the next meeting. If we don't achieve this target, then not only you but your families will feel regret.' Shofet smiled. 'Do we understand each other?'

The mayor raised her head, nodded. 'Yes.'

'And you, little princess?'

The planner peeked up and met Ghassab's eyes, staring at her in the rear vision mirror; she nodded, averting her gaze.

'Very good. Now let's get you back to Mildura and have that meal I promised you.

CHAPTER
26

'I hate these trips; they never seem to end well.' Saraf had laid his seat back, gazing at the roof twirling a pen. Ghassab paid little attention. They were almost at Horsham, the very south of the mallee. 'Do you expect any problems?'

Ghassab cast him a quick glance. 'I welcome challenges.'

'Such a strange man.'

'Here he is,' Ghassab said, checking the rear vision as flashing police lights advanced to the rear of the four-wheel drive. He slowed, pulling into a parking bay under the Welcome to Horsham sign.

Ghassab kept the motor running, waiting for their acquaintance to advance to the side of the car and hand them an incomplete speeding ticket. Just part of the game for suspicious eyes.

'How are you, Maisil? Darius, not with you today?'

Ghassab rested his arm on the open window. 'Taimur has folks to chastise for their drop in revenue, so Darius is letting me provide the muscle instead of him.'

'Anything I should worry about?'

'We have a skimmer at the club, but we'll fix it.'

'Anything else I can do for you boys?'

'We are meeting with Jack Fingleton. Any tips?'

The police officer shrugged. 'Depends on what you want.'

'He's big with the local party, is he not?'

'He ain't a supporter of Dowerin, if that's what you mean.'

'That's what we heard.' Ghassab peered up at the sergeant, but the bright sun forced him to turn away.

'You enjoy yourself in town and let me know if you need anything.'

Ghassab stretched his hand to Saraf, who slapped a tight small parcel with three elastic bands. He offered it to the police officer, who checked about before slipping it into his shirt through an unfastened button.

'Always a pleasure, Maisil.'

Ghassab gushed a smile. 'You take care, Harry. See you next time.'

'Call me if you need anything.'

'Will do.' Ghassab crawled the vehicle over the gravel, then up to speed back on the road, leaving the police sergeant with a wave.

'Is he good value?' Saraf asked.

'They all are.' Ghassab checked the mirror. 'We don't have them all, but we have most. Transfer requests are down and so is crime, so we must do something right.'

'Good for us.'

Thirty minutes later, they sauntered into the Horsham Commerce Club. They pushed past doors into the gaming lounge, where thirty players sat staring at their machine, pushing a flashing button, watching the screen spin to another loss. There had not been a jackpot won for three months. Gamblers still came every day hoping for a win.

They marched through to the bistro, surprised to see a crowd eating. The lounge bar had ten men drinking, and as they moved towards the manager's office. They spotted a blonde bar attendant duck away towards the office.

The manager strode out to greet them as the anxious attendant went back to her duties. Laurie Smithson managed the club since the redevelopment twelve years ago. He ran a tight operation with strong revenues and increasing profits. He was their best man. They often used him for staff training and development at other locations, but now something wasn't right.

'Can we use your office, Laurie?' Saraf suggested.

When they settled, Saraf hauled a laptop from his leather bag, opening it to an accounting spreadsheet.

'Laurie, this shows the trading at every register.' Smithson nodded as he watched the screen. 'These numbers get broken down further into hourly trading figures. We have analysed it even further to show ten-minute periods.' Smithson swallowed hard. 'With this information and staff coding, we can figure out where any fraud or theft may exist.' Saraf turned from the screen and gazed at the manager. 'Is there anything you would like to contribute at this stage?'

Smithson cast a glance at Ghassab, then looked back at Saraf without commenting.

'Based on the data, we think someone is skimming the till.'

'How...' Smithson swallowed again. 'How much?'

'The precise amount is three thousand, four hundred and twenty-five dollars over the last six months. We expected you would be onto it, but you're not. We came today to ask why?'

'Are you screwing her?' Ghassab said.

'What?'

Ghassab smiled. 'Are you playing hide the sausage? Are you poking her? Are you getting top shelf munga?'

'I don't know what you mean.'

Saraf sighed, rubbing the side of his face. 'What my friend is crudely saying is that we know who is stealing the money. She has been here eight months. There are complaints about her work. She has a drug problem. What we don't understand is why you are not across the losses. We assume you are in a relationship with her.'

'Who?' Smithson said.

Ghassab moved his chair closer. 'Laurie, we like you. We have no intention of getting rid of you. You are safe... but we need you to do a few things for us.'

Smithson skimmed wide eyed between Saraf and Ghassab.

'We need you to repay the money,' Saraf said.

'But...' Smithson began protesting.

'Hush now, Laurie.' Ghassab held up a silencing hand.

'I have never...' Smithson didn't finish as Ghassab fisted him, knocking him from the chair into the wall.

'You don't seem to realise... we know the truth,' Ghassab said, lifting him to the chair.

'Laurie, make this easier for yourself,' said Saraf. 'As Maisil said, we like you and we want you to work with us at our new development. But we will not tolerate any funny business with money,' he said, shaking his head. 'We thought you already knew that, but it seems not. So, for your own safety, please listen to us.' He passed Smithson tissues to wipe the blood from his nose.

Ghassab leaned on his knees, bringing his face closer. 'We want the money returned within the week. We want you to end her employment, effective now, and we want you to escort her to our car.'

Smithson peeked up, gnawing at his bottom lip.

'Are you able to do that for us?' Saraf said.

'I suppose.'

'Good lad, we'll be waiting outside,' said Saraf, as he stood. 'Be quick about it.'

The manager walked his girlfriend to the car park after explaining what had happened. They climbed into the back seat of the idling vehicle, which took off at once, heading for the river, passing the radio station, and pulling into a motel. Ghassab parked the car outside unit ten and asked them to join him in the room.

They followed while Saraf waited. He detected a shout or two, a scream, then silence, before the three reappeared, shuffling back to the car.

The woman had been upright, but anxious when she entered the room. She now appeared dishevelled, with her hair wild and eye makeup smudged as she emerged hunched over. Smithson had a towel wrapped around his left hand.

Ghassab helped them into the back seat, engaging the vehicle and crossing the river back into the town before stopping at the hospital emergency.

'Let's hope we don't have to speak to you again, okay?'

The couple plodded into the hospital as Ghassab drove off. He stretched into his pocket and pulled out a slither of red cloth, wiped his face, and tossed it into Saraf's lap.

Saraf unfolded it, holding it up to look at the string thing, smiling as he recognised it. 'Good?'

'No wonder he's in love.'

CHAPTER
27

'M' r Saraf and Mr Ghassab have travelled from Swan Hill to speak with us about the next federal election and the candidate for Mallee. Please go ahead, gentlemen.'

Ten party delegates assembled along one side of the large wooden table in the boardroom of the private golf club. Photos of office holders and memorable golfing achievements cluttered the walls.

Saraf leaned into the table. 'Thank you, Mr President.' He smiled towards the end of the table and scanned the others, recognising many faces. 'Look, I won't waste any more of your time. The fact is, the Persian Water Company would like to encourage you to consider replacing Rose Dowerin and pre-selecting a new party candidate for Mallee. We believe Dowerin is working against the best interests of the region and in recent years has not represented the electorate as she should. We think it is time for a change.'

'It's a bit rich for the Water Company to be seeking to change the member when you are the reason we want change,' said a delegate Saraf did not recognise.

'We remain willing to negotiate new water deals, but Dowerin has not acted on any representation we have made. She denied our request to arrange a meeting with the prime minister. We wanted to meet with the water minister, also rejected. Unless we get rid of the federal member, we remain unsure how to fix the challenges we all have suffered during this drought.'

'You won't get any argument from me,' Jack Fingleton said.

'What's in it for us?' a delegate asked.

Both Saraf and Ghassab smirked at the honest question.

'Darius Hassidim is keen to make this happen. He said if you arrange it this year, we will reduce leases to fifty percent of the current rate.'

Ghassab nodded, tapping the table as he scanned the men. 'We must do it this year.'

Fingleton cleared his throat. 'It's not due until next year. I'm unsure we can meet your request.'

'We can assure you, we will support the new candidate with money and resources, so the party will not be at a loss.'

'I heard Jackson is considering running,' a delegate said.

Saraf studied him, then dropped his head and smiled. 'I can guarantee Premier Jackson will not be running for preselection.'

'When do you need to know?' Fingleton asked.

'We do not want to pressure you, but if you could let us know as soon as possible, then we can plan to commence the water discount.'

A delegate with a large sweaty Akubra pushed to the back of his head, leaned into the table, and pointed at Saraf. 'You boys have been screwing us for years and now you want a favour. Smells like bullshit to me. You want something, and you want us to do your dirty work.'

'We are just businessmen trying to negotiate a deal,' Saraf said.

'Let me tell you camel jockeys something.' The delegate stood with his hands on his wiry hips. 'You release more water then we might do what you want. Until then, you can get stuffed as far as I'm concerned.'

Saraf and Ghassab didn't answer as they turned towards Fingleton.

'Right Jonno, that's enough,' Fingleton said. 'You know we want Dowerin gone and all we need to do is find a suitable candidate. These boys want us to move this side of Christmas and in return, they'll reduce our rates or give us more water.'

'I want the water first before I shake hands with the devil.'

The room was silent.

Saraf raised his hands in a conciliatory gesture. 'Fair enough. I wouldn't want to do business with folks I thought were screwing me either.' He laughed. 'Let me talk to Darius and we shall liaise through Jack.' Saraf thumbed a gesture to Fingleton. 'If we can do what you want, then we will.'

'Seems reasonable to me. What say you, Jonno?' Fingleton said.

'Okay, that'd be good. But if you screw us over, you'll never come back.'

'Fair enough,' Saraf said again. Ghassab cracked a knuckle.

CHAPTER
28

Charlotte strode into Rose's office without knocking and didn't wait to get attention. 'I've just had a heads up from John Williams down in Horsham.'

Rose hadn't lifted her head as she checked a document. 'What does Jonno want?'

'He tells me a local party meeting took place this afternoon to discuss various issues.' Charlotte sat opposite Rose, continuing to sign documents. 'Local branch presidents, delegates to state council and pre-selectors.'

Rose glanced up, dropped her pen, leaning back in her chair. 'How many?'

'Ten.'

'What's the news?'

'The Arabs were there.'

She arched her brows, tilting her head. 'Who exactly?'

Charlotte read from her notes. 'Saraf and the henchman.'

Rose laughed. 'Good title for a book.'

'According to Jonno, you may have time to write it. They want to dis-endorse you.'

'The Arabs want to get rid of me?' Rose said, scratching an ear. 'Hmm, that's interesting.'

'They want the preselection this side of Christmas. In return, they will cut a deal on water.'

'Seriously?'

'It seems a few of the delegates got stuck in and told them to stick their heads up their arse.'

Rose slightly shook her head, drawing in her lips. 'That's crap, not with Ghassab there.'

'The Iranians said they would reduce the water rates to fifty percent if you were dis-endorsed, on condition it's done this year,' Charlotte said.

'Why would that worry them?'

'The leadership challenge?'

Rose nodded. 'So, they don't want me elected leader before preselection?'

'Which means we must pressure your colleagues to get Jock to stand down this year.'

'No one would be game to stand against me in the electorate.'

'Lever would have.'

'Yeah, but he's no longer with us,' Rose said, turning away.

'He wouldn't have had the numbers anyway,' Charlotte said. 'Which means they might have someone with the numbers.'

'Like who?'

'Fingleton.'

'No one from down that end of the electorate has ever been successful,' Rose said.

'That's because your family has a mortgage on the seat. If there was a chance of a new member, I would run a cattle person from down south,' Charlotte said.

'Would an Arab run?'

'Only in the election; they don't control the numbers in the party,' Charlotte said. 'But they have a significant voting bloc in the electorate.'

'Interesting,' Rose said, rubbing a finger across her brow.

Charlotte didn't respond, tapping the arm of her chair with her long nails. 'What about Jackson?'

'Why would the premier want to move to the federal parliament?' Rose said.

'To be deputy prime minister?'

'Interesting.' Rose glanced out at the rain slashing the glass. She then straightened. 'No, they won't have a candidate. The premier wouldn't give up his job before Christmas and we are months away from an election. Nah, Jackson won't be a candidate.'

'He's close to the Arabs,' Charlotte said, the end of her pen in her teeth.

'Most folks are.'

'You aren't.'

'Yeah, but we have history.'

'What history?'

'When I was first elected, they ran an independent candidate.'

'Who?'

'Darius Hassidim.'

Charlotte pouted and raised her brows. 'If the party pulls the pin on you, he may just run again.'

'Things are different now,' Rose said. 'He has too many skeletons in the closet.'

'You don't think he had anything to do with Lever, do you?'

'Why do you ask?' Rose said.

'Pete told me he had a finger missing.'

'Yeah, so?'

'I heard it's Hassidim's traditional calling card.'

'What? Like the mafia and raw fish?' Rose glanced off with no focus on anything. 'Maybe I should go see him.'

'And do what?'

'Water,' she said. 'If I can get water, then I'm saved.'

'But he's using it to get rid of you.'

'Maybe I can convince him otherwise.'

CHAPTER
29

Peter Dowerin pushed back in his chair, resting his feet on his desk, studying the circling flies above him. Now and then he snapped a hand and caught one, rolling his fingers into his palm to make sure it died. He grabbed about five and seemed better at following the flight lines before snapping.

A colleague, observing over by the window, seemed bemused by the hunter and the manner the swarm continued their numb rotation as another disappeared. 'Busy day, Pete?' Simon Dobbs asked.

Peter didn't shift his gaze from the flies. 'I'm thinking about this Lever case.'

'Looks as if you're on the right trail.'

'These flies are providing me with valuable ideas.'

'What?' Dobbs laughed. 'You think they'll lead you to the killer?'

'They are telling me that things move in a pattern.' Peter snatched at another but missed. 'They tell me to look for a pattern. If you have nothing else, go for a pattern.'

'You think we have a serial killer?' Dobbs said. 'Wouldn't you need more than one corpse to have a serial killer?'

'This is true, but it's the pattern I'm more interested in.'

'I don't understand.'

'Lever was an irrigator. A loud voice for the release of water. As an active Country Party member, he called for a motion admonishing the local member.'

'Your mother.'

'Correct,' Peter said. 'He agitated for change to the water licence rules.'

'What's the pattern? I'm confused.'

'He speaks out against the current water leases and is murdered.'

'So, your guess is the water leases may have been the motive?'

'Yeah, could be.'

'Not family?' Dobbs rubbed his chin.

'He owed money, and folks have said he owned the reputation of being a bit of a moron. I reckon his family is not involved.' Peter snatched another unsuccessful attempt, then gave up, straightening at his desk. 'I have eliminated most of them.'

'Alibis?'

'Most of them, but zero motive for any of them. I like motives. That's why I like water.'

'Do you think getting knocked off out-of-town means much?'

'You should just say it.' Peter squeezed a frown.

Dobbs remained hesitant and checked behind him. 'Don't the folks who own the water rights also own the farm where we found him?'

'One of their community does.'

'Any link?'

'Patterns, mate; it's all about patterns.'

'I still don't get you.' Dobbs shrugged.

A uniformed constable came through the door. 'Hey Pete, your brother is outside asking for you.'

'Did he say what he wanted?'

'Said it was important.'

Peter sighed as he followed the constable. When he pushed open the outside door, a blast of heat sapped his chilled body, and he gasped for air.

'Why didn't you wait inside? It's too hot out here.'

'I needed a fag,' Bobby said, drawing deep then sucking air into his lungs.

'I don't know how you do it.'

'Stop ragging me about smokin', will ya?'

'I'm not talking about cancer; I'm talking about this heat.'

Bobby blew out another lung full. 'You get used to it.'

Peter waved away a fly. 'I never have.'

'Listen, the reason I'm here is to ask if the Lever place has any legal hold on it.'

'What do you mean?'

'Can his missus sell it? Is there any police reason she can't?'

'What's the rush?'

'I have a buyer.'

Peter stepped off the curb and leaned against his brother's Jeep, but jumped away, wringing his hand. 'Who wants to buy it?'

'Not sure I want to disclose that at this stage.'

'It could be important, given what happened to the owner.'

Bobby dropped his butt, stamping it out before bending and picking it up. 'The Persian Pastoral Company, as it happens.'

'Why are you jumping hoops for them?'

'They're not criminals; they help the community and are keen buyers.'

'They have form, you know that.'

'Anything recorded?'

Peter didn't answer. He peered down the street, waving away flies. 'They aren't the type of folks you should be supporting.'

'They pay up and on time.'

'It's not about money though, is it?'

'Easy for you to say, given you have plenty.'

Peter frowned. 'Why do you say that?'

'Mum spoilt you and made investments for you.'

'In her name.'

'Not in mine though, eh?'

'You'll get it.'

'There is nothing suggesting I will.' Bobby lit another cigarette. 'I've seen her will, you know.'

'So what?'

'I'm not in it.'

'She did it after Dad died to cover the assets she inherited. You were not yet born. She didn't want her in-laws to get any money in case something happened.'

'No change since then?' Bobby kicked the gutter. 'Sometimes I wonder if I'm even part of this family. I mean, I don't even look like you.'

'Don't be like that. She may have forgotten about it.'

'Yeah, sure she did,' Bobby said, dragging on his fag. 'Anyway, I'm making money. I get this property done and a few others out at Ned's Corner; I'll cream it. Then I get moving out of this dump and leave it all to you and Primmy. Just the way she wants it.'

'That's not the way it is, Bobby. You know that.'

'Do I? Do I really?' Bobby sucked on his cigarette. 'Look, just let me know if there are any delays with the sale of Lever's.'

'Nothing my end. Not sure about the coroner.'

'Okay, thanks. I'll take that as an opportunity to make an offer.'

'Why are they buying?' Peter asked.

'I heard they have a deal going with the state government. They want to develop an environment reserve out at Ned's, and they are buying a shitload of property along the highway and even across the river.'

'What do they want to do?'

'That I can't tell you, brother; it's above my pay grade. I'm on a need-to-know basis with them. They tell me nothing.'

'You just blindly do whatever they want?'

'When they decide to buy,' Bobby said, checking around and peering at a passer-by, 'I'm told to get it done fast otherwise they send a rocket up my arse in the form of the gorilla, Ghassab.' Bobby sucked down another lungful and spat it out, pointing at his brother. 'Now that's who you should spend time on.'

'Why?'

'When they want something, they send him.'

'Yeah, we know, but we have nothing on him.'

'Anyway brother, thanks for the tip. Take care.' Bobby opened the door and slid into his vehicle, leaning forward to start it, away from the hot seat.

Peter watched him reverse out, waving goodbye before seeking relief in the office. When he returned to his desk, he chuckled as he spotted Dobbs trying to catch a fly.

'The Arabs want to buy the Lever place.'

'Motive?' Dobbs straightened to eyeball his partner.

'Maybe.'

CHAPTER
30

Darius Hassidim stepped into the marble foyer of Parliament House and felt a surge of pride thrill through him. The centre of Australian political power, and he had access to whatever he wanted. He clipped on his security pass, reserved for politicians and apparatchiks; the water minister had organised it. He turned to wait for his colleagues Taimur Saraf and Hosmand Shofet emerge from the security alcove. Maisil Ghassab seemed unwilling to meet security requests with any dignity, so Darius leaves him in Swan Hill.

His colleagues joined him, clipping on passes giving unfettered access other than members' only sections in the building. They were early for their meeting with Clare Spencer, so agreed on an espresso, moving off towards Aussies Café, the internal meeting place for gossip and lobbyists. Saraf queued for coffee.

'It's quite a paradox, isn't it?' Darius said as they peered out an enormous window to the green garden sprinkled by a recent rainstorm.

'The greenness?'

'Yes that, but also the rain,' Darius said, glancing at a woman clomping past in heels echoing on the wooden floor. 'We own the water in the mallee and here it is falling for nothing.'

'We don't want it to rain at home,' Shofet said.

'You are right there, my friend.' Darius smiled, scrutinising the tables. 'We must leverage our influence to get our deal with the state government.'

'Now it has passed council we should have little resistance,' Shofet said.

'Only from the abolitionists and churches,' Darius said.

'Don't forget the greenies,' Shofet said.

'We have heard little since Maisil had a word.'

'We can't keep using the old ways; you know that don't you?' Shofet shifted in his chair, crossing his legs.

'Once this deal is done, we will reform and remove ourselves from criminal behaviours.'

Saraf arrived with the coffees. 'What behaviours?'

'We will have to reform our business model,' Darius said.

'Transition is the word.' Saraf passed the coffee to his colleagues. 'We can't just drop everything. Our cash flow will take a whack. We need to continue eating our bread and butter.' He tapped his nose.

'The sooner the better, I would suggest,' Shofet responded. 'It is time for us to rid ourselves of this cloud of sin that shrouds us.'

Darius laughed. 'Cloud of sin? What an image.'

'If we get the project approved and then the drought breaks, we will be in a cash bind, so we need to keep money coming in,' Saraf said

'The sooner we are unpolluted from our past the better I will like it.'

'Darius, you haven't been worried for thirty years. Why now?' Shofet said, slurping his espresso.

Darius eyed his colleague. 'We have a good life, but I want to make sure we are clear of our past activities.'

Shofet smiled, then turned to Saraf. 'I agree. I'm a little too old to be spending time in prison.'

'Everything will be fine; just let me do it.' Saraf said, then took his coffee in one swift head-back gulp. 'Another?'

Darius checked his watch. 'We have to go.'

The three men, like any other lobbyists, wandered off to the ministerial wing, stopping by the black marble water feature in the centre of Members' Hall, staring up at the flagpole. They then continued past the newspaper library and into the ministry wing.

'Gentlemen, please come in and make yourself comfortable,'

Spencer said, waving to the lounge. Darius preferred a hard chair. 'Thanks for dropping by. How can I help?'

'Minister, we need reassurance Dowerin doesn't have the numbers for the leadership,' Darius began. 'We want to make sure there is no vote before Christmas. We also seek reassurance this ridiculous idea of a referendum on water rights will not see the light of day.'

Spencer grinned. 'I can assure you no matter when the ballot is taken, I will win.' Darius nodded. 'I can also assure you the vote will be next year.'

'How can you be so sure?' Darius asked.

'Garnsworthy advised the PM he will retire next year during the summer.'

'And the referendum?'

'There has been no proposal submitted to the cabinet or even raised in the party room.'

'Are you suggesting all this talk from Dowerin is just bluster?'

'She has zero authority, very little support,' Spencer said. 'I doubt she will remain in the cabinet once the leadership is resolved.'

'Excellent news, thank you.' Darius glanced at his colleagues and smiled. 'We remain grateful for the support you offer us.'

'You know what, though?' Spencer leaned forward. 'It will help if you trade harder with the water leases. It's making the local party jumpy and motivating them to get rid of her.'

Darius scratched his head. 'What do you have to assure us any new candidate replacing Dowerin will not be demanding water if we reduce supply?'

'Release more water when she is gone.'

'And if it rains?' Darius asked.

'This is why we are moving against her. I have spoken to several people who are keen to put their hand up for pre-selection. Unfortunately, our preferred candidate died, murdered it seems.'

The directors glanced amongst themselves. 'Tragic,' Shofet said.

Saraf dragged a fat roll of fifty-dollar notes from his satchel, tossing it to the minister. She caught the roll and examined it. She couldn't close her hand around it and tossed it to the other hand like a juggler.

'What's this?'

Darius smiled. 'A bonus. Buy yourself something sparkly. You deserve it.'

As the directors passed the prime minister's media department, Rose Dowerin strolled along the corridor from the opposite direction. She slowed when she recognised them approaching.

'I've been trying to arrange a meeting with you, Darius.'

'Why would we be meeting?' He tried to pass.

'I wanted to talk about your plans for Vegas.'

The directors stopped, grouping around her, obliging her to move closer to a wall.

'We have made no announcements.'

'You know how politics works, Darius. A bit like the way you do business, but a tad more legal.'

Darius glared at her as Shofet checked about them. 'Be careful with what you say, Minister,' Darius whispered.

'Oh, I can say whatever I feel like about you folks, can't I?' Rose smirked.

'Take care, Rose,' Shofet said.

She continued grinning, her gaze not leaving Darius. 'I love secrets, and our arrangement has worked well, has it not?'

'What do you want?'

'We agreed years ago I would look after the politics. I want you to back off on my preselection.'

'We don't need you anymore; you must know that?' Darius said.

'I know that, and you know that... but you don't need to get involved with local politics. Stay out of my business.'

'We could say the same to you,' Shofet said.

'Water is my business.'

'Not anymore,' Saraf said, crossing his arms.

Rose turned to him. 'Listen here, Taimur. You know I know where your money comes from, so don't start this rubbish about water.'

'What do you want?'

'If you want your Vegas project up and running with my support, then I want water bonuses paid.'

'Meaning?' Darius said.

'I want allocations increased. Specifically, I want carting prices to fall.'

'You ask too much,' Saraf interrupted.

Rose didn't respond. She stood straighter and stared at Darius and said, 'what do you want?'

Darius averted his eyes. 'You are a ballsy woman; I'll give you that.' He raised his eyes and smirked. 'We want the project approved and we want the referendum killed.'

'Huh.' Rose cocked her head. 'Interesting choice of words.'

'If you help secure us the project, we will back off from local politics. Simple.'

'You know, if you don't, I will push the referendum.'

'You can't if you're not here,' Darius sneered. 'Your choice.'

Rose mused on him for a few moments, then grinned before stepping away. 'Nice doing business with you, Darius. I'll let you know.'

The directors watched her stride off. 'Why does this project interest you?' Darius called after her.

Rose stopped and turned.

'That little wisp of a girl you almost killed the other day. She's a friend of my daughter's. She has gone back home if you are looking for her.'

'Where's home?'

'Where it rains.' Rose turned and stepped off, smiling to herself. 'That went well,' she whispered, skipping a step.

CHAPTER

31

Rose regretted agreeing to meet with a constituent who came to see her at eight that morning and taking up most of her morning. Her constituent worried about accessing the government's drought relief funding; it didn't apply to her. Her complaint seemed reasonable. She provided credit to grain farmers, which meant, like everything else, her cash dried up. She couldn't continue to offer supplies if she couldn't get credit. The government wasn't interested.

Rose listened, taking details, advising her she would do all she could to get her funding, before delegating the file to a staffer. She grabbed a coffee from McDonald's, then hit the road to Horsham, a three-hour cruise in her government Toyota. Party delegates invited her to a meeting to discuss the next election. Rose figured it would be about preselection.

She could think of better things to do than spend six and a half hours on the road to Horsham and back. There were ministry issues to resolve. She could have been in Melbourne for a conference of local government authorities, but she thought it wise to visit the party stalwarts. Every vote is important in a preselection battle, so when the folks with the votes rang, she responded. Just like Pavlov's dog, but with greater reward. She needed them. Nonetheless, she remained uncertain whether they needed her.

Her plan to win the leadership ballot, preventing any party challengers, seemed simple enough.

Feeling a little peckish when she hit Horsham, she figured she needed a salad sandwich rather than the addictive taste of a Big Mac. It's good politics to be seen supporting local businesses, so visited a truck stop on the outskirts of town. She stretched out of the car, refilled the tank, and headed to the cashier to pay and pick up a prepacked sandwich. There wasn't much choice and settled for an egg and lettuce roll.

'You're the pollie, aren't ya, luv?' asked a loud woman behind the counter.

Rose smiled. 'Yes, that's right. Rose Dowerin, pleased to meet you.'

'When are you people going to get the water policy right?'

'No water here?'

'Where are you living, luv?' The woman accepted Rose's proffered credit card. 'Everywhere needs water and you lot are doin' nothin'.'

'We launched a new drought package the other day.'

'Can't drink money, luv.'

'But it can buy water?'

'Are you stupid or something?' The woman handed back the card. 'Melbourne folks drink all the water they like and yet you pollies expect us to buy ours. Typical.'

'I'm working on getting more water to the mallee.'

'Yeah, well, you should be doin' more. Why should we have to pay big rates for water when there is water everywhere? The dudes who own it won't let us drink it.'

Rose smiled, retrieved her card, and stepped away.

'Mark my words, if you don't pull ya finger out, we will vote for someone who will.'

In almost twenty-five years of political service, that was the first time a random voter had told her to work harder. *Always a first time, I suppose.* Rose wondered if the woman's sentiment had momentum throughout Mallee, and maybe it might be wise for her to rethink her career choice.

She tracked through the streets towards the river parking under a tree. Rose propped open the car door, brushed away a fly and unwrapped the roll. The Wimmera River flowed past as she chewed off a healthy mouthful, the egg a little too mashed.

She had an hour to kill, so dropped her seat down and lay back to think about strategy. The slight breeze coming off the river felt calming, so she became droopy. Fifty minutes later, she woke when a fly searching for food tickled her nose. She reached for the water, straightened, and checked about. She examined the rear-vision mirror, straightening her hair and wiping a small cluster of mascara away.

Rose entered the boardroom, heading for a chair facing the window. It surprised her when she realised the men were party branch presidents from all over the electorate. She waited for others to take a seat, smiling, and nodding at familiar faces. The embarrassed returned smiles tightened her stomach and her shoulders stiffened. It seemed the hyenas had come to feed.

'Order. It being three thirty, I now open the meeting,' Rod Harrison said, the electorate council president from Swan Hill. 'There is only one order of business and that is the preselection of the Country Party candidate for Mallee at the next federal election. I call Rose Dowerin to address the meeting.'

She perused the grumpy faces, thinking she wouldn't bother standing. It seemed they had already made up their minds.

'Thank you, Mr President. I appreciate the opportunity to address the leaders of the party. Whilst you are not all here, I can see the most influential are, so thank you for your time.'

Rose scanned the faces, displaying her perfect political smile. 'I am somewhat surprised by the attendance, as I thought local delegates for the southern region were meeting and not all the leaders of Mallee. I feel a little bushwhacked and wonder what the real agenda might be here today.'

'Order,' Harrison interjected. 'There is no need to toss accusations that this is a surprise meeting. We sent information to your office this morning.'

Rose scoffed and nodded. 'Whilst I drove here,' she continued, 'no matter, we can discuss the reason for the meeting so long as we do it with respect.'

'You have enjoyed yourself for too long.' A sarcastic voice came from the end of the table. Rose didn't identify who had spoken, so ignored it.

'As I perceive it, there are two issues for which I should fight this preselection. First, the powerful voice you already have in the party and the parliament representing you. Has my voice achieved policies you wanted, and does my voice remain effective?' Rose paused for a moment, spotting a few nods. 'The second issue is drought and the water rights.'

'Those are reasonable points,' Harrison said, 'but we will make our decision based on modern politics and who we think is best placed to represent the diverse agriculture in the electorate.'

'Fair enough.' Rose nodded. 'Let me address the first point.' She paused for a moment. 'Since being selected by the party twenty-five years ago...'

'More like inherited,' a voice barked.

Rose leaned in to glance down four places to identify who spoke. She recognised Michael Baldwin. 'Hi Mike. You may remember it to be competitive at the preselection and the election. I should get points for winning both and being the first woman to represent you.'

'Too long ago, Rose, and you have done very little since,' Baldwin said.

'Order. Let the member continue uninterrupted,' Harrison said.

Rose dropped her head and smirked, then moistened her bottom lip. 'Mr President, it seems I am in a meeting where minds are closed and decisions are already made. It appears to be a kangaroo court. Some sort of star chamber where my work over many years is being discounted and ignored.' Rose fanned, then tapped her red nails on the table. 'Things like redevelopment of the Henty, the establishment and funding of three hospitals, capital works on sewage and water, schools, yadda, yadda, yadda. It seems if I list these achievements, it would be a waste of time and we should get to the decision you have already made.'

Harrison hesitated for a moment, scanning around the table. Most branch presidents bowing heads to avoid providing him support. 'Well, it seems you are perceptive.'

'Perceptive? That's a joke, given Jack has been drumming up support for a motion to move the preselection before Christmas.'

Fingleton leaned forward. 'I have not been doing that at all.'

Rose turned to him. 'Jack, we all know you are ambitious. We all know you haven't decided between state or federal politics.'

'That's outrageous. I have no such ambitions.'

Rose shook her head, gazing at the ceiling. 'I see.' She dropped her head back to address them. 'Look fellas, the leadership of the party is up for determination in January. I'm considering standing, as I reckon the person positioning herself is more interested in regional towns than outback farmers.'

The announcement surprised Harrison. 'You are standing for the leadership?'

Rose gawked at him. 'Yes. Do you have a problem?'

The president peeked at Fingleton, who shrugged. 'We have never had a leader from Mallee. It would be nice to support one,' Harrison said.

Rose beamed as she straightened. 'That being the case, Mr President, can I request you decide to proclaim the preselection meeting after January? If I'm not elected the leader, then bring on the challengers. But if I am elected leader, then perhaps we could dispense with any opposition.'

'An interesting development because you are right. We are planning on bringing forward the preselection. If we do, then we can secure greater water access.'

Rose raised her eyebrows. 'You have done a deal on the preselection and tied water access to it?'

'You haven't been doing anything,' Fingleton interrupted.

Rose turned to him. 'You want to do business with the Persian Water Company? You want to manipulate standard party procedure and attack the federal member?'

'I wouldn't put it like that,' said Harrison.

'You know that's a federal offence, don't you?' Rose said.

'What? Moving the preselection forward?' Fingleton asked.

'No, doing so under the direction of a private company in return for a gratuity.'

'That's not how we read it,' said Harrison.

Rose leaned back, gazing at the president, considering options. She stood, pushing her chair in. 'I don't care what you do.' She leaned her forearms on the chair back. 'You put up anyone to challenge me, and I assure you, I will win. I'm working on a deal with the Arabs to release water and reduce the cost of carting. I do that because they want something from me. So, we will soon have water in the mallee.'

'We will have it anyway,' said Fingleton.

'Maybe so, but here's the rub.' Rose leaned over her arms and lowered her voice. 'If I do have competition in my preselection and I'm denied the opportunity to stand for the leadership, then the party will rue the day they crossed a Dowerin.'

She straightened and left. As she was about to open the door, she turned for one last declaration.

'Watch your back, boys.'

The door crashed closed, and the men relaxed.

'Okay, an interesting speech,' said Harrison. 'She seems passionate.'

'Just bluster, and I've grown tired of her tantrums,' Fingleton said. 'Let's move a motion.'

Harrison tugged a sheet of paper from his folder. 'I move that the electoral division of Mallee for the Country Party schedule its preselection for the federal seat of Mallee for Saturday the thirtieth of November. All those in favour, say, aye.'

The unanimous vote recorded.

CHAPTER

32

The Victorian Parliament is one of those grand buildings built during the gold rush, a time of great wealth. It's a building radiating powerful architecture atop a hill, and although the grandeur of the chambers and the surrounds oozes influence, it offers little modernity.

The premier completing his second reading speech for legislation approving the development of nominated lands in the mallee appeared confident of the support of the chamber. 'This project meets all its regulatory requirements, but there remains the important passing of this legislation. I know there has been talk about the detail. I am sensitive to those comments, both within this place and within the media and community.'

Jackson paused and glanced up into the public gallery, where the directors positioned themselves to watch the debate below. He nodded and Hosmand Shofet flicked a wave.

'For this reason, I would ask the legislation to be transferred to a committee to be scrutinised by parliament. It is an important project and will provide jobs and growth to the region. Whilst the federal government is yet to sign off, I am assured by the minister that such approval will not be delayed. I ask that any parliamentary inquiry be completed urgently so the developers can begin initial site works and further land acquired. I move that the motion be agreed to.'

The premier resumed his chair, glancing up into the gallery and smiled. The directors did not return his joy. He watched them push past others as they left the gallery.

As with the federal parliament, the directors enjoyed similar access to the state parliament. They positioned themselves outside the chamber to bail up Jackson when he came out. Darius Hassidim paced as they waited.

When Jackson pushed his way through the door, arms full of files, Darius began with a raised voice. 'What the hell just happened?'

'Sssh,' replied Jackson. 'Let's go through to Strangers Corridor and we can get a quiet corner.'

Maisil Ghassab growled as Darius stretched his back, relieving tension.

'Okay, let's go. We'll follow you,' Shofet said.

Jackson handed his files to a staffer then led them along a wood panelled corridor until they passed through glass doors; he spoke to an attendant, who led them to the end corner table.

'I suspect you are wondering what is happening?' Jackson asked as he directed them to sit and smiled at the waiter, ordering a bottle of Mornington Peninsula chardonnay. 'I hope you will join me in a glass?'

'This is how stupid you are.'

'Darius, please,' Shofet touched his arm.

'We don't drink in public, you idiot.'

'Oh, I'm sorry. I thought we had shared a glass or two in Swan Hill.'

'Premier, it seems you never pay attention,' Darius said, then snarled. 'What is going on?'

Jackson explained to the waiter they only required one glass, and perhaps he should serve water for the others. 'Now.' The premier focused on the directors. 'The legislation is on the table. Your project is ready to get the nod.'

'Why delay it?' Shofet asked.

'I want Dowerin gone,' Jackson said. 'I heard she is causing trouble with the party.'

'She is meeting in Horsham as we speak,' Taimur Saraf advised, his fist bouncing on his lips.

'We said she would go,' Shofet said. 'We will organise for you to transfer to the federal parliament.'

'I'll believe that when I see her gone.'

'This has nothing to do with our agreement,' Darius said, with a dismissing wave.

'Should I remind you of our agreement?' Ghassab grunted.

Jackson glanced at him and then at the others. 'Our agreement is simple enough. You get your gaming licence and I become deputy prime minister. One will come when the other is done.'

'You are being foolish,' Darius said.

'Your heavy handedness may work in the mallee, but in Melbourne your network doesn't extend to the parliament.'

'You are a simple, silly boy,' Shofet whispered. 'You don't think we have networks in Melbourne?'

'You have had the better of me on two occasions.' Jackson clenched his hands. 'I agreed, and still do, to deliver what you want, but you must cut me some slack and do what I suggest.'

'And what are you suggesting?' Shofet asked.

'I want more water released.'

'Everyone with their friggin' water demands,' Darius said, combing fingers through his hair. 'Now you want us to release water.'

'Call it a goodwill gift.'

Darius smiled as Shofet eyed him. He then turned to the premier and asked, 'If I understand you correctly, you will hasten the progress of our legislation if we release water?'

'There are several pressures on the state government to negotiate a better deal with you on the release of water.'

'Otherwise?' Saraf queried.

'Otherwise, the Feds may act with reform and take control. If that happens, the state government would not be happy. We are very pleased with our arrangement. We don't want it changed.'

'You think we should give up our control of the water?' Darius asked.

'No, just release more water into the irrigation system.'

'And then we get the approval for the gaming licence?' Darius said.

'No, you'll get that once I'm elected to the federal parliament and become deputy prime minister.'

Shofet smiled. 'A goodwill measure?'

Jackson clicked his finger and pointed. 'Exactly.'

'Interesting,' Darius said from behind steepled fingers. 'You risk damage to yourself to encourage us to do something we don't want to do.'

'I hear you have been offering deals all over the place.'

'Maybe we have,' Shofet said.

'I want ownership of any announcement. I want to receive the accolade for the water release; no one else,' Jackson said.

Shofet checked around his colleagues, gazing at Darius then flicking a nod showing they should go.

'It's nice to realise you have iron balls, Phillip,' Shofet said. 'I'm just not sure you want to test them against us.'

'We are in this deal for the new city,' Jackson said. 'I just want things to fall my way.'

'Realistic enough.' Darius stood. 'We will discuss it and let you know. We now have a plane to catch.'

The directors left without shaking hands and Jackson watched them go, breathing out a heavy sigh.

The directors lounged in a town car heading for the airport when they took the call from Rod Harrison.

'Rod, nice to hear from you. How did it go?' Shofet switched to speaker.

'We are set for the thirtieth of November,' Harrison said. 'When will you make water announcements?'

'Change of plan. We just left the premier, and he has a different idea.'

'What does he want?'

'He wants to hold any water release for a while.'

'Why?'

'Politics, apparently. What can you do?'

'He must know something, otherwise he wouldn't act like that.' Harrison seemed confused.

'Do you have a candidate?'

'Jack Fingleton is the man we want.'

'Fair enough. When will you announce the date?'

'This week.'

'Good work, Rod. You have our support.'

Darius nodded to Shofet to end the call. Shofet dropped his phone back into his jacket. 'Preselection is within two months; that is good news.'

'Excellent.' Darius smiled.

They sat for a moment, and it wasn't until they were on the Tulla-marine Freeway that Saraf asked, 'What do we do with the water?'

Darius said, 'I've been thinking about that very thing. Let's raise the price.'

CHAPTER
33

J ack Fingleton announced his candidacy for preselection a week
after the party fixed a date to select the candidate. For weeks he travelled throughout the electorate, attending party meetings,
answering questions about why he was running. His standard response
focused on the way the Dowerin family ruled the electorate, advising he
had nothing against Rose Dowerin. She had just been in the federal
parliament long enough.

The issue that riled most branch members continued to be water.
They couldn't understand why the federal government could do
nothing to provide a fair allocation of drinkable water.

For Fingleton, water wasn't an issue. His cattle property had plenty
in its dams. He empathised with what farmers told him, and his sympa-
thetic approach built support and commitment for votes.

'We want a fair water management regime, and it won't happen
with Rose Dowerin.' This statement always brought loud applause,
convincing Fingleton he could win.

The meeting at Nhill reinforced his view with delegates pledging
support by changing their vote for the first time. Perhaps he shouldn't
have accepted the extra glass of Shiraz before he left, but a delegate keen
to talk water policy offered it.

It was almost a ninety-minute drive to his property, and he looked forward to the weekend and resting at the homestead. He chalked up significant kilometres over the past week, meeting with party officials, media operatives and the money folks. He avoided the Arabs, blaming them for the water access disaster receiving much applause every time he said it.

The Western Highway carried little traffic to Horsham, convincing him to keep heading for home rather than stop at a roadhouse for coffee. There was nothing coming his way and only a distant dazzle of head-lights in his rear-vision mirror. A sudden yawn pushed him alert. He straightened, increasing the volume of his music to clear his head. As he settled back, an eyelid drooped; he forced it open, cracking another yawn.

As he approached Stawell, it was well after midnight. He checked his speed, then noticed the glare of a vehicle coming up behind. He checked the rear-vision mirror when the cabin brightened. The vehicle behind did not dim its lights, so he adjusted his mirror. He tapped his brake pedal a few times to send a message to it to back off. Nothing happened other than the vehicle moving closer, almost into his slipstream.

When Fingleton checked the mirror again, the vehicle dropped back, then zoomed forward, crashing into the bumper.

'What the hell?' Fingleton braked and slowed.

The vehicle dropped back and surged again, this time crashing harder into the back of his vehicle; Fingleton gripped the steering wheel a little harder to hold it steady.

He wanted to call the police at Stawell, just a few kilometres away, but his phone lay out of reach, so hatched a plan. He would take the Codds Flat turnoff without indicating, and then if the vehicle followed, he would drive to the bitumen at the other junction before heading back to town. *Maybe they were highway thugs.* He heard the stories but considered them to be myths. He would now have this experience to talk about at the pub.

He decelerated his vehicle, searching for the turnoff. The other vehicle had fallen back fifty metres. When he found it, he swung hard right. The tyres struggled to grip as he squealed off the highway and onto the unsealed road. Dust flew up, and he didn't know if the bandits followed. He planted his foot, searching in the mirror for lights. He almost lost traction at Yellow Box Road. He couldn't see any lights but pushed the vehicle harder.

As he sped past the turnoff, he didn't see the kangaroo. It stood dazzled by the lights in the middle of the gravel road just after the bend. It had no chance of surviving as Fingleton braked too late. The nose dipped, and the animal crashed over the bonnet, smashing through the windscreen, blurring his vision. He tried to correct the swerving vehicle, but physics kicked in, taking the gravitational pull of the roof, flipping the vehicle, tumbling it as it bounced up and down. Airbags exploded and Fingleton braced his hands against anything he could feel as glass smashed across him. He felt a sharp pain in his chest. He wanted the madness to stop, holding on as best he could. The seatbelt braced him into the seat as the car came to rest on its roof.

When he opened his eyes, he could feel pressure in his head as he acclimatised to realise he was hanging upside down. Below him lay the kangaroo, its head almost severed. He wriggled his fingers but could only feel movement in his right hand. He couldn't feel his left arm nor see it. He wriggled toes and could feel both feet. Blood dripped from his nose, and he spat out a stream of blood.

There were farms nearby. He knew them. The Hendersons were off Bevan Road, and Ray Bremner lived on Yellow Box. He trusted someone should be with him soon, confident they heard the commotion.

A vehicle appeared with its lights illuminating what the smash had left of the cabin. Above the hissing of the engine, he heard hurrying footsteps on the gravel. There was someone beside him. He couldn't see who it was. A surgical gloved hand reached and fumbled with his face. He couldn't move his head as the hand pushed his jaw down, closing his mouth. He then felt the glove stretch fingers spider like across his face, pinching his nose, the heel of the hand jamming into his chin.

Fingleton tried to resist but couldn't move. He thought about that last Shiraz as his eyes became droopy, and he embraced the sanctity of sleep that was now upon him.

When Phil Henderson found the vehicle in the morning, he reported the incident to local police. He waited for them by the front end, having a fag, passing a glimpse to his mate Jack now and then.

CHAPTER
34

Peter Dowerin stepped out of his office almost every day at eleven o'clock to have a café latte at the Stringybark café across the road. He would take his time and muse through the local newspaper, and if early editions of the Melbourne newspapers were available, he would scan them, sometimes attempting the crossword. The café attracted retired folks and mothers with babies, catching up on gossip before the lunch crowd hit.

He enjoyed sitting in the window at a bench away from the chatter where he could spread out and notice any activity outside his office. He also enjoyed coming to chat with the barista, Bianca. He wanted to ask her to come join him at a local bar for a wine, but didn't want to make her feel uncomfortable if she said no. He valued the coffee and the opportunity of the chat more than a date with her.

Air-conditioning cooled the café, yet courageous customers still took a seat in the shade outside. Most days were way too hot for Peter to even consider that as a sensible choice. The tourists enjoyed the sun and the heat, not the locals who just endured it.

The newspapers splashed federal politics over their front page, with feature stories about the water crisis and the lack of government action. He read an interesting article highlighting his mother's idea to support a referendum allowing federal regulatory control of water. He smiled as he studied the photograph of his mother with a stern expression, talking to journalists. When he was a kid, he hid whenever he saw the look. His mother might appear to have been a soft touch as a politician, but more like a dog with a bone when crossed.

He flicked over the pages and paused to read an article about a cattle breeder in Stawell killed in an accident the previous morning. It seemed to surprise the local police, and they put it down to the alcohol detected in the breeder's system. He tugged out his telephone and captured an image of the article, highlighting the name of Jack Fingleton.

'Have you finished with this, Mr Peter?' asked the familiar French voice.

Peter glanced up to see Bianca standing close, reaching for his glass. 'Yes, I have, thank you.'

'What have you planned for the rest of the day? Catching criminals?'

'Hopefully.' Peter smiled, then paused for a moment. 'Actually, I hope I have no contact with the dregs of society.'

'Not all lawbreakers are the dregs of society.'

'Are you a lawbreaker?'

Bianca smiled and stepped away. 'Maybe. Perhaps you should arrest me sometime?'

Peter nodded, wondering if she teased him or sent a message. He checked over his shoulder, watching her sashay through the tables, picking up another empty glass.

He placed his phone on the bench and texted his mother.

HAVE YOU HEARD ABOUT FINGLETON?

He checked out the window and observed an older couple at an outside table struggling with the heat, drinking water, and fanning themselves with the menu.

A text pinged.

**HE IS RUNNING AS A CANDIDATE AGAINST ME.
YOU DIDN'T KNOW?**

He's dead.

The phone buzzed with a call.

'What happened?' Rose said.

'I'm just reading a news report. They found him early yesterday in a traffic incident near Stawell. I'm surprised you don't know.'

'What happened?'

'It seems he had a few drinks and was travelling home from a political meeting. It's in today's Hancock paper on page eight.'

'Was he drunk?'

'It doesn't say, but there is an implication he may have been,' Peter said.

'That's dreadful news.'

'Good for you though, right?'

'That's a horrible thing to say.'

'Yeah righto, but nonetheless, it is good for you.' Rose didn't respond, but he could hear breathing. 'How come you didn't know?'

'No one told me.'

'That's a little odd. I would have thought you would be the first to know.'

'The party works in mysterious ways, darling, but you're right. It is good for me.'

'And there you go.' Peter said. 'Back to politics within moments.'

Rose ignored the comment, not taking the bait. 'If you learn anything, can you let me know?'

'I'm not investigating; the Stawell boys will look at it.'

'About the funeral, I mean.'

'Sure, not a worry.'

'The bells are ringing, darling. We have a division; must run.'

'Talk soon.'

Peter slipped the phone into his pocket as he stood to leave; he checked back to Bianca, who waved and smiled. As he opened the door, the older couple made their way into the cool café.

'Wise move, I suspect,' Peter said, standing aside, holding the door.

The heat hit him as he dashed across the street; a batch of flies began terrorising him, and he waved them away as best he could.

When he reached the detective's room, he called to his colleague, 'Hey Dobbsie, do you know about a TA in Stawell the other night?'

Dobbs glanced up and shook his head.

'It seems another Country Party delegate has called it a day.'

'How does a traffic accident concern us?'

'Patterns, my friend, patterns.'

Dobbs shook his head and went back to studying his file.

Peter sat at his cluttered desk and pulled a file from the stack before him. He reread the notes about the Lever case before punching the numbers of the Stawell police station into the desk phone. He snatched at a fly as he waited for the connection to the investigating officer.

'Where was Fingleton that night?'

'He was in Nhill talking with farmers and local party people.'

'Did he say anything about water?'

'Let me check my notes.' The senior constable flicked over his pages. 'He implied the recent price rise to be the fault of Mrs Dowerin, as she had gone too hard against the Water Company. He said he would get the Company to reduce their price if he was the local candidate.'

'Did he say anything about the company?'

'They reported his statements to have been provocative. He suggested they weren't locals. He said they had only grown their water business on government subsidises organised by Mrs Dowerin.'

'That is provocative,' Peter said. 'Was there anyone from the water company at the meeting?'

'Not that I am aware.'

'Are you doing an autopsy?'

'We will need to send the body to Melbourne for that to happen.'

'Can I suggest you do so?'

'Who's going to pay?'

'Since when is investigating a death considered a cost benefit equation?'

'I'll need approval.'

'That will be fine by me,' Peter said. 'Can you let me know as soon as they ship the body out?'

'Will do. Should I be concerned?'

'No, I wouldn't have thought so.'
'Then why are you?'
'Patterns, my friend, I'm looking for patterns.'

CHAPTER
35

Rose walked through the deputy prime minister's reception, then along the corridor leading to his office. She noticed his chief of staff glance up from her work and nod as if to tell her to go straight in. Jock Garnsworthy held up his hand to slow Rose, whilst continuing his conversation with an adviser, then confirmed with the staffer what he should do. He waved her to sit as the adviser left.

'Hi, Rose, nice to see you.'

'Yeah, you too, Jock,' Rose said, her jaw tightening. 'When are you announcing your departure?'

'Wow, straight into it.' Garnsworthy laughed. 'You want to chat about your electorate first?'

'It's dry, and it hasn't rained for a long time.'

'Yeah, that's what I heard.'

'Clare been briefing you from the wet north coast, has she?'

'It's a big country.'

'Not sure she has been to Mallee during her time as water minister.'

Garnsworthy shook his head. 'What can I help you with?'

Rose shook her head and blew out her cheeks as she exhaled. 'Well, for starters we can take control of water off the states, and the Feds can regulate water to stop the profiteering that is going on, especially with the water company in my electorate.'

'We can't do that,' Garnsworthy scoffed.

'We can if we have a referendum.' Rose paused for a moment, combing fingers through her hair. 'If the Feds take control, water would be cheaper.'

'That'll never happen; Brown will never agree.'

'He will if the deputy prime minister insists on it.'

Garnsworthy laughed a scoff. 'I will not do that. I'm almost out of here.'

'The next deputy PM will.'

'Not sure Clare will agree, either.'

'Who says Clare Spencer will be the next leader?'

'Who else is there?'

Rose paused, gazing at Garnsworthy, her eyes gleaming. She dropped her head, her tongue playing with the corner of her mouth, then peered up at him. 'That would be me.'

'You? You've got to be kidding?'

'What's wrong with me?'

'Profile, for starters.' Garnsworthy held up a thumb. 'Your portfolio is in the outer ministry.'

'That's been my choice.'

'Brown will never accept you over Clare.'

'That's because he's banging her.'

Garnsworthy fell back in his chair. 'You can't say things like that.'

'It's true; ask him.'

'She has the numbers.'

'No, she doesn't,' Rose said, pouting. 'I do.'

Garnsworthy's eyes darted everywhere as he tried to think of something to say. 'Jack Fingleton is about to knock you off as the party's candidate.'

'No, he's not.'

'He is working the numbers hard.' Garnsworthy said, shifting in his chair and clearing his throat.

Rose paused, studying him. 'He's dead.'

Garnsworthy shook his head in disbelief. 'He's what?'

'He's dead. Kaput. No more.'

'When? How?' he said, his tongue working his lips.

'Car accident. Too much to drink.'

'Anyone else?'

'No, just a lonely road on the way home after telling lies at a meeting in Nhill.'

'What lies?'

'That I am the reason the water price has gone up.'

'This is a tragedy.' Garnsworthy's tone changed, and he dropped his head to his hand, his elbow on the arm of his chair. 'I was only speaking with him the other day.'

'So, you were pushing for him to knock me off?'

'Brown wants you gone.'

'That will not happen. I'm standing for the leadership,' Rose smirked. 'Based on my numbers, I will be elected, so when are you announcing?'

'What's the rush?'

'I want to set out my plans for the referendum before my preselection,' she said, crossing her legs.

'I can't believe this.'

'That's politics, Jock,' Rose said, stroking under her eye. 'One minute a rooster, the next a feather duster.'

CHAPTER
36

'You know this is not the first time something like this has happened, don't you?' Clarrie McCarthy said into his beer before taking a slug.

Peter Dowerin smirked as he watched the retired police sergeant enjoy the cool drink, prompting him to take his own generous sip.

'What are you talking about, old man?'

'Political mystery.' McCarthy turned his head and arched a brow. 'It happened when your ole man fell off the perch.'

Peter shook his head. 'More like taking too much risk rather than falling off the perch, I would have thought.'

'You oughta check the file. If I recall, there was a political battle over who would take over. No one wanted your mum.'

'How did she end up winning?'

McCarthy took a sip. 'No actual competition.'

'She was a Dowerin, after all.'

'Yeah, but there is no other quality candidate who put their hand up.'

'Why's that?'

'Your grandfather remained active to get her over the line. Another potential candidate had an accident with a tractor.'

Peter eyed his confidant and occasional drinking buddy. 'What happened?'

'Crushed against the retaining wall out back of his farm. He jumped out to clear a chain he used to rip out trees. He was lying it against the wall when the tractor slipped into reverse and pinned him against the wall. The heavy-duty tyre just ripped into him.'

'Crumbs, that's gruesome,' Peter said.

'Why you would go behind a tractor still idling is beyond me.'

'Did you have a look at it?'

'We did, but we couldn't see anything that would call for further investigation. We reported it as a tragic farm accident. Anyway, your mum was free and clear to run. The other candidates had no chance.'

Peter finished his schooner. 'You want another?'

'I better not, gotta drive home,' McCarthy smiled. 'But if you're payin', why not?'

'Two thanks, luv.' Peter asked the server. 'Why would you mention that case now?'

'Coincidence.'

'With what?'

'Jimmy Lever getting knocked.'

'You think because Lever had his hand up to be a candidate for Mallee, there is a connection?'

'What else have you got?'

'Nothing much.' Peter passed over twenty dollars. 'He owed a few bucks around town.'

'How much did he owe the Arabs?'

'A bit. I'm waiting for his bank to give me details.'

'I'm not surprised. Most folks are into them for substantial amounts.'

'I'm not.'

'Your mum isn't, but what about your brother?'

'He's got nothing to spend it on,' Peter said, taking a slug of beer, then another. 'Anyway, why would you knock a debtor?'

'Stranger things have happened,' McCarthy said, sipping his beer.

'Speaking of strange things, Lever had a finger missing. Ripped off from the joint.'

McCarthy put his glass on the bar and turned around, leaning against it, wiping his chin. 'Left hand?'

'As it happens, yes.' Peter said, checking over his shoulder leaning on his forearm. 'What's that about?'

'Fingers go missing all the time on farms.'

'Yeah, but something cut or ripped this from the knuckle.'

McCarthy turned his head with a frown, gnawing at his bottom lip. 'I've seen that sort of thing before.'

'Blokes losing fingers?'

'Only dead ones.'

'How many?'

'Over the last twenty years in the job, maybe five.'

Peter stood straighter. 'Five?'

'Yeah, maybe more.'

'Why don't I know about this?'

'I'm not sure there have been any since you came here. Jimmy must be the first for a long time.'

'What? A killer just takes the finger as a trophy?'

'Serial killers do; they always take something.'

Peter turned back to the bar, leaning on his forearms, staring along the bar at the faces of men doing the same. 'Did you not connect them?'

'We tried, but the incidents were all terrible accidents. We couldn't get enough evidence to signify murder with most of them. The only link is the finger. The pinkie, right?'

'Yeah,' Peter said. 'Did the homicide boys look?'

'They did but came up with nothing.'

Peter turned and considered McCarthy. 'They did nothing?'

'The local CIB blokes were useless and the boys from Melbourne were no better. They seemed to have other things on their plate.'

'Do the files remain open?' Peter asked.

'I guess. You'll have to check, but I reckon they transferred them into the too hard cabinet and locked them away.'

Peter passed McCarthy a quizzical look. 'You think there may have been influence to put them to bed?'

'The only thing I will say is what I know,' McCarthy checked over his shoulder to see if anyone listened, 'politics got involved.'

'What type of politics?'

'Powerful friends.'

'Are you suggesting the distribution of coin?'

'Noohoohoohoo, wash your mouth out. I'm not saying that.' McCarthy took a sip of beer. 'But I wouldn't be surprised.'

'Local finances?'

'Let's put it this way,' McCarthy smirked with his glass poised at his lips. 'A couple of jockeys may have been involved.' He winked.

'Any proof?'

'None.'

'Speculation, then?'

'Have a look at the files and ask a few questions, then watch the stuff hit your fan.'

'How many had their hand out?'

'It's a hard life being a copper, you know that. Christmas gifts to buy and partners to keep happy.'

'Did you?' Peter asked.

'Nah, someone had to sleep straight.'

'So, you're telling me I should look at the Arabs?'

'Mate, let me be really clear for you.' McCarthy brought his face closer, their noses almost touching. 'I'm not telling you that and if you mention my name in dispatches on anything, I will deny it.'

'So why tell me this crap?'

'I'm just saying,' McCarthy checked over his shoulder again. 'What you are looking at seems like a remake, that's all.'

'Geezus Clarrie, you make it hard for me.'

'It's the job, young man. If you want to solve something, then study history, and the clues come falling out for you.'

'Yeah, righto.' Peter sculled his remaining beer. 'Your round.'

CHAPTER
37

Street parking remains a premium on a Friday during the summer twilight around the Commonwealth reserve. Eight netball courts were full of screaming competitors and supportive parents with other groups waiting for their scheduled start time filling most parking bays. The nearby cricket ground added more pressure, as young players plied their skills until the umpires considered it too dark.

Darius Hassidim had little choice. His wife insisted he spend Friday evenings with his children, watching them compete, but he preferred to be elsewhere. He realised that for peace at home he must do as directed.

'This game is such a waste of time,' Darius observed from his collapsible chair under a tree at the northern end of the cricket ground. 'I have never understood why they invest so much effort into so little result.'

Hosmand Shofet, relaxed next to him, sipped an iced tea from a water bottle, smiled, eyeing him. 'It's the national game, and your boys do well.'

'How are they doing well? Darius said, his hand raising, pointing to the pitch. 'One can't throw and the other backs away when they bowl the ball to him.'

'Yes, but they score runs.'

'You are crazy, my friend.' Darius said with a laugh. 'Izzy has not made over ten runs for the last two seasons, and Zana has only made one fifty this year. Allah only knows why I bother.'

'You come for peace.'

'What?' Darius said, slapping his knee. 'You call this peace not getting a car park? You call peace that intolerable noise from the courts?' He thumbed towards the netball. 'You say this is peaceful?'

Shofet tapped his nose. 'You know what peace I'm talking about.'

Darius gazed out onto the field to see a ball whipped away by a boy for four runs to end the over. 'You know me too well.'

'I know Razia too well.'

'Wish I did. She breaks my balls almost every day.'

'Happy wife, happy life.'

'Persians are not like that, Hosie; you know that. The man is supposed to be the head of the family.'

'This is why I'm not married.'

'You are a foolish man.'

'My balls are just fine, thank you very much.'

Darius chortled, then fell silent as he watched his son knock a ball to a fieldsman. He then said. 'It's about legacy, my friend.'

'You may be right,' Shofet said. 'I don't need the hassle. When I'm dead, I won't know anything about my legacy.'

Izzy slashed at a ball, and it flew over a fielder for a boundary, prompting Darius to stand and clap, shouting words of encouragement.

'Four runs, which means he'll be out soon,' he said, resuming his chair.

'You are too harsh,' Shofet said, brushing away a fly.

'If you ask me, I don't think I'm harsh enough. What is wrong with kids these days? No adventure, no spirit, no passion to discover.'

'Technology.'

'You mean the internet?'

'More the socials,' Shofet said.

'Yeah, maybe you're right. Parisha is never off her phone and the boys are always playing games rather than going outside.'

'Can you blame them? It's too hot,' Shofet chuckled.

'We had the sand, remember? How harsh was that?'

'Very hard, and yet we moved to this forsaken desert.'

'This is nothing like home,' Darius said. 'At least there is an agricultural industry here.'

'That relies on water.'

'That's why we invested.' Darius gazed out across the ground when yelping erupted. He watched his son leave the pitch, head bowed, three stumps disarrayed. 'Ah, another failure, poor kid.'

Shofet glanced over at his friend. 'What do you want to do about this water issue?'

'Hang on.' Darius watched his son. As Izzy entered the dressing room, he turned to his father, who waved until the boy disappeared. 'I think we should keep raising the price, as we said we would.'

'The natives are getting restless.'

'Stuff them; they aren't doing much for us.'

'It's the drought. It has everyone jumpy,' Shofet said, checking about the immediate area.

'There's always drought up here.'

'That's true, but this is the worst since we bought the rights, and they are getting organised against us. Dowerin is very noisy.'

'I thought we resolved that problem.'

Shofet shook his head. 'We did, but a car accident killed their boy.'

'Serves him right.'

'Why would you say that?' Shofet said, shifting in the chair peeking over his shoulder. 'He had the best chance of getting rid of Dowerin.'

Darius glanced at his friend. 'He was mouthing off about our arrangements. I never liked him.'

'He just leveraged public feeling against Dowerin.'

'He didn't have to say provocative things against us.'

Shofet squinted at Darius, shaking his head. 'Did you tell Maisil to have a word?'

Hassidim pursed his lips and winced. 'Yes, I did.'

'Did he involve himself in the accident?'

'Maybe.' Darius turned away. 'It's best you don't know.'

'Did he cause the accident?'

'Hmm, did he cause the accident?' Darius stared back at the game. 'I suppose my answer would be a qualified no.'

Shofet turned away. 'We will never get this deal done if we keep doing things like that.'

'Hosie, we didn't have a direct hand in it, believe me.'

'Given the outcome, what do we do?'

'He would never be the last candidate, you know that. Jackson is our boy. When he comes through with our approvals, we shift him to the federal seat and the leadership,' Darius said.

'For that to happen, someone has to win the preselection against Dowerin.'

'We can't afford her to win the preselection.'

'You reckon she possesses that much grunt?' Shofet asked.

'She has history, you know that. I reckon she would get the numbers she needs. She's not as lazy as people think she is.'

'Even though we own the prime minister and the minister?'

'This is the reason we need Jackson to go federal. I don't trust those bastards.'

'Are you overstating her influence?' Shofet said.

'I know her very well.' Darius winced. 'I reckon I know what makes her tick.' He gnawed at his lips. 'If she's up against it. I reckon we could be in for a fight.'

Shofet paused for a moment, gazing out to the cricket field, then said, 'Why don't we leverage the water to get our development approved?'

Darius didn't respond. He didn't even look at him as he watched the play on the field. 'I'd rather have both. If forced to choose, we would go for the development.'

'It would hurt cash flow, but in the long run it would benefit us.'

'Shot!' Darius yelled as his other son cracked a ball to the boundary.

Once he settled after letting Zana know how brilliant he was, Darius turned to his friend. 'Our plan for this shit country has always been this development. It will set us up, and once partners invested, we reap the returns, but we need Jackson's approval. If we can get that and not have Dowerin wage war against us, then so be it.'

'I still reckon you are overstating Dowerin.'

'She will do whatever it takes to get what she wants, trust me.' Darius clapped his son. 'He's looking good.'

Shofet didn't respond, gnawing on his thumb thinking through a strategy. 'We need a candidate to stand against her.'

'What we don't need is another loud-mouthed farmer, who won't do as he's told,' Darius said. 'If we can get a dud that would help our plan with Jackson. We get the dud to win and then swing in Jackson before the election.'

Shofet bounced his empty water bottle against his resting foot. 'The seat has been in the Dowerin family for decades. So why don't we get one of them to stand against her?'

'It would have to be one of her kids, and that's not likely.'

'Bobby wouldn't do it?' Shofet asked with brows raised.

Darius didn't respond as he watched his son push the ball behind a fielder for a run. 'Now that I think about it, he might.'

'He is keen for cash,' Shofet said. 'Gambling is almost an addiction.'

'I've heard he's not that close to his mother.'

'Would he go for it?' Shofet asked.

'If there's enough money in it, I'm sure he would,' Darius said. 'We only need him as the official Country Party candidate until the election.'

'Worst-case scenario, he gets elected.'

Darius smiled. 'You know something, Hosie? That might just work. He's stupid enough to do what we want, and as you say, he needs the money. I'll check with Taimur. I think he has run up considerable debt with us.'

'Maisil can talk with him.'

'Maisil wants to kill him,' Darius scoffed.

'But the bottom line is that he could be our candidate.'

'Let's get him in and put it to him.' Darius stood, walking to the boundary to retrieve the ball. 'Shot, son.' He tossed it back to the fielder trotting in.

CHAPTER
38

Bobby Dowerin packed up a home-open street sign and as he shoved it into his Jeep, he took a call from Hosmand Shofet. He checked around, bouncing on his toes as he acknowledged the call.

'Bobby, how are you?' Shofet almost whispered, sending a shiver through him. 'We want to celebrate your recent successes and would like you to visit us this afternoon for a cup of tea and cake.'

Bobby clawed his fingers through his hair. 'What's it about, Mr Shofet?'

'Nothing other than a discussion about the future,' Shofet said, responding to the anxious voice. 'This is a polite invitation, Bobby, and we do not have to talk business. We just want to put an idea to you.'

'Concerning what?'

'Let's not discuss these things now.' Shofet closed the conversation. 'Can you come see us this afternoon at Savino's?'

'I have an opening of a house at two.'

'This is fine, Bobby,' Shofet reassured him. 'Come after, we will still be there and look forward to seeing you.'

'Okay, I'll see you then.'

The directors finished a tasty lunch in their usual private room at Savino's, now waiting for Bobby. The maître d' remained preparing tea and coffee for the special guests.

'Why do we need to do this?' Maisil Ghassab asked. 'We shouldn't have to do this. He's a useless moron.'

Darius Hassidim placed his linen napkin on the table, pushed his chair out, and crossed his legs. 'Maisil, we need to set the preselection up for us and we figure this to be a sensible strategy.'

Ghassab made a noise like a growl. Taimur Saraf ignored him, wiping his mouth, head bowed. Hosmand Shofet mused on his brutish colleague, shaking his head.

'The past has long gone, my friend. We cannot be doing what we used to do,' Darius said.

'We can just take her out,' Ghassab said, stretching his neck.

'Rubbish,' Shofet said.

Ghassab flicked his head towards Shofet. 'You are too soft. We need to express our strength all the time and keep our enemies in line. We did it with Jackson. Why not Dowerin?'

'Times change,' Shofet responded.

Ghassab slapped the table, jumping the remaining cutlery and crockery. 'We are getting soft, and we will regret it.'

'Hush now, Maisil,' Darius said, with a calming hand. 'We will not be reducing our influence, but this federal politician is tricky. We must do it without raising suspicion.'

'She owes us,' Ghassab insisted. 'Big time.'

Darius raised his eyebrows and nodded. 'Perhaps she does.'

'She has done her job, now let's just get rid of her politically,' Shofet said.

'I agree,' Darius said.

'It will become messy, trust me.' Ghassab had the last word as Bobby Dowerin sauntered towards the table.

Shofet stood when he saw him. 'Bobby, please join us. Thanks so much for coming.'

Darius also stood. 'Please, Bobby, take a seat. How has your day been? Selling plenty?'

'I've made a few sales lately.' Bobby grinned, wiping his palms together.

Saraf sparked up. 'Ah, that's great news. Perhaps we can talk about your account?'

'I thought we were to talk about something else?'

'And so we are, so we are,' Shofet said, waving over the maître d'. 'Would you like a tea or coffee? We have petit fours coming.'

Darius smiled. 'Unless you would like something stronger, a brandy perhaps?'

'Tea is fine, thank you,' Bobby said, wiping his palms again.

Darius again smiled. 'Bobby, you are our great friend and you have delighted us with your work.' He leaned in and patted Bobby's hand. 'We would like to offer you a proposition.'

Bobby eyed Darius, then across the table at the nodding Shofet, then Saraf, who grinned like a conman, and Ghassab, who looked as if he wanted to hurt him.

'I don't understand. What do you want me to do?'

'Bobby, we know you have a few financial troubles, and we think we can help you.' Darius nodded to Saraf.

Saraf leaned into the table and cleared his throat. 'You owe us twenty-five thousand dollars from your visits to the club.'

Darius continued, 'We would like to wipe clean that debt.'

Bobby looked at both as if he watching a tennis match. 'You want to cancel my debt?'

Darius nodded. 'Yes, that's what we would like to do.'

Bobby chuckled. 'Who do I have to fuck to make that happen?'

'Your mother,' Ghassab grunted.

'What?' Bobby said, then swallowed.

'Well, not exactly,' Darius said, frowning at his colleague. 'We want you to run for the election against her.'

Bobby's mouth gaped. 'You want me to run as an independent against my mother?'

'Not exactly,' Shofet said. 'We would like you to run against your mother for preselection and be the party's next Member for Mallee, keeping it in the family.'

Bobby smiled as if he could not believe what they said. 'Are you serious?'

'We are very serious.' Ghassab squeezed his right hand into a fist.

'You want me to stand for preselection against my mother?'

'I told you he's a dumb bastard,' Ghassab said.

'That's right,' Darius said, nodding. 'We think we can secure the numbers for you.'

Bobby shook his head, his mouth still agape. 'I don't know what to say.'

'This is a decision for which we need an early answer,' Shofet said.

Darius rested his forearms on the table. 'In return for your agreement, we will settle your debt. We will set you up with an office and provide a team of campaign workers. We will fund your election campaign, and with our help we think you will be in federal politics by this time next year.'

Bobby pursed his lips a little, scratched his ear and glanced around the table. 'Have you spoken to my mother?'

Darius shook his head. 'No.'

'And if I don't do it?'

'Maisil is keen for you to repay your debt and wants it resolved by the end of the week.'

Ghassab grinned, nodding.

'Can I have time to think about it and maybe chat with my brother?'

'Sure,' said Darius. 'You have five minutes; take your time.'

Bobby shifted in his chair and began drumming fingers on the edge of the table. 'This is crazy.'

'You may say that, but we think it's a great idea,' Shofet said. 'The party is keen to get rid of your mother. They think she is past it and is not doing enough for the electorate. We think if she is to go down, then it would be better for the family to still hold it.'

Bobby nodded at the theory. 'She is going to lose, anyway?'

'Yes, of course she is,' Shofet said. 'We are told a farmer from down south will take over. Which means they will overlook Mildura and the river districts like Swan Hill in favour of graziers. Our community needs a vigorous supporter in the federal parliament, and we want that to be you, Bobby. We think you'll make an influential politician.'

'She'll kill me,' he said, smiling.

'That can be arranged,' Ghassab said, and the others laughed.

'What say you, Bobby? Are you the next member of parliament for Mallee?' Darius asked.

Bobby licked his lips, looked around at the others, then grinned. 'Hell, yes.'

CHAPTER
39

P eter Dowerin returned to his house late after getting lost amongst files, searching for evidence or information to assist his investigation into the death of James Lever. Evidence from the crime scene remained scant, with the obvious link to other crimes being the hacked little finger. Nothing; he had nothing.

Peter swapped into loose shorts and a polo after a refreshing shower. He appreciated the wine he sipped as the heat of the day reduced. He took up a sheet of paper from his lap, reviewing dates and crimes listed.

Five murders over the last twenty-five years interested him. The victims were random and there appeared no sign or pattern, with no obvious motive and little evidence, just like Lever. Fingers missing created a curiosity for Peter linking Lever's murder, but little else pointed to a pattern.

He placed the sheet back on his lap and plucked one of the five files from the coffee table. He kicked his feet out onto the table, resting both legs on a cushion. Opening the first file, he took another sip of wine.

Josh Malthouse served as a staffer at Peter's father's political office. By all reports, he gained a reputation as a vigorous campaigner for various causes, even getting involved in planning projects around Mildura, using the authority of the local federal member to influence decisions. Some described him as a bully, but many witness statements considered him to be a passionate advocate working on behalf of Junior Dowerin. Peter felt a little odd reading statements about his father describing him differently to the way he remembered. He knew his father as a politician but didn't grasp the many things involving him. To him, he was just dad.

A controversial approval of a local council planning decision created a political storm. Residents came to Junior for support. They wanted to reverse the decision to build residential housing on prime farming land, and Junior sent his head-kicker in to get a result. Malthouse increased community angst by organising various neighbourhood groups to advocate dissent. Every day for two weeks, the council's issue appeared on the front page of the local newspaper.

The Persian Building Company brought the submission to the council, a link Peter hadn't realised, and took another sip as he ruminated on that news. He knew the Iranians played business hard, but a pointing finger accusing illegality had yet to be thrust their way.

Police found Malthouse dead in bed after a community meeting, which resolved that a federal inquiry should investigate the matters of alleged dishonesty over the council's planning process. The housing estate was established twenty years ago, boasting best practice standards in architecture and community facilities, now enjoyed by new migrants from Iran.

Peter flipped over a few sheets to read the medical report. A finger was missing, which must mean something, but what raised interest was the blow Malthouse took to the base of his skull, likely killing him. Just like Lever. The contusion seemed comparable, but he found no opinion on what might have caused it. A scrawled file note from the investigating officer suggested it could have been a small hammer.

Peter then checked dates in the report to see if there were delays. He noted the date of the murder and finished his wine, pouring another generous serving. He twigged a thought so rechecked the date. No one would see any connection, as there was no special consequence with the date other than it was close to Malthouse's birthday. He used his fingers to work out it was four weeks before they found his father in the river.

Peter considered it a coincidence, and no written notes in the file or witness scuttlebutt suggested his father could be involved with the case.

Junior's reputation had zero innuendo of corruption. Peter took a note that he should consider the incrimination of the Iranians and any link with Lever.

He stretched to replace the file on the table and glanced out towards his mother's house, and thought he saw movement in a window. He knew his mother to be in Canberra and expected his sister to be asleep, so he slipped on loafers and headed over to the house to check on Primrose.

As he came to the house, he slowed, heightening his hearing to take in any noise. He couldn't hear anything unusual, so stepped onto the veranda, noting the fans in the ceiling still operating. He followed the veranda to the back door, trying the handle, knowing it should be open.

'Primmy, are you up?' he asked in a hushed voice.

There was no response, so he tiptoed through the house, searching for the origin of the shadow, which could be anything, including his imagination. He covered the kitchen and living rooms then upstairs checking his mother's bedroom suite and lounge when a heavy whack to his neck knocked him to the floor.

When Peter opened his eyes, he could hear the radio static of a buckled handset along with calm, deep, reassuring voices, one male and another female. He rolled onto his back, trying to lift his head, but couldn't. He identified a blurry face of a woman and felt the cool touch of a hand on his forehead.

'He seems conscious,' she said.

The blurred face of a male was now close enough to kiss him. Peter raised an arm to protect his face.

'Can you sit up?' the male voice asked.

'Of course, he can't,' she said. 'He can hardly move his head.'

'I'm okay; help me up,' Peter mumbled. Hands gripped his extended arms, pulling him up, leaning him against a wall. He bent to rest his hands on his knees, trying to focus.

'Are you okay?' she asked.

'What happened?' Peter croaked.

'We reckon someone smashed you in the back of the head.'

'Help me to a seat, please.' He felt inadequate and almost physically useless, allowing hands to lift and support him to a chair. 'Where am I?'

'You're at your mum's house, Pete,' she said.

He tried to lift his head to see who spoke, but pain limited movement, so he dropped it back down, gently touching it, feeling a swelling almost the size of half a tomato. 'My mum's?'

'Yeah. Your sister called it in. We just got here.'

'How long?'

'We took the call five minutes ago. An ambo is on its way,' the male voice said.

'Who are you? I can't see you?'

'Pete,' the female voice said. 'It's Ross and Emily.'

'How's my sister?'

'She's in her bed, a little catatonic. We've tried to talk to her, but she is unresponsive.'

'Can you remember what happened?' Ross asked.

'Um,' Peter rested his head in his hands, a throbbing headache building, 'I thought I saw someone skulking about, so came over to have a look.'

'Did you see anyone?' Emily asked.

'I don't think so.'

'We found the front door locked when we got here. The only egress was through the back door. We found you here and your sister in bed,' said Ross.

A siren could be heard, and flashing lights were now close to the house. Emily went to open the front door; two paramedics entered, moving upstairs to work on Peter, checking vitals by taking various readings.

The paramedics decided it wasn't worth the effort taking him to hospital as the patient fussed about going. They asked him to prove that he could move freely. He walked around the room unassisted, with no shakiness. He told them he had a severe headache, so they gave him a shot of sumatriptan and a sachet of two codeine tablets to use if it disturbed his sleep. They also sought an assurance he would visit the hospital before nine for a check of his neck. They remained concerned about the swelling and wanted a doctor to examine it.

Peter reassured them as they packed up and left. He accepted a steaming cup of tea from Ross as he settled on the softer couch in his mother's lounge.

'Any idea who might have done this?' Ross asked.

'I think the better question would be why,' Peter said.

'Okay,' Ross queried. 'Why do you think?'

'I have no idea.'

'Working on any case?' Emily asked.

'I'm not in my house; they weren't after me.'

'Huh,' Ross acknowledged. 'Why would they be here rummaging through your mother's stuff?'

'Anything disturbed?'

'Not that we have seen,' Emily said.

'Why here and why now?' Peter sipped his tea, relishing the sweetness. 'Primmy said nothing?'

'Not a word,' Emily said.

'The triple zero call seemed calm. I've had a listen. She seemed relaxed. No hysterics at all,' Ross said.

Peter wrinkled his face. 'That's weird. If I know anything about my sister, it's that she is protective of me, and seeing me down like that would have scared her.'

'Well, she isn't talking,' Emily said. 'Maybe we can get something from her tomorrow.'

'Let's hope,' Peter agreed. 'You know what? I think I need to lie down, maybe in my mother's room. Can you help me?'

Ross stood. 'Sure.'

The two police officers assisted a struggling Peter to his mother's bedroom. He was asleep before they turned off the light.

The sun streamed through the window onto Peter's face, causing him to stir and move away. His neck twinged, and he grunted as he rolled onto his side.

'Are you awake?'

Peter popped open his eyes, glancing towards the voice at the end of the bed. Primrose sat waiting for her big brother to wake.

'Anyone else around?' Peter rolled back and rubbed his eyes.

'A lady police officer left about an hour ago,' Primrose said. 'Do you want anything to eat?'

'No, I'm fine, thanks, darling.'

'Why are you here? The lady didn't tell me.'

'You can't remember?'

'When? Last night?'

'Yes. Do you remember calling the police?'

Primrose looked puzzled. 'I called the police? Why?'

'Someone hit me on the back of the head.'

'I remember nothing. Mum tells me to go to bed after she calls. I woke this morning with you in Mummy's bed and a lady sitting in the kitchen.'

'Anything happen last night before mum called?'

Primrose paused for a moment, gazing towards the ceiling. 'The phone rang twice.'

Peter waited for his sister to elaborate, but she didn't.

'Who was on the phone?'

'No one. I answered, and no one was there.'

'Nothing at all?'

'Nothing. Do you want a cuppa?'

Peter smiled and said, 'sure.'

Primrose skipped off downstairs to the kitchen, and Peter dropped his feet to the floor. Someone had lined up his loafers at the end of the bed, and he slipped them on before shuffling downstairs.

'When's mum due home?'

'She didn't tell me, but I think the weekend. We have plans.'

Peter smiled. 'Oh, yes? What plans might they be?'

'She wants to talk about Christmas, so we're going to do some planning.'

'Good idea.' Peter nodded, waiting for a moment. 'Primmy, do you remember calling the police last night?'

'I didn't call the police.' Primrose stepped away from the bench, kneading her hands.

'Don't worry; everything is okay,' Peter smiled, placating her with a hand gesture. 'Do you ever remember a time when strangers were wandering around?'

'There was that time when a man came to check the meter.'

Peter nodded. 'Yes, there was that time.' He accepted the offered mug of tea and took a sip. It tasted good: hot and sweet. Moving his head provoked him to rub the back of his neck. He could feel the lump and winced. Any higher, and it would have been to the base of his skull.

He took another sip and smiled at Primrose, who peered at him behind her own mug of tea, snuggled into her chest.

'How's your head?'

He nodded and smiled. 'It's okay.' He paused for a moment; his face was quizzical. 'How do you know there's something wrong with my head?'

'The lump the size of an egg on your neck, silly. You don't have something like that without having a sore head.'

'Huh, yeah, it is sore. I have to go to the hospital for a check.'

'Do you want me to drive?'

'How many times have I got to tell you, sweetheart? You shouldn't be on the road?'

'I can drive,' Primrose snapped like a child.

'Yeah, I know you can, but not well.'

'How else are you getting to the hospital?'

'I'll ring Bobby,' Peter said.

'He's useless.'

'Maybe so, but he'll help me out.'

'I've heard things about him, you know.'

'What have you heard?' Peter asked.

'He doesn't like us.'

'That's harsh; he tries his best.'

Primrose shrugged. 'He wants to leave.'

'Yeah, he told me.'

'He owes money.'

'Who to?'

'The Arabs.'

Peter hesitated. 'How much?'

'Heaps.'

'How do you know?'

'I know things.'

Peter studied his sister and considered what she raised about Bobby and the Arabs. He knew Bobby liked to gamble and hang out with shady Iranians, but it was the first he had heard about debt.

CHAPTER
40

Question time every afternoon on sitting days in the House of Representatives provided opportunity for ambitious politicians to impress colleagues with quips, witty insults, or derogative interjections. The opposition often targeting a poor performing minister, seeking to create chaos. Like a blood sport for the rabid opposition, if a weakness emerged, they verbally gnashed at the minister's throat.

The prime minister commanded the house.

Today the chamber developed high octane noise as the prime minister highlighted the weakness of the opposition's announced water management policy, having earlier declared they would review all water leasing arrangements with no guarantee of supply to the current leaseholders.

'I call the leader of the opposition.' The speaker recognised the leader, who waited at the despatch box.

'Thank you, Speaker; I direct my question to the Minister for Regional Development, and I ask: Minister, you have been silent in the debate about water. I wonder what your view about the current water leasing arrangements is; and given your own electorate has significant water management issues, I wonder what your plans are to offer security to your constituents?'

The prime minister jumped to the despatch box.

'Prime Minister?' the speaker queried.

'I will take the answer.'

The opposition leader responded.

'Speaker, on a point of order. I didn't ask the prime minister to answer my question. I asked the minister. I am looking forward to hearing her answer.'

The prime minister didn't leave his position.

'On the point of order, Speaker, standing orders allow me to direct who answers questions. I request I am called to provide an answer to the opposition leader's question.'

The speaker's lips curled into a slight smile as she recognised the prime minister's attempt to bully her. She sat forward and referred to the standing orders. 'Prime Minister, you are correct. You may decide who answers questions, but only questions asked of you. As the opposition leader asked the minister, I call the minister unless she wishes to defer to the prime minister.'

'Hear, hear,' the opposition shouted across the chamber.

Brown peered down the front bench to the very last position, reserved for the minister with the lowest ranking; he smiled, nodding with his eyebrows raised, encouraging Rose to relinquish her authority to answer the question. She stood and nodded to the speaker, striding to the despatch box to give an answer.

'I'll take it from here; just pass the question to me,' Brown demanded as she passed his chair. She reached the despatch box, smiling across the chamber, then directing her attention to the speaker.

Rose paused for a moment. She rarely received questions, but earlier convinced the opposition leader during a private phone call to ask this one. She assured her she would dump on the government.

'Thank you, Speaker; I will answer the question, for I think it time the opposition understood the demands of government and how this government will step forward with an improved water management scheme.'

'Sit down. You are about to embarrass yourself,' Brown hissed, loud enough for Rose to turn, peer down, and smile.

'The prime minister has long said the water management system in

Australia is fair for all stakeholders. He has often asked for ideas that could offer a better way. We have heard nothing from the opposition.'

'Hear, hear.' Now the government backbenchers chanted support.

'Speaker, water is at the core of humanity. We need water to live. Yet it seems the current water management system is so out of date that there are some communities within our rich and powerful country struggling to survive because they do not have access to adequate water.'

Brown crossed his arms and pushed back in his chair as the back-bench again raised voices to support Rose. He flicked a glance towards Spencer, who shrugged and shook her head.

'The Brown government has achieved massive economic results, to the envy of many, and has achieved more than any other government in increasing the wealth of this country. We have full employment, exports supplying the world, and an education system that has reversed its downward trend in standards to be within reach of the top five countries in the world. We enjoy a health and aged care system that gives confidence to all our people that we care for them, and we have a fair and just industrial relations system providing jobs.'

Brown smirked, admiring Rose's gumption for expressing the many achievements of his government. He lolled his head back, looking up at the public gallery.

'But Speaker, even though we have achieved much, we have left many who are reliant on water to be wondering about their future. In my electorate of Mallee, we have been in a drought for many years. I have heard the economists and others, some even within the government, saying that maybe we should rethink future settlement of the region. Some have said climate change will never allow the once thriving region of the mallee to recover and that it is a waste of money trying to rectify it.'

Brown smirked as he waited.

'Speaker, I disagree. I believe the people of the mallee need access to water, especially when there is plenty of water available.'

'Hear, hear,' the opposition chanted.

'The current system of water management, where speculators and stock market wealth creators suck the life from the regions, is not working, and it needs to change. I believe our federated states are incapable of managing water for the nation and the federal government must take control of water management across the country. If it's good enough for the Middle East and African countries to have effective water systems in their deserts, then why cannot the Brown federal government attain the authority to manage water? Why can't the federal government make sure all who need water can get the source of life for their families and their livestock?'

Brown sat forward, placing a hand over his mouth, hiding his grimace.

'I propose that as a nation we should move towards a federal water management regime. And Speaker, it seems the only way to ensure the state governments relinquish their rights is to propose a referendum for the Australian people to decide.

Brown swung in his seat to glare at Jock Garnsworthy, who shrugged.

'Speaker, as I finish this answer to the opposition leader's question, I can give assurance to the House that as Regional Minister, I will make sure we discuss and debate the merits of transferring management of water to the federal government. I ask this question: why wouldn't we? The Brown government provides leadership on many issues. It has achieved what it said it will do; so why not allow our people on the land to get adequate access to water and help them live a life?'

'Hear, hear,' both sides of the chamber chanted as Rose left the despatch box.

Brown rushed to the despatch box. 'Speaker, I ask that further questions be placed on the notice paper.' He then collected his files and waited for Garnsworthy to join him. 'I suspect she has tossed the leadership gauntlet right at you.'

'She's been working numbers,' responded the leader of the Country Party. 'And that's not a bad thing.'

'What the heck?' Brown exclaimed. 'Are you kidding me?' The two men turned and nodded to the speaker as they left the chamber. 'There is no way I will anoint her as my deputy.'

'You may not have any choice in the matter,' Garnsworthy said. 'They are moving away from Clare.'

'Why?'

'They think she may not pick up support.' He paused for a moment, then added. 'They think she is too close to you.'

'What do they mean, too close?'

'Tim, never try to kid a kidder; you know what I mean. Dowerin is pushing that line.'

'What do we do?' Brown asked.

'She can't be a leader if she isn't in the parliament.'

The prime minister and his deputy walked across the black marble and onto the wooden floors of Members' Hall. 'How likely is that?'

'Well, if the candidates stop killing themselves, then there is every chance,' Garnsworthy said.

'What about Jackson? I've heard whispers.'

'He would only come if we assured him of no challenge for the seat and we guaranteed him the leadership.'

'No-one supports Clare?'

'When you shit in your own nest, the pigeons rarely come home to roost.'

'What does that mean?'

'She has done some stupid things that may come back to bite her.'

CHAPTER
41

R ose relaxed back into her chair, as her numbers men shared good news about the next stage of the leadership ballot. They advised her she had the votes but needed to stay tough on water licensing to keep them. She stroked her lip, gazing at her colleagues when the desk phone shrilled.

'Prime Minister, such a pleasure. How can I help?' She smirked.

'Rosie, I'm just with Jock, and we would like you to join us for a little chat.'

'About what?'

Brown never appreciated the manner she used during conversations. Never pleasant and always with an anxiety like pulling teeth. 'We want to discuss the future, your future, and I don't want to keep talking about it on the phone, so I wonder, if you aren't too busy, whether you could join us.'

Rose picked up his sarcasm. 'I'll come right over.' She smiled at her colleagues as she left. 'We might have the deal done within the hour.'

As she entered the prime minister's office, he offered her a drink and indicated the couch between him and Garnsworthy in the leather chairs.

'Rosie, Jock and I have been talking about the leadership and who we will support when he steps away from the job.'

Rose gawked at Jock, who arched an eyebrow.

The prime minister took a quick sip of wine. 'We think you have the numbers to win a ballot.'

Rose sat deeper into the couch, surprised by the comment, but said nothing.

'And frankly,' Brown rubbed his chin, 'I have to admit, I don't want you as deputy prime minister and would like you to withdraw.'

Rose shifted her position, crossing her legs and glancing over at Jock, who stared at the floor. She paused for a moment, the prime minister waiting for her response. 'Not sure you will have a choice.'

Brown smiled a cagey grimace. 'Well, like any excellent negotiator, I wanted to talk to you about your priorities and your expectations.'

'Priorities and expectations?'

'What do you want to take a dive?'

'Prime Minister, the last time I checked, we live in a representative democracy requiring all of us to adhere to the principles of good government for and by the people.'

'Yes, yes.' Brown flicked his hand. 'What do you want?'

'I'm not prepared for this discussion, but off the top of my head, I would like something done about water rights.'

'It'll rain soon and then there will be no drama,' Garnsworthy said.

'Spoken like a city farmer, Jock.'

'Now listen here, Rose. That is no way to talk to me,' Garnsworthy said.

'Why not?' Rose smirked. 'This bloke has shagged you since you took the job,' she said with a sniff. 'You have said nothing about the drought other than to offer more money, which is useless.'

'Why is it useless?'

'Farmers need water, not money. They can't turn money into fodder and water for their livestock, and only a city farmer wouldn't know the difference.'

'Look, this type of chatter will get us nowhere,' Brown interrupted. 'Fact is, the government will not accept your appointment as leader.'

'You will risk the coalition?'

'No, we will just send it back for another go,' Brown snapped. 'Now what the hell do you want?'

'Steady, Timmy.' Rose smiled as she studied the men. She then put a finger to her chin 'Let's see, what do I want?' She paused for a moment to consider her rhetorical question. 'I want the water rights to transfer to the federal government; at the very least, I want the Arabs out of the picture.'

'You mean the Iranians in Swan Hill?'

Rose scoffed a laugh. 'You must be crazy to think they only base themselves in Swan Hill. They have an enormous population based in Mildura. They own everything in my electorate.'

Jock seemed doubtful. 'They can't own everything.'

'They migrated a little over thirty years ago and, using all the government schemes for regional development, they wrangled their way into most economic channels. This encouraged new Iranian migrants to the region, and over the years migration schemes have united families. We now have several enclaves, with only Iranians living there. Retail precincts only cater to their community because they rarely speak the language.'

'They don't have anyone in the parliament,' Brown said.

'They don't need to,' Rose said with a smirk. 'They pay for their influence in brown paper bags.'

'Pay who?' Garnsworthy asked.

Rose caught Brown's gaze and smiled, as if sending him a message. He averted his eyes. 'I hazard a guess they have some of our colleagues on the payroll.'

'You?' Brown asked.

'They tried, but I sent them away. We have not had a chat since.'

'Your husband?'

'Not sure,' Rose replied, pouting her lips. 'I think they tried to have him do a couple of things.'

'Junior took money?' Garnsworthy seemed doubtful.

'Not money, I reckon,' Rose said. 'He may have asked for support for party functions.'

'What sort of functions?'

'Like I said, they own everything from restaurants and caterers to voters. They influence everything.' Rose nodded. 'I'm even told they are very close to Jackson.'

'How close?' Brown asked.

'A knuckle,' Rose grinned.

'A knuckle.' Brown glanced at Garnsworthy, who shook his head with a shrug. 'I don't understand. What does that mean?'

'It means that if you don't do what they want, you lose a knuckle.'

'Rubbish,' Garnsworthy scoffed. 'You don't do what they want, and you haven't lost a knuckle.'

'They only do it to those who cross them,' Rose responded. 'If you owe them money or a favour and they come knocking and you don't give it to them, then they leave their mark.'

'Rubbish,' Garnsworthy said again. 'They would have the coppers down on them quick smart.'

'As I said,' Rose paused for a moment and studied both, 'they own everything.'

Brown considered Rose, then after a moment smiled. 'That's just sent a shiver up my spine.' He laughed awkwardly.

'Why?' Rose asked. 'Are you into them?'

Brown didn't answer.

'Let me assure you,' Rose said, gazing at Brown. 'They are not a crew to get involved with, and once they have you, they will never let you go.'

'Okay.' Brown stretched out the word. 'Why do you want to take water off them?'

'Because the way they are managing the licence is unfair.'

'That's it? The water management is unfair? That's why you want to take them on?' Brown asked.

Rose hesitated. 'That, and they want to take my preselection off me.'

Garnsworthy interjected. 'If they do that, then you'll never be the leader.'

'Is that what you want?' Rose asked in reply, gazing at him.

'You won't be deputy prime minister, I can assure you of that,' Brown said. 'If we have to support the party's move against you, we will.'

'Gee, you really are desperate to keep me away from you, aren't you?'

'It's not personal, Rose; you must know that.' Brown clasped his hands in front of his mouth, hiding a smirk. 'So, tell me, what do you want?'

Rose considered her options, knowing the best way to attack was sometimes to pull back. 'An ambassadorial appointment would be nice. Five years would be enough.'

'I could arrange two years.'

'Not some shithole, either,' Rose smirked. 'I said I wanted five years.'

'It is possible,' Brown said.

'Somewhere I don't have to do much work, such as the States.'

'Europe suit you?'

Rose smiled. 'Maybe. Maybe France or Italy. Or maybe Spain.'

'You pull back your rabid numbers and we can get it done.'

'That's not how it's going to work, Timmy. Surely you know that?' Rose gave him a malicious look with a fake smile. 'You give me official papers with a little financial topping and then I pull back.'

'Geez Rose, don't you trust us?' Garnsworthy huffed.

'You have got to be kidding, Jock. I'd no sooner trust you than I would sleep with the Iranians.'

Brown glanced over at Garnsworthy, who shrugged and nodded. 'Okay, we appoint you and you pull back and retire from parliament, letting in who we want as leader.'

'Is that Clare?'

Brown didn't answer.

'Just one other thing.' Rose stood with her hand stretched to shake the prime minister's hand. 'I want my preselection free and clear.'

'We cannot control the locals,' Garnsworthy said.

Rose kept hold of Brown's hand and sneered. 'I can handle the locals. I just don't want you blokes involved. If you want to get a leader you want, then stay out of my way and allow me to resign on my terms.'

'What are you going to do with the water?'

'I'll keep pushing for a referendum. It'll be up to you,' Rose said as she locked eyes with Brown. 'I suspect Australia will demand it. I will continue to demand more water for the mallee.' She dropped the prime minister's hand and moved to the door. 'It was a pleasure, gentlemen.'

CHAPTER
42

Peter Dowerin tapped through files and read reports, researching anything to link his case to other criminal activity. He searched for other crimes with fingers missing; other crimes with contusions to the head; and seeking any links with any groups in the community. In some files, information was missing, and in others he discovered references to matters not relevant, as if there existed a deliberate conspiracy to mislead. It seemed an earlier cohort of detectives in Mildura just didn't care.

'How's the head?' Simon Dobbs asked as he wandered into the detectives' room with coffee.

Peter reached to the back of his neck, rubbing the lump.

'Ya know? I was just thinking.' He stretched his neck, wriggling his head. 'Why was police paperwork crap fifteen years ago?'

'Don't know. They once told me a few boys were keen on the punt and may not have paid much attention to cases as they should.'

'What does that mean?'

'They may have spent too much time on the dark side if you get my drift.'

Peter dropped his hand to the keyboard, using the mouse to open another file. 'What are those coppers doing now?'

'Two left the job working for a local construction company,' Dobbs said, sipping coffee. 'The other three moved back to the city, now working with CIB somewhere. What have you found?'

'Slack paperwork.'

'Not surprised; it was different back then.'

Peter ignored the comment and continued his research. The desk phone buzzed, and he placed the handset under his ear as he continued to tap away. 'Dowerin.'

'Pete, it's Doug from Stawell.'

'Yeah, hi Doug, what have you got for me?'

'The Fingleton autopsy has come back.'

Peter grabbed the phone and stretched for a pen. 'Fire away.'

'It seems he had a few wines and recorded well over the limit at zero point zero nine in his system.'

'That'll do it to you on a country road.'

'The accident smashed him up pretty bad, but he died from asphyxiation. The medical folks reckon it to be a natural cause, as opposed to head or heart issues.'

'Interesting. Did he have anything blocking his airways?'

'Blood.'

'So, he survived the crash?'

'Seems that way. We have him spotted driving erratically outside of Horsham around an hour before the time of death.'

'Thanks, Doug. Anything else?'

'He had an arm torn off, which is gruesome. We think it happened during the tumble.'

'Yeah, you see that. Sometimes it's legs as well.'

'And heads,' Doug added. 'What appeared to us to be strange was his mangled fingers, and we could only find four.'

'You couldn't find his thumb?'

'No, sorry, my bad. We couldn't find his pinkie.'

Peter stretched back in his seat and cupped his chin.

'Do you have many cases like that?'

'Like what?'

'People missing fingers?'

'Mate, it's farm country. Folks lose fingers and part fingers all the time.'

'Nothing to do with a crime, though?'

'Not that I've noticed.'

'Thanks for the heads-up, Doug.' Peter readied himself to end the call. 'Are you blokes going to follow this up?'

'Nah, the city boys are taking over. One of them worked in Mildura and wanted to help.'

'Thanks, Doug. Talk soon, cheers.' Peter dropped the phone and leaned back into his chair, clasping his hands behind his head, avoiding his neck, studying the flies circling above him. 'This is strange.'

'What is?' Dobbs asked.

'There's another victim, a car accident, who has lost a finger.'

'It happens.'

'Not the left pinkie.'

CHAPTER
43

'Welcome back to the Denis Sadler breakfast program. I have the pleasure of introducing, in the studio, our next guest, the federal minister for regional development, Rose Dowerin. Good morning, Minister.' Sadler smiled in his voice, but his face frowned as he read his script.

'Good morning, Denis, and of course your listeners.'

'Minister, why are you starving a thirsty nation of water?'

Stunned by the question, Rose reacted. 'I'm not denying anyone water. The government has a water management program in partnership with the state governments.' She paused, taking a deep breath as Sadler waited, scrutinising her. 'I am sure your listeners will recognise water is precious and the essence of all life. The government has a duty to ensure there is enough to go around to all the communities that are struggling through this dreadful drought.'

'You say that, but you don't believe it, do you?'

Rose slid off her chair, pushing it away. 'There are some who take advantage of the dilemma communities face, but the government supports our regions.'

'That's blatantly not true.' Sadler picked up a sheet of paper and read from the notes. 'We continue to have problems with harvesting water throughout the country. We do not build dams anymore.

Landowners such as the poor suffering farmers out west of the Great Divide struggle to get approval to build weirs and watering holes for livestock. The Greens insist all collection of water requires a licence, which is ridiculous. These parasites overrun local government and they are killing our agriculture and you stand back and do nothing about it.'

'That seems harsh, Denis.'

'Harsh? You call that harsh? We have farmers forced to kill stock because they cannot afford fodder or water. Once we reduce our breeding stock, then this country is stuffed. It will take years and years for it to recover.'

'The government is investing in providing support for farmers. State governments look after the stock. The federal government looks after the health of our farmers.'

'Health of the farmers? Let me tell you this, Minister.' Sadler said, nodding at Rose as if acting a part. 'The health of our farmers would be much better if they had water.'

'I can't make it rain, Denis.'

'No one asks you to, Minister, but you can give greater access to water for our farmers and the rural communities left to starve by you and your government.'

'That's unfair, Denis. The government is responding to the needs of the regions.'

'Are they?' Sadler smiled, raised his eyebrows, nodding again as if all was going well. Rose shifted on her feet. 'Even your own electorate is in trouble, isn't it?'

'We have issues of water access.'

'Isn't it true the water company that owns the rights for water in the mallee has raised the price of water?'

'Yes, the company seems to think it's okay to profit from the misery of others.'

'Right, so what are you going to do about it?' Sadler winked, nodding encouragement.

Rose stalled and wondered what to say. She was confused.

Sadler observed her struggling for an answer, so prompted her. 'Minister, didn't you declare in parliament a plan to resolve these issues of profiteering by the vagabonds?'

'Vagabonds is a little harsh, Denis,' said Rose, collecting herself. 'I believe it's time for the federal government to take responsibility for the nation's water from the state governments. We have various regions competing and demanding access to water, and when it's a scarce resource, we cannot allow sectional interests to control the best interests of everyone.'

'Why can't you just legislate now?'

'The constitution won't allow us.'

'So, we need a referendum?' Sadler nodded, rolling his hand, and Rose nodded.

'Yes, we cannot continue to have profit takers making money out of drought. The federal government must manage water resources throughout this desert nation,' she said. 'If we want to harvest water, then the federal government should be able to direct state and local governments to comply. If we need to pipe water from Kununurra to New South Wales, then we should not have to go through never ending approvals to get the project done. If they can convert desert country in the Middle East to fertile land by piping water, then we should be able to do the same in Australia.'

'Kununurra has water?'

'Oh, Denis.' Rose chuckled. 'Lake Argyle is one of the biggest sources of fresh water in the world and we should be able to ship it east. We should be able to harvest water from north Queensland during flooding from tropical storms and farmers should not have to beg for water.'

'Quite right, too.' Sadler winked. 'What are you doing about it so that this can happen?'

Rose paused for a moment, then gulped and said, 'I have asked the prime minister to consider a referendum. I am sure the Australian electorate will make enough noise to convince him that water is a federal issue and not a local issue.'

'Why don't you lead the water debate and stand for the leadership of your party?'

'Politics is all about the numbers. I might have challengers for my seat of Mallee at preselection.'

'You are kidding? Which goose in the Country Party would let that happen? Who would let this talented lady out of the tent when Australia is crying out for strong leadership? Rose Dowerin is one of the strongest voices going around. Who would do that?'

'Denis, there are forces in the electorate who want change. I am a supporter of democracy, and if folks want a change, then so be it, but I can assure you I will fight until the end.'

'Fighting the company that owns the water rights along the Murray?'

'Don't forget the Darling; they own those as well.'

'How can this happen? How can a resource like water be owned by profiteers? I am told the company is the Persian Water Company; is that right?'

'Yes, it is.'

'Why is it called the Persian Water Company? Is it an international company?'

'No, it is owned by residents in Swan Hill who have grown their business holdings over the years.'

'Why Persian?'

'They are Iranian immigrants.'

'Oh, that explains it.'

'I am not sure what you are suggesting, Denis.'

'Nothing more than this: if you don't have a strong connection to the land over many generations, then is it no wonder you will take advantage of your community?'

'That's a little unfair. I am sure they have the best interests of the community at heart, as they do many good things for the community.'

'For their own benefit, I would suggest.' Sadler ran a finger across his throat to end the interview. 'Thank you for your time, Minister. I hope your plan for a referendum works out. I can assure you; my listeners will agitate for it.' Sadler checked his run-sheet. 'Listeners, that was federal minister for regional development, Rose Dowerin. I can genuinely say she is leadership material, and if she stands for the Country Party's leadership when old man Garnsworthy retires there would be no better candidate. We'll be back after these messages.'

Sadler pushed a button and removed his headphones. 'Thanks, Minister, that was great. It took a while, but we got where I wanted you to go. We will make sure this referendum gets up, and I wanted you to launch it now.'

'Perhaps you could have told me before we started.'

'No, I prefer to take you down the path and have it squeezed from you. It's makes for better listening.'

'I hope it helps your campaign.'

'Oh, it will. Are you putting your hand up for the leadership? You should.'

'I have a few preselection issues.'

'They would be mad to get rid of you. If I can help, then please let me know.'

Rose left the studio more happier with the outcome than she had expected.

CHAPTER
44

The commute home did not burden Rose in the past, but it was becoming an irritant. In Rose's mind, whoever said travelling was fun had travelled very little.

Her flights were short, not like the long hauls a minister is required to do to the west coast or far north Queensland. The frustration came from waiting. Waiting for boarding, queuing to get on the plane and then waiting for air traffic space; and that's just a departure. Arriving could be worse with a flight 'come-around', long taxiing and then having to wait for luggage. She resolved long ago to travel light and not check luggage on commuter trips. If she needed files and other ministerial items, then a travelling staffer would wait for luggage.

Rose learned to time her arrival for boarding to the minute. She normally secured the first row and was often relaxing in a waiting Commonwealth car before the last passenger disembarked.

It almost ticked over to nine when she strode down the steps from her flight, marching through the car park and hopping into her chauffeured limousine. She paid no attention to the driver, who always knew she needed to go to her home on River Boulevard.

Rose didn't pay attention and laid her head back on the leather seat, so when the car stopped outside Savino's, she asked why. The driver responded they had instructed him to deliver her to a scheduled meeting. When she demanded to be taken home, the driver pointed out his instructions were not to until she concluded her meeting, reassuring her he would wait.

Grudgingly, she left the car, descending the stairs to the cellar dining rooms, finding Hosmand Shofet, Taimur Saraf and Darius Hassidim waiting. Shofet asked if she fancied a drink, and she ordered a gin and tonic.

'What the hell am I doing here?'

Darius smiled, reassuring her they would not be long and just wanted to discuss an issue of importance. Impatient with the response, Rose snatched her drink, taking a handsome slug, then another. 'What do you want?' she asked, glaring at the men.

'We would like to negotiate a win-win political solution to your current dilemma.'

'What dilemma would that be?' she asked.

'Ambitions for a government appointment, your leadership aims and your passion to end our business model.'

'Is this about the referendum?'

'Yes, and other important matters.'

'Like what?' Rose considered Darius. 'You know I can't help you.'

'It's not what you can do for us; it's about what we can and will do to you.'

Rose shifted in her seat, crossing her legs, staring at Darius as she bit her tongue, tightening her jaw.

'We usually get what we want,' Darius continued, 'and we have the support of many to help us.'

'I understand,' Rose responded, taking another sip, the ice clinking as she swirled the liquid.

'As you may know, we have a major project we want to begin out at the desolation that is Ned's Corner station. We believe it will be good for the local economy and will deliver jobs, allowing the local community to become internationalised. We believe we are close to achieving all approvals.' Darius paused, studying her eyes. 'The only potential hitch in the entire scheme is you.'

Rose scoffed and shook her head. 'You boys kill me.'

The others glanced at each other, then convulsed a sudden laugh.

Rose interrupted their hilarity. 'You want support for this new Vegas-type community? You never came seeking my advice. Now when you think you are done, we sit down to talk.'

'We don't need you for the approval process.' Darius stroked the side of his face. 'What we don't need is you getting in the way.'

'Give my people water and I'll get out of your way.'

'Your people? That's an interesting expression. Who are your people?' Darius asked.

Rose shook her head, glancing about the men. 'I represent the mallee and we want water.'

Darius trailed a finger along the edge of the linen tablecloth. 'You represent no one.'

Rose snorted. 'Tell that to the voters who supported me for over twenty years.' She smiled. 'Come on, tell me... what's all this rubbish about?'

'We want you to step away from this referendum idea. If you don't, you won't be going overseas.'

Rose felt a momentary stab of anxiety and wondered how they knew her plan. She didn't respond, swallowing hard.

Darius noticed and smiled. 'We have the numbers to take your pres-election away from you.'

'You may have the numbers, but there currently is only one candidate. And that would be me.'

All three smiled as if they were the cat who just swallowed the canary. 'We are aware there have been a few incidents that have interrupted political careers.'

'Ended, more likely,' Rose said.

'Yes, that is true. But not everyone has met an untimely demise,' Shofet said.

Rose grinned. 'Let me guess, only the ones who would not say yes to you.'

'Rose,' Darius said, linking his fingers and squeezing.

'Yes, dear Darius?' She waggled her head and grinned.

'We want you to step away from this idea of attacking us with the referendum. We do not want to go to war with you, but if you force us, we will.'

'Give me water.'

His dark eyes did not blink, and she shifted in her chair. 'You need preselection to get your overseas appointment, and we will not let that happen if you keep pushing this idea you have, as you did with Sadler this morning.'

'Does anything ever get past you?' Rose said.

Darius turned away and tugged his earlobe. 'Rose, I am trying to give you a simple message,' he said. 'Step back from this crusade, and the diplomatic post will be yours.'

Rose raised an eyebrow, eyeing Darius. She sipped her drink.

'If you don't, then we will end your career. We have in place a keen and willing candidate ready to be the voice of the electorate. Nominations close soon and we will submit his application if we cannot get your agreement.'

'Who do you have that will beat me?'

'Please do as we ask,' Darius almost pleaded.

'I'll think about it.' She stood and moved to leave.

'Don't take too long because we have Jackson making announcements within days.'

'Why can't you just release water at a price farmers can afford?'

'We don't do business like that.'

'What, easy?' Rose snapped as she departed.

The men watched her go. 'Well, that went well,' Saraf joked.

'She has always been a hard nut to crack,' Darius said.

'We should have taken her down when we had the chance,' Shofet said.

'Used-to-be's don't count anymore,' Darius sighed.

'Yeah, and you don't bring her flowers anymore.' Shofet winked.

CHAPTER

45

The heat remained too extreme to do anything. The forecast stood to rise to well over forty degrees, with weather boffins predicting an historical record of forty-seven, but most weather predictions never eventuated. Rose looking forward to being with her boys again rescheduled Sunday lunch to an after-sundown dinner. The boys had their troubles and often she didn't agree with them, but they provided her with the sense of family she missed when younger.

Too hot to bake or roast anything Rose decided on a simple grill and salad. The front of the house remained cool, but she still turned on the cooler to chill the air. She prepared iced tea and now enjoyed a tall glass with crushed ice on the veranda below one of the ceiling fans, twirling at a comfortable speed. She spotted Peter arrive home an hour earlier, assuming he took a refreshing dip in the pool.

She brushed away a fly and took another sip of chilled sweet tea, drips of water leaking onto her shirt.

'Hello?' a voice called from the back of the house.

'Out front,' Rose yelled. 'Bring the iced tea from the fridge.'

'Right you are.'

A few moments later, Peter emerged, manscaped. Shaved, hair slicked back, skin moisturised, and with a smell of cologne. His linen clothes seemed pressed and the slip-on leather loafers a statement far removed from his usual work boots. He refilled his mother's glass and emptied the remaining tea from the jug into his glass. He sat on the cushioned lounge and kicked a foot out to rest on the glass-topped wicker table.

Rose smiled at the performance. 'She won't be long.'

'Who won't be long?'

'Charlotte.'

'I don't know what you are talking about.' He smiled into his glass before taking a generous mouthful.

'She's a nice girl. I don't want you corrupting her.'

Peter peered over his glass. 'Not sure I know what you mean.'

'Rubbish.'

'You know I am a police officer sworn to uphold the law?'

'Just be careful.'

'Yes, Mummy.' He smiled, glancing away. 'We are not even close, anyway.'

'I'm sure.' Rose smirked, studying him. 'Have you made any progress on the murder of Jimmy Lever?'

'It's weird, to be honest with you.'

Rose gnawed at her bottom lip. 'Why weird?'

'Someone took his little finger, most likely the perpetrator.'

'That is weird.' Rose turned away and saw Primrose enter the gate, walking to the back of the house, waving a gum tree sprig in front to drive away flies.

'What is weird about it is that it's not the first time we have had a corpse with a finger missing.'

Rose seemed absent minded as she watched Primrose. 'Farmers lose fingers all the time.'

'Yeah, they do, but not the same finger and not in instalments.'

'What do you mean?'

'When I researched various cases, I learned locals lose fingertips and perhaps half their fingers. It seems only dead people lose the entire finger.'

'That seems crazy.' Rose refocused.

'Crazy is a good word for it.' Peter glanced over at his mother. 'But what is crazier is that it is always the pinkie finger on the left hand.'

'Why do you think?'

'I hate to say it, but I suspect it might be a sign.'

'A sign? Of what?'

'Enforcement.' Peter rubbed the tip of his thumb across his taut bottom lip. 'We have linked it to criminal activity. It's a way to tell enemies they either comply or lose a finger.'

'You're kidding?' Rose shook her head. 'In Mildura?'

'There have been reports at various hospitals across the mallee of business operators presenting with tips of fingers wrenched off.'

'Over what period?'

'Thirty years. I have a recent report from of a similar case in Wycheproof.'

'What happened?'

'A businessman claimed he caught his finger in his truck when he was fiddling with the engine.'

'What type of business?'

'Transport.'

Rose didn't respond. 'The Arabs run transport in the region,' she finally said.

'He's a contractor for them.'

They didn't speak. The noise of the evening coming with the increasing hum of crickets and cicadas from the river.

'Would they be stupid enough to be doing things like that?' Rose asked.

'Well,' Peter sighed, 'they got rid of the bikies.'

'The boys in blue did that.'

'Yeah, nah.' Peter shook his head. 'These blokes don't muck around. They scared them off.'

'They're not that fearsome, surely?'

'They are legitimate businessmen, but always get what they want.'

'You think they take fingers?'

'I don't know what to think.' Peter peered out when he heard a car entering the property. 'Here's Charlie.'

'Just one last thing, darling.' Rose stood. 'Do you think they have anything to do with Lever?'

'I have nothing.' Peter also stood. 'Absolutely nothing, except your mate Jack Fingleton lost a finger, too.'

'In a car accident?'

'Weird, eh?'

Rose moved to the edge of the veranda to welcome Charlotte as she climbed the sandstone steps. Peter moved after his mother and grinned as he accepted the staffer's eyes, returning his smile.

'How hot is it?' Charlotte said as she hugged Rose.

'Come inside. It's much cooler.'

As Charlotte reached the veranda, she held out her hand towards Peter, who took it and felt the warmth.

'Nice to see you, Charlie.'

'You too, Pete. Nice shirt.'

'Thanks.' He didn't want to let her go as Rose moved off, encouraging them to follow.

'Bobby should be here soon. We decided on a simple grill and salad rather than a hot kitchen meal.'

'Sounds good,' Charlotte said.

Primrose was already in the lounge, lying on the couch reading, with a light blanket over her.

'Cold, sis?' Peter asked.

'It's freezing in here; can we turn the temperature up a little, Mummy?'

Rose had already passed through to the kitchen and hadn't heard her. Primrose listened for a response and seemed disappointed when none came.

'She's been stressed lately, hasn't she, Charlotte?' Primrose said.

'Under a bit of pressure, that's for sure.'

'What like?' Peter asked as he sat in a lounge chair watching her flop into the cushioned wicker chair.

'She's had preselection issues. This water thing is getting to her a little. She promised to resolve it, and nothing seems to move within government.'

'It's interesting that it is coming to a head now,' said Peter. 'What's driving it, do you reckon?'

'Age, gender, family name and maybe wanting a fresh voice.'

'Why now, do you know?'

Primrose interrupted. 'The Arabs.'

Peter peered at his sister. 'Why them and why now?'

Primrose laughed. 'I thought you were the smart one?'

Peter chuckled. 'It seems not as smart as you, Primmy.'

'They want their tourist development approved; the one Bobby is involved in,' she said.

'Out at Ned's Corner.'

'That's it. Mummy wants to stop them, or something like that.'

Peter glanced over at Charlotte. 'Is that right?'

'It's complex,' she nodded. 'Their issue is your mother's complaints about water access and pricing. They want planning approval and need to keep their water revenue strong.'

'Are they involved in mum's preselection?'

'Potential candidates keep dropping out,' Charlotte said.

'They keep dying.' Primrose giggled, dragging the blanket to cover her face.

'I'm investigating a death right now,' Peter said. 'I must admit I hadn't linked it to the preselection.'

'Why would you? I'm told Lever owed money all over the place,' Charlotte said.

'I'm not sure there is much weight to that theory,' Peter said.

'Anyway, your mum is working hard in Canberra to stand for the party leadership.'

'Only if the party endorses her, right?' Peter asked.

'Correct.'

Primrose flipped away the blanket and got up. 'She'll be pre-selected. Trust me; mummy loves a fight.'

Peter watched his sister move to the kitchen, then turned to catch Charlotte staring at him, so smiled.

'Your mum will be fine, whatever happens.'

'Are you staying with her?'

'I want her to get promoted. That's why we are pushing for the referendum.'

'What's the chances of it getting up?'

'Frankly, there is little chance if it rains.' She crossed her legs, exposing just enough thigh. Peter averted his eyes. 'If she can force greater water access for farmers and the community, then I reckon she may get what she wants.'

Car lights distracted Peter; they were moving through the gate at speed and along the pebbled drive, coming to a sliding halt.

Peter stood. 'Hey Mumsie, Bobby is here.'

'Good timing; I'm just about ready. Go sit at the table.'

Peter stood over Charlotte, holding out his hand for her. She stood close before moving to the table just as Bobby came into the lounge.

'Hi everyone,' he exclaimed, then gazed at Charlotte. 'Wow, don't you look great? Hi, Charlie.' He came to her, putting his arm around her waist and planting a kiss on her cheek. 'Nice to see you again.'

'Nice to see you, Bobby.' Charlotte stepped back, conscious of Peter's gaze.

'Why are you so happy?' Peter asked.

'Oh, nothing really.' Bobby smiled and grabbed his brother's outstretched hand, yanking him close for a hug and a manly slap on the shoulder. 'It's been a few good days.'

'That's great. Mum would like us at the table.'

'Just in time. I'm starving.' Bobby moved to the table. 'So, Charlie, tell me, what have you been up to? I hear you have been working hard to get mum the numbers.'

Charlotte seemed embarrassed, flicking a glance at Peter. 'Others do all of that. I just count when they come in.'

Rose broke up the conversation by carrying in a heaped plate of grilled meats, followed by Primrose carrying three bowls of various salads.

'Everyone crack onto this lot. Peter, can you organise a drink for everyone? Is the room cool enough?'

'It's freezing, Mummy,' whined Primrose. 'Can we turn it down?'

'It's fine, Mum,' Bobby replied. 'Just right.'

'That's right; sister always comes last.'

'Not at all, darling, but you don't like the cold and everyone else hates the heat. So, we compromise.'

Primrose sulked as she sat opposite Bobby.

The family chatted and laughed their way through the food. Charlotte always liked Sunday meals in Mildura. She missed having family meals in country Queensland. She came to Canberra an ambitious intern, now earning respect as a ministerial chief of staff, aspiring to one day be a politician.

After they cleared the table with closing wines being enjoyed, talk turned to politics, as it always did.

'So, Mum,' Bobby said, gaining his mother's attention. 'When are you planning to retire?'

Rose glanced at her son, then shrugged. 'No plans at the moment. Although I had an informal discussion with the prime minister about various jobs.'

'What sort of jobs?' Primrose asked.

'Well, they may appoint me to an ambassadorial role after the next election.'

'Why would you run for the seat if you are going to leave?' Bobby asked. 'Can't they announce it now?'

'They are doing it to get rid of me and they want to know I am returning before they move me on.'

'That's interesting,' Peter said. 'Get pre-selected, then re-elected and only then they may give you a job.'

'That's the way the system works,' Rose sighed. 'Although I am considering standing for the party leadership, which will elevate me to deputy prime minister.'

'You got the numbers for that?' Peter asked.

'What do you think, Charlie?' Rose asked.

'She has the numbers.'

Bobby dropped his head and stared at his hands in his lap. Primrose laughed and nodded. 'Mummy as prime minister; that's fantastic.'

'Deputy, darling,' Rose corrected.

'Just a heartbeat from being prime minister.' Primrose stood and clapped as the others watched, chuckling at her enthusiasm. 'How good is that?'

'Just need to get pre-selected,' Bobby mumbled.

'And that is the problem,' Rose said. 'Our Arab friends want me to stop talking about water. If I don't, they will take me down at preselection.'

Primrose stopped her celebration and sat peering towards Charlotte. 'They can't do that, can they, Charlotte?'

'If they have a candidate, they can.'

'They don't have a candidate,' said Rose. 'They've already lost two probables who were just as voracious on the water policy as I am. Nominations closed on Friday.'

'But they're dead,' Primrose blurted.

'Yes, they are, darling.' Rose patted her daughter's hand.

An air of silence hung over them for a few moments, changing the mood. Eventually, Peter asked, 'Did Jack Fingleton have any dealings with the Iranian group?'

Rose raised her eyes. 'Why do you ask?'

'Oh, nothing really, just a weird connection with Lever. Both potential candidates against you and both missing fingers.'

Bobby peered over at his brother. 'You think the directors might be involved?'

'Can't say. I don't know. Even if I did, I wouldn't be able to discuss it.'

'Why raise it?'

'It's just a little too convenient. They were both potential candidates against mum and now they aren't.'

'What?' Charlotte asked with a scoff. 'You think your mum is killing them?'

Peter snorted. 'No, of course not.' When he calmed, he added, 'but they are keen to get rid of her. The dead two weren't the ideal candidates.'

'You think they didn't want anyone to stand against your mother until they have a suitable candidate?' Charlotte asked.

'Yeah, that seems reasonable.'

'You're kidding,' Rose said. 'Who could they convince to stand against me?'

No one responded until Bobby glanced up with a crazy smile. 'Um, me.'

No one moved, all staring at Bobby, who shifted in his chair, avoiding his mother's withering gaze.

'You what?' Rose said.

Bobby opened his hand and stretching it out in front as he explained, his voice staccato. 'They told me you are likely to retire. They said you had done enough, and they will look after you in retirement.' Bobby glanced at his brother for support.

'What else did they promise you?' Rose demanded.

'They said they would clear my debts, which they have done.'

'You are going through with it?' Rose asked.

'I met Jock Garnsworthy this afternoon in Swan Hill. That's why I'm late. He said he would welcome me to the front bench.'

'You know he's bullshitting, don't you?' Rose snarled.

'Why?' Charlotte asked. 'You've shown no interest in the past.'

'I want to support the family legacy. This is best for the family. It's time to retire, Mum.'

Primrose jumped, spilling her chair back in a clatter. 'You bastard.' She pounced on the table, collecting the cake knife as she went for her brother. 'I'm going to kill you,' she shouted, raising her arm above him.

Bobby's hands were up, protecting himself from a potential slash. As Primrose thrust her arm down, Peter grabbed her, heaving her off, crashing to the floor. She moved into a fit of rage as He wrapped his legs around her as she fought to free herself. She weakened against his strength, falling into one of her catatonic states.

Peter took the knife and rolled off. Rose now cradling Primrose's head. 'I think you all had better go.'

The others checked about. It was useless to say anything. They left, walking Bobby to his car.

'Are you sure you want to do this?' Peter asked.

'No, I'm not, but it might be good for her, and dare I say, me.'

'Let's talk tomorrow once I sort this out.'

'Sweet. I'm in the office all day. Unless of course a sale comes in. You know me.'

'Yeah, I know you,' Peter said, 'and that's why I'm confused about your decision.'

'You know something, bro. I have thought long and hard about this. Whilst I get my debt paid, I can do something for myself and stop living in mum's shadow.'

'Not sure this is the way you should go about it, that's all.'

'Mum will be fine. She has her pension, plus the family name continues.' Bobby smiled. 'They are going to sack her, anyway. At least this way we get to keep the seat in the family.'

'Take care, little brother. I'll see you tomorrow, yeah?'

'Yes, you will.' Bobby opened his door and smiled at Charlotte as he got in. 'See you.'

Charlotte waved and turned towards her car as Bobby drove off.

'Are you on your way?' Peter called to her. 'I thought I might make you a coffee.'

Charlotte stopped and turned, one hand on her hip. 'Got anything stronger?'

CHAPTER
46

A little before eleven, Rose crossed the river to New South Wales, following the Sturt Highway to Swan Hill around two and a half hours away. She noticed Charlotte's car parked on the property and smiled as she drove her Toyota away. A full moon illuminating the landscape as she rushed by on a trek she didn't want to make. Bobby's announcement gutted her. She had no choice than to go see the serpent. She hoped to negotiate a deal that would see the end of the embarrassing charade. She would not allow her family being ridiculed.

She crossed the Murray River back into Victoria at Robinvale, about an hour after she left, and now travelled on the much-improved Murray Valley Highway. Ironically, she organised federal funding to improve the highway and yet the electorate was turning against her. She wanted to fight and dampen their dissent. She just needed to convince Darius Hassidim to back off.

They went back a long way.

When Darius and his cronies first came to town, Rose knew his type. She dealt with villains and lowlifes in Melbourne. When she arrived she recognised an opportunity waited for any den of thieves wanting to take advantage of the naïve folks in the mallee. They rid the area of the criminal bikies and appeared to be the ideal citizens. Rose knew what they were. She warned her husband to steer clear, but he never listened. She believed he became a potential puppet for them until his untimely death.

Rose's fingers tapped, then re-gripped the steering wheel as she thought back to the incident. She tried to tell him, tried to explain, but he challenged how she would know such things, never imagining his wife to have a history from the seedy side of town.

When Junior died, Darius approached her, offering respect and comfort, encouraging her to become part of his team. She ended discussions, negotiating her own preselection, and rejecting the Iranian community's unique number crunching methods. She knew about the price of selling yourself. Life experiences had taught her about price.

She stopped at the iron gates of Darius' rambling compound almost three hours later. She showed ID to the security guard, explaining she had a critical meeting with Mr Hassidim. The lateness of the hour did not convince him, and Minister Dowerin did not appear on his list. She played the 'call the boss' card by retrieving her phone from her leather satchel, scrolling through her call list so the guard could see, then prodding the call button. When she spoke to Darius, the guard relaxed.

'I'm just at the front gate. See you soon,' Rose said, then tossed the phone aside, smiling at the guard, who waved her through. He didn't realise she talked to a recorded message.

The small pebbles popped under the weight of her tyres as she slowly tracked through the gardens. She had only been at the property twice before and knew the residential wing was to the left of the main entrance, so continued to drive until under a familiar balcony. She left on the headlights and stepped out of the vehicle.

'Darius,' she whispered. 'Darius,' she said a little louder.

A light went on.

'Darius Hassidim!' she almost shouted.

She didn't expect Razia to come to the balcony dressed in flowing satin like a vintage movie star.

When Razia saw who disturbed her, she wasn't happy. 'What do you want, bitch?'

'Nice to see you too, Razia,' Rose replied, shifting between her feet. 'I have to talk to Darius.'

'He's not home.'

'You know that's not true; I need to see him now.'

'Why don't you just go?'

Rose stepped back, opened the door, and leaned in, turning the ignition on, then straightening with her hand on the steering wheel.

'Last chance, or I wake the neighbourhood.'

'You have no business being here. Never have.'

Rose pumped the horn like an alarm.

'Stop it. You'll wake my children.'

'I want to see your husband.'

A door below the balcony burst open, with Darius exploding from it, his satin dressing gown flowing behind him.

'Leave it to me, Razia,' he growled. 'I have got this; go inside.'

'Your whore should not be here.'

'Go inside,' Darius shouted as he got to Rose and slapped her, knocking her away from the vehicle, ending the noise. 'Get up and get out!' he demanded.

Rose touched the side of her burning face, using the vehicle door to help get to her feet. Two security guards appeared, aiding her. 'I need to talk to you.'

Darius stared with narrow eyes for a few moments. 'Take her to the bungalow.'

'You've got to be kidding me, Darius,' Rose said as they led her away. 'I just want to talk to you.'

'Time for talking is over, Rose. You've crossed the line coming here.'

A third security guard arrived. Darius requested him to wake Maisil Ghassab, directing him to come to the bungalow. 'Tell him to bring his tools.'

Rose heard the command, so struggled against the guards' firm hold.

'Where are you taking me?'

Darius tailed in behind. 'We're taking you somewhere we can talk and straighten this out.'

'You know it's a federal offence to threaten or use physical means against a federal member of parliament, don't you?'

'You're on private property. The only law here is mine.'

'You really are a hoodlum, aren't you?'

'You're on my land, late at night, screaming out to my family, and you claim I'm the criminal,' Darius responded. 'Just quieten down and this will be over in a few moments.'

They reached the bungalow at the far end of the pool. Darius entered, switching on lights; he pulled a chair from a table, turning it towards the door.

'Sit her here.'

Rose struggled against the guards for show, as she would eventually sit, but didn't want to appear too easy. She scanned the room. It seemed like a self-contained studio for pool guests.

Darius stood in front of her with a scowl, draped in a blue robe over red and blue striped pyjamas, hands clenched on hips. Rose peered up and chuckled. 'You look a little miffed.'

'What are you doing here?'

'I want to negotiate a deal with you.'

'You're a bit late.'

'What do you mean?' Rose asked. 'I'm here about the preselection.'

'You're about twenty-five years too late seeking my help.'

Before Rose could respond, Ghassab barged through the door. Darius waved the guards away.

'Ah, Minister, I now have the opportunity of showing you how skilful I am.' Ghassab walked through, squeezing her shoulder. She wrenched it away.

'Rose, ever since we first met, we have always been open to doing a deal with you,' Darius said, his hands now relaxed. 'We helped you, although we never said as much.'

'That's rubbish; you never helped me.'

'You think you remain in parliament because of the work you do?' Darius dragged a chair over and sat in front of her. 'Our community keeps you in office. You must know that?'

Rose didn't respond, knowing he could be right. Her face still felt numb as she stroked it with her fingertips.

Darius studied her, working out she seemed a little crushed. 'Why are you here, Rose?'

She peered up through her knotted brow, shaking her head. 'I thought we had an agreement?'

'We did. Then this referendum idea now seems to have gotten legs, and you have said nothing to mitigate any legislation.'

'Why are you using Robert?'

'Your son is a willing candidate,' Darius said. 'He works with us on many projects. He sees an opportunity to increase his wellbeing by being elected to the federal parliament.'

'Why don't you get someone else?'

'The answer is simple.' Darius crossed his legs, straightening his satin trousers. 'We want to use the Dowerin's name. We see benefits in keeping the legacy.'

Rose dropped her gaze, staring at the floor, shaking her head.

'You have let us down over the years. To us, you have been negligent in the support you have given our community.' Darius leaned forward, his wrists resting on his knee. 'We had to beg you in the past to help us. Because of your recalcitrance, we had to shift our efforts to others with a greater capacity to support us.'

'Garnsworthy and Spencer?' Rose asked without raising her head.

'Who we support is no concern of yours. I will tell you that our influence sits in the inner circle of the cabinet, of which you are not a member,' Darius said. 'You only ever made it to the ministry because you are a woman, not from any talent.'

'That's a little unfair.'

'Now we wish to install a local member who will work for our community, who will help us do the things we want to do.'

'Does it have to be Bobby?'

'We wanted to support other candidates, but they kept resisting our water plans and opposing the development out at Ned's.'

'They keep dying, you mean.'

'Accidents are unavoidable in politics.'

Rose lifted her head, smirking at Darius. 'More like murder.'

'I'm not sure we know anything about that.'

'Your calling card is at both scenes.'

'There is nothing implicating us; we know that.'

Rose grimaced. 'Everyone knows the punishment for people who cross you.'

'Not sure I know what you are talking about.' Darius glanced at

Ghassab, who smiled like a hyena waiting for his turn to feast. 'Why are you here?'

'I don't want Bobby running against me.'

'Too late, I'm afraid.' Darius shook his head. 'He applied before the close of nominations last Friday. The preselection is next week. So even if we wanted to help you by nominating someone else, it's too late. Just like you, Rose. Never across the detail, and too slow to react.'

Rose sniffed. 'You say.'

'Yeah, I do. We have the votes. We have our candidate, who will win next week. So not only will you be out of a job, but you will also lose your overseas posting. You will never be leader of the party, and you will trot off into retirement knowing it could have been different if you had done what we wanted you to do.'

'That could never have happened; you know that.' Rose gazed into his eyes.

'No, I suspect not.' Darius stood and shook his head at Ghassab, who seemed disappointed with the gesture.

'There is no convincing you to pull Bobby from the race?'

'He is our candidate. He will do his job.'

Rose stood. 'He won't do the things you want done in parliament. You must know that.' She pitched one last argument. 'He ain't that smart.'

'We know that.' Darius grinned as he turned away. 'Our plan is to get rid of you, and then before the election, we shall have our man in place.'

'Wait.' Rose tugged at Darius' elbow. 'Bobby won't be standing at the election?'

'Oh, he'll stand, but he will never be sworn into the parliament.'

Rose tugged harder. 'What do you mean?'

'He is our patsy.' Darius turned to face her. 'He'll run in the election. We will expose him during the campaign over something like drugs, maybe gambling, and then he'll resign in disgrace.'

'What will happen to the nomination?'

'As you know, there'll be a change before nominations close,' Darius said. 'Or we may even do it before the federal election is called and our candidate will run unopposed.'

'Oh yeah, who might that be?'

'Phillip Jackson.'

'The premier?'

Darius smirked. 'Who said you were a sandwich short of a picnic?' He chuckled. 'You are so smart.'

'He'll never do it.'

'He has already agreed. His only condition is not to run against you.'

'You're using Bobby?'

'Look, Rose, you've had a good run. It's time for you to go. You have no future in politics. I suspect you should just retire on your enormous pension. Don't waste what limp reputation you have by fighting us on this one. The deal is done.' Darius nodded to Ghassab and strode from the bungalow.

Ghassab stepped to her, gripping her shoulder. 'Time to go, sweetheart.'

Rose watched Darius move away, then dropped her head and sighed.

Ghassab prodded her. She shuffled towards the door, then onto the path back to her vehicle. As they approached, Ghassab stepped in front, opening the door. His act of chivalry confused her. She thanked him as she stepped around the door. As she did, Ghassab punched her with a blow to the solar plexus, crippling air supply. He then tossed her crumpled body into the front seat.

As Rose struggled to regain her breath, he slammed the door and walked away.

CHAPTER
47

The overhead fan fought a losing battle against the stifling midday air, doing its best to cool the squad room. They cranked up the air-conditioning unit, and the fan struggled at the highest speed to circulate air, the motor straining under the demand. Peter Dowerin could feel a waft of cool air, but it didn't calm him. The morning visit to the crime site shrouded him, and he felt queasy with his shirt sticking to him and still feeling flushed. He needed to file a report and call the victim's family, his family.

They promised him the medical report within twenty-four hours, with a more comprehensive pathology report within four days. He wasn't sure how it would help him. The victim had dinner last night, and he knew what he ate. He knew the victim deferred their planned meeting to the afternoon. And he recognised the brutality linked to other cases.

One finger severed from a victim seemed weird. Given the circumstances of the car accident a finger missing appeared to be a coincidence; but a third victim with a finger ripped from the left hand identified a pattern. A pattern now linking victims with the preselection for Mallee. That's a motive. He tossed his pen on the desk, leaning back in his rickety chair, wobbling under his weight shift.

Simon Dobbs sauntered into the office glancing at Peter staring at the fan; he slinked to his own desk, switching on the computer. He tapped a few directions before peeking over to his partner. 'Pete, got a second?'

'Sure.' Peter gazed over. 'What's on your mind?'

'How do you want to handle this?'

He didn't answer. He returned to the hard-working fan. 'I suppose we should tell the victim's family.'

'I'm more thinking I should take the case.'

Peter gazed over, pulled an unconvinced face, and shook his head.

'I mean, it's your family, and the operations manual instructs us not to get involved in these types of cases.' Dobbs leaned back in his chair, waiting for a response, then added, 'You are likely to be a witness considering your chat this morning, so it's obvious I need to manage the case.'

Peter didn't reply, his eyes staring at nothing. He then cleared his throat and said, 'I've got to go tell my mother and sister.'

'I can handle that.'

'No, I need to do it.'

'We had better do it now. Is she in Mildura?'

'As I understand it.'

'Then let's go.' Dobbs stood, collected his credentials, and waited at the door as Peter sluggishly prepared to leave. 'Let's swing by her office first and then out to her home if we need to.'

'My home.'

'Yes, of course.' Dobbs tapped on the door. 'We need to dash before the news spreads.'

Peter grimaced, accepting the urgency; he slid on his sunglasses and grabbed his keys, following his partner out the door.

The afternoon heat seemed to have increased, and they flinched against the wall of hot air as they left the building. They walked to Minister Dowerin's office, around the corner on Tenth Street. Halfway there they regretted it, as the thick air made it challenging to breathe without tongues working lips and palate.

'This is ridiculous,' Dobbs said.

'Let's get it done,' Peter said as he pushed open the office door. 'Hi Marjorie, is the minister in?'

'Is that you, Peter?' Charlotte's voice came from behind a partition.

She appeared around a corner, opening the security door to allow the detectives through to the inner office before noticing their severe faces. 'Shit, what's wrong?'

Dobbs stepped forward. 'We would like to talk to the minister if that's okay. Is she around?'

Charlotte frowned as she noticed Peter drop his gaze. 'She's been out in the electorate since this morning. I'll call her if you like, or if there is something I can do?'

Peter raised his head and shook it. 'We need to talk to her.'

'I'll call her now.'

Charlotte stepped away to a desk stacked with files. She prodded numbers with a red fingernail and waited for an answer. 'Minister, the police are here and would like to talk to you ASAP.' She glanced at Dobbs, who nodded. 'Right, okay, I'll let them know. I'll be right over.' She hung up, collected her keys then turned to Dobbs. 'She's having lunch at home. I'll see you there.'

Dobbs shrugged, and Peter sighed as she brushed past.

Ten minutes later Dobbs parked near the front steps of the homestead. Peter stepped from the vehicle, wiping his palms against his trousers, looking to the house, gnawing his bottom lip. He took a deep breath as he stepped forward.

They walked into the lounge and waited for Rose to join them. She wasn't long, and entered carrying a chilled jug of water, managing three glasses in her other hand. As the jug became uncomfortable to manage, she dumped the load on the coffee table. She poured half glasses for the police officers and filled her own before taking a seat to listen to what they had to say. Peter avoided her gaze as she cast an eye on him.

'What do you need to tell me?'

Dobbs took a mouthful of chilled water and placed it on the table. 'Minister, there has been a police incident.'

'What type of incident?'

'We are treating it as a murder, and at this stage our inquiries cover all possibilities.'

'Why are you here?'

Charlotte ducked into the room, standing behind Peter, who edged away from Dobbs, closer to his mother.

'Mum.' Peter peered at his mother, who gazed at him, searching his eyes for answers. 'It's Bobby.'

'It's Bobby what?' Rose asked.

'The victim is Robert,' Dobbs said.

'What... my Robert?' Rose brought a hand to her mouth. 'That's impossible. Where? When?'

'Out near Merrinee,' Dobbs said. 'Wheeler Road, to be precise.'

'There's nothing out there.'

'Well, there was today,' Dobbs responded, glancing at his boots.

'This can't be right. Bobby is an excellent driver.' Rose shook her head. 'Why would you treat a road accident as murder? What's happened?'

Dobbs over bit his bottom lip hard and shook his head, preferring to look at the floor, but raised his gaze. 'Someone shot him at close range. At this stage, we think they used a shottie.'

'Is he hurt? Where is he, at Mildura hospital or Melbourne?'

'Mum, he's dead.'

She gazed at her son, her face pale, eyes drained of life. Charlotte stepped forward, taking the glass from her, refilling it, and passing it back, but Rose didn't take it. She just stared ahead as if looking past the detectives. She shook her head, unable to speak.

'Minister, are you okay?' Charlotte asked.

Dobbs straightened, moving from one foot to the other, thrusting his hands into his pockets. Peter dropped to a knee in front of his mother and touched her cheek. She shifted her attention to him. A tear cascading along the side of her face.

'Bobby's gone?' Rose tried hard to say the words as eyes welled and tears flowed. Peter moved closer, draping an arm around her shoulder, and pulling her into his neck; she sobbed, then wailed, clinging to her son. He wrapped his other arm around her and peered up at Charlotte, also flushed with tears.

Dobbs let the moment pass then asked, 'I have questions for you, if you don't mind, Minister.' No one acknowledged him. He nodded, waiting a moment. 'We could do it now or perhaps later at the station when you are able.'

'Do you mind?' Charlotte straightened. 'Show some respect,' she snapped.

'Just doing my job, ma'am.'

'Well, just wait a minute will ya?'

Rose responded, straightening away from Peter. Charlotte passed her tissues snatched from a box on a sideboard. Rose dabbed at her face and fell back into her chair. 'It's all right.' Rose smiled at Peter. 'What do you want to ask?'

Dobbs cleared his throat with a stifled, gruff cough. 'Minister, there has been a pattern with several incidents, and we would like to ask some questions about your preselection.'

'What do you mean, pattern?' Charlotte asked.

Peter moved back to support Dobbs, wiping a cheek as he peered down at his mother. 'We have three dead bodies in the mallee, all killed within the last few weeks,' he said. 'All active in politics, and all announced their candidacy for preselection for Mallee. Two murdered and one in a tragic accident, all with their bodies disturbed after death.'

Rose looked up. 'Disturbed? How do you mean?'

Dobbs hurried into the briefing. 'Each victim has the little finger on their left hand amputated. In one case hacked off, ripped off in another, and in your son's case, clipped off.'

'What do you mean, clipped off?' Rose asked.

'Taken with tin snips, we think.' Dobbs nodded.

'Oh yuck.' Charlotte grimaced as Rose sat stony faced at the news.

Dobbs paused for a moment before continuing. 'So, we are wondering, is there any antagonism with this preselection that would warrant three candidates against you being murdered?'

'You said two,' Rose remarked without looking at him.

'With the finger pattern, it appears likely that the traffic crash victim would also be in this group. So, any ideas?'

'Do I know who would want to murder my son?' Rose glanced up.

'No,' Dobbs breathed deep. 'I'm trying to get an idea whether there are any groups, people or interested parties who have an interest in your preselection.'

Rose winced and cast an eye at Charlotte. 'Aside from the prime minister and the deputy prime minister, do you mean?'

'Minister.' Dobbs tightened his tone. 'We are keen to determine who might have murdered your son. We are seeking information that might be helpful.

Primrose bounced into the lounge, breaking the tension. 'Why is everyone so glum?'

'Oh shit,' Rose said, trying to stand. 'Pete, can you explain it to her?'

He glanced over at his sister. 'Sure.'

'Be gentle.' Rose watched as Peter placed an arm over his sister's shoulders and walked her to the kitchen.

Primrose turned back and checked over Peter's shoulder, raising her voice. 'What's going on?'

Dobbs paused for a moment. 'Can we continue?'

Rose watched the opening to the kitchen and listened. 'That will not go very well.'

Peter led his sister to the stone-topped island bench in the centre of the kitchen and pointed to a stool as he yanked open the fridge, pulling out two cans of her favourite soft drink, opening them and sliding one across the chilled marble top.

'What's going on, Peter?' she asked, slurping the orange drink.

'There's been a terrible accident, and it concerns Bobby.'

'What's the moron done now? He should never run against mummy.'

Peter peered at her, examining her eyes for a flicker of understanding. 'Primmy, someone has murdered Bobby.'

Her face didn't change with the news. She didn't seem stunned, sad, or anxious; she just slurped another mouthful of fizzy drink, then burped before giggling behind her fingers.

'Did you hear me?'

'Yes, I heard you. I'm not deaf,' she snapped.

'When was the last time you saw Bobby?'

'This mornin', I suppose.'

'Did you say anything to him?'

'Yeah, I did.'

Peter looked at his sister, waiting for a response, but she just kept slurping little sips from her can, seeming oblivious to what he had just told her. 'What did you say to him?' he asked.

'I told him he was a naughty for standing against mummy.'

'What did he say?'

'Nothin'.'

In the lounge, Dobbs resumed his questions. 'You've been pushing this water issue in the parliament. Has that caused any troubles for you?'

'Plenty, but most involved want to knock me off.'

'Anyone in particular?'

'The premier is making moves against me to satisfy his own ambitions. The water rights lease holders seem angry with me and want to remove me.'

Charlotte added, 'There are very few community groups supporting the minister. Any connection to her preselection is a too big a bow.'

'Yeah, you may be right.' Dobbs shifted. 'Where were you this morning, Minister?'

'What sort of question is that?' Charlotte demanded.

'I ask everyone.' Dobbs gazed at Rose.

'I was out and about in the electorate this morning.' Rose flicked a glance at Charlotte who nodded. 'I went to Culleraine to talk water with locals.'

'That's just north of Merrinee, isn't it?'

'Yeah, I guess.'

'What are you inferring?' Charlotte asked.

'Nothing.' Dobbs closed his notebook, shoving it in his trousers' back pocket. He called to Peter to leave.

Peter responded, leaving Primrose sitting at the bench. As he passed through the lounge, he hugged his mum. Then took a similar offer from Charlotte, accepting her outstretched arms. 'What time did Bobby come by this morning?'

Rose didn't look at him. 'He didn't.'

Peter shrugged before following Dobbs.

As Dobbs reached the front door, he turned towards Rose.

'Minister, we'll be able to get a log of your GPS for your car and phone, won't we? Do I have to request it from the department?'

'Pardon?' Rose said as she straightened, licking the corner of her mouth.

'What do you need that for?' Charlotte asked, frowning.

'Procedure, just eliminating all matters from the evidence trail.'

Peter stopped, shoving his hands into his pockets. 'It'll be okay; just email a name and contact and we'll do the rest.'

The detectives waited for a confirmation and Rose nodded without looking at them as they left the house.

'That was weird.' Dobbs said as they drove through the front gate. Peter didn't respond and just gazed out the side window. 'What did you get from it?'

'Nothing,' Peter said, resting his head on the window. 'I read nothing into the responses.'

'You don't think it created tension?' Dobbs asked.

Peter turned to him. 'Maybe... why did you ask about the GPS, anyway?'

'We just have to cover all bases and getting your mother out of our suspect list would make sense.'

'I suppose.' Peter watched as they passed a strip of shops. 'Who cuts fingers off victims? Why would you do that?'

'Send a message, I suppose.'

'What are they saying?' Peter shook his head and shrugged.

'Keep your fingers out of my business?' Dobbs said, tossing out a theory.

Peter shook his head, then rubbed and squeezed his chin. 'These types of killings have been about before.'

'What do you mean? When?' Dobbs asked.

'I've been following a lead.' They parked the vehicle outside the police station under the shade of a huge gum tree but left the engine running so the air-conditioning would keep them cool. 'But it makes little sense they should do it now.'

'Who should do what?' Dobbs asked.

'I suspect the Arabs of muscling their way through business deals and clipping fingers if they don't get their own way.'

'They kill people?' Dobbs asked.

'No evidence to confirm that theory. Just coincidence, and this is not the first time my family has been involved with them.'

'Why would they be helping your mother? She wants to take their water rights away.'

'That's what makes it so strange.' Peter pushed open the door, sucking a gust of warm air into the vehicle. 'Crumbs, it's hot.'

'Do you think this case involves them?'

'There are three bodies with fingers missing. Seems like a pattern to me, and historical case files show it has happened before.'

'So, if the Arabs are doing it, why?' Dobbs scoffed at the suggestion as he turned off the ignition and chasing after Peter into the building.

CHAPTER
48

The Country Party hired the conference room at the Mildura community centre, arranging over a hundred chairs to face a lectern. Members gathered after travelling from all regions of the mallee, some leaving early in the morning or coming the night before, staying at a local hotel for a discount rate. Grumbling members who arrived early asked why they couldn't start the meeting.

'We said we would begin at eleven and that's when we will start,' a senior officer announced. 'We are still taking registrations and there is a queue of around thirty delegates still to register, so get yourself a cup of tea and let's all remain calm.'

At eleven, there were almost one hundred and twenty delegates seated. The president welcomed everyone, setting out the agenda for the day and advising a substantial lunch provided by the CWA would be available in another room at midday. He then introduced the head office official who would administer the preselection. No one clapped.

Whirling fans stationed around the room did not lessen the heat, and it seemed the community centre's air-conditioning could not cope with the crowd. Colin Sullivan wanted the endorsement over as soon as possible, recognising hot delegates were unruly delegates. The tall and hunched official managed party preselection administration and assumed this meeting would be no different.

'Delegates, we are here today to select your candidate to represent you and the party at next year's federal election. I have only one nomination, Ms Rose Dowerin. Ms Dowerin being the only candidate, in accordance with party rules she is duly elected. I therefore seek a motion to approve such a decision. Is the motion seconded?'

He could hear a voice from the back. 'We want to ask the candidate questions before we vote.'

'Hear, hear,' several voices agreed.

Sullivan prowled the floor out front, looking as if his tall frame with long arms would swing like a gibbon across the light fittings and confront the voice down back. He eventually said, 'Well, this is unusual, given there is little we can achieve by questioning the candidate at this late stage. There is no constitutional variation possible within this meeting to stop her from being endorsed.'

Rose had taken a seat in the front row and now stood. 'Mr Sullivan, if I may.' She then turned to address the delegates. 'I, more than anyone else in this room, would prefer a candidate debate and discussion today.' A respectful hush descended over the delegates. 'Believe me when I say that I am the loser because of what has happened, not you. But if you would like me to answer questions, then I am more than happy to do so.'

Silence still shrouded the audience, the hum of fans and air-conditioning the only noise. No one spoke.

Rose scanned the room and smiled with a little scoff. 'There is just one message I have for you today.' Most faces turned towards her. 'I promise you I will do all in my power to bring about change to the water rights.'

'How?' a voice yelled.

Rose stepped up to the lectern. 'If I am endorsed by you today,' she breathed deep, 'I will stand for the leadership of the party when Jock Garnsworthy steps aside in the New Year. If I am successful in convincing colleagues I should lead them, I will turn my attention to establishing a referendum to ask the Australian people to support farmers by breaking the monopoly of water rights and have the federal government take control of water. This allows you all a fair share of water, which is a sovereign right and should not be a commercial deci-sion by speculators in Melbourne.'

'The owners aren't in Melbourne; they are right here in the mallee,' a voice called.

'That's right.' Rose nodded. 'They will have an obvious choice to make, and that choice needs to be made as soon as possible. I ask them: let us have our water now or lose your rights in the future.' Enthusiastic claps down the back encouraged others to approve and applaud. 'I promise you,' Rose paused for effect, 'on the memory of my murdered son, I will release water to you within months.'

It appeared a brave thing to say, given she was not deputy prime minister, had zero relations with the Persian Water Company with little chance of meeting her promise with the referendum, but she didn't care when the room erupted with loud applause.

<hr />

The sun had long gone, but heat remained, and the cicadas drove a humming screech bordering on intolerable. Locals get used to it, espe-cially near the river. Rose stretched out amongst the abundant cushions on her wicker lounge, mosquito coils drifting a trail of smoky odour across her. A glass of chardonnay with a handful of crushed ice dangled from her resting hand.

She took a long sip of chilled wine, condensation dripping onto the silk blouse she had worn to the preselection. Although it was a long sticky afternoon of meetings and shaking hands at various community events, she hadn't bothered to change when she reached home, prefer-ring a wine so she could relax under the fan on the veranda. A glass had turned into a bottle. Now she was starting her second.

The meeting finished as expected with her endorsement to run at the next federal election, but the vote wasn't unanimous. She considered sixty percent a resounding victory, but it still irked her many delegates abstained and she had not tested the vote against a competitor. *Would she have won if Bobby had run?* This question kept cranking through her thoughts.

The opportunity to carry out the plan she dreamed about since meeting Junior could now come to fruition. It had taken years; she had done the deals and deeds to get close to achieving what she wanted, and now it was within reach.

Her telephone hummed again. She had been receiving calls all afternoon and switched it to silent a few hours back, not wanting to talk to anyone; she just wanted to enjoy the moment. It hummed again and then again before she relented and answered.

'Congratulations.'

She recognised the voice. 'Thank you, Darius; unexpected, as you no doubt know.' Rose took a sip of wine.

'No competition.'

'What do you want?'

'I am keen to meet with you to discuss the future.'

'I'm not sure you have a future, especially in water.'

'Rose, this is the reason your party does not like you.' Darius lowered his tone. 'Can you come to Swan Hill tomorrow?'

'If you want to talk,' Rose said, 'then I would imagine you should come see me.' She smiled as she laid her head back on a soft cushion. 'Perhaps you could kiss my arse for once.'

Darius took the joke as a rebuke and didn't respond.

Rose then said, 'I don't want to see your thug.'

'Rose, I want to talk business with you. We go back a long way, and it would be appropriate for me to bring you into the discussions I am having with the premier.'

She paused for a moment and shook her head, turning her mouth down. 'Come tomorrow morning, after church, and we can share a coffee.'

'Church? You pray?'

'Not as much as you, Darius. Come to my house tomorrow and tell me what you have in mind.'

CHAPTER
49

The reverend stationed himself by the door, wishing the small congregation peace and love as they left the chapel, a wooden shack built a hundred years ago. His robes draining him, yet thankful for the shade of the portico. Sweaty faces attracted flies, and his wave remained ineffective in keeping them away as parishioners queued to shake hands and wish him well.

Rose attended church whenever she could, a rarity. After the previous day's party meeting, she wanted to cleanse her soul of any negative energy that may have clung to her. Her head struggled, and she regretted her second bottle of wine as soon as she sat down on the hard wooden pew. She felt vulnerable to the heat and desperate for water keen to rid herself of clothes. A swim would be ideal.

'Rose, I am sorry to hear the news about Robert. I remember him to be a good boy.'

Rose peered at him, not wanting to say anything. She hoped to squeeze past, but a group of large women blocked her escape, so she had no choice. 'Thank you, Gavin. I appreciate your thoughts and prayers.' She smiled at her cliché.

'If there is anything I or the community can do for you, then please let me know.'

Rose took his outstretched hand, regretting gripping the sweaty thing and shook it with little enthusiasm. 'I will bear that in mind, Gavin. Thank you,' she said, flashing her campaign smile.

'It's such a pleasure to see you here. I hope to see Peter and Primrose next time, perhaps. Nice to see families together.'

'Not sure my children are solid Christians, Reverend, but I do my best.'

'I pray for you, Rose.'

She twerked her head to the side. 'Why would you do that?'

'We need water and you have promised to deliver it. So, I pray you do.'

She dropped his slimy hand. 'Maybe you should ask your God for rain rather than expecting me to do your job.' She turned, stepping away, leaving the reverend frowning, staring after her, only changing his focus when someone grabbed his hand.

As she walked up the stone steps at home, Rose had already kicked off her shoes. She made her way through the house, dropping her cotton frock and discarding her underwear, grabbing a towel as she headed out the back door. The paving scorched her feet, and she danced to the pool gate, trying to keep her feet off the red bricks. As soon as she made it through the gate, she dived into the pool, the freshness of the water rushed over her. It wasn't cold, but cooler than the air and chilled her.

She turned over on her back and floated to the end of the pool, her eyes closed, allowing her skin to appreciate the refreshing water. She didn't hear the iron gate open, or the rattling of the fence when it bang closed.

'I'd forgotten about that tattoo.'

The man's voice startled her, and she straightened to tread water. She held her hand up so she could see who startled her.

'You know, for an old woman, Rosie, you still have desirable curves.'

'I wouldn't get too excited, Darius; you had your chance.'

'Too long ago, but the memory remains.'

Rose ignored him and stroked her way to the other end of the pool, using the steps to get out, and grabbing her towel, she skipped back to the shade of the house.

'Come on through. I won't be a moment. Make yourself comfortable out front; it's cooler there.'

Rose grabbed a top from the laundry and wrapped a sarong tight around her. She then went to the refrigerator and poured two iced teas, plonked a handful of crushed ice from the overlarge freezer into both, and joined Darius in the wicker lounge on the front veranda.

'How was the drive?'

'I brought my kids; they are enjoying themselves with family.'

'Yeah, nice,' Rose smiled as she took a long draught of the refreshing tea. 'So how can I help you?'

'Straight to business.'

'Well, it seems you were keen on business the other night, and you didn't want to hear what I had to say.'

'You wanted water.'

'I still do. The question is: will you give it to me?'

Darius smiled and looked away, taking a sip of his tea, careful not to drip liquid on his shirt.

'You thought you had the winning hand and now you don't, so you want a deal.'

'That's harsh,' he said, gazing out towards the river.

'Tell me I'm wrong.'

Darius turned and studied her. 'You are a beauty, aren't you?'

'Cut the crap, will you?' Rose repositioned herself. 'What do you want?'

'My only need is the state government's planning approval for the development out at Ned's Corner. I have all local approvals. I have funding ready to roll, but I still need the state government's tick to get started.'

'Jackson not going to give you what you want?'

'I can no longer give him what he wants.'

'Which is?'

'Your job.' Darius stared at her. She tried to resist but couldn't drag her eyes from their blackness.

'Not for a few years at least,' Rose said, beaming.

'I need those approvals now.'

Rose took another mouthful and rattled the ice in the glass, wondering if a deal could be done.

'My question is this: what can you do to get them for me?' Darius asked.

'You want me to resign?'

'It would be helpful if you did.' Darius laughed. 'Just like your husband.'

Rose stifled a smile. 'I'm about to become deputy prime minister.'

'You've played those cards very well,' Darius said, thumbing his bottom lip. He then peered at her. 'How did you manage no opposition for the preselection?'

'Nothing to do with me.'

Darius smirked. 'I'm sure.'

Rose took another mouthful, this time with ice, crunching the cold slivers. 'Look, Darius, I'm not going anywhere. My plan is to get the referendum approved and only then drift off to a nice little earner at an embassy in Europe.'

'Why do you need a referendum?'

'Because you wankers are screwing farmers and raising prices during a drought.'

Darius slugged a mouthful of drink. 'It's business.'

'It ain't business when you don't release water.'

'It's the rules. I can do whatever I like within the rules.'

'That doesn't mean screwing the community.'

'It is not my fault it's not raining,' Darius drained his drink.

'It may as well be.'

He leaned forward and placed his glass on a table.

'Here's the deal, Darius.' Rose also leaned over and placed her glass on the table. 'You release water to the farmers and reduce your water carting charges by fifty percent and I will hold back on the referendum.'

'I want state government approval.'

'You give me water. I'll guarantee Jackson signs the approvals.'

'I will review the water agreements once it's done.'

'No, that's not how we do things here.' Rose stood and stepped to the edge of the veranda, leaning against a rail, and peering back at

Darius, arms crossed, waiting for his decision. 'You give me what I want, and I'll give you what you want.'

He eyed her, then laughed. 'All right already, you win. I'll review the carting price and release water to the irrigators.'

'When?'

'Don't you ever give up?' Darius chuckled.

'When?'

'I'll make a statement about licence and carting pricing on Wednesday and begin releasing water by Friday.'

'If you do that, then I will get your approvals. I will announce that due to my enormous grief, I will reconsider my election providing an opportunity for Jackson,' said Rose. 'But if you don't by Friday, then the deal is over. I will move heaven and earth to bring on a referendum.'

Darius didn't move. His hands steepled in front of his face as he studied her. He sighed and shook his head. 'You are a tough girl, Rose; I have always said that. Gee, I wish we worked together.' He pinched his nose and wiped his mouth. 'Alright, deal.'

'Very good, Darius.' She moved forward and held out her hand. He stood and seized it, cementing their deal. 'Now, before you go, I want you to do two non-negotiable things for me.'

Darius sighed. 'What are they?'

Rose smiled. 'I want a clip.'

'How much?'

'Three million.'

Darius didn't respond, but kept holding her hand, frustrated with where these last two demands could be going. He then nodded. 'What else do you want me to do?

'I want a granite monument for our son's grave.'

CHAPTER

50

Journalists positioned themselves for the announced media conference in the prime minister's courtyard. Cameras secured on tripod stands with boom microphone operators checking settings. Many of the waiting journalists stood scanning phones, not bothering to chat, preferring not to engage with colleagues. Before them, behind the red velvet rope, stood two black lecterns bearing the Australian coat of arms stencilled in gold. They were expecting the announcement to begin at eleven, almost ten minutes ago, and the initial buzz of eagerness now shrouding the waiting twenty press gallery members.

Prime Minister Brown strode from the dark chambers of his office and took his place at a lectern. Consummate in his appearance, his charisma radiating his aura of leadership. When he spoke, most Australians listened with many believing what he had to say. Other politicians were not as gifted with oratory skills, and he worked his political assets throughout his career to get what he wanted.

Premier Jackson followed him, positioning himself at the other lectern. Clare Spencer and Jock Garnsworthy accompanied them, standing behind and to the side of the leaders.

'This looks a little ominous, don't you think?' Charlotte walked into Rose's office, taking up the remote and switching the broadcast to the prime minister's media conference. 'It looks like an announcement.'

Rose stood from her desk, edging over to watch as the prime minister strode to the lectern, preparing to deliver a statement. It surprised her to see Spencer, and didn't understand why the premier would be there, standing with Brown, at the other lectern.

The agreement she made with the prime minister at the Lodge the previous evening was not due to be released until the leadership politics of the Country Party had been resolved. A tight grip of anxiety took hold as she wondered what the announcement could be.

Brown invited Rose to meet him and Jock Garnsworthy at the Lodge to clear up any misunderstandings about the future. The prime minister confirming she didn't have any place in his ministry and again offering a two-year overseas appointment. 'Rose, you have no future with me.'

'Is this your money men talking or you?'

Brown swirled his Irish whiskey, ice clinking in the tumbler, considering a response. 'No matter what the party did to allow you to win your preselection, you are not part of my plans in the future.'

'I want the water issue resolved. You need to act. If you don't, then I will drive a leadership challenge and force a referendum.'

'You don't have the numbers.'

Rose smiled and sipped her chardonnay. 'As it happens, I do.'

Brown took a sip, then rested his head on the back of his leather chair as he eyed her. Garnsworthy, who had contributed nothing to the discussion so far, added, 'We want you to retire. We want to bring in our man at the next election.'

'Why would I do that?'

'Because you're useless, Rose. You may have done deals using whatever negotiating power you have to get into the ministry, but we have gotten nothing from you.'

'A little harsh, Jock.' Rose squirmed. 'I've managed the sports grants program well.'

'Did you have to make it so obvious you were favouring our marginal seats?' Brown asked.

'They may be marginal,' Rose said. 'They just happened to be in dire need of sports funding. Everything I approved went on capital expenditure and nothing for recurrent funding, which, if I recall correctly, you wanted to hand out to various clubs in your mate's electorates.'

'Your regional development plan is in crisis,' Garnsworthy frowned.

'There's a prolonged drought if you hadn't noticed,' Rose scoffed. 'Oh, that's right. You live on the coast and seldom go bush.'

'I'm always out there,' Garnsworthy said, shifting in his chair.

'Only when it rains.'

Brown laughed at the interchange.

'I will have water out to my farmers this week and I have a guarantee of a price reduction.' Rose played her trump card.

Brown glanced at Garnsworthy, who shrugged.

'This will mean I am a politician who can meet my promises, unlike some,' Rose said as she scoffed a sniff at Brown. 'So, when I campaign for fairer water rights for everyone living along the Darling and Murray rivers I will be listened to in a big way.'

'That ain't going to happen,' Brown said, finishing his glass and leaning forward to place it on the coffee table.

'We'll see.' Rose smiled at the anxious looks between them. 'When I'm deputy prime minister, I will make sure farmers get a fair share of water. The greenie stakeholders can get stuffed.' She paused for a moment. 'It's time the Arabs gave up control and we hand it back to the people.' She lifted her glass, assuming her claim was interesting enough to be convincing. 'I'm passionate about this.'

Brown glanced over at his deputy, raising his eyebrows. 'What's your price?'

'Prime Minister, I'm not someone you can wave a hand at and toss me a cheque,' Rose said. 'This water referendum is important to me.'

'Why do I feel I am being set up by a master manipulator?'

'That is so unfair.'

'Why didn't you seize these balls during your career here?'

Rose scoffed as she held the wine close. 'I didn't need to. I have been thrilled doing what I preferred.' She took a generous sip. 'It's a glorious life, being a minister of so little consequence.'

Garnsworthy winced.

'Now I'm on the cusp of being elected deputy prime minister, opening new doors for me.'

Brown stood and manoeuvred his way through the chairs to the sideboard, walking back with bottles of Bushmills and chardonnay. He splashed a generous dram into Garnsworthy's tumbler and poured wine into Rose's outstretched glass before settling back into his chair and pouring his own.

'Come on, Rosie. What's your price?' Brown insisted.

Rose lifted the chilled glass and took a small sip, looking over the rim at the concerned faces.

'My price to give up the deputy leadership of the country?'

'No, your price to fuck off out of here,' Garnsworthy snapped.

'Ease up, Jock. Let the lady speak.'

'If the Arabs do as I say, then I want three things.'

Brown smiled, the irony splashing across his expression. 'Every politician has a price, even this one,' he murmured to himself.

'I want the sign-off on all state and federal planning approvals for the tourist and gaming precinct on the river in the mallee.'

Brown tossed his head around in a somewhat approval nod with a maybe shake.

'I want five years in Italy.'

Brown now nodded.

'And ten million.'

The prime minister's expression faded away. Eventually, he said, 'The government doesn't play fast and loose with the cash drawer, Rose; you know that.'

'I don't care where it comes from. I would expect not from the federal government.'

'Where then?'

'I'm sure you have means.' Rose rolled her tongue around the inside of her bottom lip. 'I'm sure generous benefactors will stump up the funds. Maybe the Victorian government, given their ambitious premier.'

Brown glanced at Garnsworthy, who shrugged and nodded. 'We'll see what we can do.'

'You'll need to do better than that,' Rose said.

'What? You want a signed agreement? At this hour?'

'We can do that later.' Rose hauled her phone from her bag. 'Just speak to this phone and restate our agreement.'

'You're kidding.'

'Welcome to my world,' Rose said. 'Either speak clearly confirming the deal or it's over and I shall be deputy prime minister before the end of January.'

'You are a psycho, aren't you?' Brown said with a laugh.

'After twenty years, you're just getting to know that?'

'Thank you for coming,' Prime Minister Brown announced. 'I am joined this morning by the Premier of Victoria, Phillip Jackson, to announce significant matters to do with Australian water rights and the future of representation in the federal seat of Mallee.'

Rose crossed her arms, her phone squeezed into her hand as she stood before the television. She spoke to Jackson after her meeting with the prime minister the previous evening and gained agreement from him for her to step aside at the next election.

'This will make many folks in the electorate very happy, Rose. I thank you for your generosity.'

'It's not my generosity I am worried about Phillip, it's yours.'

'How do you mean?'

'I will activate my agreement to step aside when I have all approvals for the Ned's Corner development, and I receive a million in cash from you.'

'A million in cash?' Jackson scoffed.

'That's what I said,' Rose said.

They argy-bargied around the approvals and cash for an hour before

Rose recorded his agreement. Now that phone remained with her until she could download the two files.

'I am pleased to announce we have negotiated an increased release of water to farmers in the mallee commencing on Friday,' the prime minister continued. 'This has come after weeks of negotiation with the premiers of Victoria and New South Wales, which will allow our agri-industries in that vital region to produce substantial crop yields next year.'

'Jackson got the deal?' Charlotte mocked. 'Not what I heard.'

Rose smiled at the support, still watching the screen.

'I am also pleased to announce that as part of this greater release of water, the government has negotiated settlement with the companies involved for a fifty percent reduction in the water carting price effective from today. This will allow the farmers and graziers reliant on water to have their cost burden reduced.'

'Oh, good on you,' Charlotte said, sneering at the screen.

'I have focused my government on providing tangible results for those farmers suffering drought, specifically in the mallee, and I want to thank...'

'Here we go,' Charlotte said.

'... the water minister, Clare Spencer, for her tireless work in achieving this outcome.'

'Bastard.'

'Shh.' Rose smirked, stroking her staffer's arm.

'As I have announced I will activate these agreements this week. We expect farmers will see immediate relief and we thank the water rights holders for their eagerness in resolving this water issue.'

'Why doesn't he call them by name?'

Rose smiled. 'He doesn't want to open up a racist debate about who owns Australia.'

'I suppose Denis Sadler will talk about it on his program.'

Rose nodded, still watching the television. 'I will make sure he does.'

'I am also standing with the premier to announce a major development in the mallee, which in time will shift the economic model from agriculture to a more sustainable tourism model. We expect a substantial economic increase and jobs. And you know how much I love jobs.'

'Yeah, your job,' Rose said. Charlotte chuckled.

'I'll let him explain... Premier?'

'Thank you, Prime Minister.' Jackson brushed his mouth. 'It is my pleasure to announce an investment by the Victorian Government into a new tourism region in the north-west corner of the state, bordering New South Wales on the Murray River. This development will grow over the next decade and employ over one hundred thousand staff, providing a new tourism precinct and allowing the development of an international airport. We expect five- and six-star hotels will attract Australians and international visitors who want to play in a location with year-round glorious weather, helping the local economy. We don't expect the local agriculture industries to be affected. We expect jobs from the development will bring a new sustainable economic model to the region.'

'Any reason he can't do this in Melbourne?' Charlotte asked.

'Maybe there is something else to be said,' Rose said.

'The state government will release a full briefing paper with legislated approvals in the new year, and we expect the project to begin site works mid next year.'

'The Arabs will be happy,' Rose responded.

Prime Minister Brown moved closer to the microphone, clearing his throat with a quick cough behind his hand.

'Thank you Premier,' Brown glanced at Jackson, then further back to Garnsworthy. 'The deputy prime minister and I have been discussing succession planning after the next election and we have come to an arrangement should the government be successful in retaining the confidence of the Australian people.'

'Highly unlikely the other mob can win twenty-five seats,' Rose observed.

'Jock has agreed to continue as leader of his party until the election, when he will retire from the parliament after an outstanding contribution to this nation, leaving a significant legacy.' Brown turned and nodded towards Garnsworthy. 'Premier Jackson has expressed his wish to enter the federal parliament at the next election, so today I am pleased to announce he will be the Country Party's candidate for Mallee with the imminent retirement of the long-serving member and regional development minister, Rose Dowerin.'

'Wait up,' Charlotte yelped. 'Is this true?' She turned to Rose, who shrugged and nodded. 'Why?'

'They gave me an offer I couldn't refuse.'

Brown continued. 'There is never a guarantee we will win an election, but Phillip Jackson will campaign as the candidate elect for deputy prime minister. If the government is successful in retaining the government benches, then he will take his place beside me as my deputy.'

Clare Spencer gazed at her shuffling feet.

'Any questions?' Brown asked.

Charlotte switched off the television, dropping the remote on the coffee table and turning to Rose. 'I have plenty.'

'What do you need to know?'

'What about me? What will I be doing?'

'If you want it, I have organised for you to be the endorsed candidate when Jackson resigns his seat in a few months.'

Charlotte staggered back, collapsing into the lounge.

'Charlie, you have said you wanted to have a safe seat. You know Swan Hill very well. You'll have the support of the Arabs, and it is likely they'll promote you to a ministry once you win the by-election.'

'Do you think you could have let me in on the little arrangement you have made?'

'Maybe I should have,' Rose said. 'It all moved quickly last night, and frankly, I wasn't expecting the announcement this morning.' She smiled. 'I wanted to talk to you about it later today.'

'That's not fair, Minister,' Charlotte responded. 'I have given you everything.'

'You have done that and even more; that's why I'm doing a few deals for you.' Rose sat next to her, placing an arm around her shoulders. 'I thought you would be pleased.'

Charlotte's eyes welled, and a tear rolled down her cheek. 'I am, but why didn't you include me?'

'It all happened last night.'

'What happens now?'

'We continue until the election. We make sure you are pre-selected, and you begin an awe-inspiring political career.'

'What's going to happen to you?'

Rose stroked Charlotte's face with her thumb, wiping away a tear from the top of her cheek.

'Don't worry about me. I will survive; always have.'

Rose's phone hummed a message, and she peaked a look as Charlotte sank her head to her shoulder.

NOT SURE HOW YOU DID IT. THANK U. YOUR PRIZE IS WAITING. WATER TAP IS SWITCHING ON.

She swiped the window closed, dropping her head onto Charlotte's. They sat, reflecting, and planning the next steps.

CHAPTER
51

S tringybark café remained the coolest place in town for Peter Dowerin and his partner Simon Dobbs. The air-conditioning always cranked up and Bianca looking very cute again. They weren't paying particular attention to a television near them broadcasting the prime minister's media conference, but Peter noticed something as the premier began his announcement.

'Have you noticed the premier is missing some of his little finger?' Peter nodded towards the screen. 'I never noticed that.'

'What? Where?' Dobbs stared at the screen tucked in the corner above their heads. 'Why would he have a finger missing?'

'Not all of it, just part of it.'

'Which one?' Dobbs asked, leaning back to see the screen.

'His pinkie.'

'What? Wait... on his left hand?'

'As it happens, yes.'

'You're bullshitting me.' Dobbs moved closer to the television. 'How did you notice?'

'He wiped his mouth before he spoke, and I noticed.'

'You must have the observation skills of an eagle,' Dobbs said, keeping eyes glued to the set. 'When's he going to move that damn hand?'

'What do you reckon it means?' Peter asked.

'Nothing much now because I can't see it.'

'Maybe he lost it on a farm. Was he a farmer before politics?'

'Lawyer, I think. Who knows?' Dobbs said.

'Footy then?'

'Doubt it. Not likely to have a finger chewed off by an opponent,' Dobbs scoffed.

'You haven't played country football then?'

They both kept watching, waiting for the premier to raise his hand from behind the lectern. Jackson talked about jobs and visitors to the mallee, then investment before raising his left hand into a fist to strike down and make a point.

'Open your hand, dipstick.' Dobbs said to the screen.

'What's he talking about? Can we improve the sound?'

Dobbs stretched up and pumped the volume button a few times so they could hear the premier's words.

'Something to do with a development along the river.'

The prime minister shook the premier's hand and moved back to the lectern, announcing the transition of Jackson to federal politics.

'Wow, what's that going to mean for your mother?' Dobbs turned.

'Dunno.' Peter shrugged still transfixed to the screen. 'You know this is weird.'

'What is?' Dobbs resumed watching, then cheered, 'There. There, do you see it?'

'I was right,' Peter smiled. 'I thought I'd seen it.'

'What do you reckon it means?'

'This is what I was about to say; this is all very weird.'

Dobbs returned to his chair to finish his iced coffee. 'I don't get it. Why the murderous conflict over your mother's seat only to have her retire?'

'Exactly.'

Dobbs scooped whipped cream into his mouth. 'They always taught us to look for motive. I'm concluding that the perfect motive is to protect your mother.'

'Is that why you asked about the GPS data?'

'Maybe, because you have to admit it's all very strange.'

'Only one candidate, and he's my brother.'

'Yeah, but it makes sense if your mother is under threat, then maybe she needs protection.'

Peter thought for a moment. 'Maybe she wasn't under threat. Maybe they always planned for her to retire and open the door for Jackson.' He crossed his arms, leaning back in the chair, eyeing his colleague spooning cream. 'If someone else won preselection, then the premier wouldn't have the safe seat, blocking the road to deputy prime minister.'

'He announces the project's approval that favours the Arabs and then they announce he will enter federal politics, pushing your mother aside.'

Peter grinned. 'So, my mother is off your suspect list?'

'Maybe.'

'Makes little sense to be killing off your competitors including your own son, and then retire.'

'One was a car accident.'

'Why the finger?' Peter asked.

'You think it wasn't an accident?'

Peter didn't respond as he wiped his cheek. 'Maybe there was a contributor.'

'Hard to prove. Given the grog and the traffic boys report he took the bend too hard.'

'Why so reckless?'

'Frightened, maybe,' Dobbs said.

'None of the victims have been knocked the same way,' Peter said. 'We have a traffic accident, a shotgun blast to the face, and a decent blow to the back of the head.'

'Speaking of which, how is yours?'

'It's getting better. It's still tender at the back.'

'You were lucky, I reckon.'

'Yeah, suppose so,' Peter sat forward, keen to get back to the office. 'Too bad we don't have a scrap of evidence to say who did it.'

'Your sister can't offer us anything?'

'Once she takes her drugs, she travels to la la land for the night.'

'Strange,' Dobbs said, finishing his coffee and following his partner out into the blistering heat. 'Let's make a run for it; I can't walk in this.' He jogged to the other side of the road and straight into the air-conditioned office as Peter dawdled back, pondering the discussion.

As he reached the detective's squad room, he collected several files, taking them over to Dobbs' desk and dragging over a plastic chair.

'These are cold cases I have been researching. I came across similar MOs.'

Dobbs took the pile and scanned through the first. 'Fingers missing?'

'The first one was a staffer for my father, found dead in his apartment. The only suspicious evidence was the finger missing. Cause of death remains open. They thought the likely cause of death was a blow to the base of his skull, but there is a suggestion it could have been asphyxiation. The others are similar, but nothing to do with politics.'

'This is becoming weird,' Dobbs said as he gazed at his colleague. 'What stories do we know about fingers missing?'

'Plenty, but the majority are myth makers.'

'Like what?'

'No names, no pack drill,' Peter said, as Dobbs nodded. 'I've heard that cutting off a finger is a warning.'

'Who's warning who?'

'The Iranians are warning everyone.'

Dobbs didn't say a thing. He just stared at Peter for a moment before glancing away. 'They cut fingers off?'

'I'm informed they do.'

'How? Why?'

'From what I've been told,' Peter said, 'if you cross them once they take the tipoff the finger. Twice and they take the next joint. If you cross them a third time, then they take what's left.'

'Who told you this?'

Peter tapped his nose. 'I have been doing old style detective work.'

'No, seriously, where have you come across this?'

'I rang around a few hospitals and asked about finger injuries, only left-hand pinkies. It seems there are quite a few over the years, local farmers and contractors who claim they lost the joint doing dangerous work... fencing seems to be the answer most give. Strange that.'

'Left hand.'

Peter laughed. 'Yeah.'

'How many?'

'Take a guess.'

'Twenty?'

Peter smiled, linking his hands behind his head as he watched Dobbs waiting for an answer. 'This year alone, fifty and twenty of those are repeat fencers.'

'You're kidding?'

Peter shook his head. 'And you know what's really weird?' Dobbs shrugged and shook his head. 'When I called some of them, they gave similar answers.'

'What?'

'They refused to talk to me.'

'So how do you know it's the jockeys?'

'A recent case appears to be just a few months ago down in Wyche. It seems the owner of a transport company who carts water fronted at the local hospital with the tip of his finger taken. He wouldn't talk to me, but it seemed interesting that he had been winning a lot of work.'

'Don't tell me.' Dobbs sat forward. 'Off the jockeys.'

'Correct.'

The detectives considered each other. Peter smiled at his colleague who raised his eyebrows. 'Are you thinking what I'm thinking?' Peter asked.

'Why would they knock candidates?'

'To get the deal done with Jackson.'

Dobbs nodded, pondering the theory.

'They want the tourist development, but Jackson won't sign off unless he has a clear run to become deputy prime minister,' Peter said.

'Long bow to pull,' replied Dobbs.

'Remember his pinkie?'

Dobbs clicked his fingers.

Peter continued, 'The premier is their man. I would hazard a guess he has probably let them down twice.'

'Are you sure? This theory seems a little far-fetched.'

'To get what they want, they give him what he wants.'

'Yeah, but what about your brother?'

'What about him?'

'He had their support and became a late entrant.'

'Maybe they wanted to use him to influence my mother to retire?'

'But why kill him?'

The question hung in the air as their theory drifted away. 'Well, it sounded good in my head,' Peter said.

A further silence clouded them before Dobbs asked, 'Have we got a report on why Bobby broke down?'

Peter moved to his desk, searching for a sheet of paper a uniform had submitted to him. He tugged it from a stack of papers and read through the notes. 'The water pump appears tampered with. It seems someone whacked it a few times, which would have had him overheating if he went on a long run.'

'Someone called him out, right?'

'Yeah, but it wasn't a genuine call,' Peter said. 'No one knew what he was talking about when he got to the farm.'

'Do we have the number that left the message?'

'Yeah, but it was fake.'

'Can we look at any metadata?'

'I'm ahead of you. Should be a few days,' Peter said as he sat at his desk.

'So, they lured him out?'

'Seems that way.'

'Why would the jockeys do that?'

Peter screwed his face. 'Yeah, you're right. Why would they?'

'Has pathology got us a weapon for Lever?'

Peter checked his watch. 'They said it would be ready after twelve. I'll drop over now and see if it's available.'

'Sure.' Dobbs went back to reading his screen. 'Do you think there is any CCTV around your brother's car?'

'Nothing at his office.'

'What about his home?'

'Have got none.'

'Look, while you're at the hospital I might have a look to see if there are any cameras about his place. I might stop at a few cafes and see if they have anything. He might have stopped on the way out of town.'

'Okay, let's catch up back here at three.'

CHAPTER
52

Peter parked his car in the shade of a massive pine tree at the hospital, hoping it wouldn't heat too much as he hurried to the entrance, looking forward to air-conditioning and relief from the flies. A receptionist directed him to pathology, and he popped his head into various offices, searching for Dr Hammer.

'Are you looking for me?' A voice swung him around.

'Yes, as it happens.' Peter wasted a smile, as the doctor didn't return it. 'I'm just wondering if I could talk to you about a case you're working on?'

'Your brother?' Hammer kept walking, her white coat flapping him as she brushed past.

'Not so much.' Peter turned and followed a scant trace of perfume. 'I'm keen to ask questions about another, James Lever.'

'Come to my office and we can talk.'

'Yes, ma'am.'

Hammer glanced back and smiled.

'How long are you here for?' Peter asked as they walked the polished blue linoleum corridor.

'Too long, and it seems they want me to stay to do some teaching.'

'Oh well, could be worse.'

'What could be worse than this heat?' Hammer turned into an office and pushed a button for an electric fan before sitting at her desk. 'I don't know how you people put up with it.'

'Friends.'

Hammer frowned. 'Friends? That's weird.'

'You could have made some and it will be sad when you say goodbye.'

Hammer stopped fussing with files peering up, open-mouthed, shaking her head. She stared at him, then frowned and went back to fussing. 'I have friends.'

'Friends or colleagues?'

Hammer stopped again and looked through a knotted brow. 'You wanna be my friend?' she said, mocking him in a kid's voice.

'Not particularly,' smirked Peter, disappointing her. 'I'd have to get to know you first.'

'Something wrong with me?'

'No, not at all.' Peter twisted his mouth and shook his head.

'What then?' The doctor seemed confused.

'I'd need to know if you can drink a beer, and if you did, then we could be friends.'

Hammer laughed, rocking back in her chair. 'Beer?'

Peter nodded.

Hammer smiled as she rocked her chair, considering the detective. 'When?'

'Tonight.'

'Where?'

'Grand Hotel, 7.30.'

Hammer considered the challenge, thinking through options. 'Done.'

'Great,' Peter leaned forward, changing his tone. 'I'm wondering if you have identified a murder weapon in the Lever case.'

Hammer raised her brow; she wiped her eye, shaking her head and breathing deep for a moment. She then moved back into the role of pathologist, scrolling through files on her computer, clicking her way to the relevant information. 'The best estimate we have is a ball-shaped object, like a wrench or a hammer. Something hard and heavy.'

'What shape of wound was it?'

'He had a significant depression of the neck, causing a vertebral artery dissection leading to subarachnoid haemorrhage. Blood flooded around the brain, which is fatal. Death instantaneous.'

Peter scribbled a few notes. 'Where exactly was he hit?'

Hammer stood and moved to the other side of the desk, positioning herself behind Peter, placing her hands around his neck and using her thumbs to show the region.

'What's this lump here?'

'Someone had a go at me the other day.'

'Well, where they hit you is the same region for our victim.'

Hammer worked her thumbs, and Peter cringed from the discomfort.

'Did you get x-rays?'

'I had a headache for a few days, that's all.'

Hammer stepped away from Peter, resuming her seat. 'I would recommend you have your doctor look at it. You may have an issue with clotting, which could cause a problem.'

'Serious?'

'Very. I would see someone within the next day or so. Take it seriously.'

'Can I still have a beer?'

Hammer scoffed. 'Is there anything else you need?'

Peter smiled. 'This whack given to Lever, could it have been an iron bar or a shovel?'

'If I had to put money on it, I would say a hammer. A mechanic's ball hammer with its little knob on the end. Do you know the one? The claw hammer is a little too large for the circumference of the wound.'

Peter jotted a note. 'Interesting. So, a mechanic?'

'Well, at least someone who knows their way around a car.'

'Could be anyone out here.'

'Is that it?' Hammer checked her watch.

'When will you have the Dowerin report?'

'A few days.' Hammer nodded. 'Look, I meant to say to you the other day... sorry about your loss.'

Peter winced and nodded thanks.

Hammer stood, encouraging Peter to do the same, and walked him to the door.

'I must say I am surprised.'

'About what?'

'No jokes about my name?'

'Doc, we're professionals.' Peter smiled. 'Why would I give you a hammering over your name?'

Hammer smiled before pausing. 'It's Wendy, actually.'

'Hi Wendy, I'm Peter.'

'I know who you are, detective. I hear so do most single women in this sweatbox.'

'None of them drink beer.' Peter turned on his heel and strode off, leaving the doctor to sigh as she watched him go.

CHAPTER
53

'How did you go?' Dobbs asked, looking up from his examination of footage as Peter sauntered into the squad room. Dobbs visited Bobby Dowerin's apartment complex retrieving security footage from various residents. He also visited various cafes and captured footage of Bobby's breakfast stop before leaving town.

'We have a better idea of the murder weapon of Lever.'

'What is it?'

'A mechanic's hammer,' Peter said, rolling his metal chair to his partner's computer. 'Have you seen anything interesting?'

'We have Bobby getting home at the time you reported. There is nothing strange around his car, but I passed information to the uniforms about unusual behaviour before dawn.'

'Like what?'

'A couple of young lads out for a bit of trouble, I suspect.'

'They touch the car?'

'No.' Dobbs referred to his notes. 'I checked a few cafes on the route out of town and have him at breakfast on the highway. Nothing around the car, but I identified a camel jockey turning up and going inside.'

'Which one?'

'The goon.'

'Maisil Ghassab is his name.'

'Whatever,' Dobbs said. 'He didn't go anywhere near the car.' He checked his notes. 'A delivery van arrives blocking the view for five minutes, which is not enough time to do anything. I have various people walking past and a bunch of kids playing chasey using Bobby's car as protection.'

'So, nothing?'

'I have Bobby walking to his car with the jockey. Shaking hands and patting each other on the back. It's a shame they seduced him.'

'Owed them money,' said Peter. 'How long between the delivery truck and Bobby going to his car?'

'Ten minutes.'

'And nothing?'

'Just folks coming and going. No one other than the kids getting close to the vehicle.'

'Can I have a look?'

'Sure, I'll set it up for you. I need to go to the can, anyway.'

Dobbs cued the footage to before the van appeared and left Peter to it. He checked out the van delivering its goods. It took a little time before a clear view was again possible. He saw nothing so wound the video back before the van arrived. A couple walked past, then a jogger came from a pathway behind the car and ran through the car park. Something sparked Peter's attention.

'Geezus.' Peter stood, snatched his keys, heading for the door. He considered leaving a note but thought he would explain later.

CHAPTER
54

Peter cranked up the air-conditioning as the steering wheel was too hot to grip, so waited until the cabin cooled. He thought through what he had seen and pondered what he should do. A trail of beaded sweat rolled out from his temple as he stared ahead. After a few minutes, he tested the steering wheel before driving off rushing to his mother's house.

Within ten minutes, he showed up at the compound, clouding dust as he braked, sliding across the pebbles. His mother always locked the front door when away, so he headed along the veranda for the back door. He stepped through the boot room and into the kitchen.

'Primmy, are you home?'

He listened for any noise and heard nothing. He stepped back out onto the veranda and scanned the pool area, calling again. Still no reply.

Peter walked to the side of the house and leaned against a pole on the edge of the veranda, staring across to his house and checking for movement. He then scanned the back of the property but still could see no one. He tugged his phone from his pocket, scrolled through names and called Canberra, connecting with Charlotte.

'Is mum around?'

'She's just saying goodbye to a few folks on her way to the airport. Shall I get her to call you back?'

'No, I'll wait.'

Charlotte seemed uneasy with the abruptness of his tone. 'Everything okay?'

'It's fine, Charlie. I just need to talk to mum.'

'Here she is.'

'Hello, darling. What do you think? Are you happy?'

'Happy?' Peter scratched his head.

'With the announcement?'

He bumped off the pole and paced the veranda. 'What announcement?

'My retirement, darling, at the next election.'

'What?' He frowned. 'Sorry I'm confused. I thought you were keen to stand again. This whole political thing has been about you running again... now you're leaving?'

'You don't sound excited?'

'Excited?' Peter yelled. 'Excited?' He kicked out a foot as he paced. 'If you made that announcement a few weeks ago, then maybe my brother would still be alive.'

Rose didn't respond straightway. 'That's a little unfair,' she whispered. 'It's not my fault your brother has been killed.'

'He wouldn't have been standing against you if he knew you were going to retire.'

Rose remained silent.

'Is Primrose with you?'

'No, she's at home; she didn't want to come.'

'Did she arrange anything for today?'

'What's wrong, darling?'

'I need to talk to her. Do you know where she is?'

'She's supposed to be home. Is she not?'

'No, she doesn't appear to be.' Peter stopped and looked over to his house, squinting against the sun.

'What's happened? What's wrong?'

'Mum.' Peter paused a moment. 'Can I suggest you get back as soon as you can? It's important.'

'I can be there before seven. What's it about?'

'Get home real quick. You're needed here. I'll tell you then.'

He stubbed the end of the call without saying goodbye, then stepping to the edge of the veranda, his hands fisted on his hips, and called, 'Primmy!'

He heard nothing in response, so returned to the house. He stepped through to the lounge and bent over to pick up the television remote. The screen was on but muted, so he switched it off. He then moved to Primrose's wing, checking through rooms, ending at her bedroom. She had not made the bed, her clothes strewn over the floor, even though a clothes basket sat in the corner.

Peter huffed a little, but then began clearing her bedroom, picking up clothes and walking them to the basket. He lifted the lid and was about to drop them when a red colour from the bottom of the basket attracted his attention. Still holding the bundled clothes, he leaned in, pushing aside various items. Then with his thumb and forefinger he squeezed and lifted the handle of a hammer. He took the weight, lifted it out and held it up to reveal a ball hammer before dropping the bundle of clothes into the basket.

'That's mine.'

Peter jumped, startled by the voice, almost dropping the hammer; he turned to see Primrose standing at the door in her work dungarees.

'What is it?'

'It's mine.' Her menacing tone causing Peter to move away from the basket and the door.

'What do you use it for, Primmy?'

'Give it to me!' She held out her hand. Peter couldn't see the other.

He grinned, backing away, uncertain what his sister had in mind; his gaze never left her wild bug-eyed face. He tried to manoeuvre away from the bed, avoiding being tangled in its linen. 'Primmy, why don't we go have a cup of tea? You love tea. Do we have any cake?'

'It's mine and I want it. Give it to me!' Primrose stepped towards him. 'Don't make me hurt you. I don't want to hurt you.'

'Gorgeous, you'd never hurt me. You love me.' He smiled, using his outstretched hand to calm her.

'Give it to me, Peter, or I'll tell mummy.'

'Mummy said I could have it.'

'She never did. She doesn't know I have it.'

Peter shook his head, took a deep breath, biting down on his bottom lip. With a slight distraction of his gaze, she stepped closer, a kitchen knife pointing to his throat, with a crazed look, wild animal in her eyes.

'Give it to me,' Primrose scowled, a guttural noise following her words.

Peter, watching the knife and now panting, held out the hammer. Primrose snatched it, turned, and scampered from the room. He heard her run through the kitchen, tossing away the knife, clattering in the sink. Still shaken he stumbled towards the door, reengaging focus, and dashing after her. As he got to the veranda, the large black beast of the family work truck tore past, flinging dust and stones as it slid out of the front gates. Quick to his car, slapping a flashing red light unit onto the roof he pressed hard against the accelerator chasing his sister.

CHAPTER
55

C hampagne first popped soon after the premier's statement and continued during the lavish celebratory lunch in the director's restaurant in Mildura, lavishing their good fortune on leaders of the community and other key community supporters. The mood remained enthusiastic with the news of government approval for the tourist development. It meant a significant economic opportunity for Mildura, plus jobs.

The mayor enjoyed the celebrations but kept a watchful eye on Maisil Ghassab. She didn't trust the big man. She had overcame her reluctance to the development, now appreciating its opportunities. It helped that her family were benefiting through contracts for construction work. She proposed a toast extolling the virtues of the development, explaining it would not have happened without the foresight of the Iranian community.

'Baba Darius has been an entrepreneurial leader who created the vision and sought to include all of us to benefit from the development.' She raised her glass. 'This would not have happened without him. We all appreciate you, Darius: your wisdom and your leadership. Cheers.'

Darius smiled at the acknowledgement before raising his glass. His fellow directors didn't bother to respond, preferring to mutter about their own contribution. Ghassab became more vocal and proposed another loud toast to Darius, also acknowledging his work. The four recognised the dripping sarcasm, yet none of the guests twigged the insult.

After resuming his seat Ghassab turned to his colleagues and scowled, 'Why is it him who gets the glory? We did the work.'

Hosmand Shofet smiled. 'We reward your talents.'

'It's not always about the money, Hosie; never has been.' Ghassab eyed Darius, enjoying a private conversation with the mayor.

'We have got what we always coveted and now we can let the Chinese do the hard yards.'

'I thought the Americans were coming?' Ghassab said.

'It seems they want nothing to do with Iranians,' Taimur Saraf said. 'Something to do with creating problems for them in America.'

'Huh, who would have thought the Yanks have a problem with us?' Ghassab laughed.

Shofet joined him, smiling. 'Other than a little muscle, your specific talents were not required on this project.'

Ghassab leaned back in his chair and brushed back his hair with his fingers. 'You think these things happen without muscle?'

Shofet scoffed at his friend. 'You weren't required, so what are you talking about?'

Ghassab stood, his chair clattering on the floor. 'Just wait right there.' He patted Shofet's chest with gusto. 'I have something in my car I want to show you. Then maybe we could measure the roles we play for this organisation differently.'

'What have you got?' Saraf asked, shaking his head

'It's a secret, but it will show the work I have done for all of you.'

Ghassab staggered away, whacking the table, and tumbling a glass to the floor. Shofet stood to support his friend from falling.

'Are you okay? You may have had too much to drink.'

Ghassab shrugged him off, tugging away his arm and almost losing his balance over a chair. Darius came quick to his side, holding him so he could regain his composure and not fall. The two struggled against each other until Ghassab relaxed, allowing Darius the confidence to let him go. Ghassab smiled and patted his colleague on the shoulder.

'You, okay?' Darius asked.

Ghassab lolled his head back and smiled. 'I'm fine.' He looked down at Darius. 'Really, I'm fine. I just need to get something from my car.'

'Be careful, my friend.' Darius watched as the big man swayed his way through the tables to the stairs. Shofet and Saraf stood next to him, watching Ghassab stagger and trip up the stairs, before circling and studying each other.

'He is becoming a liability,' Saraf said. 'Will the Chinese accept him?'

Darius gazed at his shoes.

Shofet responded, 'He'll be okay. He just needs a little recognition for the things he does.'

'That's true,' Darius said, still gazing down. 'Maybe I could do more because he does a lot for us.'

'He gets us our money,' Saraf nodded.

'What's he got out in the car?' Darius asked, peering at Shofet.

'Beats me,' he shrugged. 'Something he said he did to get this deal done.'

'Nothing I asked him to do,' Darius turned to resume his seat. 'Razia, more champagne.' He smiled, calling to his wife.

Ghassab struggled to get outside, stumbling onto the pavement, having missed the last step. The glare squinted his eyes as he straightened to collect his bearings, remembering he secured a valued parking bay in Seventh Street under the shade of a mallee tree. He stepped off the curb, bumping into a parked SUV and placing a hand on the hot metal. He cringed away, stumbling backwards past the hot vehicle and onto the road, failing to see or hear the danger throttling towards him.

CHAPTER
56

Primrose had little time to brake as the large man dressed in black wringing his hand staggered out into the street. Her eyes flicked back to the road after focusing on her fast-approaching brother with the red flashing light. She braked hard when she saw him, but too late. The impact tossed him like a rag-doll upward; the motion throwing him onto the bonnet and headfirst through the windscreen, tumbling onto the steering wheel, killing him.

Primrose screamed as the body crashed into the cabin, pinning her arms to the steering wheel, and exploding the airbag, its impact mitigated by the body. She yanked down on the wheel, veering the vehicle hard across the road and slamming into cars parked under the shade of the mallee tree. The beast then went airborne, spinning as it left the ground. It hit the parkland grass hard, bouncing, twisting, and spinning, flaying metal and glass until it rolled to a standstill. Steam gushed from the chassis as metal noises settled and an eerie silence befell the scene.

Peter screeched to a halt across the road, scrambling from his car and rushing towards the clump of twisted metal. As he reached the hissing vehicle, he dropped to his knees to check inside the cabin. It settled upside down, a black clump of a body sprawled across the roof with Primrose dangling upside down above him, secured by her seat belt.

A distant siren from first responders blared after witnesses made emergency calls. Peter couldn't wait, squeezing into the distressed vehicle. He stretched to unclip his sister, but the pressure of weight on the buckle wouldn't budge it. He squeezed further in over the body, noticing it was an Arab clan member. By now he was under Primrose, and he tried lifting her whilst pushing the buckle release, which proved impossible. He needed to wedge against her, so tried lifting himself, but to no avail. He could see rushing feet and chaotic voices yelling instructions at each other.

'Help me; I need help,' Peter called.

A head appeared opposite. He didn't know who it was. 'Check for pulse.' The voice had his hand on the body's neck. 'This one is done.'

Peter grabbed his sister's dangling hand and felt for a pulse. Nothing.

'I'm not getting anything.'

'Try her neck.'

A woof of sound startled the voices outside. Peter fell back on the body and stretched to Primrose's neck. He noticed for the first time her lifeless face with eyes wide. He grabbed her neck and then repositioned, so his fingers could dab her carotid artery. Nothing.

'Fire, get out!' someone yelled.

Peter tried the seatbelt buckle again and still could not move it.

'Get out now.'

He tried lifting his sister again, but the weight remained too much. He stared at her lifeless face, caressing it for the last time. Peter could feel his face change and his eyes welled. Then, without warning, his ankles were grabbed, hauling him from the car.

'Wait, stop.' Peter tried to pull his sister with him, but the power of the extraction was too much for him.

When he came out, a firefighter lifted him to his feet and shuffled him away from the burning vehicle. As they got to the curb, the car exploded, sending a fireball into the air, the roiling wave of energy knocking Peter from his feet. He sat up, distraught, resting on a hand, watching the firefighters dousing the flames.

Four hours later, the professionals were done with their duties. Measurements and photographs taken; bodies already at the hospital for tests. Witness statements were recorded, and assurances made to the owners of Savino's. They cleared the wreckage from the parkland, leaving nothing but divots and scorched grass. Peter leaned against his car, watching the scene, remembering his sister, and wondering what he would tell his mother.

Dobbs had taken the statements from the celebratory guests, noting Ghassab seemed in a hurry to retrieve something from his car. As the bodies were being bagged, he asked the medical team to check pockets for car keys. An officer handed the keys to him, and Dobbs bagged them, noting the license plate number. He approached Peter, suggesting he join him to conduct a lawful search of Ghassab's vehicle.

They checked the boot, with Peter recording the search on his phone. They then searched the cabin, finding the only suspicious package under the driver's seat. It was a container, like an old tobacco tin used by smokers who rolled their own.

What they found troubled Peter.

Wendy Hammer spotted him when she arrived for her drink date, crossing the road to chat. She sidled up and leaned against the bonnet, still a little warm from the day. 'You, okay?'

Peter didn't answer, preferring to nod his head.

'This may sound a little trite, but I'm sorry for your loss.'

He didn't look at her but dropped his head. 'Thanks.'

'I'm not involved with the autopsies, but early toxicology shows the man had a skin full.'

Peter smirked and peered up. 'Is that a medical term?'

'It's the right time and place, I reckon.'

There was a long pause as both avoided words.

'You know that lump in my neck you reckon was like the Lever case?'

'Sure, what about it?'

'What type of hammer would have been used? Could it have been a mechanic's hammer?'

'If it was a hammer,' she said, crossing her arms, turning to lean her hip against the car. 'I think the injury is smaller than I would have expected if it was a carpenter's tool. I reckon the mechanic's tool would be the one. Why?'

'I may have had it in my hands earlier.'

'Where is it now?'

Peter pointed to the burnt grass.

'You're kidding?'

'Strange, isn't it?' Peter laughed and turned. 'You know what's even stranger?' He tugged a coiled plastic evidence bag from his pocket, and it spun down as he held it up for her to examine it.

'A finger? Where did you get that?'

Peter nodded towards the scorched earth. 'From the car of the pedestrian.'

'That's unbelievable.' Hammer shook her head. 'What are you going to do with it?'

'I'll drop it off in the morning for testing. By the looks of it, I doubt that it's my brother's.'

A rush of realisation washed over the doctor, and she rubbed his shoulder. 'Look, this may not be the time or the place to ask?' She studied him as he raised his head, pausing for just a moment. 'Do you still want that beer you promised me?'

Peter scoffed and smiled, nodding his head as he checked his watch. 'I have to go see my mum.' He glanced at her. 'Tomorrow maybe?'

'Sure, let's do it. I'm going to have a glass or two, anyway.' She stepped away. 'Take care.'

Peter watched as she left. 'Hey, Wendy?' She turned and looked at his smiling face. 'I look forward to seeing you tomorrow.'

She smiled and walked off towards the Grand Hotel.

CHAPTER
57

A marked police car rolled from the drive of Peter's mother's house as he pulled in. Rose nestled in a lounge out on the veranda, a glass of wine dangling in one hand and a wedge of tissues balled in the other. Her face puffy as she wiped her eyes when she saw her him climb the stone steps.

'Get yourself a drink, son.'

'No, I'm okay,' Peter said as he dropped into the large, soft cushions of a chair. 'How are you? Stunned, I'm sure.'

'I can't believe it; my two babies gone.'

'Yeah, not good.'

'Parents aren't supposed to bury their children.'

'Don't worry about any of that; I'll look after it.'

Rose wiped her face with the ball of tissues. 'I talked to her this morning after the announcements, telling her we would move to Italy.'

'Italy?'

'I'm retiring and they have appointed me ambassador to Italy. Once the election is over next year, I am off. Do you want to come?'

Peter laughed. 'Nah, I wouldn't have thought so.'

The change of subject lightened them both.

'It's time, I reckon, for me to leave.' Rose took a sip of wine. 'I know the family name has always claimed the seat, but there is no one left, and you don't want it.'

'That is for sure,' Peter said.

'It's time for me to go. To leave this place and maybe never come back.'

He didn't respond but studied Rose for a moment. 'Why did you come to Mildura, anyway?'

'I came to pick fruit. I needed the money and needed to get out of Melbourne.'

'How come?'

'Not a nice place to live if you don't have family and friends. I fell into the wrong crowd and needed to escape the nest of vipers. I came here, met your dad and the rest is history.'

'You never liked the mallee?'

'Aside from my family,' Rose smiled, sipping her wine, 'not really.' Peter shook his head and raised his eyebrows at the news. 'The payoff for me was getting to Canberra away from this stifling heat.' She drained her glass. 'It's just too hot, son.'

'Why did you want to stand for election again?'

'To force the prime minister to act, quite frankly.' She glanced at her son. 'Could you fetch me the bottle from the fridge, darling? Get something for yourself.'

Peter swung out of the chair and headed to the kitchen, taking the opened bottle of chardonnay from the fridge and a can of beer; he snapped it open and glugged a good mouthful as he strolled back to the veranda. He refilled his mother's glass, placing the bottle on the wooden floor beside her.

'Did the coppers tell you what happened?' Peter asked as he flopped into his chair.

'Most of it, but not the reason she was driving. Do you know?'

'I'm still confused by it all.'

'Were you chasing her?'

'Who told you that?' Peter asked.

'Someone told Charlotte they saw you arrive before the beast had stopped flipping. Were you chasing her?'

'I wanted to talk to her about a hammer I found in her room.'

'What type of hammer?'

'A ball type mechanics use.'

'You know she works on engines, don't you?'

'I didn't know that.' Peter said, embarrassed by the news. 'A doctor said the whack to my head the other day might have come from a similar weapon.'

'Rubbish; she would never hurt you.' Rose sipped her wine. 'Besides, why would she want to hit you? You were not a threat to her.'

'You saw her have a go at Bobby.' Peter chugged his beer. 'She had a temper and would turn if she felt threatened; you know that.'

'Rubbish!' Rose snapped. 'You're barking up the wrong tree with that theory if you think she involved herself in anything like that.'

Peter gazed out from the veranda. 'Yeah, maybe.'

'She wouldn't hurt a fly, that one.' Peter didn't respond and took another mouthful of beer. Rose studied her son and sipped her wine. 'Any closer to finding Bobby's killer?'

'Maybe.'

Rose shifted amongst her cushions. 'What have you got?'

'They sent him on a wild goose chase.' Peter sipped his beer. 'Someone tampered with his car to break down when the engine overheated. He owed plenty of money to the Arabs and nominated as candidate against you.'

'Not much then?'

'If you were going to retire, why wouldn't you let Bobby have a straightforward run?'

'I hadn't closed my deal with the prime minister.'

'What would have happened if you didn't get the deal you wanted?'

'I would have run for the leadership of the party and win election as deputy prime minister.'

Peter shook his head, surprised by the remark. 'You prefer Italy to the leadership?

Rose didn't respond, taking another sip, studying her son over the rim. 'Are you getting close in the Lever case?'

'Nope, only that someone whacked him with the same weapon used on me.'

'Who would do that?'

'That's what I wanted to talk to Primmy about.'

'Forget it,' Rose snapped. 'She would do nothing like that. She wasn't smart enough.' Rose dismissed him with a wave of her hand. 'What motive did she have?'

'Okay, okay, I'll leave it,' Peter glanced away. 'There is one thing, though. We have Primmy on CCTV acting strange around Bobby's car the morning he died.'

Rose shifted in her lounge. 'Why would she do that?' Rose spoke quickly. 'You have no right to suggest that. She would never hurt Bobby. What are you suggesting? You think your sister is capable of murder? You must be crazy.'

'Mum, take it easy; I'm only stating facts. We'll have a better idea once we have researched the metadata.'

'What?' Rose wiped the tissues across her mouth.

'Phone records,' he said. 'We are doing an analysis of Bobby's phone and we are checking the GPS on the beast and researching the Arabs' vehicles and their whereabouts.'

Rose straightened, leaning towards him with an accusing finger. 'You think Primmy killed Bobby? You have got to be joking. I thought someone killed him with a shotgun. She hates guns.'

Peter leaned further back into the cushions, holding up his hands. 'I never said that. We're just following leads.'

Rose turned away, moving to the edge of the veranda. 'I think you had better go,' she said, then after a prolonged pause murmured, 'I'm a little tired and emotional, darling. I want to sleep.'

Peter finished his beer, squeezing his can. 'Mum, it's okay. We have a suspect.' He stood, moving to the steps. 'We found a finger today; not sure whether it's Lever's, but it isn't Bobby's.'

'Where did you find it?'

'One of the Arabs had it, the big guy, Ghassab. We are checking his movements the day someone killed Bobby.'

'That'd be right.' Rose crossed her arms and watched her son step down the stairs. 'They have a habit of taking fingers.'

Peter gazed back at his mother, pouting a little and shaking his head slightly. 'Still early days in the investigation. We are searching for a shotgun at his house in Swan Hill. He has a few.'

'Those Arabs would do anything to get a deal.'

'Yeah, I suppose.' Peter stood by his car. 'Not sure why they would murder Bobby. Anyway, once we have a look at his gear we can decide.'

Rose gnawed at her bottom lip. 'Keep me in the loop if you wouldn't mind.'

'I can't do that, Mum. See you,' he said, opening his door. 'I'll drop by tomorrow.' He climbed into the car. 'Forensics wants to have a look at Primmy's room, and check the house and sheds.'

'Wasting your time,' Rose yelled.

'We'll see.' Peter didn't drive across the yard to his house. He drove out of the property, heading for the Grand Hotel.

Rose watched him go, thinking through what to do with the information. After a few moments, she stepped back into the house, moving through the kitchen to the storage cupboard off the boot room. She dragged out a set of steps and hauled them upstairs to her bedroom, placing them under a ceiling hatch. Gingerly, she climbed the steps and stretched to lift the hatch aside. Her hand then groped for the bundle she hoped to drag down. When she gripped it, she tugged it from the ceiling, dropping it on her bed, careful not to leave any smudges on the ceiling or hatch.

She then returned the steps to the cupboard, strolling to the veranda to finish her wine and wait until the sky darkened and river traffic docked for the evening. When she thought it dark enough, she checked around to see whether suspicious eyes scrutinised the property.

Once satisfied, she gathered her bundle, stepping off the veranda and heading for the river. It was late, and darkness made it difficult as she warily headed through the bush along the bank. Finding a quiet place with no houseboats nearby, she unwrapped the bundle, making sure she wiped it down to remove any evidence. She then picked it up with the oiled cloth, spun it around like a hammer thrower in the Olympics, flinging it high and long into the centre of the river.

The shotgun sank to the bottom in fifteen feet of water.

Rose watched, then turned with a smirk, sauntering back to the house, the gun cloth draped over her shoulder. Job done.

Forty years ago, she lived the life of a vagabond on the street hoping for another drug hit, dealing with the dregs of the streets, turning sexual favours for cash. A polite hint and a few dollars donated from a caring client changed her life. Now she was about to get it all.

Just thirty-five years in the mallee as a Dowerin, scheming, negotiating, and making things happen. Now free and clear to do whatever she wanted.

She chuckled as she reflected on the things she had done. She didn't care, just part of her original grand plan. They were good people, and she didn't dislike them, but they were just pawns in the bigger game she plotted. She would have preferred her family not get involved, but they did and were casualties of her grand scheme, so be it. The cash bonus and new life would soothe her grief.

The shotgun remained the last string of evidence linking her. She had already erased the GPS data; the burner phone lay at the bottom of the river and now nothing would be found implicating her. In the worst-case scenario, her darling Primmy would take the official fall.

Thank God the Arabs couldn't help themselves.

ENJOY THE READ?

Consider leaving a review on Amazon or Goodreads.

I would be very grateful if you did.

If you would like to communicate with me then please do.
I always respond and enjoy chatting about future projects

If you would like to be added to my Advanced Readers list, then please
let me know

readers@richardevans-author.com

ACKNOWLEDGMENTS

Writing a book is no mean feat. It takes creativity and grit to provide a story which opens the theatre of readers' minds. It's not easy and needs plenty of support.

I began planning this book with the idea of a political link between the federal seat and the fight for water rights in the mallee. Water remains a significant political and human issue within the district and in my view requires greater intervention by the federal government to ensure a fairer system.

I wish to acknowledge Patty Kavadias, Trish Stewart, and Anne and Michael Keaney who have again provided valuable feedback as has former colleague Phil and Cate Barresi. Deborah Daly and Michael Tate provided insight regarding consistencies, and Greg and Anthea Pelgrave provide continued support and humour. Denise and Paul Tyrrell also provide substantial support, and I remain grateful for their promotional efforts.

I thank my colleagues at Yarraville writer's group for their willingness to provide suggestions and support. Can I recommend any ambitious writer to join their local writers' community.

The team at 852 Press have been enthusiastic for the important story to be told about water rights and I thank them for their efforts in bringing it all together with their team of designers, editors, and support personnel. I especially wish to thank editor Sue Davison for her efforts. Any typos or syntax errors are mine.

It is vital to have strong family support when working on writing projects and I wish to acknowledge mine for their insight, humour, and advice during this project. Julia, Anthony, Kaitlyn, and Taylor bring me much pride.

Finally, let me acknowledge the many folks I have met during my political and business career who have all helped shape my imagination, my creativity and in some cases the stories I draw upon when writing about politics. The journey has been a pleasure to share with you.

Politics can be showbusiness for ugly people and there is always fodder within the media every day that stimulates my imagination into the exotic characters that seek and wield power. I try and bring contemporary issues forward using fiction and linking important questions that we should all ask.

We have a great democracy; it only needs a light to shine on the dark nooks to make it better.

ABOUT THE AUTHOR

As a political insider, Richard Evans served as a federal member of parliament for Cowan in Western Australia during the turbulent 1990s. He now specialises in writing political thrillers, writing about the exotic characters in the mysterious world of the Australian Parliament. He lives in the coastal village of Airlie Beach, the gateway to the Whitsunday islands, with a view from his writing desk overlooking the Coral Sea.

For more information about his other books,
or to contact Richard please visit:

www.richardevans-author.com

A plane crash begins a sequence of events which leads corrupt Prime Minister Andrew Gerrard, after a long political career, to rush through legislation designed to secure his ill-gotten gains for his retirement. Stalwart – and soon retired – Clerk of the Parliament, Gordon O'Brien, sets out to foil the Prime Minister's plan with the help of investigative journalist, Anita Devlin.

O'Brien, a stickler for correct parliamentary process is concerned by the rush to legislate and becomes aware of various incidents, which by themselves would mean little but collectively shape a conspiracy to defraud the government.

The Clerk anticipates there is a potential fraud upon the government being enacted, he has run out of time and now must act. He forces the Speaker to resign, and O'Brien takes her place, causing the parliament to prorogue, imposing a general election, preventing the fraud.

A **FREE COPY** of Deceit and to join the advanced readers team is now available from the following link:

www.richardevans-author.com

**For more information and purchasing options visit
852 Press.com.au**

The Mercantiles, a long-established, clandestine group of high-taxpaying business owners have grown frustrated by Prime Minister Andrew Gerrard's failure to meet promises, and decide the nation needs a change of government at the upcoming election. They call upon experienced and ruthless political operative Jonathan Wolff to organise their election campaign and defeat the prime minister.

Realising he cannot win the election his way, Wolff initiates an explosive campaign designed to remove the prime minister by defeating him in his own electorate using an independent candidate.

Investigative journalist Anita Devlin is appointed by her editor to promote the Stanley campaign as the publishing owner, unknown to her, is a member of the Mercantiles. She discovers the nefarious Wolff strategically working the campaign, and endeavours to expose his influence and manipulation.

For more information and purchasing options visit

852 Press.com.au

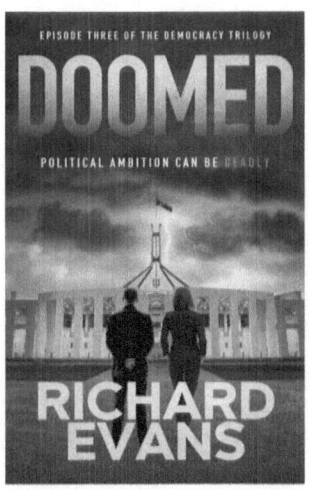

Three years after a change of government, the nation is facing huge social, policy, and environmental-related disasters yet the Australian government seems paralyzed on how to proceed. Two senior ministers resolve that a change of prime minister is essential for Australia's future and begin to lay the foundations for his dismissal.

Meanwhile, the parliament is held in a balance of power by the independent, Jaya Rukhmani, who can decide at any time if government legislation will be approved. Upon hearing the news that former prime minister Andrew Gerrard wishes to re-enter parliament, Jaya turns to Barton Messenger as an ally.

Doomed takes us behind the scenes of a parliament unaware of how ambition and political manipulation affect the everyday Australian. When the environment and economy are brought into the mix, which will be the one to flourish, and which one is doomed?

For more information and purchasing options visit

852 Press.com.au

FIRST NATIONS HAVE NEVER CEDED SOVEREIGNTY...

FORGOTTEN PEOPLE

IS CULTURE WORTHY OF REVOLUTION?

RICHARD EVANS

She wants her culture and country back. Independence was never ceded, and she will do whatever it takes to get it back, including the ultimate sacrifice. When government peace talks stop, revolution begins.

Revolutionary leader, Nellie Millergoorra, campaigns for an aboriginal homeland to preserve indigenous culture by advocating the prohibition of mining in Arnhem Land using a United Nations declaration to convince a disrespectful government to sign a treaty. Nellie will do whatever it takes to finally gain independence and end government regulation over her people.

When there is no agreement, she recruits mercenary special forces to inflame community chaos establishing an explosive aboriginal revolutionary movement.

In a surprising confrontation with a reluctant prime minister, who is threatened with an ultimatum he can't ignore, Millergoorra negotiates a treaty whilst facing her own battle for survival.

Forgotten People is gripping political thriller featuring surprising plot twists, compelling characters, and a kick-arse female heroine.

For more information and purchasing options visit

852 Press.com.au

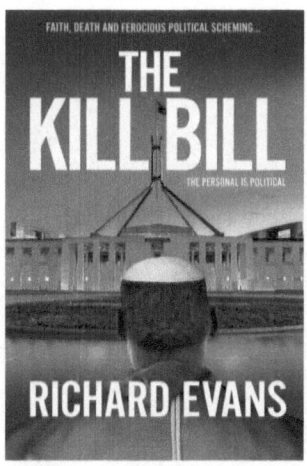

He's the nation's chief law maker. His daughter is fighting for her life in intensive care, a victim of a terrible crime. Will he ignore the prime minister's demands and his own laws to save her? Or will politics and the Catholic Church prevent him from doing his job?

Treasurer, Parker Osborne, initiates a covert plan, in partnership with Vatican emissary, Cardinal Rosseau, to guarantee proposed euthanasia legislation is destined for failure in the national parliament triggering a leadership challenge.

In a surprising development, the prime minister makes a decision which changes everything.

The Kill Bill is a gripping political thriller featuring emotional and surprising plot twists, convincing characters, and exposes the black-art of politics that will have you questioning the ethics of assisted dying. If you like fast-paced, page-turning thrillers that draw you into the story then Richard Evans' fourth book will not disappoint you.

Buy The Kill Bill today and learn how the black arts of politics really works.

For more information and purchasing options visit
852 Press.com.au

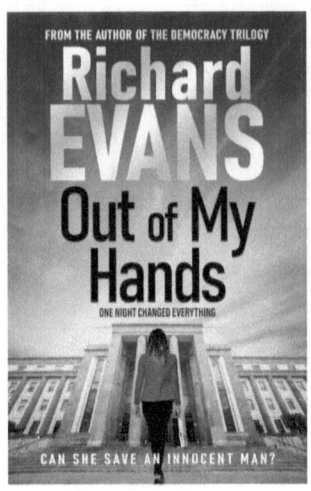

They were in the wrong place at the wrong time and will regret it forever. Nothing can change what happened, but only the lawyer can provide justice for them both. Will Anna Booth do it or will it be out of her hands?

A teenager is looking for a good time and meets a young woman who has no interest in him or his friends. Their worlds collide again when walking home. His mistake was not helping her.

After a police investigation exposing his friends, Billy Brown faces his day in court. He knows he is innocent and has little fear of the justice system. But the justice system wants a guilty accused and Billy is their patsy.

Three trials and a media storm later, his lawyer Anna Booth fights for justice for her client and the victim.

Buy OUT OF MY HANDS today and bring to light the reality of the American justice system and its faults.

Trigger warning: Out of my Hands is a gritty crime thriller and reader 18+ recommended.

For more information and purchasing options visit
852 Press.com.au

852

PRESS

ABOUT THE PUBLISHER

We are an independent publisher, helping Australians tell their story.

We are keen to share our experiences and processes with Australian writers so they can self-publish their own works. We will be launching a range of resources, services, and events for those with a story to tell.

Visit our website for more information.

WWW.852Press.com.au